Finding
Her *Spirit*

Tracie Barton-Barrett

Tracie Barton-Barrett

Book Cover Design by Tugboat Designs
Interior Formatting by Champagne Book Design
ISBN-10 : 0997025948
ISBN-13 : 978-0997025941

Acknowledgements

To Daniel, my loving husband, soundboard, and muse; Luana Russell, your astute editing skills and support helped to mold the clay; Madre, for being the best mother anywhere; my incredible Helpful Author Ladies—Padgett Gerler, Leslie Tall Manning, Michelle Garren Flye, and Heather Cobham Brewer, for your endless support and insights, especially during COVID-19 lockdown; Alice Osborn and Wonderland Book Club; Doreen Copp Campbell; Brian & Kimberly Dunlap; Stephanie Hall; Sherwood Williams; Rose Leland; Bethany Glaser.

To Deborah at Tugboat Designs and Stacey at Champagne Book Design. Thanks to Lydia Severy, Janine Mealey Nicholson, Dr. Larue Coats, and Cassie Pullin for being thoughtful beta readers.

To Edward Claflin for writing the book, *Ruffian: Queen of the Fillies* and to everyone who worked on the movie, *The Black Stallion*. Both of these instantaneously and forever changed my life.

A big thanks to Kentucky Horse Park for your help as well as allowing me to do research at the Park. I'm grateful for such a special place to honor these magnificent beings.

A special thanks to all at EasiHorse Farm, animal and human alike, for providing a peaceful sanctuary and an eye in the storm.

The biggest thanks to Dream Haven Guest Ranch for providing the inspiration and the amazing horse for this book.

Spirit, you touched my spirit,
Helping me to find it in ways you'll never being to know.

Characters

Maren Markey, main character

Caroline Fletcher, Mama
Garrett Markey, Daddy
Clint Fletcher, stepfather
Lacey Fletcher, stepsister
CJ, half-brother
Matty/Chase, guy from camp
Brody, guy at college
Brittany, Chase's girlfriend
Katie Kitty, CJ's cat

Marin Breiner, Maren's closest friend

Dallas, dog
Travis, brother

Mr. Bucky and Ms. Patsy McGee, Fair Oaks owners

Spirit, favorite horse
Jubi, Spirit's buddy
Moose & Dodger, their dogs
Penguin (*Pingüino*), their cat
Sherry, Mr. Bucky's daughter and Ms. Patsy's stepdaughter, and
Spirit's owner

Mrs. Gardner, important teacher

PART
One

July 10, 1982

Three more years.

Can hardly wait. Today is my 9th birthday! And three years
from today will be July 10, 1985 and it will be amazing. It's
forever to wait, but last year it was four years, and now
it's three. I will be twelve and that's when Daddy said he
would get me a horse.

   I just finished 3rd grade and am going into 4th grade.
I loved my teacher. Her name was Mrs. Jensen. Daddy
said once I reach junior high school that I'll be old enough
to handle the horse when I come visit him on our every
other weekend visits together. He even said we could go
and look for a horse together. Daddy knows some people.
That'll be the best gift EVER. I love all animals, but horses
are the best. They are so beautiful and majestic. They are
so free when they run!

   We have a big backyard behind our house but there
is no room for a horse. We have neighbors next to us and

sidewalks in front of the houses. But we don't have a lot of things other people have. We're not poor, but we don't have an Atari. I hope we get a VCR soon because Mama said we can rent movies from the library! I love the library and like to go where the animal books are.

I like to draw, especially horses. Mama gave me a drawing pad that I use. Everyone tells me I am a good writer. Even Mrs. Jensen said so. Mama, too. Mrs. Jensen was the one who gave me this diary for my birthday when I was in her class last year. So here it is. I don't know how much I'm supposed to write. Mama and Ms. Jensen also said that I'm independent, sensitive, and "act mature for my age." Then everyone tells me I get way too excited about things. Whatever. Whenever I get excited, Mama tells me to "hold my horses." I wish I horses to hold.

Two weeks ago, Mama married Clint. He's OK, I guess. He makes things from wood when he's not at work in Raleigh. I'm not sure what Mama sees in him except that she says she's happy he has a good job. I don't know what he does. Mama says he works for "the state," whatever that means. The only thing he knows about horses is when he says, "I have to go see a man about a horse." I wanted to go with him, but he never lets me. I didn't like their wedding because it was soooooooo long. I had to stand there forever. Actually, I kinda hated it. Except some of the songs were OK. And I got to wear my new pink dress which I loved. I love dresses, especially when they twirl. They used to call me "Twinkletoes" all the time because I would dance and sing around all over the place.

I really love music, and I love to sing. I have a different

song in my head based on how I feel. Daddy is a drummer and he sings too. He's real good. Mama sings in a choir and at church. Clint can't sing at all. He tries but he shouldn't. I want to join choir when I get to junior high. Mama said I sang before I talked.

I go to Daddy's trailer to visit every other weekend. I love the movie The Fox and the Hound and I saw it with him when it came out last year. He also got me The Fox and the Hound record, book, and puzzle. When Mama and me lived alone, Daddy didn't come around much or didn't come when he said he would. Now he wants to see me more since Clint and Mama got married. We have so much fun together.

Clint came with his daughter. I met her a few times before the wedding. Her name is Lacey and she's going into 5th grade. She is really pretty. Everyone knows it. Especially her. She likes makeup and boys and stuff. Yuck! Animals are so much better. I have to do everything with her now, when it used to be just me and Mama.

I love my new bedroom. My room used to be upstairs with everyone but now I'm downstairs near the kitchen. I like to be close to Mama but also like having my bedroom away from everyone else. I love my desk and chair in my room and I have some of my horse drawings up on my bulletin board. I have a million horse posters! My favorites are the one of two bay foals playing and then the one of a palomino galloping in the field. Daddy likes palominos, but he calls them unperdictable. Not sure what that means. Or how to spell it.

I don't think we'll ever move out of North Carolina

We still live in Garner, but we had to move from our other house when they got married. I want to move when I grow up and love it sooooo much when we go to other places.

I had to go to a new school called Garner Elementary School for 3rd grade which I didn't like. I hated gym. I felt like everyone was looking at me. I'm not the biggest person in the class, but I'm close. I hated recess too because I didn't have anyone to play with. I liked to talk to the teachers at recess. They were nice, especially Mrs. Jensen and the 2nd grade teacher, Mrs. Phillips. Sometimes Mrs. Jensen told me to play with other students. I didn't want to play with them, I wanted to talk to her and the other teachers. I usually just sat on the swing. Or, I sat at the top of the slide and looked out at everyone playing. Then, when someone came, I just went down the slide. I pretended I just got there. When they left, I went back up and sat on top of the slide again.

Animals are the best and I have a lot of stuffed animals. I want to be a veterinarian when I grow up. I used to have a kitten when Mama and I lived together. I got to name her! She was gray, but I called her Brownie. She looked like a Brownie to me. But she got sick and died. Mama said I could get another cat. I named her Jelly Bean. She didn't look like a jelly bean either, but I like the name and I like jelly beans. I even got to watch when Jelly Bean had kittens. It was, like, 10:30 at night, and Mama said I could stay up late to watch! Jelly Bean cried a lot and there was a lot of goo. The baby kittens were so cute. They were like little moving logs.

When we moved into the new house, Jelly Bean came with us, sometimes going outside. But after only being at the new house for one day, she didn't come back. I kept yelling in the backyard, "Jelly Bean! Jelly Bean!" Mama said that the people living behind us had her and named her TinkerBell. But that wasn't her name. Her name was Jelly Bean. Mama said the people found Jelly Bean and gave her an operation so she wouldn't have any more kittens. That was fast. She wasn't even their cat. Jelly Bean got sick and died from that stupid operation.

Clint had a dog and a cat before he married Mama, but he didn't really like them. He said both of them ran away the day before the wedding. I thought that was weird. Sometimes my nose runs and I sneeze around dogs and cats and horses. My lungs feel tight too, like asthma. So, they said no more animals. But I never had any problems with Jelly Bean and she would still be here if we didn't have to move. I'm mad about that.

Anyway, three more years. Daddy is going to give me a horse and it will be the bestest birthday gift ever!

Can't wait! I will stop for now. See you later!

July 25, 1982

I went on and on when I wrote before but You-Know-Who might read this, so I'm not going to write as much. She thinks she's so cool because her blue eyes are so pretty and she's thin and never worries about her weight. And, her hair is always perfect. Plus, she would totally talk about me to everyone at school and I don't want them knowing what I write about. It's *my* diary.

August 25, 1982

Mama and Clint said that I could go horseback riding! I've been on ponies before when Mama led me around but I've never really been on my own. I'm not sure what the name of the place was but I was sooooooo excited to go! We went to this place where all these horses were tied up to fences. I got a horse named Trixie. She was white with big, brown spots all over. Some parts of her mane were white and some parts were brown. My feet could hardly reach the stirrups. Trixie's head bobbed up and down when we walked, like she was saying "Yes" all the time! The best thing about being on Trixie is I was so high up! I could see everything and felt so free. I already know some horse words from my horse books I checked out at the library. You sit in a thing called a saddle and hold onto long strings called reins. That big thing on the saddle is called a horn. Michelle was our guide and she didn't hold onto the horn. No one else did but me. I was afraid I was going to fall off. Luckily, I didn't. Trixie blew out her nose a lot because there was a lot of dust. Other horses stopped and tried to eat grass. One horse tried to eat a branch! That made me laugh, but Michelle told that girl to "Pull up on the reins! Don't let him eat!" Trixie was good. She just stood there and didn't try to eat.

We went to a wide-open place with a lot of grass and no trees and we trotted. Oh my gosh! Trotting is so fast! My butt hurt so bad but it was so fun! There was a girl there who talked a lot. She told me when we trotted, I could do something about a post. I didn't know what she meant. Michelle never told us, so I didn't listen to that girl. She was annoying.

When I got off, I could hardly walk and my legs felt weird. Michelle told me to stand at Trixie's side, not in front. Horses have eyes on the side of their faces and they can't see us if we're right in front of them. That's weird. Because when I talk to Mama or my teachers, I don't stand like that. Horses are different but sometimes they are totally better than people. Trixie let me pet her mane and she blew out her nose again. It was loud and scared me. And I got some snot on me, but not too much. Trixie stood there except when she put her head down to touch her hoof. There were flies that were bugging her. Trixie was so awesome and I love her! I can't wait to draw her and see her again. Whoops! I wasn't going to write so much again but I did!

October 10, 1982

Today Mama told me she is going to have a baby in five months. Like, I'm going to have a new brother or sister. Her stomach looked big. But I don't like it when people call me fat so I didn't say anything about it to Mama. It will be weird having a baby here. There are enough people here already and living with Lacey is enough. I hope the baby doesn't cry or poop a lot.

*G*ently closing the pages of my diary, I smiled, placing my hand flat over the cover. The nine years since I started this diary seemed like a lifetime ago.

Getting ready to leave home for college afforded me the opportunity to go through my things, or at least pack up what I thought I needed. Easier said than done. When I knelt down to rummage through what was under my bed, I spotted something familiar. Stretching my fingers to wiggle it free, my heart jumped.

I recognized the front cover with the image of a bay, a chestnut, and a grey horse galloping across a field. It was my old diary I had thought I lost. Flipping through the pages transported me back in time.

A sudden knock on the door jarred me out of my thoughts. "Maren Therese Markey! How's it going in there? Down to the short rows yet?"

When Mama uttered my full name, it was time to pay attention.

"Not yet, Mama!" I yelled back through the door.

"Well, supper's been ready and it's waiting for you!"

"OK, thanks. Be right there!"

The smell of roast beef and mashed potatoes greeted me in the kitchen. "I've been calling you for a while now. It was just you and me tonight, but I'm fixin' to go back to school," she said, placing her dishes in the dishwasher. "Parent-teacher conferences. Hoping the parents won't give me too much grief tonight."

I liked it when it was just Mama and me. But it rarely happened.

"So, how's the packing going?"

"Pretty well. Just have a lot of stuff I still need to box up."

"You're telling me?" she smirked.

"I know, I know. Probably shouldn't have waited until the last minute, but there is so much to do." I paused. "I came across my old diary that has galloping horses on the front."

"I'll bet. What *is* it about girls and horses?" she asked.

"It's hard to explain. I've just always loved and felt connected to them."

"I guess you never forget your first love," she said. "You've felt that way since you were in the womb. You popped out into the delivery room asking about them! Any animals, really. But, always horses."

"I know this is out-of-the-blue," I asked, scooping peas onto my plate. "But, do you remember the very first time I ever rode one? I think I was really little and I was on a pony somewhere where you led me around."

"Hm, not off the top of my head." She turned to look at the

clock on the microwave. "Oh, shoot, gotta get going!"

"I don't either. Just wondering."

"But you went to that camp for a few years. What was the name of it again?"

"Echo Lake."

"That's it. And, you took riding lessons at one point," she said, scanning the room. "And, of course, Fair Oaks."

"Of course."

"And, I think you went horseback riding with your Daddy Garrett a lot, too, right?" she asked, reaching into her handbag.

"Yeah."

"Did you ever go riding with Aunt Mimi?" she asked, fumbling around.

"Yes, on Mackinac Island."

Mama nodded, still looking around the room. "There's my keys! All right, I'll be back about 8:00. Everyone else should be home by then. If you could put away the food, I'd appreciate it. Oh, and start the dishwasher, too."

"OK. Have fun."

With one hand on the doorknob, and the other holding her handbag to her shoulder, she said, "Love you, Baby."

I looked up from playing with my peas.

She walked over to me and hugged me harder than usual. "Just can't believe you'll be leaving us tomorrow. My baby girl," she said, kissing the top of my head.

"Thanks, Mama. But I'm just going to State. Raleigh's only a half-hour away."

"It's far enough." She gave a tight smile as she hurried out, the door closing quietly behind her.

Finishing my last bite of roast beef, I settled into the silence of the house. My diary entries consumed my mind while I loaded the dishwasher, barely registering the sound of my glass clinking against the rubber prong and my silverware sliding into the plastic holder. After turning the dishwasher on, I jogged back to my room to discover what I had written next.

March 8, 1983

Sorry I haven't written in a really long time! I was looking for you forever, Diary, and finally found you hiding under my bed! So glad I found you because today is the day Mama goes in to have the baby. They just go in and take it out of her belly. I really miss her being here. I just hope she'll be right back. Sometimes I feel left out when I'm with Clint and Lacey. It's like they don't want me around.

Details from that day flooded my mind.

Arriving home for lunch, Lacey was already waiting in the kitchen since we rarely walked home from school together.

"What do you think she had?" I asked, clanking my house keys down on the kitchen table.

"I dunno," Lacey said, grabbing a glass from the cupboard.

"Is Mama coming home today, I hope?"

"Dunno that either," she said, filling her glass from the faucet. "All I know is that thing better not mess with my stuff."

The phone rang, startling us both. Lacey practically threw her glass down and lunged at the phone on the wall. I tore up the steps to the other phone in Mama and Clint's bedroom.

"Mama! How are you? We miss you!" I squealed.

"Calm down, Maren," Lacey snorted.

"I'm just so excited!"

"I'm…good…real…good," Mama said, drawing out her words. She sounded so tired. "Daddy Clint is here with me."

"Well…what is it? What did you have?" I blurted out.

Mama chuckled.

"I had a beautiful…."

"…yeah…"

"healthy…"

"…yeah…"

"happy…"

"….yeah…"

"little baby.…"

"Mama! Come on!"

"…boy."

My heart sank in stark contrast to Lacey's rejoicing downstairs.

"Really?" I moaned.

"Yep. He's so tiny and precious," Mama said.

"A boy?"

"Yep, a healthy boy. Ten little fingers and ten little toes. That's all we really wanted." Mama paused. "Girls, you're going to love him. You're going to be great…big…sisters," she said, as the fatigue returned.

"Yeah! Can't wait!" Lacey almost gloated into the phone.

"I guess," I said, twirling the long spiral cord around my finger.

"OK, girls," Clint said. "Let your mother rest. She's had a big day."

"Oh, yeah." I snapped out of my worrying thoughts. "When will you be home?"

"I should be home tomorrow night," Mama said.

"I love you Mama. I miss you so much."

"Yeah, sure do!" Lacey echoed.

"Love y'all," she said, almost inaudibly.

"Love you, too," I whispered. Hanging up the phone, my hand held the receiver down on the cradle, processing this news.

<u>Same day</u>

I can't believe Mama had a boy today. They named him CJ after Clint James. Boys—yuck.. They're so gross. I wanted a baby sister so bad. I could have taught her about animals and we could have laughed and had so much fun. Lacey is really happy though. I don't know why. What in the world am I going to do with a brother?

April 10, 1983

Dear Kiddo,

How are ya? Things are going well here. I'm keeping busy by gardening and hiking.

Now that Spring is here, I'm so excited to tell you that they're baaaack. You guessed it—Mackinac Island's most important residents, the horses, have returned! Some stay on the Island the entire winter, but most of them stay somewhere in Mackinaw City, or maybe even the U.P. I'm sure you remember that Michigan has an Upper and Lower Peninsula. Around here, when someone says the "U.P.", they mean the Upper Peninsula of Michigan. On Mackinac Island, they say the "Horse is King." Of course, I already know that's how you feel on a daily basis!

I thought of you when I saw this tiny, tan stuffed horse. Hope you like him! Hoping to see you before Hallomas this year.

Until then, keep your spirit up!

Love, Aunt Mimi

Lodged in between the pages of my diary were a few of my Aunt Mimi's letters. Mama's older sister, and my fervent champion, Aunt Mimi wrote often. Her frequent letters, as well as birthday and Christmas cards, lifted my mood. She was not only my aunt, but my friend, as well. I could always rely on her smile and support. Aunt Mimi lives only a few hours away from Mackinac Island and relishes the opportunity to inform me when the Island's most important residents arrived in the spring and left for the winter.

Located between the Upper and Lower Peninsula of Michigan, and reachable only by ferry, Mackinac Island's only modes of transportation for the residents and tourists are either walking, biking, or horses. No motor vehicles are allowed, which made it all the more magical for me. Since Mama and I visited when I was a baby, my memories are confined to the photographs taken.

*T*urning the next page in my diary, I wondered what happened next since distant memories don't always match up to what actually happened. Packing for college still awaited me, but I thought, what was the harm in reading just a few more pages?

May 5, 1983

I am sooooo excited to be visiting Daddy this weekend. I like my suitcase. It's blue and tan and just my size. I wish it had an animal on it, but I still love it. It does get smelly at Daddy's because he smokes a lot, but we just air it out on the porch when I get home. It's harder when it's winter because the suitcase gets cold but it still has cigarette smell on it. But, it's all worth it. Daddy sleeps on the couch in the living room when I go to his trailer. He's so nice to let me sleep in the only bedroom. Plus, the pullout couch kinda smells. More than just cigarette smoke. I don't think he sleeps in his bed a lot. Not sure why, because it's like, brand new. Maybe it's because the TV is bigger in the living room. I also like to sleep with a fan on for the noise. Mama teases me about it but Daddy knows it's relaxing and helps me sleep.

I hate Sunday nights when I have to pack up my suitcase and go back home. It's hard to come back here and I secretly hope Daddy forgets. I like school and my teacher, Miss Torres, but I <u>really</u> like being with Daddy and Morris.

On the phone, Daddy asked me what I wanted to do at our next visit. I said horseback riding! Duh. That's always what I want to do. I told him about the place I rode Trixie and he said he'd take me there. I guess Mama told him where to go.

I can picture Daddy clear as day. Just shy of six feet tall, his slender build appeared to tower over everyone. Especially me. His bright blue eyes, occasional attempts at a goatee, and contagious smile were often hard for people to resist. Especially women. I definitely got my shorter height, thick brown hair, and bigger curves from Mama but she always said I had Daddy's smile and his temper. I felt fortunate to have gotten the smaller hands and feet from Mama. They joked that my green eyes came from Mama's Irish side and the grit from Daddy's Scottish side.

<u>May 7, 1983</u>

Best day of my entire life! Daddy and I went back to where I rode Trixie before. Now I know the name of it. It's called Randy's Ranch. There were horses everywhere again, but no Trixie. I was sad. Trixie was so good. They brought a horse with lots of spots on his butt over to me. His name was Snickers. Daddy got a black horse!

His name was Wildfire. The most beautifulest horse I've ever seen. Sorry Trixie and Snickers. They said Wildfire could be a handful, but Daddy can handle anything. Daddy even played a song called "Wildfire" for me on his record player when we got back. I cried it was so amazing. Snickers is the best! I sneezed and my nose ran and it was a little hard to breathe. But, not too bad and I will never forget this. The best day of my entire life!

The guy at Randy's Ranch said Daddy and I could go out on the trail by ourselves, without a guide. We walked the winding wooded trails which led to an open field with one tree. When Daddy first asked me if we wanted to go faster, I had some trepidation since Snickers' trot hurt my hind end.

It all happened so quickly. Before I knew it, Snickers' head dropped as his front leg shot out in front of him and we were moving at a pace I had never experienced before. I was just hanging on in response to the rocking motion.

"You're doing it, Mare! You're cantering!" Daddy shouted atop a cantering Wildfire.

I could hardly catch my breath, keeping my mouth closed for fear of accidentally swallowing a bug.

"That's my girl!" he yelled out. Wildfire's thundering hooves shook the ground as Daddy approached us from behind. Cantering next to Daddy and Wildfire was unlike anything I had ever felt before.

I gripped the saddle horn so tight my fingers hurt, but had enough strength to slow Snickers back down to a trot, then a walk. Daddy and Wildfire followed suit.

"That was so awesome!" I exclaimed, breathless, as I pet Snickers' sweaty neck. "Thank you so much, Snickers, Daddy *and* Wildfire!"

In the distance, a man on a horse shouted, waving his arms around. "Hey, y'all come back now!"

"Oh, man. We have to go already?" I lamented.

"Guess so. OK, thanks!" Daddy yelled back.

With every step back to the barn, I alternated between thanking Daddy and Snickers.

When we dismounted, Daddy said, "You did it, Mare! You really did it. Daddy's so proud of you." I wrapped my arms around him, trying not to cough and holding back a sneeze from the combination of cigarette and old coffee smell caked into his shirt.

"Mama! I'm home!" I yelled into the foyer.

"Hi," Mama said, tip-toeing down the steps, her finger to her mouth. "Did you have a good time?"

"Yeah, I did!" I said, setting my suitcase down. "I cantered—can you believe it?" My voice rose in volume.

She glanced upstairs and grimaced. "You did? That's great," she said, in a loud whisper. "CJ just went down for the night, so I'm hoping he'll sleep."

"Do you know what cantering is?"

"I know it's something with horses."

"Yeah, it's when you go like this." I demonstrated a gallop in a tight circle. "And, you feel like you're going to fall off, but you don't. You just hang on. It's so fast, Mama!"

"Oh, that's great, Baby." Whimpers grew from the bedroom upstairs. "Darn it," she said, looking back up at CJ's room. "But, glad you're home!" she loudly whispered, tip-toeing back up the steps.

I looked around the empty foyer, grabbed my tan and blue suitcase, and choked back a few tears. But after remembering Snickers, I galloped over to my room. Trying not to make a sound, of course.

The next morning at breakfast, I was still walking on air,

despite a short and fitful night. Clint had already left for work and Mama was warming CJ's formula in the microwave while he sat as patiently as any baby could sitting in his highchair. I was armed with my World Book Encyclopedia.

"Did you know that horses are measured in 'hands'?" I asked Lacey who was munching on her cereal, reading the side of the box.

She didn't look up.

"'Hands'?" Mama asked.

"Yeah, instead of saying they are, like five feet or six feet high, horses are measured in 'hands.'"

"No, I didn't know that," Mama said, checking the temperature of the formula on her forearm.

"See, here in the encyclopedia," I said, jumping up next to her, fumbling with the flimsy pages. "It also says that when a horse jumps, like over a fence, it's the back legs' responsibility to get them over the jump. Neat, huh?"

"Yeah, that is," she said, peering over my shoulder to get a closer look. "Lord, I hated selling those things, but those encyclopedias were a good investment after all."

"Yeah, thanks Mama. I love them!"

Lacey rolled her eyes and headed into the bathroom.

"Guess what?" I asked, following her.

"You cantered. I heard," she said, removing the blue eye shadow wand from its tube.

"Do you know what cantering is?" I asked, leaning against the bathroom counter.

"Not really," she said, applying a blue swipe to her closed left eye. I don't think she was allowed to wear makeup, but she never got in trouble when she did. At home or at school.

"It's when you go really fast. Not as fast as a gallop. But faster than a trot."

"Trot?" she asked, applying eye shadow to her right lid.

"The bouncy one."

"Oh, yeah. I think I did that once," she said, closing the compact. "Hurt my ass."

"It can," I chuckled. "Cantering is like being on a rocking horse, only way faster. It's just the most awesome thing. Ever!"

"Uh, huh," she mumbled as she applied red lipstick.

"So, if you ever want to canter, just let me know. I can tell you all about it!"

"Yeah, OK," she snickered, rolling her eyes. "No offense, Maren, just not that interested," she said, blotting her lips on a tissue.

"I know," I shrugged. "Just thought you might want to know."

"OK, sure," she said, giving herself a final once over.

I knew she never gave a damn, but anything to get her from not thinking about or admiring herself was a good thing. Give the mirror a break for once.

<u>May 22, 1983</u>

The Black Stallion is the BEST movie. Ever! There is no more to say. Except that it is the BEST movie EVER. Daddy just rented it and we watched it on his VCR. I was on the edge of my seat. Daddy laughed when he saw how much I loved the movie and it made him cough a lot. It's based on a book. The Black Stallion is the most AWESOME horse I have ever seen. He kinda looks like Wildfire that Daddy rides. You could hear the Black Stallion breathing and snorting, and when he ate from Alec's hands for the first time, his lips made a funny noise. Alec was so lucky he got to ride him. When he rides him for the first time on the beach is the best. Just the two of them and the music is incredible! The end of the movie I was crying because it was so beautiful. Just wish there wasn't a yucky snake scene when the Black Stallion and Alec were on the island but the Black Stallion protreckted Alec. I read in a magazine that there was a piece of glass between the snake and Alec, so he wouldn't get bit by the fangs. I want to be alone on an island, just me and a horse. No Lacey. No Clint. Not even Mama or CJ. Just me and a horse. I could ride all day. Best movie I've ever seen in my entire life!

June 4, 1983

Hard to believe that I'm almost done with 4th grade. Miss Torres was nice. I liked her, but I'm really excited that I might get Mrs. Smith for 5th grade!

Daddy got a new cat named Morris since the last time I was there! He said we could get another cat and I could pick out any dog or cat that I wanted. We drove to the animal shelter, but they were closed. He said we could go back some other time. Sometimes my throat starts to itch and my eyes get watery when I'm around Morris, but it's not too bad. I gave Daddy one of my horse drawings. He said he liked it and put it up on the refrigerator.

Daddy just got paid! He showed me his $20 bills. I got to count them. There were five of them. Not sure what he does though. Something with houses.

We were on a boat on Lake Jordan. Then he rode Wildfire and I rode Snickers and we cantered again. I can't get enough of riding and cantering. I could do it all day, every day! We went to Bojangles and Baskin-Robbins for my favorite Pralines and Cream ice cream. I think it's Daddy's favorite, too.

I don't like Daddy smoking. He said he's trying to quit. But I like that he remembers to pick me up for our visits now!

June 8, 1983

Sometimes I can't shut off the thoughts in my head.

Many nights after everyone would go to sleep, I'd lie awake tossing and turning, ruminating about so many things. Mama once said I was "afraid of my own shadow." I often arranged my stuffed animals to encircle me—a menagerie of cats, dogs, horses, an elephant, and even a bear.

One time, there was a huge thunderstorm when Mama and I lived alone. After a jolting thunder crash, I dashed from my room into hers.

The rain came down in sheets and the lightning lit up her room in flashes.

"Mama," I whispered to her back under the covers.

"I was wondering when you'd come," she said, yawning and rolling toward me. She lifted up the blankets and I hopped into the warm bed.

"Just remember, Baby, anytime you hear the thunder, it means the angels got a strike." She tucked the sheets and blankets around me.

"Strike?"

"Yes, remember when we went bowling with Aunt Mimi? When someone is a good bowler, they get a strike. That means all the pins have been knocked down."

"Oh. But, it's so loud."

"Yeah, but it just means they're good."

"They're *really* good."

"Yep. Now close your eyes and try to get to sleep," she said, wrapping her comforting arms around me. The rain pounded on the roof and the thunder kept letting us know it was still there. But I wasn't afraid anymore. The angels were playing really well that night.

After we moved, everyone's bedrooms were upstairs and

mine was downstairs. I felt as though my room would come alive at night. The images of the monsters I saw on television would flood my mind. Godzilla, *Gremlins, The Dark Crystal*, you name it. The thoughts of nuclear war also invaded my mind, thinking of the image of an angry bear, representing the USSR, holding onto a nuclear missile. Next to him was an angry eagle, representing the US, with a nuclear missile in its angry beak. Both standing on huge piles of missiles. When I watched some of the television show *The Day After*, I tore up the steps to Mama and Clint's room. I know they couldn't save me if there ever was a nuclear war, but I just wanted to be near Mama if it ever happened.

I also worried about Daddy and his smoking, and I relived the awful day when CJ had his allergic reaction after eating something with milk. Mama's crying out "Clint! Clint!" still haunts me. I don't think I've ever heard her so scared, which terrified me. The commercials of starving children in Africa and other places in the world also touched me. No one in our family ever talked about them and it seemed as though I was the only one who worried about them.

The only thing that really calmed me and made me feel better was thinking about, or being around, horses. I admired how they seemed to be so free, as if nothing ever held them back. They can be who they are and not worry about anything. And they never seemed to have any problems falling asleep.

July 10, 1983

Daddy said we could go to the Outer Banks for a horseback ride on my birthday! I've wanted to ride a horse on the beach my whole, entire life! I get to be like Alec and the Black Stallion riding on the island! I'm humming the music now from the first time Alec rode him on the island!

Sometimes at Daddy's, right after I shut the bedroom door to go to sleep, his front door opens and I hear a woman talking and they're laughing. Then the two of them can't go to sleep because they move around a lot because the couch starts squeaking. That's OK. Sometimes I have a hard time getting to sleep, too. I just turn the fan up on high. Maybe they need to get a fan to help them sleep.

After Daddy and I made our obligatory trip to Baskin-Robbins, we made our trek to the Outer Banks. The drive seemed to drag on since it was a long trip from Garner, but once we turned into the entrance, I knew we were driving through the gateway to the best moment in my life.

Daddy's truck sputtered up the gravel driveway, leading to a practically empty barn and stables.

"Helloooo?" Daddy's words echoed through the empty grounds. I jogged behind.

"Hey, yourself, "a girl said, emerging from the office area. Her large cowboy hat matched the size of her boobs.

"Hey," Daddy said, smiling, drawing out the one-syllable word.

"What can I do for you?" she asked, returning the smile.

"My daughter and I would like to go riding. It's her birthday."

"Happy birthday, but sorry to say you just missed the last ride of the day."

I knew we shouldn't have stopped at Baskin-Robbins.

"The thing is, we drove all the way from the Triangle to get here," Daddy said. "We've ridden before, cantered even. My daughter's really good and she's wanted to ride on the beach ever since she saw *The Black Stallion*."

"Yeah, great movie."

"And, we've heard such great things about your place," he said, looking around. His eyes landed on her. "That hat really brings out your eyes."

"Thanks," she smirked.

"How long have you worked here?" Daddy said, cocking his head as he often did when talking to girls.

"About three years. Stables have been here about five."

"You really take good care of things around here. Do you always take care of things so well?"

"I try," she said, grinning at him. "But only things I care about."

"How can we become something you care about?" he smiled, drawing out his words.

"I don't know," she said, holding back a smile, and narrowing her eyes. "What will you do for me?"

"Well, after our ride today, I'll get your number and take you out. Whenever and wherever you want to go. And, then…well, we can take it from there."

She glanced over at me and sighed.

"All right, I'll get my horse, Thunder. I'll put her on River," she said, nodding to me. "And, let's see what bucking, spooky bronco we can get for you. Comanche, yeah! He'll fit the bill. They've only been out once today and are good on the beach."

"Comanche's a stallion, I take it?" Daddy asked.

"Nope, he's a gelding. You know—no balls."

"Oh!" Daddy bellowed. "She's got spunk! I like spunk," he said, looking her up and down. "Let me tell you something—Comanche and I have *nothing* in common in that department."

There was so much I wanted to say, but watching Daddy work his magic rendered me unable to speak.

The girl brought out River, a chestnut mare, for me, and another chestnut, Comanche, for Daddy. The only difference was a blaze on River's forehead whereas Comanche had a star on his. Oh, and the fact that Daddy's horse had no balls.

The two of them talked non-stop. Luckily, Comanche and Thunder liked each other because they were walking side-by-side. I always heard it wasn't good to do that, but they seemed to like each other. Both the horses and people. River was a sweet girl, but she didn't move as fast as the other two.

Winding through the enclosed forest, we finally came to a wide sandy stretch opening to the white-capped, rolling waves of the Atlantic Ocean. A few seagulls in the distance greeted us.

"Daddy!" I squealed. It felt as though my heart was going to explode.

"Yeah, Mare!" he said, turning around to me.

"Can we really canter?"

"Once we get to the actual water, we can," the girl answered.

With every step River took in the sand, my heart beat faster and faster. I couldn't get to the water's edge soon enough.

"All right now. We can trot and then ask them to canter."

Daddy and the girl each made clicking noises and before I knew it, they were cantering down the shore. I clicked, made a kissing noise, and tightened my feet around River's barrel. Although it took a little bit more coaxing to get her to canter, when we did, it was magic.

The music of Alec and the Black Stallion galloping in the water for the first time filled my head and heart. Each note synchronized with River's hooves splashing in the water beneath us. I let out another squeal and River's ears swiveled toward me. When we finally stopped next to Daddy and the girl, my cheeks were wet, from the splashes of water and happy tears.

"So, did you like it, Mare?" Daddy asked.

"Yeah! That was the *most* fun I've ever had! In my whole, entire life!" I said, a little out of breath.

"Are you ready to go again?" the girl asked, looking at Daddy.

"I'm always ready," he smirked.

"OK, Cowboy, last one to the other end loses," she said, kicking Thunder and yelling "Ya!" The dark bay bolted into a full gallop from a standstill, like they do in Westerns.

"Oh, no, you don't!" Daddy said, squeezing his legs into Comanche's side.

Sand sprayed in all directions as the two horses galloped into the horizon. I wanted to give River a break anyway, so I held her back. She threw her head a little, but luckily, didn't fight me too much.

Finally releasing on the reins, I made a kissing noise, sending River into a trot. A little more air-kissing and we were cantering again. *The Black Stallion* music played in my mind along with images of me galloping down the island. I just had no desire to do it without holding onto the reins, like Alec did.

When River and I returned to the opening of the woods, Daddy and the girl were there laughing and quibbling about who had gotten there first. I was reveling in my post-beach-horseback riding high and was perfectly happy bringing up the rear by myself. After all, Alec and the Black Stallion rode by themselves. Daddy and the girl talked and laughed again, riding side-by-side back to the barn.

Dismounting from River, I noticed all four of our horses' legs were splattered with sand and dirt. I reached my arm under River's neck, giving her a big hug. Some of the moist gunk from her neck fell onto my arm, but I didn't care. "Thank you, River, for working so hard. I love you. Hope to see you again real soon."

Outside the mounting area, Daddy and the girl stood by the office laughing, standing closer than they had before. I felt like I was interrupting a private conversation.

"That was awesome, Daddy. Thank you," I said, side-hugging him. I could feel my throat getting itchy and I sneezed.

"You OK?"

"Oh, yeah!" I said, wiping my nose.

"You are so welcome, Mare," he said, side-hugging me back.

The girl handed a pen and paper to Daddy.

"And, thank you…"

"Roxie," she said.

"Roxie. Beautiful name. Thank you for making this so… much…fun."

"You'll call. Soon," she demanded.

"Yes, ma'am," he said, taking her hand and kissing it. "I'll be seeing you real soon."

We got into Daddy's truck for the five-hour trip home. Since I couldn't stop talking about River and my first-time cantering on the beach, the time seemed to go by even faster.

I don't know if Daddy ever took that girl, Roxie, out. If he did, I never heard about it and I never asked.

July 23, 1983

Daddy is amazing on the drums. Everyone wants to play with him. The group he plays with the most is called The Hounds. He says they are a "cover band." Daddy says that means they sing other bands' songs. They don't write their own songs, but they are still awesome!

Daddy has almost every record ever made! He kept telling me the name of a song after he played one. There was a huge pile of them all over the floor when he was done! Before I put them all back in their sleeves and back on the shelf, I wrote down the names because he said them so fast. Sometimes he can really talk fast and then other times he gets real quiet and sad.

My favorite songs Daddy told me they play were "Stormy" by Classics 4 and "Love Lifting Me Higher" by Jackie Wilson. I really like "Windy" by The Association. There is a really cool bass part at the beginning. Daddy says he gets to sing with everyone. He said that's harmonizing. I also like "Daydream Believer" by The Monkeys and "Get Ready" by Temptashuns. Those are old songs but I still like them.

Daddy says he likes songs with fun drum parts. His favorite song is "Wipeout" by Sufaris. That makes me think about what you do after you go to the bathroom. He also loves "In the Air Tonight" and "Against All Odds" by Phil Collins. Daddy said that Mr. DeAndre really likes "Against All Odds" too, because there is an awesome keyboard part. Whenever I hear those songs on the radio, I know Daddy and the guys can play it better. Mama likes to listen to The Carpenters and Andy Griffith records, but I like Daddy's songs better.

As I twirled around the room, singing with Daddy to "Sunday Will Never Be the Same," he harmonized and drummed on the side of the couch with pens. The hot summer evening and longer visitation allowed us to have the windows open, sharing our music with the world.

"Sing it, Mare. Bring it home!" Morris didn't seem to care about the commotion we were causing.

As I sang into the pen as a microphone, the kitchen phone rang.

"Hello?...DeAndre, man! What's up?...Practice—tonight?... Got my daughter this weekend...It's cool...Yeah, she'll have fun. Where at?...That's not too far...They got drums?...Nah, don't need the whole set...We'll head over soon...Later."

He returned to the living room. "Hey, Mare!"

"I heard. I'm going with you, Daddy, right?"

"Yeah, this'll be great! You'll get to meet the guys and we can all jam together. They'll love ya."

On that warm summer night, we crossed Daddy's weedy front yard, stopping at the edge of the two-lane road in front of his trailer. Bright headlights lit up the star-filled sky since street lights were few and far between.

"C'mon, we can run it now before another car comes!"

We jogged across the road and walked along the grassy edge for what seemed like hundreds of miles. In reality, it was probably about a mile, but the evening's darkness made it seem so much longer.

Daddy stopped to take a breath. We both spotted a gravel driveway to a large trailer lit up with lights, music, and laughter. "This is it."

A roar erupted as we walked through the front door. "Hey, look who's here!" a jet-black haired guy, surrounded by women, yelled from a faded green couch. Drums, guitars, and a keyboard were set up in the middle of the room with various box fans providing oxygen to the humid night. "Who let you out of your cage, you crazy son of a b—?"

"Hey, my daughter's here!" Daddy said. Numerous guys with shiny foreheads laughed from their folding chairs in the living room.

Like I've never heard that word before.

"Hey, Malik," Daddy said, throwing an arm around the shoulders of a quiet man standing next to the door. "This is my daughter, Maren."

"Hey, Miss Maren," Malik said, smiling down at me. He was a tall, broad-shouldered man with warm eyes. "Want a Pepsi?" he asked, reaching into the cooler next to our feet.

"Yes, please. Thank you, Mr. Malik."

"Thanks, man," Daddy said. "Malik here plays the bass."

"He tries anyway," the same guy who yelled from the couch said, handing Daddy a beer.

"And this wise guy is Francisco," Daddy said. "He plays the guitar."

"Acoustic *and* electric."

"Yes, 'Cisco, you can do it all," Daddy joked.

"That's right. All of it and don't you forget it, man!" Francisco said.

"How's the job goin'?" Malik asked.

"Eh, was late a few times. So, I quit. They were assholes anyway," Daddy said.

"You just started!" Francisco said, before disappearing into the large crowd.

Daddy waved him off. "Malik, hear anything from California yet?"

"Naw, man."

"When we were at The Boulevard playing the other night, they hadn't heard anything either," Daddy said.

"Fixin' to move out there?"

"Never know," Daddy said, taking a gulp from his bottle. "It's the best place for music. Love playing at The Boulevard and the groove here but nothing beats being out west. We're still playing at The Boulevard next weekend, right?"

"Far's I know," Malik said.

"Hey, y'all decided to come after all!" a guy shouted behind us.

"Hey, yeah!" Daddy said, turning around, slapping him on the shoulder and giving the lady with him a peck on the cheek.

"DeAndre, this is my daughter, Maren. DeAndre plays the keyboard and sings."

Meeting all of Daddy's friends made me feel like I was meeting celebrities.

"Nice to meet you, Miss Maren." He was tall, thin, with a smile that lit up the room, and his forehead glistened with a few small beads of sweat.

"Nice to meet you, too, Mr. DeAndre."

"I want you to meet my wife, Tiana."

"So, you're the famous Miss Maren?" she asked, extending her hand to me. "Nice to meet you." Her hand was as soft and smooth as her voice.

"Thank you, ma'am. You, too."

"Hey, Garrett, who's this lovely young lady?" A woman asked. Smelling of alcohol, she looked down at me through curly, teased hair.

"Cindy, this is my daughter, Maren. Mare, this is my friend, Cindy."

"You lucky girl," she said.

"Oh, Cind." Daddy feigned embarrassment. "Cindy here's the best," he said, wrapping his arm around her waist.

"Now don't tell him this. But, this here's a special guy."

Daddy pulled her closer and kissed her on the cheek.

"Hey, Cindy! Shake the lead out and leave your boyfriend alone!" someone hollered from the kitchen.

Daddy set down his beer.

"Well, let's do this!" he said, rubbing his hands together as he eyed the drums setup.

The first notes they played almost blew me away. I had never seen Daddy so happy as I watched Malik, DeAndre, Francisco, and

Daddy "jam," as they called it. The singing, head bobbing and clapping from the others made it feel like I was at a concert on that sticky summer night. Sitting next to Tiana made it even more fun because she really got into it. I even raised my can of Pepsi as everyone sang, "Play That Funky Music."

My Daddy was a real rock star.

When they finished playing, that Cindy woman went straight for Daddy. He gave her a peck on the lips as she stood really close to him. A grey-haired, scraggly guy joined them when Daddy motioned for me.

"Mare, this here's Mr. Red. He lives in the trailer next door."

"Hey, Miss Maren, I'm Mr. Begley, but you can call me 'Mr. Red.'" The smoke smell from his breath accentuated his yellowed teeth.

"Mr. Red's dog has puppies that are looking for homes," Daddy said. "What do you think about going over and picking one out?"

"Oh, my gosh, yes!" I said, giving a small jump despite the late hour.

"We're leaving now!" Daddy yelled to everyone. The crowd responded in one loud farewell.

"Bye, Garrett," the Cindy woman said, giving Daddy a quick kiss.

The difference in decibel levels between the inside of the trailer and the outside made my ears ring. We followed Mr. Red across the gravel to a backyard shed. Distant grunts and puppy squeaks filled the air. Mr. Red opened the door to a box containing four puppies climbing over one very patient mother.

"What kind are they?" Daddy asked.

"Heinz 57. Mama here is a Lab and we think one of the neighbor's Carolina Dogs mighta gotten to her."

"So cute!" I said, picking up a squiggly black pup. "I like this one."

"He likes you, too," Mr. Red said.

"You like that one, Mare?" Daddy crouched down next to me. "I guess we'll take him."

"Good deal. My Mrs. will be happy. We got kittens, too."

"Kittens!" I squealed.

"Geez, Red. Any of your animals fixed?" Daddy asked, shaking his head.

"Daddy, can we just look at them? *Please?*"

"Every little girl needs a dog and a cat," Mr. Red said. "Or, in your case, a dog and two cats."

"You're killin' me, Red," Daddy said, smiling. "Yeah, Mare. Why not?"

Behind and almost underneath the shed was a box of kittens, tumbling over each other. Another patient mother seemed to silently plead, "Help me!" She reminded me of the time when my kitty Jelly Bean had her litter of kittens and Mama let me stay up late to watch.

I picked up a mostly white kitten, with a few faded markings around its head, neck and belly. "I like this one. Is it a girl or boy?"

"Let's take a look," Mr. Red said, turning the protesting kitten on its back. "That is a little girl."

"Awww…I really like her." She snuggled under my chin against my shoulder as I kissed her head.

"Great!"

"All right, we're good to go!" Daddy said, hanging onto the wiggly puppy. "Do you like your new pets, Mare?"

"Yes, Daddy. Thank you." The kitten I was holding and the puppy in Daddy's arms touched noses.

"What do you think we should name her?"

"Um…I think we should call her Rosie," I said.

"Rosie's good! And, how 'bout Dino for this pup, after The Flintstones' dog."

"Yeah!"

"Now, hold on to her real tight."

"Yes," I said, hugging the squiggly kitten even closer, despite feeling a sneeze coming on.

"Thanks again, Red," Daddy said.

"No, thank *you!*"

I said it before and I'll say it again.

My Daddy really was a rock star.

Augusт 6, 1983

Going to the McCandless store always makes me happy. Maybe someday I'll get Wildfire.

The bell on the door of McCandless boutique shop jingled as we walked in. It was one of my favorite shops in Garner because even though it was August, the fall smells of cinnamon, pumpkin pie, and apple cider candles greeted us.

Marching to the back of the store, I located my favorite area—where all the stuffed animals resided. A few from my menagerie at home were purchased there and it was always a thrill to see what new ones they had in stock. My eyes studied the seemingly disorganized piles, finding a particularly special one at the very top. A huge smile grew across my face.

"Look, Daddy!" I pointed to a large, black horse roughly the size of a medium dog standing on all fours. "That is the most beautiful horse that is a stuffed animal I've ever seen!"

"Yeah, you're right."

"Can you get him for me?" I stood on my tip-toes, stretching my fingers as far as I could reach.

"Sure, you mean this one?" he asked, picking up a fluffy raccoon.

"No."

"OK, this one?" he asked, lifting up an owl.

"No, Daddy!" I tried stretching up even farther.

"What about this one? Or, this one? Or, this one?" he asked, pointing to a furry bear, frog, and monkey.

"No, Daddy!" I cried out, practically falling over. "The horse one—The Black Stallion!"

"All right," he chuckled. He was careful to pull it down from the top row of the pile, because they were packed in like sardines. A small, fuzzy bear went tumbling. "Whoops. Got him."

I wrapped my arms around the black horse, hugging him tight. "Wow, he is the most beautiful thing I've ever seen. His tag says his name is 'Wildfire.' Just like the Wildfire you ride, Daddy!"

"How about that?" he said.

Daddy mentioned to the employee that I loved horses but I didn't hear most of what they said, figuring it was adult stuff anyway. I didn't care that stuffed animals were for little kids. If I couldn't have a real horse, I'd take a stuffed one. Meandering up and down the aisles with Wildfire safely tucked under my arm, I introduced my new friend to other things in the store. The candles, books, cards, knick knacks, and more stuffed animals.

"Sir, we're going to be closing," the clerk said.

"Just a few more minutes? She's really having fun."

"Sorry, man."

I was busy showing Wildfire the cash register because, you know, he had never seen that front area of the store before.

"OK, time to put him back now, Mare," Daddy said.

"Oh, Daddy, can I have him though? I would love him." I pressed my face deeper into the horse's neck.

"It's $50.00. That's a lot of money."

"I know," I muttered.

"C'mon, we'll come back sometime to see him," he said, tugging the horse from my arms.

He nestled the black horse back on the shelf, propping him up between two teddy bears. I couldn't stop staring at Wildfire.

Daddy took my hand. "C'mon, now. Let's go."

From the exit door, I turned back around. It almost looked like Wildfire was saying, "Please don't leave me."

Blinking hard against the tears, I pushed on the door, jingling the bell once again.

<u>August 7, 1983</u>

I got to see a baby horse get born! It was exciting! Hopefully when I'm a vet, I'll get to do this, too. They said the mama's milk was coming in. I guess horses have boobs, too. They're just closer to their butt than ours are. The mama's name was Gypsy and she was in pain. I didn't like that. Her tail was wrapped up so all the goo wouldn't get on it. When Gypsy was on her side, she held it up so the baby could come out. She pushed really hard and sometimes grunted. She farted a lot but all horses do that. A lot. She definitely pooped, but horses do that a lot, too. She kept pushing and her hole looked like a big slit that got bigger and bigger. It looked like pee coming out, but they told me that was "allantoic fluid." I'm glad they told me the real name. I'm big enough to know. It got kinda weird at the end but it was amazing!

"Wake up, Mare!" Daddy whispered, nudging my arm.

"Daddy?" I blinked several times to focus on his face peering down at me.

"I've been trying to get you up for the last five minutes!"

"What's wrong?" I asked, looking over at the clock. 2:36 am. Dino, the puppy, jumped up on the bed and the soft mews from Rosie helped snap me out of my deep sleep.

"It's time!"

"Time for what?" I asked, with dry lips and a crackly voice. "Dino, stop licking me."

"Time for the baby horse!" he said.

"Baby horse?"

"Yes, c'mon. We're gonna see a baby horse be born!" he said, tugging on my arm.

"Oh my gosh! Where is it?" I asked, stumbling out of bed and fumbling around. "I need a sweater."

"At my buddy's barn. I was talking to him the other day and he told me his mare, Gypsy, was going to give birth."

I braced myself on the bureau and struggled to open a drawer.

"Here," he said, tossing one of his sweaters to me. "So, I told him, 'Let me know when Gypsy's about to give birth. My daughter Maren would go ape sh—I mean, 'She would love it'. So, he did! Really good guy."

"This will be so awesome, Daddy," I said through a loud yawn.

"I knew you'd love it. Wanted it to be a surprise."

"I do, Daddy. Thank you."

"You're welcome, Mare," he said, hugging me tightly. "I love you, you know. You're my pride and joy."

Through bleary eyes, I smiled up at him.

"But, c'mon—we don't wanna miss the action!" he said, motioning to the door.

*I*n the pitch-black night, we drove up a long, curvy driveway leading to the barn. The outside lights almost blinded my still sleepy eyes as they struggled to focus on a man emerging from the barn to greet us. The gravel beneath our feet crackled as Daddy extended his hand, saying, "Thanks again, man. She's really happy to be here." Turning to me, Daddy said, "Mare, this is my friend, Mr. Gary."

"Nice to meet you, Mr. Gary. Thank you for letting me watch a baby get born." My excitement intensified after hearing my own words.

"You're welcome," he laughed. "I understand you want to be a vet."

"Yeah!" I said, realizing again how loud my response was.

Daddy smiled at me and asked Mr. Gary, "How's it going?"

"This definitely is the foal time of year. Misty just had one, but poor Daisy's didn't make it," he said, casting a long shadow.

"Oh, man. That sucks."

Enough of this chit-chat! I twisted my body trying to peek into the barn.

"Eh, it happens," Mr. Gary said. "Gypsy's about ready. Are you ready for this, Miss Maren?"

"Yes, sir. I can't wait! I've seen a baby kitten be born, but never anything as spectacular as this!"

Both of them snickered. Maybe they didn't know I knew the word "spectacular."

The dimly lit barn provided just enough light to see Gypsy. She walked in circles in her stall, frequently stopping to look at her side, occasionally stopping to paw at the ground and then stomp her front leg. She then stretched out both of her front legs and dropped her head between them while her butt was up in the air. It looked like she was bowing. I heard the guy say she was "foaling down." I thought he said, "falling down," because that's what she did next.

"Oh my gosh! Is she dead?" I asked in a loud whisper.

"Nah, this is all part of it," Mr. Gary said.

It was scary watching her go through it, since it looked as though she was in agony. It hurts me to see any animal in pain, regardless of the reason.

A whoosh of fluid spewed out like a hose turned on full blast. Something white emerged, encased in a sac, like it was encased in thick plastic wrap. Gypsy tried to stand, but couldn't, grunting the entire time. On the next contraction, I realized I was seeing the baby's front legs inside the sac.

"She's coming!" I squealed, gripping the side of the wooden stall door.

"Shhhh, you're right, Mare. That's the baby's front legs," Daddy said.

With each contraction, more fluid, poop, and what appeared to be blood came out, but Mr. Gary said there was nothing to worry about. The first sign of the head made me squeal again. "She's really coming now!" I said, jumping up and down. From the get-go, we all thought the foal was a girl.

"Yes, she's really coming," Daddy whispered, kneeling next to me.

It's hard to believe that, at one point, the foal's head and front legs came out at the same time. Poor Gypsy. I remember having such empathy for her; it must have been excruciating. She rolled on her side, with her legs stretched out, looking very stiff.

After a few more pushes and contractions, the foal's entire body emerged on its side, accompanied by more buckets of fluid. Even though Gypsy was big, it's hard to believe how large her baby was at birth. Almost the size of a large dog. The foal wiggled around, trying to free her face from the sac. Her wobbly movements accentuated its cuteness, especially with her ears pointing down, like a floppy-eared dog. Despite being on the earth for only a few minutes, it was as though something deep within her was pushing her to stand. Still on her side, Gypsy looked back at her new baby. She must have been so relieved. I know I was.

Gypsy licked her newborn's ears which the foal seemed to enjoy. The baby appeared as though she was attempting to stand up because her slightly-bent front legs were stretched out in front. Gypsy faced her unstable baby, briefly touching noses. It was one of the most adorable things I had ever seen.

"Do we have to help her?" I asked.

"Only if I think she needs it. Better to just let her do what she does," Mr. Gary said. "Should be standing within one hour, nursing within two, and pooping within three. The 1-2-3 Rule." He paused, watching the foal. "If she doesn't start walking soon then I'll—"

Almost on cue, by sheer force the struggling foal uncurled one front leg, and then the other. She hopped to the side, landing on all fours, that splayed in opposite directions. She wiggled her butt, appearing to jump forward, but it was just an exercise in maintaining balance. Her front legs started sliding forward as she slowly lowered to the ground on her belly, like Bambi when he wiped out on the ice. Her back left leg kicked out again to regain traction, and she hoisted her body forward again on all fours. Gypsy licked her baby's back and by the time she got to her face, the foal seemed to say, "Oh, Mama—I got this!" She even shook her head for emphasis, like her mama's licks were annoying her. After the exhausting exercise, the foal rested all her weight on her butt, like she was sitting. After taking a few steps, the sac finally disconnected itself, freeing the wobbly foal. It wasn't until then that we could actually confirm that the foal was, indeed, a "she."

"Is she OK?" I asked.

"Yep, she's doing what needs to be doing. Just let her go," Mr. Gary said.

"Her legs were so long. Like her body should have been bigger."

"Yep, they're not going to grow much longer. When they're born, the legs are almost the same length as an adult's. They grow in tone and muscle, but not too much longer." He paused. "Dammit. She's a 'parrot mouth,'" he said, shaking his head.

"What's a 'parrot mouth'?" I asked, rubbing my tongue over my slightly crooked back tooth.

"See how her top lip goes over her bottom like that? And, the teeth don't line up real good?" he asked, peeling the foal's top lip back. "That's it."

"Can she get braces?" I asked, immediately realizing there was no such thing. From Daddy and Mr. Gary's faces, I was right. Guess she'll just have to live with it.

"Well, what should we name this little one?" Mr. Gary asked.

"Spirit!" I yelled out, thinking of how Aunt Mimi talked about my spirit in her letters.

"Yeah. 'Spirit' fits her," Daddy said.

"She's got that, that's for sure. She—Uh, Garrett," Mr. Gary said, interrupting himself.

He motioned his head to Daddy to get me out. I wasn't sure what was happening, but Gypsy was on her side, with labored breathing. She didn't look very good.

"OK, then. Thanks, Ms. Maren for coming," Mr. Gary said, rushing me out the barn door with Daddy following behind.

They walked a few feet away from me and spoke in hushed tones. Mr. Gary gestured toward Gypsy in the barn and then back to me. The beautiful colors of the sunrise on the horizon contrasted against the tense and awkward mood. Daddy shook Mr. Gary's hand, jogged back over to me, ushering me into his truck.

"So, Mare, wasn't that the best?" he asked, closing his creaky truck door.

"Yeah, Daddy. Is everything all right?" I asked, clicking my seatbelt.

He looked over at the barn. "Oh, yeah. Sure, sure," he repeated, turning on the ignition.

"You sure?"

"Yeah." He paused. "Let's get some shut eye before the sun comes all the way up."

It was almost impossible to sleep after everything I had seen. And heard.

<u>August 19, 1983</u>

I went to Daddy's trailer last weekend. I love being with all the animals but I wanted to see little Spirit so bad. Ever since she was born, Daddy said we couldn't go see her. I asked him why not over and over. He FINALLY told me that they sold Spirit. I was so sad because I love little babies and because I got to see her get born. Now she's gone. I'm so sad. To make it up to me, Daddy said I could get another kitten. So, we went to the animal shelter, but they were closed. Again. I could tell he was tired and he slept a lot last weekend, but we went horseback riding and I got to ride Snickers again and Daddy rode Wildfire. That made me happy. Hope Daddy was happy, too.

<u>September 1, 1983</u>

I miss summer. A lot. It was awesome being with Daddy, Dino, Morris, and Rosie and especially seeing little Spirit get born, even if she's gone now. I'm still sad about that. But, I'm so excited that I'm getting Mrs. Smith for 5th grade! She's so nice. Part of our class goes to Mrs. Nichols for English and then Mr. Bevins for math. Mrs. Nichols is OK, but not friendly like Mrs. Smith. Mr. Bevins is super boring, so I draw horses in my notebook in class. I'm glad I have Mrs. Smith for my main teacher.

September 3, 1983

I found the most amazing book at the Garner library. The name of the book is Ruffian and the guy who wrote it is Edward Claflin. Ruffian is the most incredible horse EVER.

Nestling into one of the library's bean bag chairs, I was completely engrossed in learning about this miraculous horse. Born on April 17, 1972, Ruffian was roughly a year older than me. A striking dark bay with a star on her forehead, Ruffian was large for a filly. After she won all ten of her races against other fillies with very little effort, people couldn't believe Ruffian wasn't a stallion. On July 7, 1975, the people around her decided they needed to prove how magnificent a horse she really was. They ran her in a match race at Belmont Park in New York against a colt named Foolish Pleasure, 1975's Kentucky Derby winner.

Countless buttons were made to celebrate this media-created "Boy vs. Girl Race," which was televised to millions. The starting gate opened and Ruffian and Foolish Pleasure were practically nose to nose for a majority of the race, with Ruffian slightly ahead. But down the back stretch, Ruffian's jockey said he heard a loud crack, like a stick snapping. Ruffian had shattered her right front leg, but her spirit kept pushing her to run on three legs. Her head bobbed up and down as her damaged leg dangled. While her jockey tried to pull her up, Foolish Pleasure ran across the finish line. Alone.

They took Ruffian to surgery, but when she woke up, she

thrashed around so violently, the cast fell off. After more attempts to console her failed, she sustained another injury, leading them no choice but to euthanize her.

Turning to the last page of the book, I wept seeing Ruffian's burial grave on the infield of the Belmont track. Wiping my teardrops that had fallen onto the pages I closed the book, staring at her picture on the cover. I traced the outline of her magnificent head, imagining petting her neck, and telling her what an amazing horse she was. At the check-out counter, the librarian asked me for my library card. At least, I think that's what she asked me. I was in such a fog. This magnificent horse, that died when I was two years old, was all that dominated my thoughts. My anger grew thinking about how her handlers, owners, and others ultimately killed her by making her participate in the match race. At the moment of her fatal accident, she was in the lead; no one had ever beaten her. Her final strides reflected her passion for running and she died doing what she loved. She will always have my heart and I don't know if my spirit will ever stop crying thinking about her.

September 15, 1983

Dear Kiddo,

I'm very interested in the new book you found! Ruffian sounds like she really was an amazing horse. I seem to remember reading about the match race years ago in the newspaper and hearing about it on TV. Although I didn't actually see it, I heard it was tragic. Try to enjoy Ruffian's life and her accomplishments and not focus so much on her death.

Today is the day that most of the important residents of Mackinac Island, the horses, are leaving the Island and heading back up to the U.P. for the winter. The signal that summer is over.

They're finally getting a well-deserved rest since they worked all sum-
mer long for all the tourists. Not all of them go—some do stay on the
Island. They'll be back in the Spring. I know that's sad for you, and
you have a hard time in the fall and especially winter. It just means
that Hallomas is coming and I'll be there to visit with you soon!
*   Keep your spirit up!*

Love you to the moon and back,
Aunt Mimi

October 8, 1983

Aunt Mimi is finally here! I love that she listens to me and
I can tell her anything. She gave me the best Hallomas
presents! Horse statues! I've been playing with them in my
room. I wanted to take them to Daddy's to play with and
show him, but Mama said no. I'm not sure what Aunt Mimi
got Lacey and CJ. I was sad when she left, but I'm always
sad when she leaves. She is the best and now I have the
best gift from her!

Every year around Halloween, Aunt Mimi stayed with us
on her annual trek from her home in Michigan to her condo in
Florida for the winter. Since we'd celebrate Christmas while she was
here, we called the annual tradition "Hallomas."

This particular year she gave me the Breyer set of Black Beauty
horse figurines. It included Black Beauty, Ginger the cantering
Chestnut, Duchess the dark bay, and Merrylegs the dappled pony.
They were intended to be collected and displayed on a shelf, but
I often played with them, making up my own stories. It felt like
I had four new friends to play with. Not wanting to risk damag-
ing them in a college dorm room, however, I made the decision to
leave them at home.

Halloween 1983

I love when Mama brings out the Greenwich Bay Trading Company Apple Cider liquid hand soap. She gets it from Mitchell Hardware in New Bern when we go to their yearly festival, MumFest. Mitchell Hardware is such a cool place and makes you feel like you're back in the olden days. I love the soap because it's orange and there is a black cat on the front. It makes my hands and the room smell like cinnamon. Sometimes I just squirt a little in my hand and smell it. Makes me so happy!

Halloween always signaled the beginning of the "Trifecta of Holidays." Halloween, Thanksgiving, and, the best—Christmas! These special days were the only thing keeping me sane during that time of year due to the earlier sunsets and colder temperatures. However, Mama always outdid herself to create a fun atmosphere.

Every Halloween, I'd reach into the large plastic orange bin searching for the flat, cardboard skeleton whose arms, legs, and head moved on metal circles at the joints. I also loved the decorations she placed on the tables that lie flat but open to orange tissue-paper pumpkins. I always taped the cardboard "Happy Halloween" across the kitchen doorway, and the orange and black tablecloth helped make a fun pumpkin-carving experience. The ironically dull knives with plastic orange handles allowed us to create any face we wanted. I typically carved the standard triangle eyes and nose, with a smiling mouth that displayed one tooth on top and two on bottom. Mama usually carved CJ's pumpkin so his looked better than mine. Surprisingly, Lacey participated, but wasn't as invested. Not surprising. The only ick part was reaching into the pumpkins, feeling its stringy and cold insides, and pulling out all the gooey contents onto the cookie sheet. After picking out all the hidden seeds, Mama sprinkled salt on them and baked them in the oven. The yummy crunch of the seeds made the whole mess worth it. I loved when Aunt Mimi was there for pumpkin carving. Some years she was in a bigger hurry to get to Florida, so she missed it.

After trick-or-treating on Halloween, we would return home to Mama's yummy spicy meal. Halloween wasn't always a chilly night, but it was always a chili night. Lacey often trick-or-treated with her friends. Sometimes she'd eat Mama's chili and sometimes she was vegetarian. I'm just glad there weren't too many beans. If she had added them, I would just pick around them. I never dared say anything bad about the food because if any of us did, then we'd have to cook the next meal. So, my lips were always sealed.

When our bellies were full, we'd spill all our candy out onto the living room floor, grouping them together. Little piles formed of Smarties, Nerds, Runts, Lemonheads, Fruit Stripe gum, Jolly Ranchers, Milk Duds, Spree, and Bazooka gum. My favorites were Skor, Twix, and Reese's Peanut Butter cups, but I never liked Almond Joys and Mounds. Coconut. Bleh. Ironically, I never liked Snickers, the candy bar—just the horse. It was fun giving them to Mama since they're her favorite.

After the sorting, the trading negotiations began with Mama trading on CJ's behalf. Even if Lacey went with her friends, she wouldn't miss this part. Luckily, she didn't like the chocolate bars, so I gave away some of my candy cigarettes and necklaces in exchange. I always tried to offload the candy corn and those taffy-like orange or black pieces of candy. Just seemed like the neighbors who handed them out never felt the Halloween spirit. Or, they were really angry about having kids come to their door asking for candy, so they channeled their frustration into giving out crappy treats. In the end, everyone usually seemed happy with their trades.

If we ever got an apple, Mama sliced them into pieces before we ate them. She said we had to be careful there weren't any needles, pins, or razor blades inside. It wasn't just in our neighborhood, but in other places as well. It was scary, but fortunately, we never experienced any problems with Halloween fruit.

<u>November 25, 1983</u>

Thanksgiving was so much fun! Mama said we could use the good china and glasses. She cooked so much but I'm so happy she is good at it and likes to cook! She made turkey, stuffing, seven-layer salad, macaroni and cheese, green-bean casserole, sweet potato casserole, mashed potatoes, corn pudding, biscuits and gravy, and cranberry sauce. My belly just hung out after all the food! Everyone but CJ had a wine glass for water and another for soda. Mama and Clint drank wine in their wine glasses. Mama dipped her finger in her water glass and rubbed the top edge of the glass. It made a cool angelic sound. We all tried it, too. Even Clint for a minute. Everybody laughed. Lacey and I sang songs and I said I liked the song "Holiday" by Madonna. She said she did, too! She even said my hair looked good. She's fun when she's nice. Doesn't happen very often.

<u>December 17, 1983</u>

Christmastime at Crabtree! CJ was so sweet.

Every year, Mama took us to see Santa at Crabtree Valley Mall in Raleigh. That year, when she placed the nine-month-old CJ down on Santa's lap, my brother looked up at Santa, and his little face crumpled up. Tears and whimpers morphed into deafening screams, and his face turned a bright red, an almost perfect match to Santa's suit. The person in the elf costume asked if Mama still wanted the picture taken.

"Absolutely!" she said. "Take it now!"

I could hardly hear Mama over CJ's blood-curdling screams. As soon as the picture was taken, Mama ran up to her son's chubby, outstretched arms. He clung to her as he looked back at a waving Santa.

"Wave bye to Santa, CJ," Mama said, smiling.

He jerked his head around to face Mama, hugging her even tighter. She handled that much better than I would have! Whenever I heard CJ cry, I wanted to cry, too. Not out of frustration or annoyance, but out of a deep sadness. It was as if someone was stabbing me in the heart. I chalked it up to being "too sensitive and put my hands over my ears since no one else seemed to be bothered by it. Or, *that* bothered, anyway. Mama was the Queen of Redirection and by the time we left Santa's House area, she had CJ enthralled with other Christmas lights and trees in the mall. I felt better, too. That was one of her superpowers.

December 30, 1983

I was at Daddy's for a few days over Christmas Break. I told him about Ruffian. He said he watched the match race and that it was really bad. He said he was glad I didn't see it but glad I knew about her.

Daddy and I hung ornaments and tinsel on his tree. He doesn't have as much as Mama does. We also danced to the Christmas songs on the radio. They play Christmas songs starting right after Thanksgiving. My favorite song "Sleigh Ride" came on. Daddy told me it was by the Ronettes. It's like one of my favorites. I think it's his favorite, too!

As we decorated, Daddy had taped a Christmas bow to my head. It complemented the jingle bell necklace around my neck. When he stooped over to get more Christmas tree lights out of the box, I returned the favor and placed a sticky bow on his head. Daddy's deep belly laughs often morphed into wheezing and coughing from all his smoking, but he never let that stop him. His laughing always made me laugh more.

Once we finished, he said, "Guess what we're going to do now?"

"What?" I jingled the bell around my neck for emphasis.

"We're going to get a Christmas tree."

"But we just decorated one."

"Yeah, but we're going to get *another* one!"

"Oh my gosh, Daddy!" I squealed. "Two Christmas trees?"

"Yeah, we get to choose our own, and then bring it home!"

"But where are we going to get more decorations? We already used them all," I said, looking around at the bins.

"We'll just go to Kmart and get more."

"Yay, Kmart!" I said, dancing around.

"Let's go get us a real tree!" he said, grabbing his car keys.

Cradling Dino in my arms, I said, "We'll be back, and when we do, we're going to have another tree." His deep brown eyes and wagging tail nub were all I needed. Morris received my obligatory kiss on the head, leaning into it, rubbing his cheek against mine. Rosie was still tearing around the room when I reminded her, "Rosie, no going after the tree."

We climbed into Daddy's old green Chevy LUV truck. After a few attempts to start it, the ignition finally caught, and a plume of black smoke shot out behind us. The heater wasn't quite functional, and the stale cigarette smoke smell inside was hard to mask, but singing Christmas songs on the way there helped.

Arriving at the farm, the trees were lined up like soldiers as far as I could see. Daddy found a parking spot in the almost-full parking lot.

"Oh my gosh, Daddy. Look!"

"Yeah, we'll get whichever one you want, Mare," Grabbing a saw from the back of the truck, he closed the rusty tailgate door behind him, throwing his weight against it.

"Over here, look at this one!" I held onto Daddy's hand, using my entire body to direct him to the perfect tree. "Or this one over here." I turned back around to see even more.

"Yeah," he said, with the saw over his shoulder.

"Oh, Daddy. This one is perfect!" I stopped in front of another tree, bending my neck back to see the top. "Yeah, this one is the most beautiful tree I've ever seen." He said it was seven feet high which might as well have been 107 feet, as far as I was concerned.

Daddy did most of the sawing, but he let me try a few times just to say that I helped. After paying for the tree, he placed it on an angle and finagled it into the truck's bed. We turned our heads after hearing a woman arguing with three kids in the distance. "Mommy, we want this tree."

"We can't afford that one, honey."

"Please, we were good this year. You said if we were good, we could have a big tree this year."

"I'm sorry."

"Hang on a second, Mare. I'll be right back," Daddy said, closing the truck door behind him. I ran after him wondering what he was up to.

We strolled up to the woman heading toward the rows of smaller trees.

"Excuse me, ma'am. A little birdie told me you might want a bigger tree?" Daddy asked.

"Yeah," the woman said, sighing. "We'd love one, but just can't do it. Not this year."

Daddy reached into his pocket. "Here, take this."

All I saw was a bunch of bills hidden in his fist.

"Oh no, sir. We can't," she said, shaking her head.

"Please take it," Daddy said. "Go get yourself a big tree. How about this one here?" he said, pointing to the nearest one. "Everyone needs to have a Merry Christmas."

"Sorry, sir. We just can't," the woman protested. "Thank you just the same."

"Well, then," Daddy said, shifting his weight. "I'd say we have a problem here. See, if you don't take this, my Christmas won't be merry. And, so that means your Christmas *and* mine won't be merry," he said, with a coy grin, outstretching his hand again. "And, I *know* you wouldn't want that to happen."

"There is no way we could possibly repay you," she said, smiling.

"You can by having a very Merry Christmas."

"Pleezzzz, Mama. Pleeezzzz," The pleading choir of children clinging to her legs included a Carolina Blue, knitted-capped boy, his blonde sister in matching ear muffs, and a hooded toddler.

She looked down at her children and sighed. "Oh, all right. Bless you, sir." In tears, she hugged Daddy. "Thank you so much. I did promise them a big tree this year. But when they cut my hours at work to almost nuthin'—"

"—but now the kids have one." Daddy smiled in a way I hadn't seen him do in a long time. He turned, pointed at the kids and said, "And, you give lots of love to that tree, OK?"

"We will. Thank you, sir!" they said, jumping around, flailing their arms.

"You really helped to make this a real Merry Christmas for my babies and me. Thank you again."

"Glad to hear it." He turned to me and said, "Let's go, Mare!"

I waved good-bye, yelling "Merry Christmas!" and jogged after Daddy.

He jumped back into the driver's seat again, shutting the creaking door behind him.

"That was awesome, Daddy."

"Mare, just remember: whenever you can help someone out or make their day, you should."

*T*hat Christmas Day, Mother Nature made herself known. It was so cold, it almost felt like it could snow. Not only was the blowing wind outside rattling Daddy's windows, I could actually feel the wind inside the trailer.

Wrapping Daddy's heavy blanket around me, I snuggled next to Morris on the living room couch. He didn't seem bothered that I interrupted his nap.

"Yeah, get comfy," Daddy said. "Gift time!"

I opened my presents from Daddy which included a horse pen and pencil set that looked like the Black Stallion and horse socks that looked like Ruffian. I also gave him socks, but the ones he gave me were much better. "Santa brought one last gift. You know you gotta believe to receive," Daddy said, heading into the bedroom. Mama said something similar, especially with CJ around. "Close your eyes and wait right here."

"OK, Daddy," I said, closing them tight, rocking back and forth in excitement. I knew it was another puppy or kitten and I kept thinking about what to name him or her. If it was going to be a big dog, I like the name Titan or Brutus. But if it was going to be a kitten, I liked the name Boo Boo or Taco.

"Still shut?" he asked, each word accentuated his cigarette-smelling breath.

"Yep."

"No peeking."

"Nope," I said, trying to listen for a kitten's meowing or a puppy's whimpering.

"Sure, they're still shut?"

"Daddy!"

He laughed. "Put your hands out, palms up," he said, moving them closer to each other. "And, keep them together."

I prepared for the weight of a squiggly animal. But the thing just sat there in my hands. I frowned, trying to balance a weird, strangely large, fuzzy thing with my eyes shut.

"Now open them!"

What I had felt on my hands finally made its way to my brain.

It had been about six months since I first saw him at McCandless store, but there in my hands was Wildfire, the most beautiful horse stuffed animal I had ever seen. I hugged him so tight as tears fell onto Wildfire's fuzzy side. Daddy completely understood my love of horses—both real and stuffed.

January 18, 1984

I'm so excited that in three more days I get to be with Daddy! The first visit of the new year! He couldn't come get me for our last visit, but I think we'll be doing something really fun, like seeing a movie. And I can't wait to see Dino, Morris, and Rosie again. My nose does run a little and I sneeze sometimes but I hope they will remember me from Christmas. I think they will. I definitely remember them.

January 21, 1984

Well, Daddy didn't pick me up. I stood by the front door with my suitcase, and waited forever. It was dark and every headlight I saw coming down the road I thought was him. But it wasn't. Mama finally came up to me and asked how I was doing. She said she called Daddy but there was no answer. Then like two hours later, he called here, asking about next weekend for a visit. But that's when I have to study for my big math test. So, I didn't go. I don't like unpacking my things from my suitcase, especially when I don't go to Daddy's. I cry when I unpack anyway. I don't understand, how could he forget about me?

February 27, 1984

Winters are hard. I'm glad Spring will be here soon. Mama gave me a gift. I guess I like it.

In my bedroom, I sat at the desk Mama had bought from one of the local schools when it was revamping. It was an exact replica of my desk at school. The desk's top could be lifted open on a hinge and this is where I usually kept my diary. There was a stand underneath the desktop that popped out to make the writing surface level. The attached chair swiveled and I had pencils in the built-in pencil holders. Finishing up learning about exponents in math, I heard a knock at the door.

"Come in."

"Hey, Baby."

"Mama!" I said, swiveling my squeaky chair to face the door. I was so happy to see her especially since she rarely visited me in my room.

"How was your day?"

"Good."

"What are you working on?" she asked, peering over my shoulder.

"Just studying Math. Bleh."

"But, you're such a good student."

It always felt good when Mama complimented me. Didn't happen as much as it used to.

"I wanted to give you something I got at work," she said. Her hands hid something behind her back.

"Really?" I asked, getting up from the seat. "Whatcha get me?"

"This."

She presented a small, strange figurine wearing a tiny cowboy hat, topped off with a tiny feather. Its solid body had googly eyes, pipe cleaner legs, and little feather arms attached to a tiny pedestal. Squinting to get a closer look, I tried to make out the words printed on the front.

"It's a Billy Bob's Texas Turd Bird," she exclaimed.

"Yeah, but—what is it?"

"It's a shellacked piece of horse crap!" she chuckled. Handing it to me, I twisted it around to get a 360-degree look.

"Isn't it cute? Someone was going to throw it away at work and I said, 'Please let me have it! My daughter would love it.'"

"Um, thank you, Mama."

"Sure, it's not a horse, but it's the closest thing to a horse we can getcha!"

I placed my Turd Bird on my dresser next to a small horse figurine Aunt Mimi had gotten me at Mackinac Island.

I wasn't sure whether I felt honored that Mama had thought of me, or hurt that she wasn't kidding.

Λpril 8, 1984

Daddy apologized for missing so many visits this year. He totally made it up to me because I had the bestest trip with him!

"Guess where we're going?"

"I know, Daddy. Horseback riding!"

We did that every time, but he always seemed to love it.

"Well, not exactly. But we'll see horses at a really fun place."

"To see Snickers?"

"Nope."

"Or Wildfire?"

"Nope. Not this time."

"To see River and Comanche!" I said, jumping around, thinking about the horses from the Outer Banks.

"Nope," he grinned.

"Then where?"

"We're going to....dum, dum, da. Kentucky Horse Park!"

"What?"

"Kentucky Horse Park."

"Is that in—?"

"—Kentucky! My buddy was telling me about it. You're going to love it. Be sure to pack up your stuff. I already have mine in the back of the truck," he said, grabbing his keys.

"Is it far away?"

"Well, it's a good drive," he said.

"Are we staying overnight somewhere? Where are we staying?"

"Um, not sure, but we'll find a place along the way. C'mon, let's go!"

"Do I need my pillow?"

"Yeah, and grab the blanket, too," he said, motioning to the couch.

"Will Dino and Rosie and Morris be OK?"

"Yeah, they'll be fine. Mr. DeAndre and Ms. Tiana will look in on them."

"Will I still go back home Sunday night?"

"Yeah, Mare," he said, irritated. "That's why we need to get going now. We're burning daylight here!"

"OK, Daddy," I said, sprinting to the bedroom, grabbing my suitcase and pillow.

"You guys be good," I said, squatting down to hug Dino and Rosie. Morris was hanging out on the couch. He didn't seem to mind, or frankly care, about what was happening. Such a cool cat.

Reaching outside the open window as Daddy drove, the spring evening kissed my hand. Since it was around supper time, we stopped at a Waffle House.

"Hi, y'all," the hostess said.

"Hi, April," Daddy said, squinting to read her name tag.

"Smoking or non-smoking?" she asked, grabbing the menus.

"Non-smoking," Daddy said, smiling down at me.

I reciprocated with the biggest smile, full of pride.

"OK, follow me."

Sitting down at the booth in the squeaky teal booth seats, Daddy said, "Thanks, April. You have a good night."

"What are you hungry for, Daddy?" I asked, opening the large, laminated menu.

"Not too hungry, Mare."

"Hey y'all," a thin lady with huge hair and thick eyeliner greeted us. "Welcome to Waffle House. My name is Josie."

"Hey, there...Josie." Daddy said, reading her name tag strategically placed next to her large cleavage as she poured our waters. A smile grew across his face.

"What can I get y'all to drink?" she asked, with a similar smile spreading in response.

"I'd like a—"

"—Josie. Now, that's a pretty name," Daddy interrupted.

"Thank you," she said, tapping her pen on her notepad, narrowing her eyes. "I bet you say that to all the girls."

"No, not at all, Josie," he said, smiling. Cocking his head, he said, "I peg you as a musician. Or, maybe a singer. I say…a singer. I'm right, aren't I?"

She smiled.

"Betcha you wonder how I knew that," he said, spreading his arms behind the booth.

"How did you guess?" she asked, clasping her necklace.

"I just have a really good feel for people. And, I'll go one step further—I'll bet you are a country singer."

"I sing a lot in church. But, you're sorta close."

"I'll bet you sing as pretty as you look," he said, stretching his arms out again, shifting his weight back on the booth seat. "I know a beautiful soul when I see one."

"Do you sing, too?" she asked, her face blushing.

I rolled my eyes.

"Yeah, but mostly I'm a drummer."

"Daddy's really good!" I piped up.

She shot me a look. I slid back in the seat, pulling the straw to my mouth.

"What kind of music do you play?" she asked.

"All types, but my favorites are 60s rock, Motown, country, church…"

I furrowed my eyebrows trying to remember the last time Daddy went to church.

"Great, what can I give you? I mean, get for you?" she asked.

"I have a few ideas," Daddy laughed.

"You're so bad!" she said, tapping his hand with her pencil. Her cheeks turned even more red.

"I'm not too hungry. What would you like, Mare?"

"I'll have the hot dog, fries, and a 7Up. Can I get a milkshake, Daddy?"

"Sure. Whatever you want. I'm here to make you happy," he said, smiling at Josie.

"I'll get right on that. I'm here to serve," she said, locking her eyes onto Daddy.

When Josie returned, Daddy definitely wasn't looking at her eyes when she leaned over. Or, during the numerous times he requested more coffee, resulting in their mutual laughing.

After a fun supper with Daddy, he motioned to Josie.

"Josie, sweetheart, we have to get going, so we'll need the check," he said. A smile crept back again.

"Awww....so soon," she pouted. "OK, I'll be right back with it." She turned back toward the cash register and Daddy's eyes fixated on her backside as she sauntered away.

"Mare, go ahead and use the bathroom, then we'll get the show on the road."

I took one more slurp of my milkshake and scooted across the vinyl-padded booth seats.

When I was done, I looked around for Daddy but didn't see him anywhere. Another waitress with a full tray and red lips motioned her head to the back and said, "They're out there. Go out, turn left, and follow it around to the back."

"Thank you," I said, rushing out the door. I followed the side of the building to the back, passing the large garbage receptacles. The stench of decaying food and garbage attacked my nose.

Making another left, I peeked around the corner to see Daddy's back. Between him and the building was Josie with her back against the wall. Her arms ran up and down his back as he held her thigh, rhythmically pressing into her.

Ducking back around the corner, I tried to catch my breath from shock and embarrassment. Clearing my throat, I pretended to have just gotten there.

They were still locked in a deep kiss, but Josie caught sight of me and pulled away.

Daddy looked at her, confused. Following her eyes to me, he said, "Hey there, Mare."

"Daddy, it's time to go."

Josie quickly buttoned up her blouse as he gave her one more deep kiss. Moving toward me, he said, "Time to get the show back on the road."

"Call me!" Josie yelled out.

Her perfume still clung to his shirt as we drove away. "Not too much longer and we'll be at the Kentucky Horse Park. Aren't you excited?"

"Yeah," I said, feeling a little awkward.

Josie was never mentioned again.

J never realized how long North Carolina was until that trip. I often asked how much longer we had to go. Daddy said we still had to go through parts of Tennessee before even getting to Kentucky. It felt like we'd never get there.

Daddy drove all night while I slept in the truck's carpeted covered bed area. Fortunately, I had my pillow from home, but the blanket from the couch, as well as the truck bed itself, stunk of stale cigarettes. The few occasions Daddy rolled the window down to blow out his smoke provided a little ventilation. Just as I was finally falling asleep, I heard Daddy exclaim, "Mare, we're here! Look at this place!"

I blinked hard out the window to take in what I was seeing. The endless rows of white picket fences dotted with grazing horses sprung me out of my slumber. It was Disney World for horses, except instead of Mickey and Minnie, it was Secretariat and Seabiscuit.

Bleary-eyed, my heart raced with excitement as we walked under the "Kentucky Horse Park" sign, past a distant Man O' War statue, and into the Visitor's Center. After highlighting some of the attractions, the girl at the counter handed me a park map, pointing us in the direction of the auditorium entrance. In the darkened theater, the short film, "Thou Shall Fly Without Wings" celebrating horses was the fastest twenty-two minutes of my life. The birth of the foal was my favorite part, reminding me of Gypsy and Spirit's birth. Daddy's eyes were closed for most of the movie and I secretly hoped his occasional snoring didn't bother other people.

"What do we do next, Daddy?" I asked as the auditorium lights turned back on.

Daddy stretched and smacked his lips. "Whatever you'd like, Mare."

"Can we do the tour?"

"Sure," he said, pulling down his shirt. "On to the tour!" As we stood in line, the sound of clip-clopping hooves announced its arrival. Two large, chestnut draft horses pulled a carriage donned with a blue and white awning, as rows of people loaded, slightly rocking it.

"What're the horses' names?" I asked the driver.

"George is on the right and Charlie's on the left."

"Awww...what kind are they?"

"They're Belgians."

"I've never seen a Belgian horse before!" I said, turning to Daddy.

"Isn't this fun, Mare?"

"Yeah, we get to see horses from other countries!"

Over the microphone, the driver said the Kentucky Horse Park, built in 1978, consisted of 1,200 acres, and held various horse events and tournaments as well as a nearby campground. Passing by the Parade of Breeds arena, we saw the Big Barn that was built in 1897—one the largest horse barns ever built. On the way back to the trolley stop, we rode by the Hall of Champions barn. He said there were discussions about building a future Saddlebred Museum with a sculpture of the famous Saddlebred, Supreme Sultan, in front. Each exhibit mentioned was accompanied by my saying, "I wanna do that!" to which Daddy belly laughed. Even though I heard some of the tour highlights, my focus was primarily on Charlie and George and all they were doing. It dawned on me how much work horses do, and have done for us, throughout history, from pulling a plow on the farms to transportation to fighting in wars. We literally wouldn't be where we are without them.

Once the tour was done, Daddy and I jumped off the carriage. I asked the driver about petting Charlie and George.

The driver didn't mind, but reminded me to stand to their sides where the horses would know I was there since they had blinders on.

"Thank you, Charlie and George, for all your work. You are awesome." Due to their size, I was only able to reach their shoulder, but was astounded that their hooves were about the size of my out-stretched hand.

"They really are awesome, aren't they, Mare?" It surprised me that even Daddy seemed dwarfed by these two gentle giants.

"Bye, Charlie! Bye, George!" I said, pulling out the park map again. "Where can we go now, Daddy?"

"Well—"

"What time is it?" I interrupted.

"Not sure. Excuse me, ma'am, what time is it?" Daddy asked a lady standing nearby.

"Let's see…it's about 10:20," she said, looking at her watch.

"Thank you. Hope y'all are having a good time."

"Yeah, my little one here loves horses," she said, motioning down to a child holding her hand.

"So does mine," Daddy smiled. "More than anything."

Pretending not to hear him, as I often did, I was happy he thought I was little. It was a rarity to be called that.

"Well, there is the Hall of Champions at 10:30 up this way. Then, the Parade of Breeds at 11:00. Let's go to both!" I said, grabbing Daddy's hand.

At the Hall of Champions barn, we sat in bleachers as they introduced the two most famous horses there: Forego and Rambling Willie. I felt like I was meeting celebrities.

"Before we bring them out, we want to thank you for coming," the employee said. "We want you to know how much these horses mean to us. These are our athletes. As far as we're concerned, they're no different than Joe Namath or Magic Johnson."

I furrowed my brow, looking over at Daddy.

"Joe Namath is a football player and Magic Johnson plays basketball."

I didn't understand how those two guys could ever measure up to these two horses.

"Without further ado, please put your hands together for Rambling Willie!"

I could hear the trumpets sound as the handler led out a beautiful bay.

"As a racing Standardbred, Willie raced mostly in the Midwest. He had the most starts and wins of any Standardbred. He was also the Champion Aged Pacer of the Year for three years and was inducted into the National Harness Racing Hall of Fame. Willie even has a book named after him, *The Horse That God Loved.* He's also been on TV and has visited many places to meet his fans."

Does that mean God doesn't love the other horses?

I raised my hand to ask a question. "What's the difference between a Thoroughbred and a Standardbred?"

"A Standardbred can pace rather than trot," the employee said. "It's where the front leg and back leg of the same side go forward at the same time. Most horses will go opposite for a trot: front right leg, back left leg go forward at the same time. Thoroughbred racing is usually galloping. Good question. We can't forget that Willie also has his pet goat, Billy."

"Willie and Billy!" I cried out.

"Yes, they're always together, those two. We wouldn't take him without his goat. And, he wouldn't have come without him. Let's hear it for Rambling Willie!"

The audience clapped as Willie returned to the barn while another guy led out a massive dark bay without any distinct markings. "Ladies and gentleman, please show some love for the wonderful…fabulous…. Forego!"

The audience cheered as I was hypnotized by this gorgeous horse.

"As a gangly and tall youngster, Forego was gelded early in his life. This helped to slow his legs from growing too long as well as getting rid of some of that stallion temper. He was voted for eight Eclipse Awards, as well as three Horse of the Year titles. Winning many of his big races by coming from the outside, he was often handicapped to carry more than 130 pounds. Despite all his awards, leg issues plagued most of his life. Eventually ankle issues brought him here to Kentucky Horse Park, and he's loved it ever since. He loves his bananas, but we're careful not to give too many. Just enough to make him happy."

I couldn't help but picture Forego peeling a banana.

"Forego's trainer was Frank Whiteley, Jr, who also trained the most amazing filly, Ruffian."

"Ruffian!" I exclaimed, snapping my head to look at Daddy. "My Ruffian? The filly who died in the match race?"

He nodded.

"Wow," I said, tears building in my eyes. In a strange cosmic connection, I felt like looking at Forego was like looking at Ruffian incarnated.

"Thank you, ladies and gentlemen, for coming today. And, please enjoy the rest of your day here at Kentucky Horse Park."

I was transfixed. Daddy unknowingly snapped me out of my fog.

"Ready for the Parade of Breeds?"

"Yeah," I said, heading toward the arena, yet twisting my head around to get one last look at the barn that held these magnificent creatures.

Following the sidewalk down the slight hill to the Parade of Breeds, we found a seat on the bleachers in the outside arena. The announcer introduced each breed as they cantered into the arena with music playing in the background. Since we were sitting next to the entrance, we heard the clip clop of hooves as each breed was individually announced. Although everyone else was clapping, initially I was so mesmerized that clapping seemed to be a distraction.

"Ladies and gentlemen, boys and girls—put your hands together for the Appaloosa!"

"Daddy, it's Snickers' brother or sister!"

The Appaloosa cantered around as the announcer shared information about the Appy, as it is often called. My thoughts went to Snickers, missing many of the details. When he left, a cowboy riding on a Quarter Horse galloped full tilt into the arena, then slid to a halt. Galloping back to the opposite side, he did the same. The rider spun the horse around, then backed him up. He exited just as a team of Percherons entered pulling an old-time carriage around the arena. A Saddlebred with its high-stepping gait circled the arena, followed by the finale of a Standardbred pacing with a driver in silks.

"Rambling Willie!" I exclaimed.

At the end of the show, my hands finally appeared to be clapping. Daddy later said it was the quietest I had been the entire day.

After the program, the horses re-entered the arena, lining up along the periphery, allowing us to pet them and ask the riders questions. All my silence had built up and came gushing out in a barrage of questions. Fortunately, each rider was patient in answering them.

We walked around the stalls lining the arena, each housing a different breed, including the Morgan, Friesian, and the adorable Miniature Horse. I just wanted to have a conversation with each horse, but time didn't allow.

After we left, I made sure to wash my hands several times, using toilet paper as Kleenex. Even though my nose ran a little, I was cognizant not to touch my face after petting the horses. That seemed to make my nose run even more, leading to sneezing and even some wheezing. My determination was strong not to let any issues dampen my day.

Watching the horses graze in the distance, Daddy asked, "Is that your stomach growling? You want something to eat?"

"Um, well…." I said, pulling out the map for our next attraction.

"Tell you what, let's grab something to eat and then we'll go horseback riding."

"OK!" Only at that moment did I become aware of how hungry I really was. With so many horses to see, who had time to eat?

Daddy ate his hot dog and fries slowly, whereas I gulped mine down in preparation to go riding. Part of me already felt we had wasted time eating, but it did help me to feel a little less lightheaded.

Passing by the Dressage Complex, we saw various people on horses warming up for their events. Daddy had to urge me along since I just wanted to stare at the horse and rider combos moving together as one.

For our horseback riding experience, I was on a chestnut gelding named Sunny and Daddy was on a chestnut gelding named Tango. Every fiber of my being wanted to at least trot, but since there were many children and first-time riders, it was in everyone's interest to just walk. Everyone's except mine. Riding along the circumference of the Park gave an even wider perspective of this wonderland I never wanted to leave.

After our ride, I was only slightly interested in visiting the farrier. It seemed to me that was like watching someone get a pedicure—something I have never gotten, nor have a desire to get. The fact that it dealt with horses made it a little more interesting, but not enough to listen to the entire presentation.

We snuck out early, which made me feel so rebellious.

But then it hit me—"Oh, no. Is that it?"

"Nope, still got the Museum to go through," Daddy said.

"Yay!"

I hadn't noticed how warm it had gotten outside until we stepped into the cool museum lobby.

"Hi!" I chirped. "I absolutely love it here at the Kentucky Horse Park. It's amazing!"

The older lady behind the desk smiled. It was clear it wasn't the first time she had heard a young girl say that.

"Here is a map of the museum," she said, handing it to Daddy who immediately passed it onto me. "The entrance is right here. You'll be sure to find many interesting things."

"Thank you, ma'am. Is Ruffian buried here?" I asked.

"No, honey, she's buried at Belmont Park."

I knew that. I guess I just hoped something of Ruffian was there so I could pay her respects.

"Oh, yeah. Where's Belmont Park again?"

"New York."

"Guess we can't see her," my voice trailed.

"Not this weekend, but we'll get out there someday," Daddy consoled me. "Thank you, ma'am."

"Yeah, thank you!" I said, jogging toward the entrance.

The Legacy of the Horse started at the first floor and spiraled upward to the second floor. Starting with the very first horse, Hyracotherium (Eohippus) 45-55 million years ago that were no bigger than a dog, progressing to what we now think of as a horse. The exhibit included how horses were first brought to America, examined their role in the Old West, and in various wars. Endless rows of horse-drawn carriages highlighted the numerous ways horses were used in transportation. The spiral ramp added to the feeling that you were moving through time, truly experiencing the innumerable contributions horses have made. And they did it all without wanting anything but love, safety, and a few carrots as payment.

The museum underscored the insight I'd had earlier in the day on the carriage tour. We literally could never repay horses for everything they've done. We are, and will forever be, indebted.

A visit to any place must end with an obligatory stop at the gift shop, especially at Kentucky Horse Park. An enormous life-sized drawing on the wall of a horse and a jockey greeted us.

Christy, Glenda, Eunice, and Beverly were so lucky to work at the best place in the world. I loved their blue-collared polo tops and beige skirts. The same Kentucky Horse Park logo of a white foal cantering next to a trotting dark horse adorned their tops, matching a larger version on the walls. At the register, a magnificent mural of a galloping race horse seemed to emerge from behind the wall.

Shelf after shelf of horse items filled the store. An open trunk with countless horse pillows, spilled over its sides. As a small souvenir, Daddy got me a tiny black horse keychain.

Pushing through the exit doors of the Visitor's Center, sadness grew when I realized that my marvelous day was soon ending.

"Wait, Daddy—Man O' War!" I exclaimed, so grateful we still had more to see before we left.

Various signs about Man O' War punctuated the tree-lined walk and the bricked walkway leading to his sculpture.

"He had a stride of twenty-eight feet. Most Thoroughbreds are twenty feet and his was twenty-eight!"

"He was a real stud!"

"Yeah," I wasn't sure what that meant at the time, but was excited that Daddy sustained enthusiasm, even at the end of the day.

Man O' War is one of horse-racing's most famous champions. Encircled by a fountain and various plaques about him, his sculpture was enormous, fitting of a horse who was also larger than life. His death on November 5, 1947 was a media event where racetracks observed moments of silence and a local radio announcer provided burial details that were heard across the country. Man O' War was one of the first horses buried and embalmed whole. Near the end of his life, he was inseparable from his groom, Will Harbut. In fact, when Will suffered a heart attack and died shortly after, Man O' War died about a month later.

A nearby memorial held the remains and a tombstone honoring one of the greatest jockeys of all time, Isaac Burns Murphy, a black Hall of Fame jockey. Although he died before Man O' War was born, Murphy's remains are interred near Man O' War to honor all his contributions to the early days of the sport. He rode many races, winning three Kentucky Derbies and was inducted into the Jockey Hall of Fame.

Following the memorial circle back around to the entrance, Daddy said, "Well, Mare..."

"Noooooo, Daddy," I said, fighting back a yawn.

"Let's try to come back again sometime."

Although I had a feeling that wouldn't happen, it felt nice to hear him say it. The magical day had to come to an end. Much too soon by my estimation. On the drive back home, the deluge of "Which would you rather" questions to Daddy were answered until I hit a wall and fell asleep. I don't think Daddy slept all weekend and I was pretty worn out too. But once I got a little more sleep, I sure talked about my trip to anyone who would listen, even if it was primarily to my stuffed animals.

April 9, 1984

I hated coming home from the Kentucky Horse Park yesterday. CJ cried a lot and Lacey and Clint ignored me. I wanted to be with Daddy. He listens to me and cares about horses. Sometimes I really feel like I'm on the outside looking in and Mama just goes along to get along. I keep thinking about all the horses I got to meet and pet and the horses I learned about. I've never been in a place where there were so many horses and horse stuff! Felt like my head would explode. Now I have so many other horses to think about when I can't get to sleep besides Trixie, Snickers, River, Wildlife, Ruffian, and the Black Stallion. Even Gypsy and little Spirit. Now there's Man O' War, Secretariat, and so many others. I don't ever want to stop thinking about them. Now I'll never get to sleep but it's because of good things, not because I'm worried!

May 5, 1984

I get to watch the Kentucky Derby with Daddy this weekend! I'm so excited!

In anticipation of the big race, Daddy muted the television to listen to songs we chose from his record collection.

"Daddy, have you heard the cool song, 'Video Killed the Radio Star'?" I asked, leafing through the albums on the shelf.

"Yeah, you've heard it?" he said, pouring his cup of coffee.

"Yeah, who sings it?"

"The Buggles."

Their name made me giggle. "I love it. There is a big drum part. And the guitar. And when the lady sings at the end, I get goosebumps!"

"It is a fun song. Did you know it was the first video MTV ever played?"

"Wow, can y'all play it?"

"No, don't think so. Too much synthesizer."

"What's that?"

"The keyboard," Daddy said, looking through some of the other albums on the floor.

"But Mr. DeAndre would love it. And, there's even the piano part."

"Yeah, just not our style, Mare. Sorry."

I twisted my face. "What about 'Owner of a Lonely Heart'?"

"Yes."

"So, you can play it?"

Daddy laughed. "That's the name of the band. 'Yes' is the name of the band."

I furrowed my brow. "Band names are so weird. So, can y'all play it?"

"Not sure."

"But Mr. Francisco would love the guitar part and there is a huge drum part, too!"

"Yeah, not sure they'd go for that either, Mare. They don't like the newer stuff as much."

"Oh." I shifted my disappointment to the television watching the huge Kentucky Derby crowds.

"But, you're right, it is a good song. Here, let me play you a really awesome song," he said, pulling a record out of its sleeve. "It's called 'Beginnings' by the band Chicago. Man, it has such a smooth beginning. Maybe that's why they called it that! Listen to this drum part right here," he said, closing his eyes, air-drumming on each beat.

"Can you play *this* song?"

"Nope, because we would need a bigger horn section. But man, this song is one of my favorites."

"Daddy, the horses! Can we turn the volume back on?" I exclaimed, seeing the horses lining up on the field.

"Sure," he said, sitting down on the couch.

"Is the Kentucky Derby near the Kentucky Horse Park?"

"It's about an hour and a half away. The Derby is at Churchill Downs. We should go there sometime."

"That would be so much fun! Wow, look at all of them," I said, completely spellbound by all the horses.

"It's a big field this year. They're showing us all the horses before they load them in. All twenty of them and there's a filly running."

"Really?" I snapped my head around.

"Yeah, Althea, and she's favored to win. This could be her year. The last time a filly won the Kentucky Derby was four years ago with Genuine Risk."

"I'm rooting for Althea," I said. "If Ruffian can't be there, Althea can run for her. But I'm happy for anyone who wins!"

"Yeah, me, too. There she goes—first one loaded in the gate," he said, scooting to the end of the seat, resting his elbows on his legs. Althea's striking dark color against her white bridle made me think of Ruffian even more. It seemed to take forever for all the other horses to load.

"And, they're off!" Daddy said, in lockstep with the announcer.

Seeing twenty horses released at the same moment across a wide track nearly took my breath away.

"Althea's in front right away!" I said.

"Yeah, just look at her go!"

With mouth agape, I watched the herd of horses gallop down the track.

"Swale's really staying on her heels, though," Daddy said.

"But she's still in front!" I said, dancing in front of the television.

Althea stayed at the front until about the half-mile marker.

"Oh, no, Mare, he's passing her."

"That's OK. She was first for a long time," I said, sitting on my knees, pulling myself closer to the screen.

Around the three-quarter mile marker, the almost black Swale took the lead and Althea dropped way to the back.

"Look at Swale go!" Daddy said.

Pulling ahead down the backstretch, the announcer echoed Daddy's sentiments, "It's...all...Swale!"

Daddy and I jumped up and down in celebration, simultaneously exciting Dino and scaring Rosie. Morris might have raised his head to see what we were up to, but not much ever really excited him. Watching #10 Swale cross the finish line by three lengths was mesmerizing. There was a photo finish for third place and a disqualification between fourth and fifth places. But, since it didn't affect Swale or Althea, Daddy and I didn't pay too much attention.

"Sorry Althea didn't win, but she gave the boys a run for their money," Daddy said.

She really did, figuratively and literally.

"I'm just glad it didn't end like it did for Ruffian," I said.

"Yeah," he said, wrapping his arm around me and kissing my head. "We had fun, didn't we?"

"Yeah, Daddy!"

Although I later learned more about the darker side of horse racing, especially for those horses who didn't win, doing anything with Daddy and horses was the true definition of fun for me.

<u>June 17, 1984</u>

I am so sad. Swale won the Belmont Stakes a few days ago. But after a normal exercise he got a bath and then collapsed on his way back to his stall. Just a regular day and now he's gone. He just won the Kentucky Derby last month. How could he be gone? First it was Ruffian dying after the match race back in 1975 and now Swale. Why do all these incredible horses keep dying?

"Oh, no!" I exclaimed from the kitchen.

"What's wrong, Baby?" Mama asked.

"Swale died."

"Who died?'" she asked, with a full laundry basket on one hip and CJ on the other.

"Swale, the horse. He died," I said, rattling the newspaper's Sports section.

"Is he a horse you rode?—CJ, where did you get that? Not in the mouth! Honestly, everything ends up there."

"No," I said, talking to her back, as she waddled down the hall. "He won the Kentucky Derby *and* the Belmont."

"Oh, those big horse races?" She turned to CJ again, "I told you—Out. Of. Your. Mouth. Now!" She set down the basket, sweeping her finger around CJ's tongue as he whimpered in disagreement.

"He won both of them," I muttered, propping myself against the wall, allowing the newspaper to droop.

"Would you mind grabbing the laundry basket and bringing it upstairs? I gotta make sure everything is out of his mouth." CJ swayed his head back and forth in protest.

Tucking the newspaper under my arm, I picked up the laundry basket, and made my way up the steps.

"Sorry, Baby, about your horse," Mama yelled down to me.

"I wish he had been mine," I muttered.

"Did you hear the bad news, Daddy?"

"Yeah, so sorry, Mare," he said, motioning for me to sit on his lap. I didn't normally do that, but that's really where I wanted to be. "Swale was a good horse. Amazing horse, really."

"He just won the Kentucky Derby..." I said, tears welling in my eyes.

"...and the Belmont," Daddy finished, hugging me close. "I know, Mare. I know."

"He was right there and now he's gone," I said. "First Ruffian, and now Swale. Why do they have to die?"

Daddy kissed the top of my head. "It sucks, Mare. It really does. Look at it this way: think of how much better we are because of them. Think of how strong they both were. How powerful Swale and Ruffian were on the track. Swale won by three lengths in the Kentucky Derby and—"

"—But he didn't win the Preakness."

"No, but that's OK."

"But he should have. He *should* still be alive and *should* have won the Triple Crown. And now he never will."

"Nope, and horses only get one shot. For those races, anyway."

He sighed. "It really *is* hard. And, the sadness can swallow you whole if you let it. I know about that. But there are so many other horses out there that need our love and attention." He cleared his throat and gave me a quick hug. "Hey, I have a great idea."

"What," I mumbled, wiping away a tear.

"I think there is another horse that needs some Mare Time."

I looked up at him.

"Let's go see what Snickers and Wildfire are up to."

"Really?" I said, swiping my tears with the back of my hand.

"Yeah, grab your shoes and let's go."

Daddy always seemed to make things right. Except when he didn't.

June 13, 1984

CJ is turning out to be not that bad of a brother. Actually, he's super adorable.

"Maren, do you mind watching CJ?" Mama asked. "You're so good with him. Daddy Clint is still working on his project at work. Lacey is over at her friend's house and I have an end-of-the-year meeting this afternoon."

Looking over at my little brother, he was sitting in his playpen, cooing, and clapping his tiny hands. His legs, full of numerous fat rolls, formed a V on the ground.

"I guess so."

"You'll do great. I'll give him lunch and put him down for his nap. When he wakes up, check his diaper, which I'm sure will need changing. Then put him in the stroller and take him to the park or just walk around the neighborhood. I'll be home before supper."

It sounded like it could be fun, although I wasn't sure how good he was. Or how good I'd be.

Fortunately, he slept for a while and Mama was right—he definitely needed his diaper changed when he woke up. After watching Mama do it a thousand times, it seemed as though he went through a thousand diapers every day. I could never figure out how a little body could make such stinky stuff. Mama reminded me to put something over his little thing when changing his diaper, otherwise you'd see "The Fountain of Youth," as she called it. She said she got hit once, but that's all it took.

Pushing CJ in the stroller turned out to be fun as I mentioned a few areas of interest in the park. He pointed to them with his chubby little fingers, babbling the entire time.

It's amazing how much a little thing could start to grow on you in such a big way.

July 10, 1984

For my 11th birthday, Mama gave me an awesome gift—English riding lessons! All the riding I've done on Snickers and with Daddy has been in a Western saddle. The opposite of Western riding is called English, not Eastern. I'm kinda scared because the saddle is so small. Where's the darn horn? Why did they cut it off? It's going to be like riding a cornflake with a strap! And, one more year from today before Daddy gives me the BEST birthday gift!

July 15, 1984

My first English lesson was so fun and I had the best pony. Her name is Friday and she's dark all over. I want to say she's black, but there aren't many pure black horses or ponies. My teacher, Alicia, said that. I like her. I learned to post! Posting is when the horse trots and you basically stand up in the stirrups for a second. I think I'm getting it which is good because I don't want to boink my butt on Friday's back. You hold one rein in each hand for direct reining instead of neck reining. I kept wanting to put both reins in my left hand. It's so different, but I like it! I love learning all these new things. It's like a new language that I never knew existed. I do feel bad, because I really like riding Friday and it feels like I'm betraying Snickers. That's OK. I don't think they mind sharing me.

July 21, 1984

I miss Friday so much.

Before that English riding lesson, Mama dropped me off to run her errand. I peeked inside the barn, trying to find Friday because they usually let me curry comb and brush her before they tacked her up. Scanning the barn and the outside arena, I hardly saw anyone, so I sat on the nearby picnic table.

Still waiting for some movement on the property, Alicia finally emerged from who-knows-where, and sat down next to me. She said that Friday was being used at an event and that I'd be riding Patches. Disappointed after waiting all week to ride my favorite pony, it also miffed me to think of someone else riding "my" pony.

Alicia went back inside the barn and led out a very tall, yet somewhat slow, horse. Patches must have been almost fifteen hands. Although he wasn't as tall as Ruffian, after riding a twelve-hand Friday, a fifteen-hand horse felt as though I could touch the sky. His name confused me, however, because he was a completely chestnut horse with the tiniest of stars on his forehead. But then again, none of this made sense to me.

Patches was sweaty, but it was a warm, summer day, and they said he was a good horse to ride. I grabbed my helmet, Alicia helped me to mount him and she instructed me to walk him around the arena. I had to squeeze him much harder than Friday, because he wasn't responding to my air-kissing and clicking. When she told me to trot, I squeezed my legs even tighter. He relented for a minute, then slowed to a walk.

"Keep him goin'!" she yelled. "Kick him, if you have to!"

"OK."

"He's slowing down. Do it again. Keep him goin'!"

"I'm trying!" I yelled back through his bouncy and uncomfortable trot.

He slowed to a walk on his own again and I exhaled loudly in frustration.

Then he stopped.

I glanced down to see if something was bothering his hooves, but I didn't see anything. Just the arena sand filled with numerous deep hoof prints.

Just as I opened my mouth to speak, Patches' front legs buckled under me, lunging my body forward. His back legs went down, whiplashing me backward.

"Git your leg outta there!" Alicia yelled, rushing toward me.

Maintaining my seat in the saddle as Patches and I went down, I yanked my leg out in time, hobbling over to the side.

Patches' legs kicked out as he rolled to one side, then the other. Back and forth. The originally dark brown saddle and bridle were now a lighter shade caked in dirt and sand. The more relaxed horse stood up, shook himself off, jingling the bridle and saddle that were still attached to him.

I stood about six feet away watching in shock. He looked back at me, chewed the bit a few times, and walked away. My pounding heart felt like it would come clear out of my chest.

"You all right?" Alicia asked, following him.

"Um, I think so," I said, dazed, touching my helmet.

"Guess he really didn't want to be here today. He worked a lot this morning, and they didn't give him a break before they gave him to us."

I barely saw her grab Patches' reins when she called out to someone to bring us another horse. I found that strange since I thought he was the only horse available and ready for lessons.

Another girl brought out a bay horse who was already tacked up. "OK, here's Rocky," Alicia said, taking the reins from the girl. "He's a good boy and hasn't been ridden today. Let's get you up."

"Um, I don't really wanna."

Alicia turned to face me, holding onto the reins with one hand and her other hand on her hips. "If you don't get back up on Rocky now, I guarantee you will never ride another horse again."

"I'm OK with that," I quipped. "Didn't you see what just happened?"

"Yeah, that was exciting," she chuckled.

"Exciting?"

"Yep. Now it's time for you to get back up. C'mon," she said, motioning to me with her head.

"Are you serious?"

"Absolutely."

"No, thank you," I said, shaking my head.

"Maren, I'm not going to let you just walk away from this. You're a good rider. I don't want you to fear getting back up on a horse."

My throat began to tighten. "But didn't you see—?"

"Yeah, I did. But, if you don't get back up, you will never ride again."

"You said that already," I muttered through my growing tears. "When will Friday be back?"

"Not sure. But she'll be here for the next lesson."

"All right, so, I'll see you then," I said, unsnapping my helmet.

"No, Maren. You need to get back up. Now."

"Why? Patches almost kicked me in the head!"

"Yeah, we all got bumps and bruises. I've had broken bones, cracked ribs, been stepped on, bucked off, reared up on. That's what can happen. Welcome to the horse world!"

"Wow, sounds like so much fun," I said, rolling my eyes.

"It *is* fun. And now, it's time to get back up."

"Whatever, "I muttered, looking down at my boot, kicking the sand around.

"Maren, I'm not going to let you just walk away."

I raised my head, ready to protest again, and got a really good look at Rocky. Strangely enough, I was impressed with how calmly he was standing. With a lowered head and his ears turned toward our conversation, he stomped a fly away. For a second, I felt bad for him—like he was being rejected. I knew what that felt like and didn't want to do that to him.

"Time to get back up."

Snapping my helmet on again, I relented.

"Up you go," Alicia said, holding Rocky's head.

I could hardly see and catch my breath through the tears that flowed as I grabbed the reins in my left hand.

"I can't get my leg in the stirrup," I said, hopping around on my right leg.

"Here, I'll give you a boost," she said, pushing up on my butt.

I threw my leg over his back and lowered myself down into the saddle. His head jerked up as if I had awakened him.

When Mama got back from her errands, Alicia told her what happened. Mama agreed that getting back up on the horse was the best thing for me. Rocky walked and trotted when asked, even trotting over some ground poles. He really was a good horse.

He just wasn't my Friday.

August 4, 1984

I can't wait to see Friday again. Definitely missed her when I had to ride Patches and then Rocky a few weeks ago. We've had two more lessons together, but I wish we had more. It's my last lesson and Daddy is going to have to take me there.

The afternoon summer breeze swept through Daddy's open front door. It relaxed me as we sat at his kitchen table grabbing a bite to eat before my lesson. He usually loves it when I try to make him laugh. And, since hearing his loud belly laugh always made me laugh, I did it whenever I could. He picked up a saltine cracker and when he chewed, little flakes from the cracker landed in his developing moustache. Using a funny voice, I imitated what he just did, spewing out cracker crumbs that landed on the table. He snapped his head over at me, standing up so fast, his chair fell over. Pointing his finger at me, he yelled, "You don't appreciate all I do for you!"

Wiping the small amount of cracker from the sides of my mouth, I looked at him with shock and disbelief.

"You never appreciate anything I do for you. You never do!" he repeated, marching over to the front door.

"Yes, I do, Daddy," I whispered.

"I take you to your horse lessons. We go horseback riding. We do all sorts of things!" His voice increased in volume as his face turned red, and one particular vein on his face popped out. "I take you out to eat, and you don't appreciate anything! And your mother—she's the worst!"

The suddenness of his reaction made my heart pound not only in my chest, but also in my throat. I swallowed again to prevent tears from falling as my mind tried to process what had just happened. At the same time, it felt like my mind went somewhere else, and I was underwater, hearing him yelling from above. He threw open the front screen door and stomped outside, still yelling at the top of his lungs. "You never appreciate anything!"

I sat in the kitchen chair, unable to move, yet following him with my eyes through the windows as he paced outside. His piercing words dissolved any remnants of the relaxing breeze.

After what seemed like an eternity, the front screen door unlatched.

"Sorry for losing it, Mare," he said, a little calmer. "You ready to go?"

"Yeah," I whispered, slinking away from the chair, pulling up my riding boots as silently as possible.

I held my breath, not making a peep, since I didn't know when or if he would go off again. I felt like I was holding a ticking time bomb as we headed out to the truck.

"What do you want to listen to?" he asked, turning the radio on as we got onto the road.

"Whatever you want, Daddy," I whispered.

"What?"

"Whatever you want, Daddy," I said, a little louder after clearing my throat.

"Let's just find something. Here we are. 'Baker Street,' Gerry Rafferty."

Just as he seemed to calm down, someone in a blue car passed us, then pulled right in front of us, slowing way down.

"Dammit!"

Jerking the car back into the left lane, Daddy sped up, shaking his fist and screaming as we passed the blue car.

I don't remember everything that he said since it felt like I was underwater again. Since I had sunk lower into the seat, I didn't see them as we passed.

"He's such an idiot, he could throw himself down on the ground and miss," Daddy said, pounding the steering wheel. "He thinks he can just drive like a...a...jerk? He's got another thing comin'!"

Still sitting low on the seat, I heard, "Oh, my god. Drive the friggin' speed limit!" I could see Daddy pressing the gas pedal to the floor, but the truck's engine needed a minute to catch up. Clutching the side door handle even tighter, I prayed that we'd be OK.

Even though we arrived at the stable quicker than the normal twenty-minute drive, it felt like it took twenty days.

I had never been so happy to see Friday in all my life.

<u>Same day</u>

I know I already wrote in you today, but I couldn't get to sleep. I keep thinking about Daddy. I didn't mean to hurt his feelings. I thought he liked it when I made him laugh. I'm sorry I made him mad. I didn't mean it.

I know it's been a few months since Swale died, but

sometimes I can't stop thinking about his death. Then, I think about Ruffian. I always try to remember Ruffian in her glory. Running so fast and leaving everyone in the dust. But sometimes all I can see are the pictures of her eyes, showing her intense pain after she hurt her leg. Then I think about her being put to sleep. Sometimes it's hard to get the thoughts out of my mind.

August 10, 1984

Lacey got back from cheerleading camp. How boring. She told me she met a new friend there, Jamie, and guess what? Jamie has two horses! I asked Lacey what breed they were. She said she didn't know. I asked her what the horses' names were. She didn't know that either. She doesn't know a lot. I asked if I could go over and ride sometime. She didn't answer. Can't believe SHE is the one that has a friend with horses. I'm glad I can go horseback riding with Daddy and next year at this time for my 12th birthday, I'll get my horse from him! I don't need to have a friend with a horse. I'll have the horse myself!

September 6, 1984

School has been fun even though being in 6th grade feels weird. I like being the oldest in the school and I like my homeroom teacher, Mrs. Hayes. She's really cool. My math teacher, Mr. Evans, is SUPER boring. Why are all these math teachers so boring? I draw pictures of horses again, especially Ruffian, which helps. Thinking of horses anytime always helps me.

September 22, 1984

I am totally embarrassed. TOTALLY! Mama seemed to enjoy the whole thing!

"Time to go, Baby!" Mama said, quickly knocking then opening my bedroom door.

"Why do we have to do this now?"

"Baby—it's time. We really needed to do this a month ago, before school started."

"But I have to work on my language arts homework, and study for my math test. Oh, and I also have a social studies worksheet."

"I know. We won't be long."

"Oh, man," I bemoaned.

"We can stop by McDonald's for a Happy Meal."

I sat up. "I'm too old for that. But, can I have a nine-piece Chicken McNuggets? Or, share a twenty piece with you?"

"Well, we'll see. Let's get goin' here."

"Where's CJ?"

"He's staying here with Daddy Clint."

I was suddenly more open to this idea.

"So, what is your language arts assignment about?" she asked. I grabbed a baseball cap off one of the hooks at the front door, choosing one with a long bill to hide me.

"We're learning about research skills and how to evaluate sources."

"How is math going?" she asked.

"OK, I guess. Mr. Evans is kinda boring, so I just draw more horses."

"We'll need to work on that," Mama said, ushering me into the car.

Pulling into the big parking lot, I never really noticed how large and bright the "Kmart" sign was until then.

"Do we really have to do this today?"

"C'mon, it'll be fine," Mama consoled.

"Right," I guffawed.

Walking past the women's clothing, shoes and athletic sections, we stopped at an area splattered with pastel colors and half-dressed mannequins. We had arrived at the dreaded section. The bra section.

Mama sauntered up and down the aisles like she owned the place. I trailed behind her, far enough away so I could keep her in sight, but making it seem like we weren't together.

"OK, so you're probably a—come closer here, Baby!" she seemed to shout.

"Mama, I'm right here. And, stop looking at me like that!"

"I need to see what size you are. OK, let's try a 34A and... here's a 36A." Every word seemed to increase in volume.

She might as well have spoken Greek because I had no idea what any of that meant. "Here, take these," she said, handing me three hangers. I briefly pulled them in closer to marvel at how tiny they were.

"I really don't want to hold on to them. Can you?"

"You're fine," she said, picking out a dressing room. "This room's free. Go on in and see what you think."

I poked my head into the fluorescent-lit room with a smeared mirror. "Um, Mama, can you...?"

"Sure, I'll come in," she chuckled.

Having her in there with me really helped since I had no idea she was so talented. She twisted straps around and fastened hooks like she was tying down a tarp. The 34 one was a little tight but the 36 one fit better. Mama cocked her head to the side, studying my proportions.

"How does that feel?"

"Feels weird," I said, examining myself in the mirror. "But my boobs seem happier!"

Mama really laughed. I hadn't heard her laugh that way for a while.

"Let me look for a different color."

"Um, OK. But shut the door!" I said, hiding behind it, closing the door behind her.

I looked at myself in the smudged mirror.

I'm really getting a bra. A real bra.

A loud knock interrupted my thoughts. *"Special Delivery for Miss Maren Markey!*

"Mama!" I scolded, opening up the door, motioning for her to come in.

She laughed. "How about this?" she said, holding up a white one.

"Nah," I said, twisting, with my hands on my hips. "I like what I have on better."

"OK, now I need to walk you through how it goes on."

"Good because it's like a puzzle," I said, fumbling around the straps. "Why do they make it so complicated?"

"You do the back clasp in front, then twist around so the cups are in front. Then, pull one strap over one shoulder, and then the other."

"Oh, yeah!"

"Now, you try it." I managed to do most of it with some of her help at the end. "See you got it."

"Thanks, Mama," I said, hugging her. "OK, now let's get out of here before..."

"Before what?" she smirked.

"You know, before anyone sees us."

"First we need to go to the men's section to get drawers for Daddy Clint."

"Aw, man."

"Just pulling your leg!" she laughed. "Let's go get some lunch."

I definitely earned my Chicken McNuggets that day.

October 16, 1984

Hallomas was so much fun this year. I just love Aunt Mimi. And, I'm so excited! I get to be a horse for Halloween!

The Halloween that Mama wasn't able to make our costumes was the year we made our own. She brought home a large box that measured about two feet by three feet, along with a few large cans of paint and brushes. I decided this would be the perfect year to be what I had always wanted to be—a horse.

After I decided to be a pinto, like Trixie, I painted the box with white paint and used light brown paint to create spots over the body. Mama and I stuffed brown pantyhose with crumpled newspaper, each leg becoming the horse's back legs.

I was all dressed in my costume when Mama dropped me off at school.

Since Lacey and I were at different schools, Lacey had already left earlier. She wanted to dress up as Madonna but Clint said that wasn't going to happen. So, she decided to be a princess. That was fitting. But it was the first and only time I really heard him say "No" to her.

"Sorry I can't be part of your Halloween party today, Baby," Mama said.

"It's OK. Thanks for coming home at lunch to do my makeup. I just can't wait!" I was so proud of my makeup and my yarn mane. I realized later that Mama didn't eat lunch that day to help me.

"Now, be careful. You got it?" she asked, as I slightly stumbled out of the car.

"Yep. Bye, Mama!"

Stepping on to the school lawn and trying to avoid ruining my makeup, I maneuvered the box over me. Placing the wig on, I was ready for our Halloween party. I kept looking at my watch, waiting for the lunch bell to ring so we could go inside. At the same time, I noticed Jesse Laur, one of the meanest kids in school, standing nearby with some of his friends. Luckily, he was not in my class, but I was very aware he was a bully.

"Hey, you in the box!" he yelled my way. "What are you?"

I pretended not to hear him or all the laughing from his friends, just like what Mama told me to do whenever someone made fun of me.

"Hey, you must be a cow! Or, a deaf cow!" The laughing around him got louder. "Hey, deaf cow!"

I blinked hard as the welling tears rolled down my face.

The bell finally rang and I walked as fast as I could to my classroom. Jesse and the rest of his friends followed me down the hall, repeating, "Cow, cow, cow, cow, cow."

I felt relief finally reaching my classroom. My teacher, Mrs. Hayes, stood at the door welcoming students, dressed as the prettiest witch I had ever seen.

"Hi, Mrs. Hayes."

Her eyes followed Jesse and his friends as they passed by looking and laughing at me.

"Happy Halloween, Maren," she said. "Here is your treat."

"Thanks."

She leaned in closer. "You all right, darlin'?"

I shrugged, twisting my face, and blinking hard.

"Well, come on in. This afternoon's Halloween parade and party will be fun."

As soon as she took afternoon attendance, our class walked down the school halls, joining with other students doing the same. Every classroom showed off their costumes, which included many rabbits, mice, princesses, Supermans, He-mans, and Spidermans. The only time the masks could be worn in school was during the parade. I just hoped we wouldn't pass Jesse Laur. At least I'd be with my class if we did.

After the parade, Mrs. Hayes gave out prizes. I struggled to sit in my seat, tucking my pantyhose "back legs" under me.

"Today's scariest vampire costume goes to Chad. C'mon up, Chad, and get your prize."

He smiled a toothy grin as we all clapped.

"The most sparkly costume goes to Heidi...the costume with the biggest wig goes to Melissa...the costume with the most elaborate makeup goes to Angel..."

I heard Mrs. Hayes speaking, but it sounded as if she were underwater. Even though I was having fun, I couldn't stop replaying what Jesse and his friends said to me.

"And, last, but not least. The most unique horse costume goes to...Maren!"

I snapped out of my thoughts and navigated my way to the front of the class.

"Congratulations, darlin'," she whispered, giving me a side-hug. "You worked so hard on your costume. This is well-deserved."

"Thank you, Mrs. Hayes," I said, choking back some tears.

<u>December 3, 1984</u>

I didn't see Daddy at Thanksgiving since he didn't say anything about a visit. I still try not to upset him because he might get mad all of a sudden again. But, at our last visit, we had fun and danced around to the new song, "Do They Know It's Christmas?" by Band Aid. Dino, Morris, and Rosie also danced around and we were careful not to step on their tails. Daddy even played that really cool drum part near the end of the song with pens on the table and side of the couch. The song just came out this year and Daddy already knows almost all of the singers. When I asked him how he knew, he said just by hearing their voices he knew who it was. Mama probably doesn't even know who Band Aid is. She probably thinks it's something you put on your finger after you cut it. I love all of their voices and the cool thing is the singers are all from other countries. Someday Daddy wants to visit other countries, and I do, too. That seems almost impossible. I like to think about people in England and Ireland and Australia and New Zealand and Norway and Switzerland celebrating Christmas, too. Daddy said Norway has a horse named Norweegan Feeyord Horse. I know what a Ford is but I don't know what a Feeyord is.

We listen to Christmas music here, too. Mama has Bing Crosby, Johnny Mathis, and Andy Williams albums. I also love listening to the radio to hear other Christmas songs that Mama might not have. Daddy will probably eventually have all the Christmas records like he has other records!

December 8, 1984

CJ really makes Christmas fun!

My favorite holiday had once again returned! Our annual trek to see Santa at Crabtree Valley Mall had morphed from a practically traumatic experience for CJ to an almost enjoyable visit. It was interesting to see the progression in his pictures laid side-by-side. The blood-curdling screams from his first Santa visit transitioned to a silent, but wrinkled and pinkish face, highlighted by a jutting bottom lip. The year after that, he mustered a small smile. In the following years, he'd look directly into the camera, flash a huge grin, and wrap his arm around Santa's neck. If that's not growth, I don't know what is.

Looking back at 1984, CJ seemed to enjoy the season as much as I did, adding to the overall fun. A few days before Christmas, everyone was watching *A Christmas Story* in the living room. I snuck into the hallway, took my red winter coat off the hook, and buttoned it shut. Grabbing the pillow from my bed, I pulled off the pillowcase, set it on top of my belly and stretched my coat over it. Rummaging through the bathroom, I located a package of cotton balls, and glued them to the beard I cut from the construction paper I found in my desk. As the sweat began to develop under my warm coat, I wished I had created the beard first. Placing a small gift in my empty pillowcase, I threw it over my shoulder.

"Ho-ho-ho! Merry Christmas!" I yelled down the hallway.

Mama laughed.

"What is this?" Clint asked.

In my deepest voice, I bellowed, "Well, I heard CJ had been a good little boy this year and I wanted to give him a present this way."

"Mawen!" CJ squealed.

"Yes, Santa Claus told me he wanted you to have this gift early since you've been so good this year."

I pulled out a small, plastic boat and handed it to CJ.

"A boat!" Mama exclaimed. "What do you say, CJ?"

"Thank you!"

"You're welcome, CJ," I said. Some of the cotton balls were jumping ship from my makeshift beard. "I must be going now. You continue to be good and I'll see you next year. Ho, ho, ho!" I couldn't believe how fun that was and understood why the Santa at Crabtree Valley Mall did it every year.

*L*ater that day, I located a $5 bill I had received from Aunt Mimi. I placed it in an envelope and gave it to Mama as she was cleaning up the kitchen after supper. "Thank you for my stuffed animals and everything you gave me for Christmas."

"You're welcome, Baby," she said, bending down to put a plate in the dishwasher. "They're from Daddy Clint, too."

"I know, but I wanted to give you this. Merry Christmas, Mama." After practically dropping the envelope on the counter next to her, I dashed back to my room, knowing that she wouldn't take it.

I was right.

Mama knocked on the door and opened it. "Baby, this is so thoughtful of you. But this is *your* money."

"I want you to have it. For everything you've done."

She studied my face. "OK, but I'll keep this for you in case you need it. Or if you need it for something else, it's yours."

"OK, Mama," I said, humoring her, knowing that wouldn't happen.

December 23, 1984

I'm going to Daddy's for Christmas tomorrow. That's why we celebrated early. I kinda do want to go and kinda don't. Everyone was watching "Rudolph the Red-Nosed Reindeer" and eating popcorn tonight. I actually didn't want to leave. That almost never happens. I'm sure it will still be fun at Daddy's because we can dance and sing again! I'm excited to see Dino, Morris, and Rosie, even if my nose runs a little bit.

Mama drove me to the Kmart parking lot where we were going to meet for Christmas visitation. I wasn't sure why he didn't pick me up at home.

After sitting for over a half hour, we eventually saw Daddy's green truck pull up. And heard it long before we saw it.

"I'll see you soon, CJ," I said, reaching over and hugging him.

"G'bye, Mawen." He removed his soggy thumb from his mouth and reached his arms up to hug me.

"Oh, don't worry. I'll be back before you know it. Have fun playing with your presents!"

"Bye, Mama!" I said, scooching over, giving her an awkward side-hug.

"Bye, Baby. Got everything you need?"

"Yep, love you both," I said, opening the door and high-tailing over to Daddy's truck.

"Hi, Daddy!" I pushed the outside car door handle down as hard as I could. It wasn't opening, so I knocked on the window. He reached over the passenger seat, yanking up on the knob.

"Hey, Mare." Easing back into his seat, he rolled down his window. "I'll have her back on Sunday," he said to Mama.

Mama and CJ waved back as we left the parking lot.

"How are you, Daddy? Do you have your tree up yet?" I did

my best not to take too deep of a breath because the smell of cigarette smoke was stronger than usual.

"Yeah, it's up," he whispered.

"Well, if you don't have your tree up, I can help! And, Morris
and Dino, oh and Rosie, too. And..."

"I just said it was up," he said, rubbing his face.

"Oh, OK. Does Morris still try to jump at the tree? He's so
silly. Oh, and I can—"

"—Yeah," he said, forcing out an exhale.

"Well, next year I'll be twelve," I said, studying his pale face
and disheveled hair.

"I know."

"And, that's when ..."

"...you said..."

"...I'd get...my...."

I waited for him to finish my sentence. He didn't, so I finished
it for him.

"Horse."

"Yeah, that's right." He scratched his scalp, messing up his hair
even more.

"I'm *so* excited about it. Just cannot wait," I said, looking for
some confirmation.

"Yep, should be good," he said, emitting an audible exhale.

Christmas Day, 1984

I'm writing at Daddy's. I opened my eyes to see the time of
9:01AM and Morris staring down at me. He's so sweet and
his orange fur matches Daddy's couch. 10:30, Daddy still
sleeping. 11:54, Daddy still sleeping. 1:34, I think he's finally
up. Lots of times he sleeps in, but not like this time.

The first time I looked at the clock at 9:01AM, I petted Morris's
face which he really enjoyed. Opening the bedroom door as quietly

as I could, I tip-toed past a sleeping Daddy. I left the fan on in the room, hoping that might absorb any sound I may accidentally make. Morris led me past the partially-decorated Christmas tree through the living room to the animals' food bags and bowls in the kitchen. I hoped his soft meows and jingly collar wouldn't wake Daddy on the couch. The floor creaked and I turned to look back at him. He drew in a large breath, exhaling in a slight snore. Dino, who was sleeping next to him, jumped down when he saw Rosie following me. The rambunctious puppy went out to the backyard through a new doggie door Daddy installed, quickly returning for food. Although Dino had calmed a little, he was still a puppy.

I quietly opened the cat and dog food bags, grabbed handfuls and placed each kibble one at a time into all three of their bowls. After each food nugget's clink onto the stainless steel, I looked back at the couch. Still asleep. I carefully folded over the top of the food bags, Morris smelled his bowl, then crunched his food so loud, I swear that it echoed in the kitchen. Tip-toeing to the bathroom, past my horse drawing on the refrigerator, I sat down on the cold toilet seat just as Morris decided to talk to me through the closed door. With no time to dry my hands, I opened the door, scooped up Morris to keep him from meowing, and headed back to the bedroom. With some residual fur on my still wet palms, my hands were full of a nuzzling, purring cat while at my heel was a floppy puppy and happy kitten en route to the bedroom. Taking a few steps closer to the couch, I saw a big lump of a man whose thin, light-blue blanket was slipping off of him. Amazed by how different someone appears when they're lying down, I had never realized how big Daddy was. Balancing Morris on one arm, I gently pulled the blanket over Daddy's shoulders. He inhaled again followed by a wheezy, quick exhale. Shifting Morris to my other arm, I turned around and glided back over the creaky floor. Leaving the bedroom door ajar for the animals, I hopped back into bed and rested my head on the pillow. Setting Morris down, he snuggled next to my head—his favorite spot to curl up.

10:30AM. A small pile of Morris' striped, orangish hair

accumulated near my pillow. Sneaking out of bed, I peeked through the small crack to see Daddy on the couch. He was still asleep. I got back into bed, closed my eyes, wishing he would get up. At least the animals were there with me, although I did sneeze and felt a little wheezy. When I laid down, Dino thought we were playing and momentarily licked my face until I nudged him away. He eventually settled and the vibrations from Morris and Rosie's purrs lulled me back to sleep over the sound of the fan.

11:54AM. I got up and opened the door just enough to see the rise and fall of the light-blue blanket over Daddy and closed it again. Safe with my menagerie of animals, I turned on the radio, hoping Daddy got a few stations. Luckily, one of them was playing a song I liked, "Last Christmas" by Wham. After listening for a while, I turned on the one television channel that barely came through the rabbit ears.

1:34pm. I heard the living room floor creaking outside the door. Turning off the fan, I opened the bedroom door to see an empty couch. Daddy was coming out of the bathroom, just in time to hear the microwave "ding" signaling his coffee was done.

"Morning, Daddy," I chirped.

"Hey, Mare. How'd you sleep?" he mumbled through a yawn, stretching his arms to the ceiling.

"Good, Daddy. How about you?"

"Good, longer than I wanted."

"That's good," I repeated, trying to keep the conversation light.

He pulled his shirt down over his hairy belly and ran his fingers through his matted hair. "Did everyone sleep with you?"

"Yeah, most of the time. They're so sweet and Morris stares at me when I sleep!"

"He loves you so much." Daddy smiled at Morris who had joined us in the kitchen. The feline looked up at Daddy with soft eyes while Dino jumped around and Rosie mewed up at us. "They all do, and so do I." He hugged me with the pungent odor of fourteen hours of sleep and stale cigarette smoke caked on his clothes.

"Daddy? We're still going horseback riding today, right?" I asked, following him into the living room.

"Oh, Mare," he said, gripping his coffee cup. "Probably not today."

My heart fell. "But you said that we could go today because the weather was going to be good."

"I know," he said, collapsing onto the couch, rubbing his head again.

"But we have to go today," I protested through growing tears. "If we don't go today, we can't ride for a really long time!"

"Sorry, Mare. Just can't do it today," he said, lighting up a cigarette, picking up the remote and turning the TV on. "Want me to take you back home early?"

"Well, I dunno," I said, looking around the trailer. "I guess so."

"You do?" His head snapped around and he turned off the TV. "I thought you liked it here. With Morris and Dino and Rosie. And horseback riding, and…"

Uh-oh. I don't want him to explode again.

"I do, Daddy, but—"

"—And, we have so much fun. Don't we?"

"Well, yeah, but—"

"I make sure of it. And, it'll be this way when you come and live with me."

"Yeah, but—"

"C'mere, Mare," he said. I sat down on the arm of the couch when he reached for my hands. "Please don't go away. Please promise you'll never leave me."

I couldn't respond.

"I'm serious. Please don't ever leave me," he said, as he tightened his grip, with tears welled in his eyes. "You're the only good thing I have in my life."

I still couldn't find any words.

"OK?" he pleaded, with a quivering voice.

"OK, Daddy. I promise." It was hard seeing him get choked up. Unsure of how to respond, I kissed him on the forehead.

"Thanks, Mare. That's my girl," he said, patting my arm.

"But, are you...like...sick?" I asked, coughing through the new clouds of cigarette smoke forming in the living room. "Because I can take care of you if you're sick."

"Nah, just tired," he said, drawing in another hit from the cigarette, blowing away from me.

"That's what you said yesterday. And, last time, too."

"I'm fine."

I furrowed my brow.

"There is so much hatred and evil in the world. People lying. People dying. Feel the weight of the world on me. I don't feel like doing too much. Sometimes it's just hard. You know? Sometimes Life can get so hard."

"But we can take a walk and get outside. The sun's out today. It would be fun!"

"Maybe later."

"You're OK, right? You don't have, like, cancer, or anything, do you?"

"Nah, I'm OK," he said, rubbing his face with the palms of his hands. "I just don't like the pills the doctor gives me. Don't feel like myself. Feel like I can't drum and sing like I used to. There's no excitement. I used to get all these awesome ideas—they'd come a mile a minute. I can hardly keep up with them. Felt so alive! But now, all my creativity seems gone. I can't feel anything. I'd rather feel something than nothing at all."

"You don't feel anything?"

He exhaled. "Don't worry about it, Mare. I'm fine."

"You sure?"

"Yeah, c'mere," he said, scooting over and patting the slightly torn couch cushion next to him.

I plopped down on the couch, resting my head on his shoulder. Morris joined us, curling himself on my lap. Dino tried too, but just jumped around in circles.

"Dino, you're OK," Daddy said. "See, we're good, right? We have fun." He pat my hand and took another drag from his cigarette.

"Sure, Daddy." I found momentary comfort feeling Morris' soft fur, even though I felt a sneeze coming on. I was just glad we avoided another blow up.

<u>January 1, 1985</u>

Another new year! I'm so excited that in three more days I'll be at Daddy's. I hope he is happier this time and I hope he doesn't forget. I can't wait to see Morris, Rosie, and Dino again. I miss them. Then school starts again soon. I'm excited to see everyone again and see my teacher Mrs. Hayes again.

January 4, 1985

Well, Daddy didn't pick me up. AGAIN. After waiting FOREVER and calling his number that rang and rang and rang, he finally called me. He said he was really sorry and that he couldn't pick me up tonight, but asked about tomorrow night. I said no. This pisses me off. Sorry for the swears. Why does he say he can do something and not do it? At least my suitcase won't stink to high Heaven. I can't wait to go back to school tomorrow after Christmas break. I hope I can talk to my homeroom teacher Mrs. Hayes at recess. I don't like it when she tells me to go play with other kids. I'm excited to see her!

PART
Two

January 7, 1985

So glad to be back at school today! There's a new girl in my class. Her name is also Marin but with an "I," not an "E." So weird, because I've always been the only Maren I know. Now, there's two of us but I like my "E" better. She said she moved here because of her Daddy's work. Her mama doesn't work, like Mama does. But, guess what? She loves animals and she loves horses, too! This is so awesome!

Nearing the end of our science lesson, I was grateful for an interruption. Mrs. Hayes stood at our classroom door talking with Principal Winters who had a new girl next to him. Although she was wearing fashionable Jordache jeans and an Esprit shirt, my eyes were immediately drawn to her backpack with a small horse head on it, matching her Jordache logo.

"Class, I want to introduce you to your new classmate. This is Marin Breiner," Mrs. Hayes said. She escorted her to the front of the class and wrote her name on the chalkboard.

Another Maren? Or, Marin? How could that be?

"She just moved here from Texas, so let's be sure to welcome her."

Marin politely smiled after seeing all the eyes staring back at her. She was much thinner than me, long blonde hair, with hardly any boobs. From my front row seat, I saw small remnants of acne on her cheeks and forehead. I felt bad for her because even though I wasn't a size ten, at least my skin was clear.

"Go ahead and sit in the third row," Mrs. Hayes motioned.

I watched Marin as she walked past me to her new desk. I resisted the intense urge to turn around.

After what seemed like an eternity, we broke for recess. I eagerly wanted to talk to her. Part of me felt like I kinda had to anyway since we both had the same name.

"Hi, Marin, I'm Maren, too," I said, giving a quick wave. "But I spell it with an 'e' instead of an 'i.'"

"Hi."

"How do you like it here?"

"Well, we just got here a few days ago. But, so far, I like it," she said, smiling.

"I love your backpack. That is the best!"

"Thank you. I love horses."

"Me too!" I practically squealed. "I totally want one."

"Yeah, I love all animals, but bunnies are my favorite."

I rarely think about bunnies, but whenever I do, I'm always glad I did. They are the most precious bundles of fluff, outside of kittens, that is.

"Bunnies are sweet," I said. "Do you have any animals?"

"We have a dog and—"

"—What's his name?"

"Dallas, where we just moved from. He's a Lab and so goofy. Makes me laugh a lot."

"You're so lucky. Sometimes I'm allergic, but I totally love animals. I don't care if I start sneezing or wheezing. I'm still going to be a vet when I grow up."

"My mama said that since we moved here so fast without a

lot of time to get ready, we could get a dog," she continued. "So, at my last school, she came to my classroom and I got to leave school early so we could get one."

I couldn't imagine Mama ever doing that.

"Maren," Mrs. Hayes said, startling me a little. "Why don't you show Marin around during recess?"

Mrs. Hayes knew how I felt about recess so I was happy to do it. Win-win for me.

I showed Marin where everything was from the pencil sharpener to where she would pick up a hall pass. She also followed me down the hallway to see where the bathroom, library, and gym were. It was fun to be a tour guide, and although she didn't say much, I think she was grateful. Through my numerous questions, I learned that she lived near the school, roughly a mile from me.

When we returned to the classroom, everyone was still outside at recess. "Well, that's Garner Elementary School. But, if you wanted to come over sometime, here is my phone number," I said, walking to my desk and tearing out a piece of paper from my notebook.

"Thank you."

"I'm excited because I might have my own phone line soon," I said.

"Really? Your own phone line? That's awesome!"

"Well, I'd have to share it with my stepsister, Lacey, but it would be better than what we have now."

"You have a stepsister?" she asked.

"Yeah, my mama and Daddy are divorced. I've also got a little brother that my mama and stepdad had. I have a long family history."

"Well, my mama and daddy have been together for like forever, or fifteen years. Something like that."

What would that be like?

"I have a younger brother, too. But, he's annoying," she said.

"My little brother will be two years old pretty soon."

"He's still a baby!" Marin said.

"Yeah, but he's really cute!"

"My brother is already six years old. My family moves around a lot. We came here because of my Daddy's job," Marin said. "But he told us that we'll be staying put for a while."

"Well, if you want to come over some time, let me know."

"Yeah, that'd be fun," Marin said.

It felt good to talk to someone about horses who wasn't Daddy.

"**M**ama!" I yelled, flying through the kitchen door.

"We're in here!" she yelled from the living room.

"Guess what? There is a new girl in our class who moved from Texas and she loves animals and horses, too!" I said, practically throwing my backpack on the floor.

"Baby, that's great."

"And, I got to show her around. And, she got a new puppy!"

Mama exchanged a coy smile with Clint.

"What?"

"Are you going to want one now?" Mama asked.

"In your dreams," Clint said.

"Well, it would be great to have one," I quipped. "But, can she come over sometime? She doesn't live very far."

"Of course," Mama said.

"Yay!" I jumped around and ran into my room, tidying it up in preparation for the possibility of a new horse-loving friend coming over.

<u>January 15, 1985</u>

I'm going over to Marin's for supper after school tomorrow! Mama talked to Marin's mama and I'm going over!

"Hi, Mama!" Marin said as we walked through her large, stained-glass front door. She hugged her mama as her daddy came in from the living room, with a dog leading the way.

"Hello, Maren, I'm Mrs. Breiner and this is Mr. Breiner," she said, extending her hand.

"Hello, ma'am. Hello, sir," I said, mirroring her actions.

"Maren, this is my brother, Travis," Marin said. He gave a weak nod, barely looking up from his handheld video game.

"And, this is Dallas," Marin said, trying to keep the black Lab from jumping up on me.

"Hi, y'all and Dallas. Thank you for letting me stay for supper."

"Sure. Leave your things there and c'mon back," Mrs. Breiner said. "We're ordering pizza."

"Is it someone's birthday?" I asked, following everyone down the hall to the kitchen.

"No," Mrs. Breiner chuckled. "What do you like on yours?"

"Mama!" Travis said. "I want—"

"Travis, Miss Maren is a guest here. We ask our guests first," Mrs. Breiner said. Mr. Breiner was a quieter man and nodded.

Travis glanced up at me and twisted his face.

"Whatever y'all like on yours is good," I said.

"Do you like pepperoni?" Mrs. Breiner asked.

Does a bear poop in the woods? Aunt Mimi would say this all the time, but she wouldn't say "poop," she'd say the "s" word.

"Yes! I want pepperoni!" Travis yelled.

"Travis, geez," Marin said, nudging her brother. "We asked Maren."

"Yes, that would be great. Thank you, ma'am," I said.

"OK, so we'll get one large pepperoni for Travis and Maren and one large sausage with green peppers on one half and without on the other half for Daddy, Marin, and me," she said, jotting her thoughts down on a piece of paper. "Do you like breadsticks?"

Again, does a bear...

"Breadsticks!" Travis exclaimed. "I want tons. Tons of breadsticks!"

I watched in disbelief as he skipped in circles, wondering if CJ would be like that when he got older.

"Yes, ma'am. Thank you."

"Great. I'll call this in. Marin, show Miss Maren your room," Mrs. Breiner said. Again, Mr. Breiner simply nodded.

"C'mon, M," Marin said. "No, Travis. Stay down with Mama."

"Oh, man," he pouted.

"He's just ornery as all get out."

"No, I'm not!" he yelled from the bottom of the steps.

"Ugh. Must be nice not to deal with this, "Marin said. She was right. One thing I had that she didn't—a not-annoying brother. I followed her up the sweeping staircase, watching Travis get smaller and smaller.

"So, this is my room."

My jaw dropped. "Wow, this is huge!" My voice practically echoed in the massive bedroom that included a bird cage, an aquarium, and an attached bathroom. Her room could have fit two of my rooms in it.

"You can just put your backpack over there," she said, pointing to a bureau.

"Awww….so cute." I crouched down to get a better look at the white-headed, light-blue bodied bird inside the cage. "What's his name?"

"*Her* name is Skye."

"That's pretty."

"She's a girl. You can tell because her cere isn't blue."

"What's a 'cere'?"

"That's the part where her nostrils are," she said, indicating the area above the beak. I narrowed my eyes to see. "She's a budgie."

I giggled like when I first heard the band name Buggles. "I love that word. Just fits how cute they are. Does she like to be held?"

"Sometimes," she said, opening up the cage door and reaching inside.

Skye, perched on the rod, hopped to the opposite side of the cage.

"C'mon, Skye." The miffed budgie pecked at her hand.

"Does that hurt?"

"Nah." Skye eventually relented, hopping onto Marin's finger. "You can pet her." I was surprised that her feathers were as soft as they were blue in color.

Marin placed her on the bed, and the parakeet hopped up to Marin's pillow, pacing back and forth.

"Is she going to poop on your pillow?"

"Maybe, but it's not a big deal if she does," she said.

"Does she fly around the room?"

"She might but her wings get clipped."

"Ow, why?"

"So she doesn't get away."

"Does it hurt them?" I asked, watching the hopping budgie.

"I don't think so. We just take her to the vet to get it done."

"Like, how often?"

"I don't know. Every once in a while."

"Wow, I never knew so much went into taking care of parakeets."

"There's actually not too much," she said, scooping the hopping Skye back into her cage.

"Bye, sweetie," I said, giving her a quick wave.

A soothing, bubbling noise caught my attention from a large fish aquarium on the other side of the room.

"Look at all the different kinds of fish. We only had a goldfish CJ named Fishie! And, he didn't last too long!"

She laughed.

I sat mesmerized as she pointed out the Black Mollies, Angel Fish, and Neon Tetras swimming around the treasure chest and plastic greenery in the aquarium.

"Is that one a goldfish?"

"Actually, that's a swordtail," she said.

"They look almost the same. What's this guy down here called?" I asked, indicating a speckled little fish cleaning the bottom rocks. He was on the aquarium floor, seemingly uninterested in the fish swimming above.

"That's a Corydora."

"Looks like a catfish."

"I think they're kinda the same," she said.

"It's funny, I don't know much about fish, but it's crazy that they all have their own lives. Just doin' their own fish things."

I spotted a horse poster hanging above another bureau on the opposite side of the room. Even though I had more posters than she had, this particular one was more eye-catching than any of mine. It had a chestnut and a bay galloping in the water with sand flying up behind them. "Wow, I love your poster!"

"Thank you," she said, sitting on the bed.

"What's your favorite kind of horse?"

"I don't know," she said, looking up at the poster. "Maybe the brown ones, like there."

"Yeah, that's a 'bay' and this one is a 'chestnut'. Have you ever heard of a horse named Ruffian?" I asked, sitting down next to her.

"I don't think so."

"Ruffian was a racing thoroughbred who lived a long time ago, but she was the most amazing horse. She ran like the wind and won all her races. But then the stupid people ran her in a match race against the horse who won the Kentucky Derby. It was just the two of them and she broke her leg and died."

"That's terrible," Marin said.

"Yeah, I cried when I found out."

"How do you know all of this?"

"I go to the library a lot," I said.

Spotting a large stereo system in the corner, I got closer to see its record player and cassette player. Both mine and Daddy's were much smaller. I don't think Daddy even had a tape player.

"Do you like music?" I asked.

"Yeah, especially on the radio. Mama's got the 'Islands in the Stream' record downstairs."

"That's so cool! Does she like Kenny Rogers and Dolly Parton?"

"Yeah!"

"I absolutely love music and my Daddy plays the drums. My *real* Daddy. Do you think your mama would let us play it?"

"Probably, but it's still new so we'd have to play it downstairs," she said.

"OK. What songs do you like?" I asked.

"'Flashdance'!"

"Yeah! That's fun! How about 'The Reflex'?" I added.

"Yeah, and 'Like a Virgin!' Madonna is so pretty!" she said.

"And what about…'Ghostbusters'!" We both sang the title together through giggles.

"Have you seen the movie?" I asked.

"Yeah—so scary!"

"I know, but the song is fun! And, what about 'Footloose'!"

"Haven't seen the movie, but totally love that song!" she said.

"'Footloose! Footloose! Take off your sweater and shoes!' Are those the words? I can't tell what they're saying!"

"I'm not sure, but what about 'Careless Whisper'?" she asked.

"*Please stay!*" We sang in unison with closed eyes, fists held close to our chests.

We fell onto her bed, laughing.

"Marin." We both jumped when Mrs. Breiner tapped on the door. "Pizza will be here in about five minutes. Time to get ready for supper. C'mon, Dallas." Their beloved dog seemed upset that he couldn't be with us.

"OK," Marin said, sitting up, still giggling. I was still trying to catch my breath.

On our way downstairs, I saw that the upstairs hallway had three more bedrooms. My favorite part of the house was their sweeping staircase that led to the welcoming foyer and couldn't wait to walk back down it.

Their downstairs hallway seemed to go on forever before we finally arrived at the kitchen. They had a bar area with stools, a kitchen table, and then steps leading down into their family room. This led to the biggest TV I had ever seen, complete with a VCR. Dallas led the tour, happy to be part of the pack. Luckily, my allergies weren't bad at Marin's house.

Pizza for supper on a random Wednesday night was quite a treat. I got the impression that Marin and her family did a lot of things we didn't.

January 18, 1985

Well, it happened again. Daddy didn't show up. I didn't really want to go anyway. I'll miss Morris, Rosie, and Dino but I don't like when he "loses track of time." I want to say, "Don't say you're going to pick me up and not do it." I get mad. Then, I get mad when Clint and Mama get mad at me. I ate some chocolate chips out of the bag, Mama said I ate too many. There was another bag in the pantry, and she can always get more. What's the big deal?

February 26, 1985

Winters are still hard but I love when Marin and I go over to each other's houses. We've done it like a million times now, especially since I haven't heard from Daddy in a while. I hope he remembers the awesome gift of a horse he promised me this year for my birthday. Marin says she likes to come over to my house because our house smells "homey" but I go over there a lot.

"Can I go over to Marin's after school tomorrow?" I asked Mama as she was cooking supper.

"That would be fine. Just make sure you're home when the street lamps come on."

"Thanks, Mama!"

"And, park your bike on the front sidewalk if you don't want to put it in the garage. Daddy Clint almost ran over it when you parked in the driveway."

"Um, OK," I said, furrowing my brow.

"So, just park it on the sidewalk," she said, smiling.

I was too excited to question.

atching every minute slowly tick by in school was unnerving. The last bell finally rang and Marin and I headed outside to the bike rack.

"Can't wait to go over to your house," I said.

"Yeah, Mama said we're going to get Bojangles tonight."

As usual, my growing excitement of going over to her house and eating food from a restaurant funneled into questions.

"Did you know that a horse's top lip is 'prehensile'?" I asked, opening the long, glass school door with my hip.

"What's 'prehenses'?"

"'Prehensile.' It means that it can grasp things. Like a lemur's tail. And, that horse trailers are called horse floats in Australia? They're just so cool over there in Australia and in other countries like England and Ireland."

"Can they really float like our boat?" she asked.

"You have a boat?"

"Yeah, we got one down in Texas and it should be delivered here soon."

"Wow, I'd love to be on a boat," I said, raising my voice over the kids hurrying to the bike rack and buses.

"It's fun," she said, turning her bike's combination.

"I'm sure. I've always wanted to be a horse. Did you ever want to be one?" I asked, unlocking my bike.

"Not really."

"I have. They're amazing and free!"

"My parents are talking about getting a horse," Marin said.

"Oh, my gosh! When?" I said, snapping my head around.

"Not sure, but they're looking around and talking to people. My daddy knows people at work."

Wow, she has a boat, possibly a horse, and Jordache jeans with the horse's head on them. She really is lucky.

"My Daddy said he'd get me a horse this year when I'm twelve, but we'll see," I said, shrugging. "I've got books and magazines if your parents want."

"Thanks," Marin said, taking the lead. I hopped on my bike, excited about what yummy things from Bojangles were on the menu tonight.

March 6, 1985

Mama and Marin's mama finally said we could have a sleepover this weekend! They said I could go over there. Her house is bigger and Marin has Pepsi-Free all the time. We only get soda at home when we get good grades. I packed up my suitcase but I'm happy it won't come home smelling like smoke this time. I don't think Marin's parents smoke. I would smell it if they did.

It's weird how I can smell smells. I wonder if other people are the same way. What's also weird is that some smells are way too yucky, but the smell of hay or horse poop doesn't really bother me. The wild onions outside are really smelly now. Now that spring is coming, it's everywhere. Yellow pollen is everywhere too. It looks like yellow snow. Like the kind that Clint says not to eat! I'm so excited for the sleepover!

"Have a good time," Mama said, pulling into Marin's circular driveway.

"I will!"

"Don't forget to thank her mother, too."

"I won't," I said, grabbing my suitcase from the back.

"And, mind your manners. You're a guest in their home."

"I always do. Bye, Mama!" I said, slamming the door with excitement.

Marin answered her large front door under the enormous brick entry. Her house seemed to get bigger every time I visited.

"Hey, M," she said, hugging me.

"Hey, y'all!" I said, seeing her whole family lined up to greet me again.

Dallas tried to jump up on me, but I prevented him by blocking him with a raised knee.

"You girls take Miss Maren's things upstairs and then wash up. Daddy's on his way back from Bo's."

Bojangles again, which always made me happy. Other things that made me happy were gliding up and down her staircase and seeing her room and her horse posters.

"Look what I brought!" I said, setting my suitcase down on her bed and removing the Black Beauty horse statuette.

"You brought them!"

"Yeah, Mama said I could this time. So, here is Duchess, here is Merrylegs, and here's Ginger." Next to Black Beauty, I lined up the cantering chestnut figurine next to the grey pony and the dark bay. "Which ones do you want to play with?"

"Well, I have some here, too," she said, reaching into her closet. "My mama and daddy got me these." Emerging from her walk-in closet, she placed a box on her bed that said "The Black Stallion Returns."

"I *love* The Black Stallion!" I said. "He's like my favorite horse, next to Ruffian. Haven't seen *The Black Stallion Returns* yet though."

She pulled out The Black Stallion, a sorrel chestnut, and an almost white horse statuette in a standing position. "I haven't seen it either. But we were shopping and I really liked these, so Mama got them for me."

Their shininess almost prevented me from wanting to play with them.

I looked down at my figurines lined up on the bed. Even though Marin's were in pristine condition, we preferred to play with mine since the legs on Black Beauty and Ginger were easier to maneuver for pretend canters and gallops. And, my Black Beauty group showcased a lot of wear from the many adventures we had. Sometimes things that are well-loved really are better.

"Supper's ready. Go wash up," Mrs. Breiner announced through the closed bedroom door.

Marin ran down the massive staircase and I tried to keep up.

"Do you want to play our Atari after supper? It's downstairs."

"Wow, you have an Atari *and* a basement? We just got a Tandy."

"What's a 'Tandy'?" Marin asked, turning on the main floor's bathroom sink.

"Well, it's a silver and grey computer thingy. I think it's made by Radio Shack," I said, lathering my hands.

"Can you play Ms. Pac-Man on it?"

"I don't think so. But we have Clowns and Balloons, which is fun! And, Clint and Mama love the game 'Bust Out.'"

"My mama loves to play Ms. Pac-Man," she said.

"I know some guys really love Pac-Man, but I like horses better."

"For sure!"

*T*he next morning, Mrs. Breiner made waffles with grits, homemade buttermilk biscuits, and what she called "Popeyes." They were toast with a hole cut in the middle, just big enough for a sunny-side up egg. Lacey and I were usually left to our devices for breakfast because Mama and Clint had to get to work. Sometimes I had a bowl of Cheerios from the box Mama intended for Clint, or just skipped breakfast altogether.

"When is your mama expecting you home, Maren?" Mrs. Breiner asked.

"I don't have any specific time."

"We'll need to drop you off before our reservation at Circle Bowl. Once Marin does her chores, we can go."

"Awww, Mama," Travis protested at having to wait for his sister.

"I can always help," I offered.

Mr. and Mrs. Breiner exchanged glances. "You really want to help with chores?"

"Yeah, Mama," Marin pleaded. "Can Maren help me with mine? It will make it go faster. Then she can go bowling, too?"

My heart pounded in anticipation as I studied Mrs. Breiner's face.

"You *really* want to help Marin with her chores?" she repeated. "You know, she has to make her bed, vacuum the living room and steps, clean the downstairs toilet, and clean out Dallas' food and water bowls."

"Yes, ma'am. I don't mind at all."

"Suit yourself."

I really didn't care what I had to do. I was just happy I got to stay longer.

Marin played their "Islands in the Stream" record as we sang along with Dolly and Kenny over the roar of the vacuum and the scrubbing of the toilet. Marin had a good voice, too, but I didn't think she was as interested in being in choir as I was. Noticing how thin her whole family was, I figured it was due the consistent chores they did together. At any rate, it felt fun being part of a family.

March 30, 1985

It was weird seeing Daddy in the hospital.

Deep in thought while trying to decide whether to pack my jeans for my visit with Daddy, Mama knocked on the door.

"Baby, your Daddy won't be picking you up this weekend."

My shoulders slumped. "He forgot again."

"Well, no. It's because he's in the hospital."

"Oh, my gosh! Why?"

"Well, uh, he hurt his back and is recuperating from surgery. So, you won't be going to his place this time. But he still wants to see you."

"I really wanted to see Morris, Dino, and Rosie."

"I know you did, but not this time," Mama said. "We can go to the hospital now, if you want."

"I guess," I said, looking around at my open drawers and clothes strewn out on the bed.

Mama was silent on the short ride over. However, she was

open to the idea of swinging by Burger King to pick up Daddy's favorite—the Whopper.

When we checked in at the hospital's reception desk, I wrote down both Mama's and my names on the sign-in sheet. They gave us badges that said "Visitor." It felt so official. We also had to leave our stuff with them at the front which was fine with me. The less I had to carry, the better.

We weren't allowed to go to Daddy's room. That was fine because hospital rooms seemed so freaky to me. We met him in the cafeteria, where he was sitting at a table by himself. Other people milled around, and one guy in particular talked to himself a lot. Another guy was practically yelling at something in the corner until some nurses came and took him away.

"Hi, Daddy," I said, leaning over and giving him a quick hug. He seemed heavier than the last time I saw him.

"Hey, Mare," he said, bleary-eyed, talking slower than usual. "Caroline, thanks for bringin' her."

"You're welcome, Garrett," Mama said, quietly standing to the side.

"How long will you be here, Daddy?" I sat down, placing the Burger King bag in front of him.

"Well…until the doctors say it's OK for me to go home." Reaching for the bag in almost slow motion, he asked, "Is that for me?"

"Yeah, we got you a Whopper on the way over, Daddy."

"Thanks," he said, smacking his lips a few times. "I'm so thirsty. Do you have any Pepsi?"

"Sorry," I said, spotting the empty glass in front of him. "Do you want more water?"

"Nah, I'm OK."

"But you can have the Whopper. It's yours," I said, showing him the bag again. With slightly shaky hands, he reached inside, but struggled as if he couldn't grasp it.

"Nah, that's OK," he said, setting the bag aside. "Thanks anyway."

"Well, how's your back? Did the surgery hurt? Can I see your scar?"

Daddy looked up at Mama.

"Not right now," he said, as tears formed. "I'm so sorry that this is our visit." All three of us were momentarily distracted by the guy talking to himself again. We were glad when he finally stopped.

"It's OK, Daddy. Next time. How is Morris?"

"He's good. He misses you."

"Is Dino still adorable?"

"Yeah, he's still chewing a lot and causing a ruckus," Daddy said. He smacked his lips together again. "Man, I'm so thirsty."

"What about Rosie?"

"Yep, they're all good. Ready for you to come visit again." Daddy stretched with a loud yawn.

"Baby, we should get going," Mama said. "Your father is getting tired."

I looked back at him.

"You'll see him soon."

"I hope you feel better, Daddy. I love you," I said, hugging him in his paper-thin hospital gown.

"Love you too, Mare." He clumsily threw his arms around me. "My pride and joy."

"Bye, Daddy."

After taking a few steps, I turned around and he was staring at the table, all alone. His back shook a little as if he was crying.

It wasn't until years later that I realized Daddy wasn't in the hospital because of back surgery.

April 17, 1985

Guess what? Mama found out there is another horseback riding place nearby! I think a teacher at work told her. It's called Fair Oaks Stables and it's not very far! It's awesome having someone to share horses with again. Daddy hasn't called in a long time. I hope he's out of the hospital and feeling better. But I'm so excited to go horseback riding and Marin is excited, too! Mama said we could go this weekend! Hope Marin's mama says it's OK, too.

I vividly remember this moment. Marin's mama, indeed, said, "Yes."

In preparation for our ride, I wore my yucky tennis shoes, jeans, and my t-shirt with a bay horse's head on the front while Marin wore a t-shirt with nicer shoes. On the drive over, Mama said that Marin and I talked a mile a minute. From my position in the passenger seat, I was on high alert and was the first one to spot the Fair Oaks sign when we turned the corner.

"There it is, Mama!" I squealed, pointing at the weathered wood and slightly chipped paint.

Turning into the long driveway, the gravel crackled underneath the tires, creating a cloud of dust in our wake. The driveway twisted and turned several times, making me wonder if we would really find stables at the end. When the clearing finally came, there was a two-story house next to a large barn. It had a small, attached office and a few small paddocks with a couple horses inside. Directly in front of the parking area were a few saddled horses tethered to the fence. Stomping occasionally, their tails swished from side to side. It took every last ounce of restraint not to run up to them.

When we got out of the car, a tall, thin woman with short, dyed black hair and blue eyes greeted us from the house, escorted by two dogs. The first dog was large and white, with almost black eyes, a deep chest, and a fluffy tail that stood straight up. In contrast, his white, silky ears flopped down close to his face. He maintained some distance from us, sniffing the air.

The smaller dog's coat had different shades of gray, accentuated by tufts of brown. Unlike the other dog, his black triangle ears stood straight up, like an Australian Cattle Dog mix. He seemed more interested in getting closer to us and sniffing our legs.

"Hey, y'all," the lady said, shaking Mama's hand. "Welcome to Fair Oaks Stables."

"Hello, Mrs. McGee. I'm Caroline Fletcher," Mama said. "We spoke on the phone."

"Please, call me Patsy."

"Sure." She managed to fit in a few words over the continuous barking from the large, white dog.

"Moose!" Ms. Patsy said, turning around towards him. The canine stopped, swallowed, slightly relaxing his tail. "Don't you mind him. Great Pyrenees. He's all bark. Dodger, the other one, is good, too. I suppose you two young ladies are riding today?"

"Yes, ma'am," we said simultaneously.

"Great! C'mon in."

We followed her into the tiny office where a small window gave us a perfect view of the horses. They seemed so close, I felt like I could reach out and touch them. The wood-paneled walls held old faded pictures of horses, certificates, and plaques. Mama signed papers that asked our addresses and phone numbers as well as how much riding we had done. Despite the underlined warning that horses' behavior can be unpredictable, my excitement grew with each passing moment.

"Marin, your mother is going to pick y'all up when you're done," Mama said, slipping her wallet into her purse.

"Thanks, Mrs. Fletcher."

"Yeah, thanks, Mama!" I hollered. Using my "inside voice" just wasn't going to happen here.

"You lookin' forward to goin' out today?" Ms. Patsy asked.

"Yes, ma'am!" I exclaimed.

A girl, probably a few years older than Marin and me, entered from a door behind their counter. The man with her was tall, thin, grey-haired, complete with a cowboy hat, boots, and a mustache to match. He looked like he walked right out of a Western movie.

"This here's my husband, Mr. Bucky, and my stepdaughter, Sherry," Ms. Patsy said, stapling the forms we filled out.

"Ma'am," he said, tipping his hat.

"Hey," Sherry said.

We said our hellos.

"Miss, you've ridden before?" Mr. Bucky asked me.

"Yes, sir! I've ridden Trixie, Snickers, Friday, Sunny, and River." I turned to Mama. "Have I ridden any others?"

"I don't think so."

"And, I've trotted…"

"OK."

"…and cantered! And, when I cantered, Snickers went really fast!"

"OK," he chuckled. "And, you?" he asked Marin.

"Well, I've ridden a few times and have also trotted. I think I've cantered, sir."

"Now, then," Mr. Bucky turned to Sherry speaking in hushed tones. I could make out "Go git…for her, and…for her," nodding to me then Marin. I couldn't make out the names because of his hushed voice and thick Southern accent.

"All right then. Follow Sherry out and she'll gitcha ready to go. I've got to make a quick phone call, but will be right out," Ms. Patsy said.

We approached a large tree-shaded paddock. Sherry opened the gate and I followed her in.

"You stay back until I call you," she said, turning around to me.

"Oh, OK," I said, slinking back behind the gate. Mama smiled at me.

Sherry untied a dark brown, almost black horse from the fence. Walking to the large water trough, the horse stretched his long neck, placing his muzzle in the water. The loud slurps could be heard from where we stood behind the gate.

"Ya 'bout done?" Sherry asked him.

Nope, he stuck his long neck back in again, drinking even

more. Raising his head, his tongue shot out of his mouth, trying to slurp up the drops dripping from his muzzle. He looked around at us as she removed the bridle that hung off the side of the saddle horn. He took the bit well; sometimes they don't always do that.

"OK," Sherry said, turning to us.

I unlatched the gate.

"No, actually, he is for her," she said, motioning to Marin.

My heart fell. Again. Both the dark horse and I were chomping at the bit.

"It's OK, Baby," Mama said. "She's getting your horse."

"My horse." Loved the sound of that.

Marin unlatched the gate and mounted him. I knew it was a him because, well, I looked. You kinda have to look to know for sure.

The horse shifted his feet and Sherry asked Marin about her stirrups. They were fine because she had longer legs.

Sherry then untied a beautiful, golden horse with a shiny, black mane and tail and black stockings that came to his knees. She walked him to the water trough, and he too, drank. Looking around, he pricked his ears toward me. I waved to him and he dove his head into the trough again.

"Want any more?" Sherry asked. He turned his head away. "*Now* you can come in."

"Bye, Mama!" I said, running to them.

"First thing—don't *ever* run around horses," Sherry said, pointing her finger at me.

"I know," I mumbled. "Just got excited. Sorry."

"They see things different than we do and they could spook. That would be bad for everyone."

"Sorry. So, who is this?"

"This is Spirit."

I couldn't believe it. I really wanted to tell her what that name meant to me since that's what I named Gypsy's baby when we saw her give birth. But I was pretty sure she wouldn't be interested.

"Hi, Spirit," I said, rubbing my hands along his thick, golden neck. I loved how portions of his dark mane just flopped to the side. "What color is he?"

"He's a buckskin."

"Buckskin," I repeated. "He's beautiful."

"You're a good boy, aren't cha?" Sherry said, patting his neck. "He's actually my horse."

"Really? Do you mind me riding him?"

"Nope, he goes out on the trails with people all the time. Daddy and Patsy got him for me when I was a kid, and he'll be my baby for life. But I've been riding the other horses more and they're more fun to ride anyway. So, let's get you up."

I slid my left foot into the stirrup, then hopped on my right for momentum. She nudged my butt help me into the saddle.

"Do your stirrups feel OK? Think they're a little long," she said, placing her hand on my calf. "Stand up in them. There should be some air between your butt and the saddle when you stand."

I did, and there wasn't.

"Yep, they need shortening." She unbuckled some things on the side of each. It's mind-boggling: I'm on this huge, incredible animal with nothing more than big belts holding everything together. "Good now?"

I nodded.

"Also, keep the ball of your foot in the stirrup. And heels down," she said, adjusting my foot into that position.

I nodded, since I knew some of this from riding before.

"All right, now!" Ms. Patsy said, emerging from the office. She muttered a quick "Thanks, Sherry," before Sherry nodded and returned to the house. "Let's get 'em going!"

She untied her horse, a chestnut with a lighter mane and tail with a slightly different build than our horses.

"Hey, M!" I said, twisting around in the saddle to face her. "Can you believe we're actually here?"

"No, I can't!"

"What's your horse's name?"

"I don't know."

"Mine is Spirit and he's a buckskin."

Ms. Patsy mounted her already-walking horse. "I'm going to be in front. Just don't let them eat. Jubilee will try."

"Jubilee—that's your horse's name," I said, turning to Marin.

"We call him Jubi for short," Ms. Patsy said, steering her restless horse. "He'll go right behind me, and then Spirit. Give Jubi a small kick. With Spirit, all you need to do is make a kissing noise and he'll fall in line."

She was right. Marin gave a slight kick, and I made a loud kissing noise and we were off.

Once the three of us were lined up, I asked Ms. Patsy, "What's your horse's name?" raising my voice to be heard from the back.

"This is Lady Bird," she said, twisting around in the saddle.

"What kind is she?"

"She's a Thoroughbred. A little more spirited than Spirit and Jubi. But, you're a good girl, aren't cha, girl?" Lady Bird snorted out.

Ruffian was a Thoroughbred, too! I really wanted to know if Lady Bird was related to Ruffian, but didn't want to ask. I felt a little weird that I had to talk so loudly, like I was talking past Marin. But I just had so many burning questions.

"What kind is Spirit, besides a buckskin?" His ears swiveled toward me when he heard his name. "You're a good boy," I said, scratching his neck.

"Plain ole' Quarter Horse," she said.

"What kind is Jubi?" I asked.

"Appendix."

"'Appendix'? Like what we have?"

"Strange name, isn't it? That's what they call a Quarter Horse-Thoroughbred cross."

"And, the three of them like each other?"

"Maren, c'mon..." Marin said, uncomfortable with my questions.

"You can ask as many questions as you want! That's how you learn," Ms. Patsy said. "As long as Lady Bird is in front, she's fine. Jubi and Spirit are best pals. They came in together from people who just let them waste away. They were underweight and their hooves were in terrible shape."

"Poor Spirit and Jubi," I said, petting the side of Spirit's neck. I really wanted to wrap my arms around him and give him a huge hug. But we were on a trail ride, after all.

"It broke my heart. I've seen worse, but it wasn't the best. But the Old Man and I worked with them and now they're great. Eating us out of house and home!"

"That's just so sweet." I couldn't stop staring at the chunk of mane that flopped to the opposite side of his golden neck. Like he had a cowlick.

"Makes it easy because they don't care who's in front either," she continued. "Some horses do. The only reason Spirit is last is because he's faster. If he was in front, he'd leave both Jubi and Lady Bird in the dust. Jubi would be fine, but Lady Bird would surely have something to say about that. It wouldn't be good!"

Sounded kinda cool.

"Or, he'd be so far up Lady Bird's butt, she'd probably kick out."

Well, not so much that part.

"Jubi isn't slow by any stretch of the imagination. Spirit is just faster. Faster walker, faster trotter."

"Faster canterer, too?"

"Yes, that too. But we won't be doing that today."

My heart sank. I thought the fact I mentioned that I had cantered on Snickers during check-in would have been enough.

The trail wound through the woods, leading to an occasional open space where we could look down over the small hills. There was one oak tree that stood in front of a larger open area. I preferred the wider spaces to the thinner, more root-filled trails. Either way, I was just happy to be on Spirit since it had been a few months since I had last ridden a horse.

"Oh, man, we're back at the barn already? That was the fastest hour I've ever had," I said.

Sherry emerged from the office and held Spirit as I dismounted. Ms. Patsy helped Marin.

"Whoa, my legs!" I said, wobbling around.

"I know," Marin said.

We both returned to the office in true, bow-legged cowgirl fashion.

"Yeah, that can happen," Ms. Patsy said. "You used muscles you didn't even know you had." I remembered that from riding Trixie, Friday, River, and Snickers, but I think Spirit was wider than them.

"So, what did you think?" Ms. Patsy asked.

"That was fun!" I exclaimed.

"Yeah," Marin said, smiling.

"Happy to hear. Your mama will be here soon," Ms. Patsy said, motioning to Marin. "In the meantime, let me show you girls the farm." The three of us passed Sherry in the paddock tending to our recently-ridden horses.

I was glad Mrs. Breiner was going to pick us up. She was always late for things which worked in our favor this time. I could feel my throat start to get itchy and a sneeze come on but did my best to suppress it.

I couldn't take my eyes off Spirit. I was about to ask another question when Ms. Patsy said, "See in that other paddock? A paddock is the fenced area where the other horses are. You see a brown horse with black mane and tail out there?"

"That's a bay!" I blurted. I could hardly control myself and a sneeze got out. Only one.

"Right, that *is* a bay. That's Deuce, Mr. Bucky's horse. He's a handful, and a turd most times. That's why we call him 'Deuce'!" She laughed. "But, he's still fun to ride and has a big heart. Do you see the dark horse next to him?"

"Is that Jubi?" I asked.

"Nope, he's still tied up at the gate. That's Shadow. She's mine and a complete mess. But, wouldn't have her any other way."

I smiled but Marin appeared less interested.

"The pony with her is Little Bit. Sometimes we do pony rides with her. She can be a booger, too, but she's a doll with the little ones. The other dark horse with a white stripe down his face—that's Ebony. He's a Tennessee Walker Horse."

"Tennessee Walker," I repeated.

"A real sweetheart who gets along with Jubi and Spirit really well. Guests love to ride him, too. He's what is called a gaited horse. That means that they have another 'speed' between a walk and a trot called a running walk. It's as fast as a trot, but not as bouncy. Poor guy's been dealing with some lameness, so he's healing. Then, over yonder, that bay is Beau."

"What is Beau?"

"He's an Arabian mix."

"I think the Black Stallion is Arabian!" I said.

"You saw that movie, did ya?" Ms. Patsy asked, through a not-so-hidden smile and tiny wink.

"Yeah, like a million times with my Daddy. Best movie ever!" I turned to Marin. "Did you ever get to see it?"

"Not yet."

"You totally have to see it. You will love it!" I gushed.

"See a whitish horse over there?" Ms. Patsy asked. "That's Frosty. He's what you call a 'flea-bitten' gray."

"Ewwww," I said.

"Yeah, hateful term, but that's what he's called. Good horse, though. And, do you see that chestnut over there next to Frosty?"

"Yeah?" I said, craning my neck, gripping the side of the fence.

"That's Kiwi. We call her that because she has a mark on her face. It's called a blaze, and it's in the shape of New Zealand."

I furrowed my brow.

"They lovingly call people from New Zealand 'kiwis.'"

"Oh!"

Marin didn't say much. She mostly looked at the ground, occasionally glancing at her watch.

"The Old Man, Mr. Bucky, also rescued Frosty and Kiwi when they were neglected and really thin," Ms. Patsy continued. "The people who had them before just dumped them. Since they came together, we kept them together. Jubi and Spirit are that way, too. But, for Frosty and Kiwi it can be a real problem. They can be buddy sour."

"What's 'buddy sour'?"

"That's when they can't be away from each other without the other one losing their minds. Some folks call it separation anxiety. Since they only had each other where they used to live, they bonded. Everyone needs friends."

I looked over at Marin and smiled.

"We're still working on them. Always a work in progress with horses. They're huge animals, but they're actually quite fragile and sensitive creatures."

I could relate. On both accounts.

"Can we go in and see them?" I asked.

Ms. Patsy laughed.

"Please?"

"Maybe some other time."

"OK." My bounciness ceased, which was probably a good thing. Just like you're not supposed to run around horses, bouncing around them wasn't good either.

"Here's our chickens," Ms. Patsy said, pointing down at a few hens running by. "And, here are the goats, Chocolate, Chip, and Cookie. Hello, ladies!"

Although the chickens were adorable when they ran and the goats were just funny creatures overall, they weren't as interesting to me. With every fiber of my being, I wanted to return to the horses again. Just to see them made my heart sing.

I was just about to take a step when I felt something swish past my ankle. Rubbing against it was a fuzzy black and white cat.

"Oh, my gosh!"

"That's Penguin. He's one of the few barn cats around here to keep the mice population down," Ms. Patsy said. "There are other cats, but he's definitely the most outgoing. I think he thinks he's a dog!"

"He's so soft," I said. The feline stood up on his haunches, nestling his head into my hand. Although his markings were different, thoughts of my kitties Brownie and Jelly Bean briefly returned.

"M, you gotta feel him. Isn't he soft?" I was careful not to touch my face after petting him.

She crouched down, petting his back. "Yeah, he is." Marin was more of a dog person, but I thought maybe she would like a cat that acted like a dog.

"He loves people and horses," Ms. Patsy said. "He'll follow us around. Nothing much scares him. Even Dodger and Moose don't scare him. Sometimes he'll lie down smack dab in the middle of the paddock, just watching the horses, who never seem to mind. He never gets underfoot and is respectful. With them, anyway."

She crouched down to pet Penguin who was now rolling around on his back from side to side. "You're a good boy, aren't cha, Penguin?"

They had a few other cats; Oscar, a gray tabby, Mr. Kitty, an orange tabby, and Mouse, a gray, fluffy boy. But Penguin was my favorite. In my head, I called him *Pingüino,* Spanish for penguin.

Pingüino loved us loving on him, but the crackling gravel signaled Mrs. Breiner's arrival.

"Your chariot has arrived," Ms. Patsy said.

"Thank you, ma'am," Marin said, heading toward the car.

"Yeah, thanks, Ms. Patsy. And, thank you Penguin," I said, giving a quick pet. "Bye, Moose and Dodger," I said waving to them, slowly making my way to the car.

"...and Spirit and Jubi...and Chocolate, Chip, and Cookie. And bye chickens—!"

"All right, now. You git!" Ms. Patsy joked. "Don't make me come over there and give you a giddy up!"

"Thanks, Ms. Patsy!" I said, closing the car door.

"How was it?" Mrs. Breiner asked, waving to Ms. Patsy.

"The best time! Wasn't that the most fun?" I asked Marin, strapping myself into the back seat.

"Yeah, I loved Jubi. He's great."

"Spirit is awesome, too! I just wish we could have cantered," I said. "Maybe next time."

"Have you ridden before, Maren?" Mrs. Breiner asked, looking in her rearview mirror.

"Yes, ma'am. I used to ride with my Daddy a lot."

"Mr. Fletcher?" she asked.

"No, my real Daddy. But I haven't seen him in a while."

"I see."

I was grateful she didn't keep asking questions, because I really didn't have any answers.

"What was your favorite part, M?" I asked, trying to change the subject.

"Well, when Jubi started trotting, I didn't even have to really kick him or anything."

"Spirit, too! He was just like, 'OK, I guess Jubi and Lady Bird are going. Guess I will, too'!"

"You girls sound like you had a good time."

"The absolute best!" I exclaimed.

May 13, 1985

Our mamas said I could sleep over at Marin's Friday night and go horseback riding at Fair Oaks on Saturday! I'll ride my bike over. Sunday morning they're leaving to go boating. I wish I could go with them sometime, but they don't ask me.

After Mama read my English paper the other day, she says my writing has changed a little bit. I guess so. I can't wait until Saturday!

May 18, 1985

Riding at Fair Oaks was the best! We got to canter! I don't really like Sherry, but I still love Spirit and everyone else there!

When something is amazing the first time, one never knows how the second time will be. Luckily, riding at Fair Oaks did not disappoint.

Calling ahead, I requested Jubi and Spirit after being told by Sherry they couldn't be "reserved—only "requested." As Mama dropped us off, seeing the tacked-up horses at the hitching post still gave me fluttering butterflies.

Once we mounted up, Sherry got us out on the trail. I had hoped Ms. Patsy or Mr. Bucky would have been our guide, but at least we were horseback riding.

My mind wandered to thoughts of Ruffian and how amazing Thoroughbreds were. Thinking about how cool it would be to actually be one, I asked, "M, what breed of horse do you think you are?"

"Probably a Thoroughbred," Marin said.

"Yeah!" I said. "I can see that."

"I'm a Quarter Horse," Sherry interjected.

I was talking to Marin. But whatever you say.

"Well," I said, "I think I'm a—"

"—You're definitely a Shetland Pony!" Sherry guffawed.

My heart fell. I didn't want to be a short, squatty Shetland Pony, I wanted to be a sleek Thoroughbred.

A girl could still dream.

We walked a little more and Jubi and Spirit started trotting at the oak tree.

"Do you want to canter?" Sherry asked, turning around in her saddle.

"Yes!" I said, nodding my head with such force, I think I overextended my neck. It took three steps for Spirit to canter, and we were off! *The Black Stallion* music played again in my head as pictures of Ruffian galloping across the finish line flashed in my mind. The strength and energy from Spirit's canter forced me to balance myself more than I had to with Snickers and River. In an attempt to prevent Spirit's nose from going up Jubi's butt, I veered off to the side, committing a huge no-no by completely passing him. Spirit and I got too close to Lady Bird, whose ears flattened and tail swished in response.

I pulled back on the reins with even more strength and Spirit slowed, just as Sherry yelled, "What are you doing? You could have gotten kicked!"

Although Sherry was right, the exhilaration of cantering was something I had sorely missed. We all slowed and I waited for Marin and Jubi to pass me as Marin mouthed the words, "It's OK."

After returning to the barn and dismounting, Ms. Patsy emerged from the office. "How'd it go?"

Dodger sniffed curiously at my shoes, while Moose still kept his distance.

"Still sooooo much fun!" I really wanted to say that going back the second time felt as if I were going home, but I decided not to.

"She's *got* to remember to stay in line," Sherry said, pointing at me. "Lady Bird almost gave them a piece of her mind."

Ms. Patsy saw my fallen countenance. "Yeah, Spirit-man likes to move."

"It's OK," Marin said, whispering to me and squeezing my hand. "Jubi didn't mind. I watched his ears."

"Thanks, M," I said, trying not to let Sherry ruin my good mood. I felt my throat getting itchy and a sneeze just waiting to be released again.

"While you're waiting, feel free to say 'Hello' to our other residents, or just watch Spirit and Jubi," Ms. Patsy said.

True to form, Marin's mama was late in picking us up. But I had started relying on it, and frankly, hoping that would happen. As we waited, we watched *Pingüino* jump on the fence where Spirit jutted out his top lip, nibbling on the feline's ear. I noticed the cats seemed to relax the horses whereas the dogs tended to be the horses' playmates or, at times, irritants. *Pingüino* leaned into the horse's lippy nibbles, bracing himself on the fence and enjoying this cross-species grooming.

A symbiotic relationship. That was the phrase for the day.

The ride back to Marin's house was chock-full of our lively chatter, including a little Sherry-bashing. Pulling into Marin's driveway, the awe I felt the first time I went to her house returned. The sheer size of her house and property was stunning. I had started anticipating that Dallas, her dog, would greet us. He also didn't disappoint, with his usual forceful, wagging tail and playful hops.

S inging along with the radio had become one of our favorite things to do. Sometimes we'd even throw in an interpretative dance, spinning and twirling around.

Marin's stereo was on when the radio station played "When I'm With You" by Sheriff. "I love this song!" I said, turning it up. "Baaaabbbyyy!" Marin laughed, as I sang.

Then on the next, "Baaaaabbbbbyy!" she stood up on the bed and sang along with it, closing her eyes and making fists.

"Wait—here comes the key change!" I said, jumping up on the bed next to her. "Baaaabbbyyyyy!"

Singing in unison, we stood on our tippy-toes to reach the last high note. Ironically, the singer is a guy and even we struggled to reach it. We both collapsed on the bed, giggling.

In the laughing-induced high, I said, "Oh my God! I just found out that boy horses, geldings, can get something called 'beans.'"

"'Beans'?"

"Yeah, that's what they call them!"

"Like jelly beans?" she asked.

"Not really! You *do not* want these in your Easter basket!" I said, in the loudest belly laugh.

"What? Tell me!" Marin laughed, falling onto the bed.

"It's stuff they get in their...well...you know."

"Their butts?"

Hearing her say that made me collapse onto the bed from laughter. I think some drops of spit landed on her comforter.

"Actually, in their...well, ding-a-lings!" I said, sputtering to get the words out.

"Ewwww, gag me!"

"Yeah, sweat and dirt and stuff can get up in there and it combines into this like stone-like thing," I explained, fumbling my hands over each other.

"Why?"

"I dunno. It does hang down, after all!"

"I know. One time Jubi was standing there and I was about to get on him and it was totally just dangling out there!"

"And Spirit was thinking, 'Dude, what is that?'" I quipped.

"He wanted to say to him, 'Put that thing away!'"

"You'll poke someone's eye out!" I added.

We erupted into laughter again, doubled over, with tears streaming down our cheeks. Marin nudged me, which is something she did when she couldn't stop laughing. I opened my mouth to talk again and another little droplet of spit flew out, almost landing on her ear.

We both slowly exhaled to catch our breath, holding our sides, and wiping away a few tears. It's funny how often uncontrollable laughing brings physical reactions similar to crying.

"Now I'm never going to be able to look at them the same way," she said.

"No wonder the fillies and mares run from them. I would too! Poor guys, they can't help it. But, daggum!"

I began laughing again so hard, I started wheezing. "Oh my gosh, I can hardly breathe!"

"Are you OK?" she asked, placing her hand on my back.

"I'm fine," I hacked.

"Are you sure?"

"Yeah, this is awesome!"

"So, can girls get 'beans'?" she asked. Her question caught me by surprise and I laughed and coughed at the same time.

"Not sure. Maybe! Grody, huh?" I said, trying to take in deep breaths.

"Yeah!"

Even if it got harder to breathe, it was all worth it. I couldn't remember the last time I laughed that hard. All I know is that, when it happened, I was with Marin.

*A*fter breakfast the next morning, Mrs. Breiner asked me, "Are you all packed up? Time to take you home."

"Aw, man," Marin said. She reached down and pet Dallas who just loved to be wherever his people were.

I walked back up the stately staircase and gathered the rest of my things. I had graduated from my previous blue and tan suitcase to a backpack.

"Thanks for coming over," Marin said.

"Yes, we'll see you real soon," Mrs. Breiner said. "Let's take the minivan. We'll put your bike in the back."

I peeked outside and saw their boat already attached to their truck. Guess it had arrived from Texas.

"Honey, I'll be right back. I'm taking Maren home," Mrs. Breiner said to her husband.

"That's OK. I can ride my bike home," I said.

"It's no trouble."

"It's OK. Thank you, ma'am," I said.

"Bye, M," Marin said, hugging me.

"Bye."

Have fun.

Wrapping my fingers around my handlebars, I watched them

carry a cooler to their truck then pedaled down their driveway home.

<u>June 2, 1985</u>

Horseback riding is awesome! I love how Spirit and Jubi are best friends and Marin is my best friend. Horses are like people. They have different personalities, too. Spirit is perfect on the trail and Ms. Patsy says he's an easy keeper, is practically bomb-proof and doesn't crib, or chew on things. But he could be mean to other horses or animals, and I don't even know it! I don't think so because Spirit is the most amazing horse! Horses are awesome because if they like you, they'll show it. If they don't, you'll know. They are pure. Animals are that way. People aren't. Animals aren't going to give you a fake smile or talk behind your back. Or, say they'll come pick you up when they don't. I wonder what Daddy is doing. I don't miss him since I'm riding with Marin now. I do miss riding Snickers and Wildfire and seeing Morris, Dino, and Rosie. I don't miss smelling like smoke and everything. And him being weird sometimes.

<u>June 10, 1985</u>

Even though I love school, I'm really happy that we're out for the summer! It's been super fun with CJ. Who knew playing with a sprinkler could be so great?

Reminds me of CJ's second birthday last March. He was so cute with the cake Mama made and all the balloons around. Mama rented a huge bubble machine and we all had fun in the backyard. Well, at least Mama, CJ, and I did.

Playing with the sprinkler was entertaining as a child, but CJ made it extra-special. On that humid June day, CJ was clothed only in his diaper, waddling bow-legged from its inherent bulkiness.

"OK, CJ, here we go!" I said, turning on the spigot.

The sprinkler shot out thin tubes of water, spinning around in a circle. Pretending the water was something to avoid, I jumped around, squealing.

CJ looked up at me, studying my face for a minute. He clapped as a huge smile grew across his face. Dipping my toe into one of the streams of water, I jumped around, pretending to recoil.

"Don't let it getcha!"

Reaching out to one of the ribbons of water, he laughed, holding his head back.

"It gotcha!"

He giggled and clapped, as small droplets flew off his tiny hands.

After a few more games of dipping our toes into the water and faux-running away, CJ toddled back to the front door. Sprinkler time was over. For now.

June 13, 1985

Mama found a horseback riding camp—sleepover and everything! It's called Echo Lake Camp. Marin's mama said Marin could go too and we're so excited!

We're going at the end of July. I can't believe I'll have my own horse by then! I'll be so excited from everything, I'll hardly be able to sleep!

July 6, 1985

For my 12th birthday, Mama is giving me a horseback riding party at Fair Oaks! After we go riding, we'll eat at the firepit in front of their barn. We'll have hamburgers, hot dogs, chips and we'll roast marshmallows. Mama even said that I could have my favorite candies, Wispa and Rolos. It will be me, Mama, CJ, Marin, and unfortunately, Lacey.

Why does Lacey even have to be there? She doesn't even like horseback riding and she's not good at it. Plus, there won't be any boys there, so why would she want to come? I'm glad Clint won't be there, but I did thank him for the party since Mama told me to. I don't think he really likes horses anyway. I wish his daughter would do the same and stay home. While we're out on the trails, CJ is going to ride Little Bit while Mama holds onto him and Sherry walks them around. So exciting!

July 9, 1985

Tomorrow is my 12th birthday. I cannot wait! I haven't heard from Daddy in a long time. He obviously knows it's my birthday and I'll be getting the best gift EVER from him! I'm supposed to be, anyway. Wonder what my new horse will look like? Will I get a mare or a gelding? And what will be his or her name? Maybe I could get one like Spirit? Wish I could have him, but he's Sherry's horse and I definitely know she wouldn't share him. Maybe I could get a dark or almost black horse, like the Black Stallion or Ruffian. I'm so excited because now I can gallop all the time! That would be amazing. I can't believe that I'm talking about having my own actual horse! It's so real, I can almost taste it!

On the way to Fair Oaks, the song "Down Under" came on the radio. We all sang along with it, including Lacey.

"What is a vegemite sandwich?" I asked.

Marin looked over at Lacey. "Dunno," Lacey said.

"Is that like a vegetable sandwich because that sounds gross!"

"I. Don't. Know," Lacey repeated, slower for more emphasis.

Those were my exact words when I wondered why Lacey was even there.

The crackling gravel under the tires meant that the fun was about to start. Seeing Spirit, Jubi, Ebony, and Shadow tacked up still made my heart soar.

Ms. Patsy welcomed us. "Hey, y'all! Happy Birthday, Ms. Maren and good to see you again, Ms. Fletcher."

"Thanks, Ms. Patsy!" I squealed, without diverting my attention from the saddled horses.

"You know the drill. Paperwork to sign and then we'll be on our way. While we're gone, Mr. Bucky will get the fire going. There's plenty of hot dogs, chips, sweet tea, and s'mores. I know Ms. Maren likes to be in front. I'll ride Ebony because Lady Bird really does not like Spirit on her behind."

My chest puffed with excitement since I really loved being in front. It meant a lot that Ms. Patsy knew that and even changed the horse she was riding to accommodate me.

"And, you, little man," she said, turning to CJ. "Ms. Sherry will help you with Little Bit. You can ride for as much or as little during that time as you want." She turned around and smiled at Mama. "We'll be back in about an hour."

Almost on cue, Sherry seemingly came out of nowhere, helping Marin and me to mount our horses. Ms. Patsy stood next to Lacey since she needed a little more help, despite her obvious disinterest. I turned my focus to Spirit, pet his neck and noticed how his golden ears were outlined in black, like eyeliner for the ears.

"OK...Spirit, then Jubi, then Beau," Ms. Patsy said, mounting Ebony. "All these geldings are good together. On this ride, we got fillies and one old gray mare in the saddles!"

I think I was the only one who laughed.

Ms. Patsy moved from walking next to me back to walking next to Jubi and Beau. I think she was checking on Lacey, in particular, because sometimes Beau dragged a bit. I was grateful Ms. Patsy was there to instruct her. I'd love to tell Lacey, but it was probably better received if it didn't come from me.

After a few minutes on the trail, I turned around and asked, "Isn't this fun?"

"Yeah!" Marin said.

Lacey smiled, which is a more positive response than I thought I'd see from her.

After trotting twice, my heart raced when we saw the big oak tree that led to the open and spacious clearing. Once inside the clearing, there is only one tree in the middle that seemed to stand with confidence. I sometimes wondered if it was lonely.

Ms. Patsy passed me and swung Ebony around to face us. "Do you girls want to canter?"

I was about to answer.

"I know full well you do," she said, smiling, pointing to me. "How about you two?"

Marin looked over at Lacey.

"No thanks," Lacey said.

"No thanks," Marin mirrored.

"You don't want to?" I asked.

"Naw, not today," she said, glancing over at Lacey again.

"Just the Birthday Girl then" Ms. Patsy said. "The three of us will keep walking around the edge. Just stay on this side of the tree. Have fun!"

"Thanks!" I kissed the air and Spirit and I jogged off. He didn't seem as eager to be away from his buddies, especially Jubi. But we did canter a few times. The familiar images of the Black Stallion and Ruffian filled my mind and the love for Spirit filled my heart even more.

On the way back, Ms. Patsy and I walked side-by-side on the wide trail. Fortunately, Ebony and Spirit got along well. No pinned ears or swishing tails.

"My Daddy said he would get me my own horse when I turned twelve. I hope I get one as good as Spirit!" I said.

"Hope you do, too," Ms. Patsy smiled.

Once we arrived at the barn, Sherry and Ms. Patsy helped us dismount, then tied down the horses. I gave Spirit a quick scratch while Lacey and Marin headed for the exit toward Mama. She was sitting with CJ on the picnic table by the firepit. The hot dogs, chips, paper plates, and soda were all set, and the smell of a low-burning fire set the stage.

"Hey y'all, how was it?" Mama asked.

"It was awesome! I totally got to canter!" I said, galloping in place.

"She sure did," Ms. Patsy said.

"That's great, Baby. Glad you had fun."

"It was fun," Marin said.

"Yeah, wasn't too bad," Lacey said. She headed toward the pile of food at the end of the picnic table, with Marin as her shadow.

"Did you like Little Bit?" I asked CJ.

He shrugged.

"Well, it wasn't as fun for CJ as it was for you," Mama said, standing up.

"How long did you ride the pony?"

"About five minutes," Mama said.

"That's it? I was hoping he'd like it more. Well, at least you tried."

"Yeah, up high!" he said, pointing to the sky. I guess eleven hands would have seemed high for a little guy like him.

"We've been enjoying watching the chickens and the goats."

"And kitties!" CJ exclaimed.

"Yes, and the kitties. We also helped Mr. Bucky get things ready for dinner," Mama said, handing each of us a plate and napkin.

"I caweed the ha dawgs!" CJ said.

"Yes, you carried the hot dogs. You sure did," Mama said, smiling down at him.

"Looks like you have everything," Ms. Patsy said, glancing over the food and necessities. "I'm going to leave you to it. Holler if you need anything. We're all set," she said, nodding to Mama.

"You're not gonna stay?" I asked.

"No, this is your time," she said, heading toward the house. "We'll be seeing y'all soon. Happy Birthday, Maren!"

"Bye, Ms. Patsy," I said, with a twinge of disappointment.

After opening the clammy hot dog bags, we all laughed trying to slide the wiggly things on the roasting sticks. The shape of hot dogs really does lend itself to numerous jokes. Even Mama laughed a few times. Although Marin and Lacey talked mostly to each other, it was fun to feel connected to everyone, even if it was by way of inappropriate comments. Mama's homemade birthday cake, heavy on the frosting, was my favorite and was always my birthday wish. However, it was obvious what my *real* birthday wish was.

July 12, 1985

My 12th birthday is over. Didn't hear from Daddy. Maybe this weekend. I didn't get my horse, but I got my period. What a birthday gift. Everyone has a name for it. I call it "Bertha." Glad I knew about her from Mama and those totally awful classes at school. I'm so glad boys weren't there for that. Totally embarrassing. Now I'll definitely know when not to wear white pants. The absolute worst thing of all is I didn't get my horse. Dammit! I know I shouldn't swear, but I'm really, really mad.

Although I was angry, my new physical development initially intrigued me. It helped that Mama was so cool when I told her. She was at the kitchen sink, cutting carrots when I asked, "Guess what came last night?"

She turned around, wiping her hands on the dishcloth. "You mean?"

I nodded.

"Oh, Maren, congratulations!" she said, hugging me. What she had failed to mention were the stabbing, excruciating pains that would accompany Bertha every month. Wish I had known about that ahead of time. Thank God for Ibuprofen, or I would have died. Or, it sure felt that way.

> <u>July 13, 1985</u>
>
> Daddy actually remembered to pick me up for my visit this time. He was even a little early, which was weird. Just not sure about everything he's asking though. I'm still so mad. When I got home, Mama asked me if I was OK because my eyes were puffy. I told her it was because my allergies were really bad. They were bad at Daddy's but it was because I just couldn't stop crying. I only cry now when no one else is around. Usually at night which makes it hard to sleep.

Despite the increasing sputtering and jerking of Daddy's truck on the way to his trailer, he seemed to be in a good mood. Once we arrived, he said, "Everyone here is so excited to get some Mare-time! Going to be a great weekend!" he said, turning the key to his front door.

"OK, Daddy." I feigned a smile but it was all worthwhile to see the animals again. Dino jumped around with a thumping tail, Rosie observed the excitement from the corner of the couch and Morris sat on the couch's arm, watching everything happen.

"Now that it's warm, there is so much more we can do!" he said, throwing the keys down on the table. "And…. since it's a special someone's birthday…."

"Yes! Thank you, Daddy!" I said, looking around for some sign of a horse.

"Turn around," he said, walking into the bedroom.

Was my horse in the bedroom? Or, was Daddy just pretending to forget, like he sometimes did?

"No peeking."

I've been waiting for three years and it's finally here!

"OK, turn around and open your eyes!"

In his hands was a dog stuffed animal.

"Here you go!"

"Um, thanks," I said, turning it around to get a look.

"What's wrong?"

Setting the floppy dog down on the couch, I drew in a deep breath. "You totally said you'd get me a horse for my twelfth birthday."

He ran his fingers through his hair. "Well, gotta tell ya, Mare. Daddy couldn't swing it now. OK?"

"OK, Daddy," I said, trying to prevent him from losing his temper.

"But, next year. Definitely next year. All right?"

"A whole year?" I asked, regretting my words as soon as they left my mouth.

"Yes, but it'll go by fast. You'll see," he said, seemingly trying to convince himself.

It felt like a heavy rock was forming in my gut. Yet, at the same time, I was relieved he didn't explode.

"And, don't forget, you will be able to come live with me then."

"We'll see." I know what that really meant when Mama said that.

"And we need to put our heads together to find another place to go horseback riding now that Randy's Ranch closed down."

"They're closed?"

"Yeah, the guy there wasn't taking care of the horses. So, they went right in there and shut him down. All gone. Nothing left."

Poor Snickers and Wildfire. This was getting worse.

"No problem, we'll find another place! Plenty of them around here. We can check Cary or Durham. Or, Chapel Hill. Even outside the Triangle, if you want."

"OK but—"

"—And, I think Wake Forest might even have a place up there! Of course, we can check the rest of Johnston County. And

Harnett County, too. You know I have no problem going outside the Triangle. There are tons of places. Remember when we went to Kentucky Horse Park?"

"Yeah."

"That was fun, wasn't it?"

"Yeah, but—"

"—And, when we went to the Outer Banks? Now that was rockin'. Riding on the beach!" he said, opening his arms.

"Yeah, I wonder how River and Comanche are doing—"

"—Oh, and we could even go to Virginia. Or, South Carolina. Or, we can even try Tennessee, if you want." He nodded. "Yep, tons of places. Every place has got horses. Next year will be great! You'll come here, and you'll have your horse. You'll be able to ride him or her whenever you want! It will kick ass! Whoops—shouldn't swear in front of you."

Pu-leeze.

"But, where would he, or she, live? There's not much room behind the trailer," I quietly added.

"He can live with Mr. Gary. Or, we can move!" Daddy said, throwing his arms open again. "Malik and the guys talked about another place we could move to in Johnston County that sounded good. Or, we can stay. We'll figure it out. And, they also told me about a new job that pays so much better than that other one and the boss isn't a…well, jerk. Yeah, this will be great!"

"Well, we'll see."

There it is again.

The reality of not getting a horse dominated my mind, creating many depressing days and sleepless nights. All his promises. Empty and meaningless.

It finally sank in. It wasn't going to happen.

I would never get a horse from Daddy.

July 15, 1985

I'm still really sad and mad. Luckily, playing with CJ helps as well as getting together with Marin, even if we don't talk as much as we used to. I told her about not getting a horse, but I'm not sure if she knows how hard this is. When I can't stop myself from crying, I'll go to my room because I'm not going to do it in front of other people. I've been listening to the song, "Birds Fly (Whisper to a Scream)" lately. It seems to fit.

I still hate going to bed because everyone is asleep but me. The nights seem to take forever. I'm tossing and turning and going through tons of Kleenex. The images of Ruffian and Swale's deaths keep haunting my mind. It's just not fair that amazing animals have to die. I came across the song, "I'm Free" by Kenny Loggins. Even though it's from the movie, Footloose, I cry thinking of Ruffian running free whenever I hear it. At some point, I should be cried out. I'm trying to be excited about camp, but it's hard.

A few days later, after another big cry, I sat on my bed and organized my stuffed animals, hoping it would alleviate the sadness and frustration. It really didn't.

Mama's knock on the door startled me. "Hey, Baby. How are you doing?"

"Fine." My tone dripped as much as my eyes had earlier.

"Are you organizing your stuffed animals?"

"No, Mama, I just have them all out on my bed for nothing!"

She placed her hand on her hip. "Maren. Therese. Markey. You've been hateful and absolutely impossible since you got back from your Daddy's."

"Sorry," I whispered, lowering my head.

"What is wrong with you?" she asked, closing the door.

"I was going to get a horse."

"You what?"

"Daddy totally said he was going to get me a horse for my twelfth birthday. A real live horse," I said, voice cracking.

"Oh, Baby." She set a few stuffed animals to the side and joined me on the bed. "That man. I tell ya."

"Yeah, for the last three years. Like almost every time I'd go there," I said, wiping away a few tears.

"Three years?" she asked, her lips almost disappearing. "Unbelievable. Honestly, he is just—"

"—So, when I went to visit him this time, I thought he'd have one or we'd get one together. Like he said we would."

"Baby, your Daddy...well, he's not the most reliable person," she said, tucking her hair behind her ears.

"I know."

"He means well, but doesn't always pull through."

"Then, why did he say he would? Why even get my hopes up?"

"Again, he tries."

"Geez, Mama. How can you even stick up for him?" I barked.

"I learned after living with him for many years. The hard way."

"He promised you a horse, too, huh?" I joked, trying to cut the tension.

She chuckled. "No, but there were things he said he'd do and never did. You know...arrive on time...get a job...be nice to me." She paused. "Again, he means well."

"He just shouldn't say anything at all. Just keep his damn mouth shut," I said, slightly pleased at my use of a swear word.

"I know, Baby," she said, touching my shoulder and kissing my head. "I know it's hard. Listen, unfortunately, I need to head out for a meeting."

I rolled my eyes.

"But you and Marin will be going to horseback riding camp soon. Then, there is horseback riding at Fair Oaks."

"I know," I sighed.

"And you can see the horse you love. What's his name again?"

"Spirit."

"Yeah, Spirit. Your face lights up when you say his name."

"He's the best," I said, with a quivering smile.

"That's something to look forward to," she said, placing her hand on the doorknob, tightening her mouth. "And, again, Baby. I'm so sorry about your Daddy. I really am."

"Thanks, but I don't know if I want to go see him anymore."

"We'll see," she said, closing the door behind her.

July 15, 1985

Hello, Kiddo,

Thank you for your letter. I hope you had a good birthday, despite the fact that Garrett didn't deliver on his promise to give you a horse. Same old, same old from that SOB. Probably shouldn't say that around you. Caroline is much more understanding than I am. To me, he will always be the guy who hurt my baby sister. I will never forgive him. She can, but I won't.

Anyway, you are so welcome for the book. I knew you'd like the Horses-in-Color book because it has all the horse breeds you like. Thank you again for your thank-you card! That is so thoughtful of you. You are so loving and every horse you are around is lucky to have you loving them.

Have fun at your new horseback riding camp!

Hang in there, Kiddo and keep your spirit up!

Don't forget to breathe.

Love you to the moon and back,

Aunt Mimi

July 22, 1985

Today's the day for Echo Lake Camp! I am excited about it and am trying so hard to forget about what happened with Daddy.

*E*ven though it was only about two hours away, turning into the wooded entrance of Echo Lake Camp felt as though we were driving into a whole new world. It didn't seem possible that the gravel crackling underneath the tires could create even more excitement and anticipation than going to Fair Oaks. In our usual way, Marin and I talked nonstop, except for the moment when we arrived. Mama rolled down her window to talk to a woman with a clipboard. I hardly paid attention to what Mama was saying because standing right next to the lady was a girl on a horse. I was enchanted by the brown splotchy pinto horse's calm nature. Once she told us where to park and go next, I learned from the rider that the horse's name was Dudley. Dudley's long tail swayed back and forth as he trotted, escorting us down the drive that was more dirt than gravel. Dudley's rider directed us to the cafeteria where they would give us our cabin assignments. When we were done, we tossed our luggage into a nearby horse-drawn open wagon. It took everything in me not to ask the names of the two draft horses pulling it.

After saying goodbye to Mama, Marin and I hopped onto a different horse-drawn wagon to our cabins. The bumpy journey felt like a hay ride and smelled like it too, which was soothing in a strange way. After a minute, my curiosity overtook me.

"Excuse me, sir?" I asked. "What are the names of the horses?"

"That's Mike on the left and Ike on the right."

"Aww, are they Belgians?"

"Yes, they are," he said, smiling. "You know your breeds."

"Well, I was at the Kentucky Horse Park and they had Belgians there pulling wagons, too."

"I'll bet they did."

Marin nudged me and smiled.

Pulling up to our cabins, we saw three Conestoga wagons, like what they used in the 1800s to settle the West. Each wagon housed four bunk beds with an attached shelf for bathroom items. Our counselor said the outhouse was around the corner and we could take a shower two times that week. Yes, two for the week, which seemed a bigger issue for some of the girls than for Marin and me.

The stables where the horses lived were up the hill behind the wagons. The enthusiasm I felt knowing we would see horses that evening made the walk up the hill much more manageable. Spotting the barn and countless horses tacked up in the distance got my heart racing. I could hardly catch my breath, unsure if it was from my asthma or excitement.

The campers from the three other Conestoga wagons gathered with us on the picnic tables under a large oak tree. The main wrangler, Jenny, came out in her cowboy hat and bolo tie. She told us that every day we would have one hour in the arena, one hour on the trail, and one hour for class. That evening, I rode a bay named Dolly and Marin rode Blue, a horse with faded spots that appeared blue.

We were told we needed to ride different horses every day but it was hard not to choose the same horse once you connect with them.

I just couldn't believe that we were there.

<u>July 23, 1985</u>

Today in horse class, we learned about the parts of the horse, like the cannon bone, and the frog which is on the inside of the hoof. The wranglers are so nice and for class they usually bring out Dudley because he's so sweet. It was neat to see him again from when we first arrived at camp. There are other girls from the other wagons. One girl is so annoying. She just runs up to the horses and throws her arms around them, after the wranglers just told us not to. Duh! I already knew that. We also sing and have campfires at night. I love the smell and crackling sound of campfires. The girls in my cabin are awesome. I think Marin is having a good time, too.

I can't sleep because I'm so excited, not because I'm scared, like at home or at Daddy's. It's like my brain and heart are going to explode! Sometimes my nose runs and I sneeze and my asthma comes back. But now I have an inhaler and a lot of Kleenex. I don't care—I'm around horses all day! It's Heaven!

<u>July 24, 1985</u>

Every night after supper we have an activity in the arena. Last night we played "Red Light, Green Light." The first one who reaches and touches the wrangler wins. The wrangler stands on one side of the arena and we're all lined up on the other side. She has her back to us and yells, "Green light!" Then turns back around facing us saying "Red Light!" But, if your horse is still moving when she yells "Red Light," then you're out. I almost won it but Dolly took a quick step at the end. So, I was out. I love Dolly though. Even though I wasn't supposed to ride her again, I did.

In class we learned that horses have a hock that's like our ankle, and their stifle is like our knee. Wonder why they don't just call it their ankle and knee? We learned how to brush them. I love when their back haunches ripple when you brush them. My least favorite part of the horse time are the trail rides. They're OK. I had Inky, who is a dark bay with handlebar ears. He's sweet but just a little slow. My favorite is the hour in the arena when we work on our form. I'm still working on keeping my heels down.

Our daily arena, class, and trail hours had ended for the day, feeding our need for supper. Fortunately, the mile-long walk to the cafeteria passed quickly with everyone from our wagon singing and laughing. The decibel level continued and even increased once we got inside the cafeteria. The sound was amplified by the loud buzz of talkative and hungry campers, and clinking of silverware and glasses in the soapy plastic bins. The smell of fried hamburgers, hotdogs, and french fries filled the wide-open space. Fortunately, the long food line kept moving. I grabbed a tray and plastic cup, looked up, and noticed someone in the distance.

"Hey, M, look at that guy over there," I said, handing a tray and plastic cup to her.

"Which one?"

"The tall guy with blondish, brownish hair standing by the fries. He's kinda cute."

She tilted her head. "I guess. A little skinny, though."

I furrowed my brow. "I don't think so."

"The guy over there, now he's cute," she said, pointing to a tall, well-built, dark-haired guy talking to two other girls by the exit.

"Well, why don't you go talk to him?" I said.

"No way. You go talk to your guy!"

"Nope! We're here for horses. Boys are so weird anyway," I said, pushing my tray down the line.

<u>July 25, 1985</u>

On the last night at Echo Lake, many different camp programs come together for a rodeo. Not a real one. Just a lot of arena games for all the campers there. I signed up for the "Dudley Mount" and the "Dizzy Stick." I'm nervous because I don't like running or doing physical things in front of people. My nose has been running a lot and I've been sneezing a lot, but I don't care!

My first event, the "Dudley Mount," required three campers to mount Dudley bareback in the quickest time. We didn't do too bad, finishing third out of seven teams. The other option was the "Boney Mount" which was the same event using Boney, the nearly black Percheron-Quarter Horse mixed horse. The white stripe down his face made the large horse look even sweeter. He was at least seventeen hands, whereas Dudley was closer to fifteen. The "Boney Mount" was harder and I was more concerned about hurting him, since he was definitely older than Dudley.

The "Dizzy Stick" didn't go as well. It's a foot race where a person runs from one end of the arena to the other, picks up a stick, leans over it, runs three circles around it, then runs back to their team. Since they're dizzy, the return is often on a slant, with an occasional person falling down. The next person in line would do the same thing until everyone on the team has gone.

Let's just say, it didn't end well. I didn't like that there weren't even horses around, but we didn't even get on the board. And, note to self: don't have a huge meal right before the event, especially if it's Mexican.

<u>July 26, 1985</u>

I'm so sad to be leaving Echo Lake. I'll miss all the horses here and the people and singing and food and our wagon. I don't want to go home. I hope Marin and I can come back next summer. A whole year is so long to wait.

<u>August 1, 1985</u>

I hate being home from Echo Lake Camp. No horses. No nothing. Everyone does their own thing. Lacey's gone. Mama is busy. Clint is...who cares. Kinda wonder what Daddy is doing, but then, sometimes I don't want to know. CJ is still adorable, but I miss the horses so much. Dolly and Blue and Dudley and Boney. The wranglers were great, too. Now Mama says I have to get tested for allergies before I go back to school. I will be starting Garner Junior High School. I hate my sneezing, runny nose, itchy throat, tightness in chest. What kind of test is it? It's not a true or false or multiple-choice. Nope. It's a scratch test. Even its name sounds ominous. I guess Mrs. Hayes was right. We eventually do use our vocabulary words.

My heart pounded on the drive over to the allergist's office. Luckily, CJ was with Clint, although I would have appreciated my little brother being there to distract me from the seemingly unending wait. When we finally got into the room, the nurse said, "Put this gown on. Doctor Baker is going to make small scratches on your back. Then, he'll put a drop of liquid of an allergen on each scratch. It will be everything from dust mites, to mildew, to foods, such as cheeses, to dogs and cats—"

"Dogs and cats?" I asked.

"Yes, and horses, too."

"Horses?"

"Yes, we need to check everything," the nurse said.

"It'll be OK, Baby," Mama said.

My nerves started to get the best of me. On top of that, ever since Mama told me that dust mites actually feed off our dead skin, I couldn't get the disgusting image of mites out of my mind.

Slipping into the paper gown, I let my legs dangle over the side of the examining table. Mama tried to divert my attention again, but everything seemed like meaningless chatter. Despite the fact that I was waiting for it, the knock on the door startled me. Dr. Baker wheeled in a cart with endless eye-dropper bottles on it. He shook my hand and explained what was going to happen. His warm demeanor helped alleviate a little of the anxiety. Just a little.

I eased down on my belly onto the cold table.

"Try and hold still. This will be a little cool," Dr. Baker said, opening my gown from the back.

Shuddering at each icy cold drop on my back, I gripped the side of the table. The forked-prong scratch over each drop provided a small relief.

Dr. Baker left the room and my only job was to stay as still as possible. The initially cool drops on my back morphed into intense itchy sensations.

"Mama, how long do I have to be like this?"

"Dr. Baker said it would be about fifteen minutes."

"How many minutes have passed?"

"About three."

"Oh, my gosh." I said, resting my hands beneath my chin to prevent myself from accidentally or involuntarily scratching. "It's really starting to itch."

Mama stood up from her chair and checked my back. "Oh, yeah, it's starting to get red and bumpy on your lower back. Is that where it's bothering you?"

"Yes!"

"I'll bet it is," she said, sitting back down. "So, what was your favorite part of camp?"

I know what she's doing but this is becoming unbearable.

"Well, I loved the horseback riding. And, this one horse—Oh my gosh, Mama. It's getting *really* bad." I clutched the side of the table, scratching it in hopes that the movement would somehow relieve the extreme itchiness.

"Not much longer."

"Oh my gosh. How much longer?" I said, flipping my head to the left and right and back again.

"Not too much longer, Baby," Mama repeated.

"Can you scratch it pleeeeezzz?"

"Sorry. We have to see what grows."

"Oh, my gosh," I whimpered. "I can tell you *everything* is growing!" It had become almost painful.

"What if I just scratch near it?" she asked.

I felt her finger scratching right beside one of the itchiest areas on my lower back. It brought instant relief and I released an audible exhale.

"Yes! Please do that again, especially on my lower, right part," I said, trying to show her.

"Yes, now hold still."

I pushed my butt up in the air, hoping an air current could provide a reprieve. Anything to alleviate this agony.

She scratched up and down along the side of my back again, allowing me a moment of relief. I just wanted her to dig her nails deep, driving them deeper up and down my back.

Dr. Baker finally knocked and entered the room.

"Oh, thank God!" I squealed.

"Hello again! Yeah, I know it can be itchy."

Duh!

"Let's have a look. Oh, yeah..." he said, his voice trailing off. "Does it itch on your lower right?"

Does a bear...?

"Yes!"

"I'll bet. It's pretty red, and the bumps are really raised."

I could have told him that. And, he's a doctor?

"Just need to make note of all the numbers. 2, 13, 14, 15, 16...."

Hurry up! Take a picture. I'm dying here.

Once he jotted down all the information he needed, he said the magic words.

"OK, now you can scratch."

Without missing a beat, I flipped over, driving my entire back against the table like a bear against a thick-barked tree. The white tissue paper that lined the table folded up underneath me.

"Flip back over on your belly, Baby," Mama said.

She drove all her fingers into back. Once she got to the lower right part, I almost cried. Then I laughed and almost cried again.

"So, what is it, Doctor?" Mama asked.

"Maren had a reaction to mold."

Yep.

"And, pollen."

Definitely.

"Mildew."

Whatever that is.

"Dust mites."

Yep. Knew that one. Still super gross.

"Cats."

Oh, no. Morris, Rosie, and Pingüino!

"Dogs."

And, Dino!

"And, horses."

Damn.

The initial relief I felt from scratching was now replaced with a very heavy heart and an empty feeling in the pit of my stomach. I had hoped all the I sneezing I did was from dirt getting in my nose, or because Dino, Morris, and Rosie weren't always clean. But I'm not telling Daddy. And, what about being a vet now?

"So, we recommend injections."

He might as well have said they recommended amputations.

My hatred of needles was visceral and primal. Mama once told me when I was little it took two adults to hold me down and another to actually give me a shot.

I worried this might not go well.

August 8, 1985

Today is the day I go get a...I don't even want to say it. The needles are going to be so friggin' huge. I'm going to bleed everywhere and I'll double-over in pain. I just know it.

Why does time seem to crawl at doctors' offices and fly when I'm horseback riding? Luckily CJ was with us this time, so he was a great distraction from the scrubs, medical posters, and other nervous patients.

The door to the exam rooms opened and an older, round Hispanic woman with shoulder-length, jet-black hair and the warmest smile emerged.

"Miss Maren Markey?"

"That's me," I said, standing up. Like preparing for my execution.

"Do you want me to come back with you?" Mama asked. The lady shook her head at Mama. "OK, Baby, we'll see you in a jiffy!"

"Hi, Maren, my name is Ms. Yolanda. How are you today?" she said, escorting me to the back. As she put on gloves, I scanned the counters full of glass jars with tongue depressors and cotton balls. My eyes landed on the syringes and I gulped.

"Well, I'd be better if I wasn't here. How much is this gonna hurt?"

"Oh, you'll be fine," she consoled. "These first ones are so little, you probably won't even notice."

I know they tell everyone that lie.

I rolled up my sleeve, slightly coughing as the pungent smell of rubbing alcohol accosted my nose.

"OK, I need you to look in the other direction. Good, now take a deep breath and exhale slowly."

I did what she asked as slowly as I could.

"What grade are you going into again?" she asked.

"Seventh."

"There, we're done."

"You're done?" I asked, snapping my head back around.

Her warm smile had grown even bigger. "Told you it wasn't going to be bad. Especially at first."

My eyes darted from my arm, back to her, then back to my arm again. "I literally didn't even feel it!" I said, jumping up and down, giving her a big hug. Her scrubs smelled like strawberries, a nice contrast to the rubbing alcohol.

"See?" she said, tossing something in the garbage.

"Yeah, I'll see you next week!" I said, practically skipping.

I never thought I'd utter those words so cheerfully leaving a doctor's office.

*T*he following week I entered the doctor's office the same way I left—by skipping.

"Hi, Ms. Yolanda!"

"Hi, Miss Maren. How are you?" she asked, with the same warm smile and strawberry-scented scrubs.

"Good. I have a question. Hope it's OK," I said, as we walked down the hall.

"Sure."

"Do you know Spanish?"

She laughed. "Yes."

"Cool! I want to learn Spanish."

"Will they teach you in school?" she asked, pulling latex gloves over her hands.

"I can take it in ninth grade, but I don't want to wait."

She smiled. "Tell you what—every time you come in, I'll teach you a new word."

"Thanks!"

"So, what would you like to know?" she asked, grabbing a cotton ball.

"Well, I learned some Spanish from a girl who came in and taught us some words, like 'hola' and 'caballo.'"

"'*Caballo*'? You like horses?" she asked.

"Oh, yeah. They're my favorite. Even though I'm allergic and stuff."

"So you are," she said, peeking into my chart. "Well, these shots will help."

Shots. I really hate that word.

"I love learning about different languages and places and will definitely take Spanish when I get to high school," I said, trying to get my mind off the word "shots" pinging around in my brain.

"That's good. Learn as much as you can."

"Um, do you know any bad words?" I whispered.

She gave me a side eye. "You know I can't really teach you that. Now, roll up that sleeve."

"I know, just wondering," I said, folding my sleeve. Out came the pungent smell again as she wiped down my arm.

"OK, all done."

I swear, she didn't even have a needle in that syringe.

"See you next Tuesday," she said, putting on a band aid. "Oh, and Miss Maren?"

"Yeah."

She motioned to me to come closer. "*Caca.*"

"What does that mean?"

"It's the word for 'poop.'"

I laughed into my hand.

"Now, don't tell your mama!" she said, pointing at me.

"I won't!"

All I could think about is *caca*. I'm so happy Ms. Yolanda taught me that, because Lacey was sure full of it.

<u>August 27, 1985</u>

Tomorrow is my first day at Garner Junior High School! We have different teachers for different classes in different classrooms now. I'll miss Garner Elementary and all my teachers. But Mama says that it will be fun and Garner Elementary is right next door. Lacey will be there, too but Mama said I don't have to see her. Marin and I are both nervous and excited. Thank God we'll be in the same school. It would be terrible without her. We don't have any classes together, but at least we have the same lunch.

September 5, 1985

School has been fun. It took me a few days to learn my schedule, but the teachers are really nice and I like my classes. I still have a hard time going to sleep at night, especially when I know everyone else is asleep. But I'm not crying as much over not getting a horse. I just think about other horses, especially Spirit and some from camp. Even though they're not mine, I like to think about them.

Lunch is really busy and noisy, but they have new things to eat that they didn't have in elementary school, like Swiss Cake Rolls. I usually have that and Doritos for lunch. We don't have a lot of time to eat, especially because the line for food is so long. But I get to see Marin and luckily don't have to see Lacey.

There is one guy I kinda like. Jake Creech. He is cute and funny and smart. He's in my English class. We sometimes talk and laugh.

Wonder if he knows I like him?

September 10, 1985

I can't believe I just told Marin! I hope I don't regret it!

The school day ended, and Marin and I met at our usual meeting place: the bike rack.

"I have something to tell you," I said, taking in a deep breath. "But you have to *promise* you won't tell anyone. Not even your dog, Dallas. Not anyone, or any dog!"

"OK, I promise," she said, crossing her heart.

"I think I like Jake Creech."

"What?"

"OK, I do like him," I said, scrunching up my face.

"Oh my gosh!"

"Yeah, but you *promised* not to tell anyone!"

"I won't!" she said, crossing her heart.

"Now that I've spilled my guts, who do you like?" I asked, unlocking my bike.

"I kinda like Derek Cooper."

"Wow, he's super cute. And, on the football team!"

"Yeah, he kept looking at me the other day when I went to practice," she added.

"You went to their football practice?"

"Yeah, after school one day when you had to get your allergy shot."

"That would have been so much fun."

"It was," she said. "So, Jake Creech, huh?"

"Yeah, it's so weird being in English. He's like, right there and he smells so good, too. I think he wears Drakkar Noir cologne. One time when Lacey and I were shopping we smelled it at the counter. Smelled the same. And Jake is so funny! The other day, he read his story in class and I could *not* stop laughing. There were other people laughing, too, but just seeing him makes me giggle. And, all tingly inside!"

"I know! That's how I feel when we have pep rallies and they have all the football players there."

"We definitely can't tell Jake and Derek," I said, throwing my leg over my bike.

"No way," Marin said. "Way too embarrassing."

"Really is fun to talk about, though!"
"For sure!"

<u>September 23, 1985</u>

I'm so nervous because this Friday we're having a Back-To-School dance in the gym and I'm going to ask Jake Creech if he wants to go with me. Marin is going to ask Derek. It's a Sadie Hawkins dance—so the girls ask the boys. I'm so nervous Jake will say, "No."

<u>Same Day.</u>

Well, I just called Jake and I didn't even get a chance to ask him.

I said, "So, are you going to the dance this Friday?"
"I think so." Then he quickly said, "Well, I'll see ya at school, OK?" I bet he said that fast so I wouldn't have the chance to ask him to the dance. But, in a way I'm happy because it might have been too complicated. You know, where and when to meet and all that jazz. I'll just ask him at the dance. That way I wouldn't have to dance with him on every slow dance. He might get sick of me. Plus, I don't want to jeopardize our friendship.

Daddy sent me a letter and hopes I can come visit soon. Not sure if I will, but he said he's down to one cigarette a day! I know he's going to quit!

<u>September 28, 1985</u>

YESTERDAY WAS THE BEST DANCE EVER! HE ASKED ME TO DANCE! I CAN NOT BELIEVE IT! Jake Creech came up behind me and Marin and said, "Maren?" I turned around. "Do you want to dance with me on the next slow dance?" While he was saying that I was thinking to myself, "I hope he asks me to dance with him." I said, "Sure!" but Marin said I didn't smile, but I'm almost positive I did. Marin said she looked away once, so that's probably when I smiled. We danced to "Nothing's Gonna Stop Us Now" by Starship.

The second time we were standing by Jake, Marin pushed me toward him. The next thing I knew, we were face to face. We danced to "True Colors" by Cyndi Lauper. But, then on "Broken Wing" and another song he danced with Tina and then Lynette. I sure hope they asked him. But I'm still glad that I'm his first at this school dance!

Derek said "No" to Marin when she asked him to go to the dance with her earlier in the week. But they totally danced with each other three times! But then he also danced with Tina and Lynette. Man, those girls get around.

Lacey asked Junior to go with her to the dance. He said yes, but she didn't have a good time. On the last dance he was with a girl named Crystal plus he didn't talk to Lacey—only when she asked him a question. Lacey ALWAYS has to have a boyfriend. This year, her boyfriends have been Kyle, Cory, and Junior. I'm not sure how much longer Junior will be her boyfriend.

This should have been shorter, but I don't care if Lacey reads this or not. She probably won't because she really doesn't care. That works for me. I'm just so happy because Jake Creech asked me to dance!

November 2, 1985

It was fun having Aunt Mimi here for Hallomas. I love her so much. She even taught me that when I get sad *and upset to take deep breaths. Take a deep breath and count to 4. Hold it and count to 4. Then exhale it and count to 8. It does help. Maybe one year she can actually stay for Halloween night. But I know she wants to get to Florida as soon as she can. I don't blame her. Mama and I are just so glad Mimi comes to visit us. CJ was so cute this Halloween.*

CJ morphed into Superman after sliding into the costume Mama made for him. Although he didn't have the plastic mask that a came with a store-bought Superman costume, he didn't need it. What Mama made was enough. She applied gel to his hair and created a small curl on his forehead. The red cape, blue shirt and pants, and red underwear-looking thing completed his Superman ensemble. Mama said she knew his costume was supposed to be a onesie, but going to the bathroom would be better if it were in two pieces. Although it didn't lie as flat on his little body as a store-bought costume, it was just as authentic. Neighbors commented on how precious he was. Mama showed me how to use the sewing machine one time, but it actually made me nervous. I was afraid I'd get my finger caught in the moving needle thingy. Although I was too old to trick or treat, Mama made me a bear costume so I could go out with them, since Mrs. Breiner wanted Marin to trick or treat with their family. Lacey had no interest in going with us, as usual.

Dashing from one neighbor's house to another, CJ swung his plastic pumpkin candy bucket around until the accumulating candy was too heavy for him. Only then did he want us to carry it. Nearing the end of the night, he resorted to crawling up the steps leading to the neighbors' front doors.

The Jones' household was one of our last stops of the night. CJ rang the doorbell and Mrs. Jones answered, leaving the door ajar.

Fascinated by her Halloween decorations inside, he stood silent.

"CJ, what do you say?" Mama asked.

"Candy in house." He pushed himself inside, his red cape flapping behind him.

"CJ, come back here! Oh, my goodness, I'm so sorry," Mama said, making her way to the door. "Mrs. Jones gives us the candy out here."

"That's quite all right, honey," Mrs. Jones said. She turned around into her foyer to retrieve my caped brother.

I nearly bent my wooly bear costume in half from laughing so hard.

December 7, 1985

This year over Christmas Break, Mama said we're going to the Biltmore! It's the first big family trip we've had in a long time. I've never been there before but people at school have said it's beautiful!

That particular Christmas was vivid. Although the Biltmore was in North Carolina, the five-hour drive was unrelenting torture with all the family trapped together in the car. Lacey broke up with Junior and her sour mood hung thick. I think she had gotten her first "Bertha" too.

Focusing on the green mile markers and the beginning of the beautiful Blue Ridge mountains, I rejoiced when we saw signs for Asheville. Tudor-style stores in that area of town practically hid Biltmore's admission gate. Twisting down the long driveway through the woods felt as though we were literally going to a different time and place, leaving the 20th century behind. I could just imagine riding a horse, hearing the clip-clop of the hooves on the paved path.

After parking the car, we followed a wooded walkway that opened to an enormous lawn. Bordered by gardens to the left, the lawn was accentuated by lit-pine trees along the perimeter with a large fountain in the middle. I gasped when I saw what appeared to be a castle, which at 175,000 square feet is known as America's

Largest House. Behind the Biltmore, the Blue Ridge mountains stood, dwarfing it, tricking the eye even more.

"Look at the Biltmore, CJ? See all the trees?" I asked. Unhooking him from his stroller, I twirled him around in a circle.

"Twees!" he exclaimed.

"Yeah, aren't they beautiful!" I said, giving him a tight hug and kissing his pudgy cheek.

"C'mon," I said, to everyone, motioning to the house. Our winter coats squeaked against each other as I jogged with CJ in my arms.

"Careful, Baby," Mama said.

"Maren, stop running!" Clint said.

I jogged for several feet and got winded, stopping to catch my breath. Lacey took her own sweet time catching up. CJ wasn't a big kid, but the cold air aggravated my asthma. And, let's face it, running wasn't my strong suit.

After walking around the grounds and gardens, we stood in line for the evening Christmas tour. Passing through the regal entrance, green garlands with red bows hung along the hanging chandeliers, matching the bright red poinsettias on the floor. The acoustics were perfect for the carolers in the alcove singing "God Rest Ye Merry Gentleman" as we meandered into the dining room. The opposite side of the room housed a huge fireplace encircled in garland, book-ended by two towering Christmas trees.

"Y'all go over there for a picture," Mama said. Standing next to the towering trees, CJ looked like he could have been a prize inside one of the wrapped presents underneath. Even I looked small.

As the tour progressed to the library, I marveled at the numerous decorated trees guiding our path. It was hard enough trying to get just one Christmas tree decorated at our house. They probably didn't have a little brother trying to "help" and an older stepsister who wanted nothing to do with it.

The library consisted of bookshelves upon bookshelves that led our eyes to beautifully drawn angels on the ceilings.

"This is reminiscent of the Sistine Chapel," Mama added.

"What's the Sixteen Chapel?" I asked.

"No, the *Sistine* Chapel. It's a church in Rome."

"Oh, I want to go see it!"

Mama chuckled. "We'll see, but the ceiling was painted by Michelangelo."

"Is he still alive?"

"No, he lived a long, long time ago. Back in the 1500s."

"Yeah," Lacey added, with a tinge of indignancy.

"Like you knew that," I hissed. She smiled and moseyed over to another area of the library.

The long black ladder resting against the bookshelves looked so classy. Then again, everything about the Biltmore was classy. A picture on the wall of a foxhunt caught my eye. Although I felt badly for the foxes, I couldn't take my eyes off the horses surrounded by numerous foxhounds.

Leaving the library led us to a beautiful, sweeping staircase, encircling a chandelier hanging a few floors from the ceiling to a Christmas tree below. Peering down from the highest step, the chandelier appeared to be a halo on top of the tree. It reminded me a little of Marin's staircase. Not quite, but very similar.

We came upon a portrait of the Vanderbilt family, the former residents of Biltmore. Continuing along the tour we visited Mr. and Mrs. Vanderbilt separate bedrooms, connected by a long sitting room. A small flight of steps led to an Artist's Suite that actually had a toilet in it which was unusual for this time period. Good thing Clint stopped CJ from almost using it. Again, beautifully decorated Christmas trees greeted us at every turn.

In the basement, we made our way to a large, eerie, empty pool. CJ yelled, "Hello!" to hear his voice echo to which I answered back. After another guest mentioned this area might be haunted, I kept moving.

The gym, adjacent to the pool area, had some almost dainty pieces of workout equipment, including some hand weights. I'm not sure how often they were used or how hard they worked out. It definitely wasn't "Sweatin' to the Oldies" or "Buns of Steel."

Motivated by the late hour and CJ and Lacey's growing restlessness, we hurried past more rooms. Stepping back outside, I turned around to take in this magnificent building illuminated by outside lights. If I had lived there, I would have loved to run up and down the staircases. And saunter, too.

But most of all, I would have had as many horses as I possibly could. Then I wouldn't have had to rely on Daddy to get me one.

January 4, 1986

Now that the fun of Christmas is over, I'm eating waayyy too many chips, both potato and chocolate. We heard thunder last night. Mama said that means it will snow in the next week or so. We'll see.

January 12, 1986

It actually snowed last night! School was cancelled. Mama called Aunt Mimi and she couldn't believe that because in Michigan they have way worse weather than here. I'm just glad it didn't interfere with getting together with Marin because we haven't gotten together much lately.

February 2, 1986

Winters sure are hard. I don't like writing in my diary as much because the more I write in it, the sadder I get. It's really hard whenever I think about Daddy not getting a horse for me. I know that he does the best he can, but sometimes it feels like he's not doing the best he can. He just got mad so fast, it doesn't feel like he really loves me. I also don't draw as much as I used to. It just doesn't seem like anyone else has ever felt this way, especially in the winter when it seems worse. Marin and Lacey and Mama sure don't.

I try not to think about Ruffian now because then I might not be able to stop crying. Or, if I do think about her, I try to focus on when she was little and younger and winning her races against other fillies, not her horrible death. But imagining the horrible sound when she broke her front leg still haunts me.

And it was really terrible because someone at school committed suicide today. He was a nineth grader and I didn't know him very well. Seventh graders don't usually hang out with freshman, but he was going with someone in my class. Tomorrow there is going to be an assembly and counselors will be there if we need someone to talk to. I think other counselors are coming in from other schools. It would be so terrible to feel like he did. I wouldn't do what he did, but I know how it feels to feel sad and lonely.

February 16, 1986

I wonder what Spirit and Jubi are doing now. I picture them running around in the paddock. Pingüino is rubbing against Spirit, and Dodger and Moose are doing their doggie things. Seems like it's been forever since we went riding. I would love to ride but it's way too cold for them. For me, too. Plus, it rained last night and Mama said it could be slippery. Thinking about everyone at Fair Oaks and camp does cheer me up so I try to do it as much as I can. Of course, thinking about the Black Stallion always makes me smile. Spring will be here soon. That's what I keep reminding myself.

<u>April 22, 1986</u>

Marin and I finally got to go horseback riding today! It feels like it's been a gazillion years since we were there. It was so awesome to see Spirit, Jubi, and everyone again! I learn more from Ms. Patsy every time I go. I think my allergy shots are helping, too because my nose didn't run as much and I didn't sneeze as often. Now that spring is coming, I feel so much better!

<u>June 23, 1986</u>

I know it's been a while, but 7th grade ended pretty well. Onto 8th grade in a few months! And, it's almost time for Echo Lake again! I cannot wait because Marin and I will be in Advanced Horsemanship this year! Mama will take us and pick us back up. I may have a hard time sleeping, but for good reasons. I wonder if Dolly and Blue will be there? Maybe I'll get to gallop like The Black Stallion!

I love the song "I can't Wait" by Nu Shooz. They spell their name wrong—on purpose! I taped it off the radio and I have played it a gazillion times. Just love the synthesizer at the beginning and I really can't wait!

Turning into the entrance to Echo Lake, the familiar greetings never got old. It was like returning to Fair Oaks for the second time—it was still thrilling. Marin and I were more confident and excited because we knew what to expect, like where to check in and put our luggage. We looked forward to the wagon ride to our Conestoga wagon. Once we arrived, we met our counselor, Joanne, and the other girls, Jessica, Heather, Angela, Kimberly and Carrie. Everyone seemed to get along well as we rolled out our sleeping bags and set out our sundries. Except for one girl—Shae. Her bright blue eyes, perfectly-brushed long, blonde hair, and tall, thin body matched the fact that her nose was so high in the air, she'd drown in a rainstorm. The only big thing on her were her boobs. At least we had that in common. I had graduated up from the first time Mama and I went bra shopping.

After the introductions, we all sang on our way to the cafeteria. Observing all the hustle and bustle of the people inside on our way to the food line, my heart jumped.

The cute guy I pointed out to Marin last summer was there again standing by the exit.

"Oh, my gosh, M! There he is!" I said, nudging her.

"Who? Where?" Marin asked, looking around.

"The guy from last year—by the exit. Don't look!"

We both kept our heads down as we each grabbed a tray.

I slowly looked back at him, studying his every move.

"Oh my gosh! He just looked at me. What do I do?"

"Smile and wave!" Marin said.

Pushing my food tray down the line, I followed Marin's suggestion then lowered my head. "He waved back! What do I do?"

When I glanced back up again, he was leaving with the rest of his cabinmates.

Although he was gone, just seeing him again put me in an even better mood. I was beginning to decipher the excitement I felt between thinking about horses and thinking about this guy. This guy made me stand up a little taller and straighter.

I definitely giggled more.

*I*n the Advanced Horsemanship program, we were given one horse to ride the entire time. I got Fiddles, a Thoroughbred mix who stood about sixteen hands. She was a pretty dark bay with dark mane and tail. Maybe an Appendix, like Jubi back home. Suzy, the wrangler kept saying to me, "Keep Fiddles moving. She's going to want to talk to her friend, Steve, in the next pen. Keep her movin." I did the best I could. Fiddles wasn't a bad horse; she just did her own thing. Although it was frustrating, I could relate.

Shae rode Wispy, a smaller, chestnut horse who was almost a hand shorter than Fiddles. He was stocky, possibly a Quarter Horse mix, with a white stripe on his nose and two white socks on his front legs. Shae complained about how slow he was. But, after watching her in the arena, he didn't look that slow to me.

Because we both were having problems with our horses, the wranglers had us switch; Shae was now on Fiddles, and I was on Wispy. It was a little awkward, but Suzy thought it would be best.

<u>June 27, 1986</u>

I'm so sad this is my last full day at camp, but what a day! I don't even know where to start!

For this year's rodeo, Marin participated in the "Dizzy Stick." Since that didn't work for me last summer, I thought I would try the "Horse Relay." With two people on a team, one person rides her horse half way around the arena where, at a certain place, she hands a baton off to the team member. That teammate holds onto the baton and rides to the other side of the arena. Whichever team crosses the finish line first with the baton, wins.

I was so nervous the night before, I could hardly sleep. I was trying to ignore it, but my heart raced. Guess who had the last leg of the race against me? Yep, Shae.

We mounted our horses and walked into the arena. Jessica, who was riding a horse named Cash, would hand the baton to me and Michelle, on Red, would hand the baton to Shae.

Shae mounted Fiddles and I got on Wispy. We were positioned next to each other as we waited for our respective teammates to come around the corner.

"Fiddles, see that little horse? That's who we have to beat," Shae said, motioning to me. "That little runt." The cheering from the bleachers almost drowned out her taunts.

Almost.

"C'mon, c'mon, c'mon, Jessica," I muttered, keeping a close watch on her. "Keep Cash moving."

The Michelle-and-Red team approached Shae and Fiddles, gave her the baton, and off they went. Fiddles broke into a fast walk, then a trot, then a canter.

After what seemed like forever, Jessica and Cash finally got to us. I reached out, grabbed the baton, and tucked it under my arm. I loosened up the reins, gave Wispy a slight kick, and yelled "C'mon, Wispy—let's go!"

He broke into a fast trot, then immediately into a canter. Rounding the corner past the orange cone, I squeezed my legs even tighter around his chestnut barrel.

Tapping into something dormant, the little horse lunged into a full-on gallop. He was wide open, moving at such a speed, I hunkered down in the saddle and held on—to both the baton and the reins. With an outstretched neck, his legs dug deeper into the dirt, pulling us closer and closer to Shae and the dark bay. Within several seconds, we were galloping neck and neck. I yelled out one last time, "C'mon, Wispy!" and he pulled into high gear. We shot past them across the finish line as I pictured Ruffian leaving her competition in the dust.

The crowd erupted and so did the pride in my heart.

Pulling back on the reins, Wispy threw his head a few times resisting the signal to slow down. When we finally stopped, I threw my arms around his sweaty neck, thanking him for all he did. He didn't like that snooty Shae and Fiddles in front of us any more than I did.

Shae, still on Fiddles, approached us and mumbled, "Um, good job."

"Thanks!" I squealed.

"I really thought we would win, since Fiddles is taller and all."

"We're small, but we get it done!"

*A*t supper later that evening, I waited in line for the soda machine. Placing my cup under the 7Up nozzle, someone behind me said, "Hey, you were great at the rodeo today."

I turned around to see who it was. I could hardly believe it.

It was him!

"Oh, my gosh, hi. You were there?" I asked, staring into his brown eyes.

"Yeah, you were great."

"Thanks," I said, still holding my cup under the nozzle.

"I'm Matty Williams, by the way. Short for Matthew."

"I'm Maren Markey," I said, biting my lower lip.

"Maren," he said, pausing a bit. "That's a cool name." My eyes fixated on the floor as an awkward silence grew. "Yeah, the way you and your horse outran that girl. That was awesome."

"Thanks," I giggled, looking past his right shoulder to avoid eye contact.

"Uh, Maren?"

"Yeah?" My eyes met his brown eyes and inviting smile.

"Um, the soda is—"

Snapping my head around, a deluge of 7Up bubbled up over the sides of my cup, pooling around the slots underneath.

"Oh, my gosh! I can't believe—" I shook the soda off my fingers, splattering drops around me. A few of them landed in my eyes forcing them shut. "Oh, man!"

"Here're some napkins."

I reached for them, bringing them to my eyes.

"Thanks. I'm so embarrassed."

"It's OK," he chuckled. "I think it's…kinda cute."

I smiled under the wet paper products.

"Matty—time to go, man!" another camper yelled.

I peeled the napkins off my face, which I'm sure revealed pink, watery eyes.

"Well, see ya around, Maren. Great job again today."

I stood there processing what just happened when I heard someone running up behind me. "Hey! Did you just talk to that guy?" Marin asked.

"Oh my gosh, M. I *cannot* believe it. He said I did a great job at the rodeo today!"

"Are you serious? Oh my gosh!" Marin squealed.

"And, then…" I couldn't get the words out.

"What?" She almost screeched through her slight jumps.

"I totally got 7Up in my eye!"

She stopped jumping. "How'd you get 7Up in your eye?"

"I got it because I was looking away and it overflowed. And then when I shook it off, it like, got in my eyes!"

"Oh, my gosh. Did he see you?"

"Yeah."

"Oh, no."

"Yeah, but it's OK. Because when he grabbed napkins for me—"

"—Aww, he got you napkins? That's so sweet!" she said.

"Yeah, so, when he got the napkins, he said I was cute."

"Oh my gosh!"

"Well, he actually said 'kinda cute,' but I think it still counts!"

"Yeah!" Marin threw her arms around me. Luckily it was loud enough in the cafeteria that our squealing was drowned out by the constant cafeteria noise. All anyone saw were two happy campers jumping around.

*A*fter supper, the girls from our Conestoga wagon were back at the barn where Suzy, the wrangler, explained our evening game. She motioned us to sit under the oak tree where the picnic table were.

"Have a seat, ladies. Tonight, you're going to play a game called 'Catch the Flag.' We'll slide a tiny flag under your calf. Your goal is to try to get as many flags as possible from your fellow campers. Whoever gets the most flags, wins. But it won't just be you playing against yourselves. You'll eventually be playing against the Ranchers."

We all furrowed our brows. "Who's that?" Shae asked.

Just as she asked, we saw a group of guys coming up over the hill.

"Those are the boys," Suzy said.

Marin and I exchanged looks as I bit my lip.

Within the approaching gaggle of guys, I saw a tall, thinner blonde-haired guy among them.

Sure enough—there he was. Matty Williams.

"You're going to play against yourselves and they're going to play against themselves. Then, each winner will play each other in a reverse course. We'll play Fox and the Hound."

I got excited, thinking it had to do with Disney.

"It's basically Tag on horses."

Whomp, whomp. Guess not.

"One of you will try to get the flag from the other. So, basically it will be Conestoga Wagons versus Ranchers. Guys against girls. Go ahead and pick your horse. Ladies, first."

I tried to find Wispy, but he was already grazing in the pasture for the night. Many of the horses we usually rode were taking a well-deserved rest. Luckily, I found Dolly and stood behind her, trying to keep myself together, thinking about seeing Matty again. My shaky hands reflected the excitement inside my tingly body. It made it more difficult to grip the reins, but muscle memory kicked into gear. I was happy Marin got to be on her favorite horse, Blue.

Without averting my gaze, I watched as Matty picked Blaze, a chestnut gelding, whose name fit the big white blaze on his forehead. I have no idea who the other people rode, nor did I care.

After Suzy gave us each a flag, Marin whispered to me, "I'm just going to let you have mine." She never really liked games like this anyway.

"You sure?"

"Yeah, but you have to beat Shae, OK?"

I nodded.

Once we were spread out in the arena, Suzy gave the signal and we were off. I walked Dolly after Blue, grabbing Marin's flag. She pretended to be upset, but smiled as she and Blue left the arena.

Then, I got Jessica's. Then, Heather's, Angela's, and Carrie's. Kimberly's was a little tougher since she's ridden much more than I have, but I eventually got it. That left me with Shae on a horse named Candy. This seemed quite familiar. She trotted over, cornered me, and reached down to grab my flag. In my attempt to avoid her, I stretched out, grabbing her flag. I beat her—twice in one day.

When the Ranchers got into the arena, they were definitely more aggressive. I was captivated by Matty and Blaze. Someone went to grab his flag and he cut left, trotting off. Focusing only on him, everything and everyone else seemed to fade into the background. I think Marin said some things to me. Matty's flag count went from one to two to three to four to five to the last one.

I wanted to cheer with a full-on throttled scream, but all my energy was channeled into not showing any emotion. It was like trying to keep a volcano from erupting or trying not to vomit.

The realization set in—we were going to be playing against each other.

"All right, Maren, bring Dolly up here," Suzy said. "Matty on Blaze—same thing. Congratulations, you two. Now you have to choose. Who is going to go after who?"

Looking over at his inviting smile, my tongue felt as though it had swollen ten times its natural size, rendering me unable to speak.

"She can try to get my flag," he said, smiling.

"Does that work for you, Maren?"

I think I muttered, "Sure."

"OK," she said, handing a flag to Matty. "You have three minutes. Winner takes all. Maren, go to one that side of the arena. Matty, you go to the other."

Walking our horses side-by-side, he asked, "You ready to do this?"

"Oh, yeah," I smiled, trying to hide my still-trembling hands in Dolly's mane. Our horses then separated, each of us taking our positions in the arena.

"And—go!"

Matty made a kissing noise and Blaze broke into a fast walk. Fortunately, Dolly had an even quicker walk and I followed right behind. Matty, spotting us on his tail, turned Blaze completely around, heading in the opposite direction.

Surprised at his quick changeup, I steered Dolly to an even faster walk after them. Again, he cut to the left, zig-zagging, leaving me in the dust. This happened a few more times.

"C'mon, Maren! You can do this!" Although various cheers came from the Conestoga Wagon side of the arena, Maren's voice was louder than the others.

The support helped me to momentarily forget my anxiety. Squeezing my legs a little tighter around Dolly's barrel, I trotted after Matty. "Oh, no, you don't!" I said.

Matty laughed, responding in kind as we both trotted. The palpable excitement and electricity between the people on their backs I'm sure was evident to our horses.

I trotted up within a few feet of Matty who suddenly steered Blaze to the left. Dolly and I cut to the left too. He turned Blaze to the right. Dolly and I were now right in sync.

"C'mon, man!" The other Ranchers bellowed from the side of the arena. "Don't let her getcha!"

Cornering them, I reached out to grab the flag when he made a hard right on Blaze, trotting away.

"Dang it." Similar moans came from the fellow Conestoga Wagon ladies while cheers came from the Ranchers.

More determined than ever, I gave Dolly a slight kick, sending her into a canter after him.

When I was within reach of the flag, Matty abruptly stopped Blaze, sending Dolly and me cantering past. I think Dolly had some Quarter Horse in her, because she swung around on a dime. When we broke into a canter after them, the applause grew louder, almost drowning out the thundering hooves. Dolly was on the verge of a gallop next to Blaze when I reached out, snatching the flag from under his leg.

"Yippee!" I said, waving the flag in the air, immediately regretting my jubilant reaction. The Conestoga Wagon ladies erupted into cheers while the Ranchers booed.

Matty threw his head back, but smiled as he slowed Blaze. Slowing Dolly as I praised her and pet her neck, I trotted back over to him. "You really know how to do it! Good job," Matty said, as we walked Blaze and Dolly back out the gate. "You got me."

"Thanks," I said, biting my lip.

"Don't mention it," he said, smiling.

I don't remember exactly what happened after that or the walk back to our wagon. All I know is that tingly feeling intensified every time I thought about him.

*D*uring the evening's campfire right outside our wagon, Marin had to nudge me back to the present moment since my thoughts were consumed with Matty Williams.

"All right, girls, get your stuff for the bathrooms and be back at the wagon for bed. You have fifteen minutes," our camp counselor, Joanne said.

"M, I really have to use the bathroom now. Can you bring me my toothbrush and stuff?" Marin asked.

"Um, sure." Even though they just built a new bathhouse with flush toilets, I didn't enjoy the trek between the bathrooms and our wagon. It was always too dark, even with our flashlights. But today had been a good day so I decided to feign bravery.

Holding Marin's and my sundries bag in one hand and my flashlight in the other, I focused on the ground in front of me until I could see shadowed figures by the bathroom.

A person, almost out of breath, ran right toward me. My heart raced until I realized it was Marin.

"M, he's there and he's waiting for you!"

"What?"

"Matty! He's behind the bathrooms, now. Around the corner. Go!"

I gave Marin both our sundries bags and jogged over to the bathrooms, not as worried about the darkness as before. With the search light attached to the side of the bathrooms as my only light, I peeked around the corner and saw him.

"Hey, Maren," he said, leaning against the wall.

"Hey, Matty," I said, biting my lower lip again as my throat dried up. I glanced down to see if my heart was pounding through my chest, since it felt that way. No one ever calls me "Maren," except when I'm in trouble. That's when I hear my full name.

"So...." he said, slowly walking toward me. "You want to sit down?" He motioned to a fallen log nearby.

"Um, yeah." Those were the only words I could speak. The outside lights created heavy shadows making it difficult to see details of his face as we sat. My t-shirt stuck to my body as the warm summer night deepened my personal heat wave, but the crickets provided a soothing soundtrack.

"How can you ride so well? Do you have a horse?" He smelled of Drakkar Noir and hay.

Take a breath.

"Thank you, but no, I ride at a barn nearby."

"Could have fooled me."

"Thanks. You're really good, too."

He smiled.

"Do you have any horses?" I asked, fiddling with a piece of bark from the log.

Thank you, tongue, for letting me form words.

"Yeah, we have a Quarter Horse and Morgan cross named Ray and a thoroughbred named Olive. Part of my chores are to clean out the barn, but they're worth it," he shrugged, picking up a stone.

My head was about to explode with everything I wanted to mention—Spirit...the Black Stallion...the fact I felt like I was going to faint. Or, vomit. Wasn't sure which.

"I almost got a horse, but I didn't. So, I ride a buckskin quarter horse named Spirit. He's amazing." I hoped I hadn't said too much.

"That's cool. Our guys are a handful, but my father lets me barrel race them when I can," he said, tossing the stone to the side.

"Really?"

"Yeah, Ray does better than Olive. But, if she's in the mood to run—nothing can stop her."

I marveled at how easy it was to talk to him. "I can't imagine life without horses. Just love them so much." I tossed my hair to the side involuntarily. I don't remember ever doing that before.

"Yeah," he said, scooting closer to me.

"Um, yeah." I tried so hard to suppress the giggles that were bubbling up inside of me.

The Drakkar cologne on his shirt intensified and I could feel his breath as he moved in closer. His soft, but filmy lips touched mine and he kissed me. In that moment, I understood why adults enjoyed kissing so much because the longer we kissed, the sliminess seemed to fade. He reached his arm around my waist to keep me from falling off the log as my body weakened.

"Whoa, I gotcha."

After steadying me, we looked at each other again and the kissing resumed. Part of me was there on the log and part of me felt as though I were watching myself from the outside.

We stopped when we heard rustling in the woods. It was Marin. "Maren!"

I pulled away from Matty, still feeling him on my lips.

"M—you gotta come now! Joanne's asking about you!"

"Oh, man."

He took his hand off my waist. "Yeah, guess I should go, too."

"Sorry! See ya around?"

"Definitely, Maren."

Every fiber of my being wanted to stay and lose myself in his smile. But reality called. Marin grabbed my hand, and together we sprinted through the wooded area, using the outside bathroom lights as our guide.

"He kissed me!" I yelled in a hushed tone, dodging the branches at our head and feet.

"Oh my gosh! Are you serious?"

"Yeah, I thought that he was just going to like, hold my hand. But he totally kissed me!"

We arrived at our wagon, carefully placing each foot on each creaky step. The sound reverberated louder than during the day.

"Are you two OK?" Joanne asked, meeting us at the top of the steps. The outside lights around the wagons provided enough light to make her shadowed face seem menacing.

"Yeah, we're great. But, uh, I think I ate too much," I said.

"You hardly ate anything for supper," Joanne said, furrowing her brow.

"Well, maybe I needed to eat more." I grimaced my face, hoping Joanne was buying this.

"Do you need to eat something now?"

"No, I'm good." I paused. "Really good."

"Huh," she said, looking over at Marin, who was hiding a smile.

"Maren, do you need to go to the nurse?" Joanne asked.

"What?"

"Do. You. Need. To. Go. To. The. Nurse?"

"No, thank you, I'm great! I mean, I think I'm feeling better now." *Although I wouldn't mind going to the bathroom.*

"Because if you have something, we wouldn't want others to get it, too," she said.

"I'm pretty sure this isn't something that others can catch."

"Uh, huh, I see. That seems apparent."

"Besides, tomorrow's the last day," I added.

Looking directly at me, she smiled. "I just hope it's not too serious."

"I think I'll be all right," I said, walking back into the wagon with Marin behind.

It felt good to be bad, for once in my life.

June 28, 1986

Damn Matty Williams.

The next morning was our last day and as part of the checkout process, we had to clean the wagon for the next campers. Rolling up my sleeping bag, I overheard Shae say to Jessica, "Matty and I were talking and he said he wanted to, like, kiss me. But, I'm like, no thank you."

I looked up from rolling my sleeping bag, and Shae and I locked eyes.

"Yeah, he's really been following me around," she sniffed. "I'm like, back off. I have a boyfriend!"

"You already said that," I muttered to myself. Marin heard me from her bunk and mouthed, "Sorry, M."

"The dude needs to get a life," Shae continued. "It's sorta sad, really."

With my sleeping bag under one arm and my backpack over the other, I strode past her, knocking her into her bunk.

"Geez, watch it next time!" she said, stumbling around.

Ha—in your face!

"Whoops, sorry," I said, trying to hide a devious smile.

She found her footing and reached for her mirror. "Just want to make sure…Yeah, still looks good," she said, fluffing up her bangs.

Lumbering down the cabin steps, I struggled to process everything I felt and just now heard. My previously elated heart now broke thinking that Matty wanted to kiss Shae, too. I said it before and I'll say it again…

Damn Matty Williams.

July 5, 1986

I'm so glad I got to stay over at Marin's house. It was like being at Echo Lake Camp again, even if there weren't any horses or Matty Williams.

"Ugh, I really miss Matty," I said, flopping onto her bed.

"It really sucks that you'll probably never see him again." She walked into her bathroom to change into her pajamas, leaving the door slightly ajar.

"Thanks for reminding me," I said, sitting up. "I even wrote Echo Lake Camp and asked if they could give me his phone number."

"You did?"

"Totally. Then I called their number from their brochures. But they said they couldn't give out his information."

"Did you ask your mama if you could call?" Marin asked, peeking her head out.

"No way. She and Clint would totally tease me. Nope. Just really bummed out. I mean, what do you think he's doing right now?"

"I have no idea," she said,

"I totally miss him. His lips, were, oh my gosh!" I fell forward on the bed.

"There are so many guys out there," Marin sniffed. "And, didn't he like, kiss, that other Shae girl anyway?"

I sighed. "I know, but I really like him and I think he liked me." I threw up my arms. "I thought he did."

"He's still too skinny," Marin said, after flushing the toilet.

"I don't think so. He did get bigger from last summer. And a little taller."

"I guess. Anyway, time for you to get over him. Move on to better ones," she said, gliding over to her bureau.

"I guess."

"What about Jake?" She brushed her long, blonde locks in the mirror. I noticed most of her acne had cleared.

"That was last year! Plus, after the dance, he was totally into Lynette. So, no more Jake for me. But, Matty, on the other hand..."

"He's still too skinny." The irony of Marin repeating that about someone else was not lost on me. I wondered if it was lost on her.

"Here, this will cheer you up," she said, putting in her *Top Gun* soundtrack cassette tape.

"Yay, Mighty Wings!" If the strong bass and drum beat didn't lift my spirits, then not much would.

Except for horses. And remembering Matty Williams' kiss.

July 11, 1986

Well, yesterday was my 13th birthday. I'm technically a teenager now. Woo-hoo, I guess. Thought I'd be more excited. I'm just bummed about a lot now. But CJ gave me a huge hug and Mama tried to make it a good birthday. She gave me a few presents, including a small, adorable horse stuffed animal and a pretty deep blue shirt. She also made her famous birthday cake and we got real Breyers ice-cream. Two things I love are named Breyers and Breyer—ice cream and horse statues! Marin stayed overnight, which was fine, but it feels like we don't laugh as much as we used to. Daddy called and wished me a Happy Birthday. Not that I thought he'd get me a horse this year. Well, maybe I did hope a little bit. But, at this point, it's not going to happen. I'm mad at two guys right now. Well, three, counting Clint. That one never goes away.

August 28, 1986

This past summer wasn't my favorite, but I do like 8th grade. Unfortunately, Marin and I don't have any classes together again, but at least we have lunch together like last year. Otherwise I wouldn't be able to see her all day and that would be totally awful. I'm eating too much again, and sometimes my head and belly hurt afterward. But my clothes still fit, so it's OK. Luckily, there is some elastic in all my clothes. Time (Clock of the Heart)" by Culture Club is what I've been really listening to. It's an older song, but I still love it. Beautiful melody makes me cry. How can thinking about Matty Williams make me excited and stressed at the same time?

In hindsight, my head and belly probably hurt from eating anything that wasn't tied down as a direct result from the "Summer of Matty Williams Humiliation." Interestingly enough, inhaling vast amounts of ice cream after eating a full meal didn't create any further issues for my belly. At least, that's what I told myself.

<u>October 3, 1986</u>

I'm so happy my allergy shots really have been helping for the last year or so. I still wash my sheets and blankets every week. To get the dust off my stuffed animals, I put them in a garbage bag, then stick the vacuum in there. It can be weird to see them shrink down so small in the bag, but they're cleaner when I'm done. Glad Aunt Mimi will be here soon and the "Trifecta of Holidays" will begin!

<u>December 26, 1986</u>

What a whirlwind this fall was! Aunt Mimi's visit was amazing, as usual. And, she actually got to stay for trick-or-treating! She is the best and always makes everything better. She makes me laugh and think. When I got upset by Lacey, she reminded me to breathe. I'm not sure if she really likes Lacey either! But she can't say it because she's an adult.

Thanksgiving was full of delicious food and we started watching the Macy's Day Parade. I guess it's been on forever. That guy from Wheel of Fortune hosted it. Glad we saw it because they had cool floats like Alvin & the Chipmunks and Garfield. I like the Tom Turkey one too, because he's the oldest float they have. There were tons of bands from around the country, even one from Fort Mill, South Carolina. I'm not sure there were any from North Carolina since we didn't see the whole thing. It would be incredible to have the opportunity to play there.

This Christmas was awesome! I FINALLY got my own phone line! But I have to share with Lacey. Yuck! Clint and Mama said it was time since our friends call so much. The telephone guys will come after the New Year and put a phone line in each of our rooms.

Haven't heard from Daddy in a long time. I wonder how Morris and Rosie and Dino are doing. I miss the animals so much and love all the fun we had, especially at Christmas. But then it's kinda easier not having to go over there, It's so strange. Sometimes I want to be with Daddy and other times I don't want anything to do with him. Then sometimes I would give anything to hear Daddy's voice again, especially his laugh. He had such a big, belly laugh. It's like I can hear him, but I'm not sure if it's really what he sounded like. Like how we technically can't hear our own voices like other people hear them.

Can't wait to get the new phone line, so that's something to look forward to.

January 2, 1987

Four more days until the worker guys come and add our new phone line!

<u>January 6, 1987</u>

The phone line is finally installed! We had to wait FOREVER for the guys to come and add the line. But we have it now and it's the best! I called Marin and she called me back. She was the first person I called. Lacey had an attitude when she knocked on my door to tell me the phone was for me. But it is fun just having the phone line to ourselves. I always wait for Lacey to hang up before I start talking.

<u>February 2, 1987</u>

Now, when the phone is for me, Lacey just stomps the floor, since her bedroom is above mine. One time when I picked up the phone, Marin and Lacey were talking and laughing about cheerleading. It was weird. Marin just told me that she got her period for the first time. I wonder if she told Lacey, too?

I still don't like the winter. I eat too much and have a hard time getting going. It's also hard to focus. So, I just watch a lot of Golden Girls and Muppets Take Manhattan or any other movies we have. My clothes are starting to get tighter, so I need to be more careful.

February 22, 1987

Dear Kiddo,

Your letter arrived today. Thank you for writing to me. I can understand how hard it is for you during this time of year. I understand because I enjoy being in the warmth and love the summer breeze from our back porch. I heard from my friends in Michigan that they had a lot of snow up there. Spring is coming soon and you know what that means!

Hang in there and keep your spirit up!

Love you to the moon and back,
Aunt Mimi

April 28, 1987

I'll be horseback riding again tomorrow! Yippee! Fair Oaks has worked out a program with Campfire Teens for a one-time, after-school horseback riding option. Marin said she couldn't go that night, which was weird. I'll be with other people on the trail, and I'm sure none of them will know what to do. They'll say, "He won't walk." Well, you gotta squeeze your legs, or even kick! Or, they'll say, "He's eating." Well, pull up on the reins. That's what they're there for—use them! But, I'm so excited—I get to ride Spirit again! At least, I think I'll be able to. I'd be happy riding Jubi, if Spirit isn't available.

I still haven't heard from Daddy. That's fine. My stuff smells a lot better now. Tomorrow, I have an English test and math homework assignment due in class. They shouldn't be too bad. We also have "Field Day" tomorrow. Yuck! They divide the 8th graders up into teams to play a softball game. You can also run a track event or do things like use the shot put, but no way! Marin and I won't be seeing each other there because our teams didn't match up. I hate everything about Field Day: sports, running, and balls. At least I can hit pretty well and I think I've lost some weight! At least my pants don't seem as tight.

Just can't wait to ride Spirit again. Fingers crossed! Just have to get through the day...

<u>April 28, 1987</u>

Well, you'll never believe it. This day did not go as hoped.

*A*t the softball game, Missy Rhinehart was up to bat and I was next in line. Awaiting my turn, I picked up a bat and swung at the air. I would have given anything to have someone play in my place, but I asked and that was not an option. Missy got two balls and a strike. On the next pitch, she swung, hitting far into the outfield. Before she ran to first base, she threw the bat behind her—right at my head.

The barreling bat bounced off my forehead, on my chin and back to my forehead before falling to the ground. Releasing a blood-curdling scream, I doubled over, crying out for Mama. Mrs. Gardner, an English teacher helping out, ran over to me while the rest of the students gathered around. Everyone's words were jumbled, but I think some of them asked if I was OK. Mrs. Gardner told me to get up slowly as she put her hand on my back. I did as she said, blinking hard to focus.

Staggering across the playground, I was arm in arm with Mrs. Gardner. She led me through the principal's office to a quiet room with a cot in the back.

"How are you feeling, Miss Maren?" a nice lady asked me. She might have been a nurse. I wasn't sure how she knew my name or when Mrs. Gardner had left.

"My head hurts a little, but I'm OK. I'm going horseback riding after school today," I slurred.

"Here, lie down," she said, motioning to a cot.

Easing down onto it provided some relief, especially when she adjusted the pillow. I failed to mention my belly wasn't feeling too well.

"I'm going to check your eyes now. You're going to see a bright light."

"Why?" I asked, flinching and blinking.

"We need to examine your pupils. Make sure everything is OK."

I was OK, but that light sure didn't help. Someone brought an ice pack wrapped in a towel and she placed it on my head.

"Still doing OK?" she asked, adjusting it.

"Yeah."

"Can you tell me your name?"

"Um, Maren Markey."

You just said it earlier.

"Where do you live?"

Pretty sure you have that information.

"I live at 1311 Dilloway Drive, Garner, North Carolina 27529."

"Do you know where you are now?"

You're sitting right next to me!

"The principal's office."

"Do you know what day it is?"

"Tuesday. The day I'm going horseback riding on Spirit!"

She laughed, which was fine with me. I just wanted the questions to stop.

She stood up for a moment and walked into the other room where the secretary's desk was. I heard shuffling papers, people coming and going, chatting and laughing. My eyes struggled to focus on the clock as the ice pack wasn't lying flat against the curve of my forehead. A small bump had formed.

After a few minutes, a familiar voice cut through the buzz from the front area. "Maren?"

"Mama!"

"How are you, Baby?" She kneeled down next to me and the nurse lady returned. "Here, let me see. Oh, that's a big bump."

"Yeah, OK," I said, turning my head away.

"How are you doing?"

"Fine. So, um, I'm still going horseback riding today, right?"

She looked up at the nurse-lady who tightened her mouth. "Oh, Baby. I don't think so."

"What? Why not?" I dropped the ice pack and towel. The nurse-lady picked it up, wrapped it in a fresh towel, handing it back to me.

"That's a huge bump. We don't want you to go if you have a concussion," Mama said.

"What's a 'concussion'?"

"It's like a bruise on your brain," the nurse-lady said. "We need to make sure you're OK."

"What if, God forbid, you fall off? Or, the horse takes off?" Mama said.

I blinked hard, as the warm tears began to form.

"That won't happen! That would never happen with Spirit. He's so good. Plus, I'll be really careful. I'll really hold on to the horn really tight. I promise!"

Mama looked over at the nurse-lady again.

"Please, Mama. Please." I studied Mama's face. It didn't change.

"But, Spirit...." I whimpered.

My head really started to hurt.

"Sorry, Baby. Some other time."

I knew there wouldn't be another time. Campfire Teens only had this horseback riding event one night. And, I'd have to wait until who-knows-when before they had it again. If they ever did.

The nurse-lady told me to slowly and carefully sit up on the side of the cot. Mama linked her arm in mine and we made our way out of the school and over to the emergency room. When the doctor said a cat scan was in order, I got excited. But it wasn't anything like I thought. No kitties at all. After I lay down in a cold, metallic machine and they took the tests, he said everything seemed OK, but that I needed to "rest and take it easy." It was amazing how quickly the small bump morphed into a bigger, blacker and bluer lump. Although it looked like I lost a brutal fist fight, I was more upset that I didn't get to go horseback riding or see Spirit that day.

Missy Rhinehart never did apologize.

May 6, 1987

Only three more days until Marin sleeps over and then horseback riding to see Spirit and Jubi again! It feels like forever. I'm totally excited and my bruises are finally almost gone! Mama watched me a lot right after I got hit in the head, but I'm feeling so much better now. They sure turned different colors as they healed.

This week is taking FOREVER!

The night Marin slept over at my house brought torrential thunderstorms. The next morning, heavy, gray clouds smothered the sky, reflected in the newly formed puddles on the lawn.

"We're still going horseback riding today, aren't we?" I asked Marin.

"Yeah, I guess. It's just…I think it's going to rain again."

"Not sure. But, if it's still wet, Jubi and Spirit will be fine," I consoled. "Horses can ride when there is a little rain."

"I know they can, but…"

"It shouldn't downpour or anything."

"I don't think I brought the right shoes," Marin said, rummaging through her overnight bag on the floor.

"You can't wear the ones you brought?

"Not really. I guess I could, but they could get muddy and stuff."

"Well, if they're horseback riding shoes, they'll get yucky regardless. Mine are dirty from horse poo and who knows what else!"

Marin grimaced.

"Maybe your mama has some boots you could borrow?" I asked. "We could swing by your house, if you want. I just know that my mama doesn't have any and mine would be too small. I definitely know Lacey doesn't have any."

"Is she here? I thought she was staying overnight at Jamie's," Marin said, perking up.

"Yeah, she's over there," I said, furrowing my brow.

"Guess I'll just wear what I have," she said, slumping on the bed. "Hope they don't get too messed up."

"Well, I called Fair Oaks and requested Spirit and Jubi on Wednesday, so we should be set! Remember that one time when I asked to 'reserve' them and Ms. Sherry said, 'Can't reserve, only request.' OK, Ms. Sherry!"

My attempt to break Marin's contorted face, as well as the tension, failed.

*M*arin was quieter than usual on the way over to Fair Oaks, barely averting her gaze from the window. Fortunately, CJ's constant narration of Life as a four-year-old broke up the awkward silence. The beloved sound of the gravel crackling under the tires provided its usual joy. My heart jumped even more when I saw Spirit and Jubi tacked up, ready to go.

"I'll be back in about an hour and a half. Ask them to use their phone if you need to be picked up earlier," Mama said.

"Bye, Mawen," CJ said, releasing his thumb from his mouth just long enough to speak.

"Bye, y'all!"

"Bye, Mrs. Fletcher," Marin said, closing the car door behind us.

Ms. Patsy greeted us in her usual warm and welcoming way, while Mr. Bucky gave us his usual nod. "You ladies ready to ride?" she asked.

"Yes, ma'am," I said, bouncing on the balls of my feet. "A little rain won't keep us away."

Ms. Patsy pointed at me. "So, you're on…."

"Spirit!"

"Right, and Marin, you're on Jubi," she said. "Let's get you two up and out before the real rain comes later this afternoon. Mr. Bucky is going to take you out today because I have some errands to run."

Secretly wishing Ms. Patsy would have taken us out to help cut some of the tension, I quickly turned my focus to the excitement of riding Spirit. After hurdling over puddles of water that had gathered from last night's storms in the mounting area, we got in the saddles just as the sprinkling started.

"It's starting to rain!" Marin exclaimed.

"Not too hard," Mr. Bucky said, mounting Deuce. "Sure you wanna go?"

I looked over at Marin.

"Yeah, should be OK," she muttered.

He nodded. "Bring Spirit behind me. Keep him there, with Jubi in back. Been acting lazy. Jubi will keep him goin.'"

I wondered what Marin thought about this change in configuration since I'm usually the one in back. Sometimes I even tried to hold Spirit back a little, then trot to "catch up," creating even more fun for me. Most times I just have to kiss the air to get to him to move, but I actually had to almost kick him which woke him up.

The sprinkling stopped once we got to the tree-covered part of the trail. The sloshing sound of horses walking through the puddles lulled me into a more peaceful state of mind.

Luckily Spirit and Jubi have no problem going through water. Deuce, on the other hand, stopped in front of a few puddles, pacing back and forth before Mr. Bucky kicked him. Once Deuce decided there was, indeed, no Boogie Man at the bottom of the puddle, he walked right through it.

On a drier part of the trail, Spirit slowed and stopped, spreading out his back legs.

"Stand up, Miss," Mr. Bucky said. "He's peeing."

Right on cue, down came a faucet of pee, as if he hadn't gone in days.

I flashed Marin an awkward smile since Jubi's face was almost in Spirit's butt.

Marin pulled Jubi's head away. I wondered why Jubi didn't move his face on his own. Spirit is peeing—give him some space!

After what felt like an eternity, Spirit brought his back legs back under him, and we proceeded through the trails.

"You girls wanna trot?" Mr. Bucky asked, turning around in his saddle.

"Yeah!" I said.

"Canter, even?"

"Oh, yeah!" He said the magic words.

Mr. Bucky kicked Deuce and the horse's head shot up. We were off. The sloshing increased in volume and a small splattering of mud flew from Deuce's hooves to my face. A cantering horse was my favorite place in the world, but this time I had to balance between wiping my face to see the trail and balance myself on Spirit. He was good about following the horse in front of him and not taking off into the woods. But the Quarter Horse in him made his stops pretty sudden. Just needed to be ready—which I was for this stop.

Reaching into my pocket for a tissue, I noticed mud splattered all over my jeans.

A fallen branch draped over the trail, forcing me to hold it back to pass through. This created a spring action, so by the time Marin arrived at that spot, she received a branch flying in her face.

"Sorry, Marin!"

Mr. Bucky turned around.

"There was a branch…"

"Y'all look like Paints."

My stomach fell. I could only imagine what Marin looked like and could feel her dour expression burning a hole in the back of my head. I turned around to verify. Yep. She, too, had clumps of mud on her cheeks, calves and in her hair. Fortunately, she was looking down at her legs, and missed my glance. I quickly turned back around in my saddle, deciding to let Mr. Bucky be the one to turn around for the rest of the ride.

Cantering had jostled the contents inside Spirit's belly. When we arrived at the barn, he raised his tail and pooped, right in front of Jubi's face. One by one, each turd plopped into a large puddle, creating a different pitch based on the amount released. It's as though he waited to go until we got to the puddle. This was not helping Marin's mood. Not one bit.

We found a drier area to dismount when Ms. Patsy came out of the office. "Good Heavens!" she exclaimed.

"Told 'em they was Paints," Mr. Bucky said, dismounting Deuce.

I feigned a smile as Ms. Patsy handed us paper towels to wash up, still holding my breath from Marin's silence. She was eerily quiet from the time we dismounted to when Mama picked us up. Ironically, the big rain never came and our shoes never really got muddy. But I was wondering if our friendship was starting to.

June 1, 1987

Dear Kiddo,

Thank you for writing. You certainly have a lot on your plate now. There could be many reasons why your friend doesn't want to go to camp this summer. Sometimes people change. Don't let that stop you. If you want to go, and your Mama and Clint say it's OK, then you go to camp and have yourself a ball!

Clearly this Matty guy...whoever...isn't good enough for my niece. There are plenty of fish in the sea. Men are like buses—there's always another one comin' around! And, if he's at camp again, he can see even more of the good things I see in you.

I thought you might like this cute stuffed animal. It's not a horse, but I know you still like kitties.

Keep your spirit up and don't forget to breathe!

Love you to the moon and back,
Aunt Mimi

<u>June 5, 1987</u>

I really want to go to Echo Lake Camp but I'm still bummed that Marin doesn't want to go. It's some of the most fun we've had, outside of going to Fair Oaks. What if Matty is there? That would be so weird. What would I say? I think I'd just ignore him. After all, he kissed me and then kissed Shae. He broke my heart. Maybe Aunt Mimi is right. Anytime I can be on horses for tons of hours each day, I'm there! And, I'd have so much fun— with or without either of them.

<u>July 10, 1987</u>

Today's my 14th birthday! Again, it was fine. Nothing too exciting. But I'm feeling better about going to Echo Lake by myself and I'm just counting down the days. 11 more!

<u>July 21, 1987</u>

Echo Lake today! Horses, here I come!

*A*s was the case from previous years, simply seeing the Echo Lake Camp sign made my heart pound with excitement. Campers said good-bye to their parents, some with tears and some without. Wranglers rode the horses around the camp and the hustle and bustle was exhilarating. A feast for my eyes. Mama said I talked from the time we left the house to the time we arrived.

Breathing a sigh of relief, I didn't see Matty. All that worrying for nothing. But I was still disappointed Marin wasn't there with me.

July 23, 1987

I don't like Candy.

Although there wasn't another "Shae" in my wagon that summer, I wasn't really close to any of the other girls. They were fine. Kind of like a saltine cracker; not terrible, but not great. For the trail ride, I was the last to pick my horse since everyone ran to their respective horses. I couldn't believe there were still people who still did this. Nonetheless, it left me horse-less.

One of the wranglers yelled, "Candy's right there! Stand next to her!" My heart fell. It was well-known that Candy was stubborn and I wasn't in the mood to deal with that. I really wanted Dolly, my favorite beautiful bay, or Inky, the dark bay with the handlebar ears, or Jack, the cool pony, or Chicoby, the chestnut, or anyone else. Anyone else. Heck, even Deuce back at Fair Oaks.

Since my options were gone and the clock was ticking, I shuffled over to Candy. To make it worse, I was last in line for the trail ride which I never liked. It was fine when I rode Spirit, but I didn't like being the caboose on a long line at camp.

Much to my surprise, however, the trail ride actually started out well, despite the fact that the night before, a large and windy thunderstorm knocked down branches and even some trees. One area on the trail meandered right by one of the campers' cabins, which included many screaming kids. Our wrangler yelled out to them to keep it down, since horses were coming through. Luckily, I was the last one, so all the loud screaming and carrying on happened before I got up there. One good thing about being last.

I could see the clearing from the woods and most of the horses were making the trek back up the hill to the barn. At the edge of the woods, a huge tree had fallen across our path. The horses had to literally lift their legs high to step over it. Every one of them walked over it with no problem. When Candy and I approached, she stopped in her tracks.

"C'mon, Candy. Walk over it." I gave her a slight kick as she smelled the tree.

She lifted her front leg and rested it on the thick trunk. Then she took a slight step back, pawing right in front of it.

"Candy, let's go." I scooted my body forward in the saddle, watching everyone else walk on. My heart pounded harder.

She smelled it again before pacing back and forth. There was no other way around it except over it.

Just as I was about to give her another, "C'mon, Candy," she lunged her body over the tree, flinging me out of the saddle. I landed hard on the ground, directly on my back. Barely processing what happened until I looked up at the sky, Candy stood off to the side of the trail.

"Maaaammmmmmaaaaaa!" I yelled out. Turning my head to the right, the wrangler at the front of the line galloped full force. His bay horse stopped on a dime right in front of me, spraying a little dirt on my face.

"Oh, my gosh!" he said, leaping out of the saddle. "Miss Maren, are you all right?"

Since the shock of everything knocked the wind out of me, I struggled to speak.

"Don't move, but can you move your feet?"

"Yeah," I said, struggling to get air.

"Anything else hurt?"

"Nah, I'm OK." I mustered enough energy to attempt to roll over onto my side.

"Just take it easy. Just take it easy," he said, helping me up. "Let's get you to the infirmary."

He said something into his walkie-talkie. I'm assuming the rest of the campers on their horses and Candy were taken back to the barn but it was all a blur. I just wish Marin had been there. I really missed her, especially after this. And, I wondered if Matty would have come and said anything to me if he had been there, too.

Guess I won't be riding Candy again.

Totally fine by me.

July 28, 1987

Echo Lake is awesome! There were so many nice people there who asked me how I was doing. My back was a little sore, with some small bruises, but nothing was broken. The wranglers even let me pick whatever horse I wanted for the trail ride. I picked Dolly again. I guess Alicia, my instructor when I rode Friday, was right. You gotta get back up. Although I was nervous, I knew that being on Dolly would be great. And, she was.

August 1, 1987

I'm sad to be home from Echo Lake but I can't believe I'm going into 9th grade. My last year at Garner Junior High. I remember how afraid I was to start and now I know the school like the back of my hand. Plus, this year I'm going to join choir.

I'm going to like being the "big fish" this year! We'll rule the school!

September 20, 1987

Marin is having a big birthday party! I've always loved her parties, even if I haven't written about them. I'm sure she'll have yummy pizza, cake, and even ice-cream. She said they might even rent a video camera! It's weird because she also invited Duffy Palmer and Rachel Mellin. She's been hanging out with them more. Duffy and Rachel are cheerleaders and both really popular. Plus, Bertha is going to be here for me during that time. Bleh. But I love Marin's parties and it will be fun.

Well, it wasn't.

My ability to stay up late waned as the night progressed. Whenever I slept over at Marin's, I usually conked out first and was often the last one to wake up in the morning. Having Bertha didn't help, especially when I was the only one who was dealing with my monthly visitor that night. Earlier in the evening, we all shared when Bertha would be "visiting." It's strange and unique that is something that can connect all girls together.

The next morning, when I joined everyone already sitting at the breakfast table, I was met with snickering and side glances. Marin stood up from the table and marched right up to me.

"Hey, M," she said, standing so close to me I could tell that she hadn't brushed her teeth yet.

"Yeah?"

"Last night. Well, actually this morning, Dallas had a....a..."

"A what?" I looked over at the grinning dog, wagging his tail at me.

"Well, this morning when we woke up, we found out he went into the trash and got into one of your—" She cleared her throat, and whispered, "Pads."

"He what?" I threw my hand over my mouth. "You mean in the bathroom?"

"Well, that's where it started. But he brought it into the living room and started, like, ripping into it and stuff."

"Oh my gosh." I placed my fingers on the bridge of my nose, trying to ignore the tittering at the breakfast table.

"At first we didn't know what it was. We thought it was a new toy. But, then..."

"'*We?*' Did everyone see?" I asked, inaudibly.

"Well, there's me."

"OK—"

"And Mama and Daddy. And, Travis."

"Oh, no."

"And, Duffy and Rachel."

I groaned.

"Don't worry, I took care of it."

"Oh my gosh," I repeated.

Even though the giggling at the breakfast table subsided, all I wanted to do was hightail it out of there. But since Mrs. Breiner had made her famous shrimp and grits, and buttermilk biscuits, I was willing to swallow my pride to have some. I was ready to swallow anything at that point to wash down my humiliation.

November 12, 1987

Hallomas and Halloween were fun this year. But I'm really nervous because I'm sleeping over at Marin's again this weekend. It's the first time since her birthday party, but it should be better this time.

"Bye, y'all," Mrs. Breiner said, with her hand on the doorknob. "We'll be at the Meyers' house. Their number is on the fridge. Travis is at Billy's house. Be sure to let Dallas out before you go to bed. Be good! We'll be back in a few hours."

"Bye, Mama. Bye, Daddy," Marin said, hugging and kissing them goodbye. We watched them back out of the garage and drive away.

"The whole house to ourselves," I joked. "We should dance in the living room and turn up the music really, really loud!"

A large smile grew across Marin's face. "C'mere."

"What?"

"You'll see." She sprinted through the kitchen, running across the living room, stopping in front of a cabinet I never noticed before. Inside were countless bottles of alcohol all lined up.

"Is that—?"

"Yeah, let's have some!" she said, reaching in.

"I don't know."

"Why not? It's no big deal. Like, everyone has tried it. Like Duffy and everyone."

Mama let me try her gin and tonic a few times, but I thought it tasted like cough syrup. I also tried a few sips of her beer. Just didn't get the big deal. It tasted like I would imagine pee would taste.

I'd rather have ice cream.

Marin lunged for a bottle of vodka, unscrewed the top, and gulped right from the bottle. I couldn't believe what I was seeing.

Her face grimaced and she yelled out a loud *Woooweeee!* "Here," she said, shoving it into my hand.

"Um, OK." I raised the bottle slowly, taking a whiff. I crinkled my nose and dabbed the bottle to my lips.

"C'mon!" she said, tipping the end of the bottle into the air. "Really take a swig!"

A giant mouthful slid down my throat, burning as gravity pulled it down. I coughed, wiping a small trickle that had oozed out the side of the mouth.

She laughed, took the bottle from me, and downed another large gulp.

"M, when did you start doing this?"

"I don't know. A few weeks ago, maybe," she said, taking another drink. "I've seen Mama take gulps when I was supposed to be asleep. She didn't see me. I just wondered what all the fuss was. I get it now. It makes you feel so silly and relaxed."

I tried not to breathe too deeply to avoid smelling my own alcohol-laced breath.

"You really like it?" I asked, following her into the kitchen.

"Yeah, don't you?" She turned on the faucet, filling the vodka bottle with water to refill it to its original amount.

I twisted my face, hoping the stinging sensation would subside.

"Give it a minute. You'll feel real good in a minute."

That "good feeling" never came. Watching Marin take several more swallows, swaying as she walked and acting super giggly all night made my head hurt. What started out as excitement that the Breiners left us alone for the evening ended with me keeping a watchful eye on Marin the whole time. I counted the minutes waiting for the adults to return.

December 8, 1987

Things feel a little weird with Marin. But I'm excited because tomorrow our choir sings at the Apex Tree-Lighting ceremony! All the Christmas lights will be up and they'll serve hot chocolate and donuts after. Mama will drop me off since I need to be there early and then run her errands. But she'll be back for the whole concert. I'm so excited!

That cold, star-filled night was a perfect setting for a tree-lighting and Christmas carols as the enormous main Christmas tree swayed in the breeze. Bare maple trees and surrounding pine trees were wrapped in strings of twinkling white lights, a beautiful contrast to the red Santa Claus display with his brown reindeer. Although it was too cold for CJ to come, Mama found a place to stand up in front next to the other parents. Watching her participate in the sing-along portion while waving to me made my heart grow. Like the Grinch's. At the end of our program, she clapped harder than any of the other parents. Everyone clapped as the main Christmas tree was lit.

"Mama, did you like it?" I asked, dashing over to her past the concession table.

"I did, Baby. You did so well." Her hug felt so warm on a chilly night.

"What was your favorite song?"

"Let's see. I really liked the—"

"—Was it the 'Silent Night' one? I loved that rendition. It was just enough of the original melody, but it had different harmonies to it."

"That was good and I also liked the 'Deck the Halls' number."

"That's one of my favorites, too! Oh, do you want some donuts or—?"

"—Listen, Baby," Mama practically whispered. "There is someone who has come to see you."

"Really? Who?" I craned my neck, examining all the people laughing and talking. "Where?"

"No, waiting at home," she sighed.

"Who is it?"

Studying her expressionless face, I knew.

"Like at our house?"

"He's waiting in his truck parked in front of the house," she said, adjusting her winter hat.

"I really don't want to see him."

Mama tightened her lips. "I know, Baby. But, just say 'Hi.' Maybe he'll even have a gift for you."

"I doubt it's the horse he promised."

We both knew it wouldn't be that. On the drive home, the only hint of communication that cut the silence was when I shook my head in disbelief as I stared out the window. Pulling into the driveway, our headlights illuminated his parked truck in front of the house. After parking in the garage, Mama met him at the end of the driveway and I went inside the house.

After a minute, Mama came inside. "He's coming up the sidewalk. He just wants to see you," she said, as she headed upstairs.

I peeked outside the living room curtain, hearing CJ and Clint's distant voices upstairs. I don't know why I let Daddy get all the way to the front porch and ring the doorbell. Guess I wanted him to wait for me for a change. He lumbered up the sidewalk. His body was heavier than he was before and appeared much older.

"Hey, Daddy," I said, holding the front door open. His graying beard covered an even bigger double chin.

"Hey, Mare. How are ya, sweetie?" he wheezed, kissing me on the cheek. The ever-present cigarette smoke smell attacked my nose again.

"Good."

"Got you something," he said, handing me a plastic grocery bag. Inside was a pretty turquoise and white striped sweater—two sizes too small.

"Thank you, Daddy," I said politely. The cigarette smoke smell from him permeated our foyer.

"How have you been, Mare?"

"Good, good. I just got back from singing at a tree-lighting."

"That's great," he said, with a slight wheeze.

"Are you still playing the drums?"

"It's been a while. But the guys know they can call whenever they need me. There is some talk about something happening for them out West. California or Oregon, even."

"That's good. Um, how are the animals?" I asked, sighing.

"Well, Dino died..."

"Oh, no! He was so sweet."

"Yeah, but Morris is still doing good and Rosie is goofy as ever."

A slight chuckle between us sliced through some of the awkwardness.

"I heard that the Kentucky Horse Park has their Saddlebred Museum open and has a sculpture of Supreme Sultan in front."

"That's great. Do you want to sit down?" I regretted asking him as soon as the words left my lips.

"Nah, I should get going," he said, playing with his jacket zipper.

"OK," I said, probably too quickly.

"Mare," Daddy whispered, "You know, you can come and live with me now."

"What?" I asked, with one hand on the doorknob.

"Yeah, you can decide now. You're old enough."

I furrowed my brow. "I don't know, Daddy."

"I thought you always wanted to come live with me?"

I shrugged, running my finger over the crinkly plastic bag.

"It's just—you said you'd get me a horse for my birthday. You promised," I muttered.

"Is that the only reason you wanted to live with me?" he asked, raising his voice a little.

"Well, no, but..."

"Yeah, sorry about the whole horse thing," he said, wiping his face. "This is what we can do. How about for your next birthday? I promise I can do it then. How does that sound?"

"Well…"

"You can come live with me and then we can look at horses together. I know Morris would be so happy and we can get another puppy. Or, kitten. What do you think?" He coughed as his voice began to rise. "Next year will be great! You'll have your horse and can ride him anytime you're there. Or, her—whatever you want."

This sounded familiar. Too familiar.

"We'll see." I couldn't believe I resorted to using Mama's phrases.

"OK, next weekend is my weekend and we can talk about it when you come."

"I guess," I said, opening the front door.

After giving him a small side-hug, he said "I love you, Mare. You are my pride and joy, and always will be," he said, tearing up.

"Thank you, Daddy."

He sighed. "Goodbye, Maren." His sad eyes held my gaze before walking out the door.

Mama gingerly walked downstairs as I shut the door behind him and CJ followed close behind her.

"Sister!"

"Hey, CJ," I said, giving him a hug. I loved that he started calling me "Sister" since he called Lacey by her first name.

"You OK, Baby?" Mama asked.

"I guess."

"What did he get you?"

Unwrapping the grocery bag, I pulled out the sweater.

"Well, it's a good color on you at least," she said.

"It's way too small." I seethed.

"Well, his heart is in the right place."

I shook my head.

"Do you have any tests tomorrow?" she asked, picking CJ up and resting him on her hip.

"Yeah, I have another English test."

"Another one? Didn't you like, just have one?" I knew Mama was trying to lighten the mood. "I enjoyed your program tonight."

I forced a smile. "Thanks. I think I'm going to bed."

"All right, Baby. Good night."

"G'night, Sister," CJ said. I hugged both of them, quite aware of the cigarette smoke residue clinging to me.

Heading to my room with the plastic bag still in hand, I gently shut the door behind me. I know Daddy said that I could live with him. I guess I could have. The thing is, I just didn't think that I ever really wanted to. In fact, even though I loved him, I was OK with not seeing him again.

December 27, 1987

Christmas was pretty fun this year, but it's been weird. Just got off the phone with Daddy who wished me a belated Merry Christmas. That's the first time I heard from him since the night of the Christmas-tree lighting three weeks ago. He didn't pick me up for our visit. Still feel weird about the last time I saw him. Not sure if I feel sad or what. I am so glad that Marin wanted to sleep over during Christmas break because I wasn't sure she wanted to. Haven't talked to her as much. We used to talk about horses and a little bit about guys but lately we've been spending more time on guys, or not really too much at all. I've been listening to "Is There Something I Should Know" by Duran Duran now. Great song and I have the biggest crush on Duran Duran, like everyone else in the world.

That December weekend when Marin slept over was unseasonably warm. Turning on the radio, I was surprised to hear a non-Christmas tune. "La Bamba" was playing and I sang along as best as I could. Apparently, I didn't get the lyrics correct. "Bada ba dum la bamba. Bada ba dum la bamba! So, it can't be done, it can't be done!" I sang, twirling around.

Marin snickered. "I don't think those are the words." Marin's Spanish was really good, especially after living in Texas.

"Well, maybe I'm close," I said, turning down the dial. "We haven't learned this song in Spanish class yet. I'll have to ask Yolanda when I get my next shot."

"You're still getting shots?" she asked.

I thought you knew that.

"Yeah, they said I'd need to get them for a few years. But they've been helping so I don't have to go as much."

"That's good."

"So, do you like anyone now?" I asked, hoping to find a topic she might want to talk about.

"Yeah, Trevor Anderson," she said, brushing her hair in the mirror on the back of the door. It was strange to be talking to her back, while seeing her front reflected in the mirror.

"You mean, like the Quarterback?"

"Yeah," she smirked. "We talked and he called me the other night about going out."

"Really?"

"I thought I told you," she said, tucking her brush in her overnight bag.

"No, but after you go out, you'll tell me everything, right?"

"Sure," she said, rummaging through her bag.

"Oh, I have a good question for you: If you could ride any horse, fiction or real, alive or not, who would it be?"

"I don't know," she said, folding her pajamas.

"For me, it would definitely be Ruffian. And, the Black Stallion, too!" I stopped myself. "Sorry, how about you?"

"Don't really know. Just really like Jubi."

"No other horses then?"

"Not that I can think of," she said, placing her pajamas in her bag.

"Not like Secretariat or Black Beauty?"

She shook her head.

"Or, Phar Lap?"

"Who's that?" she scowled.

"A movie came out about him. He was a really amazing Australian horse who died from—"

"—Nah, I just really like Jubi. And, I guess I also like Blue from camp." She zipped up her bag. "I think I have everything."

"I'll call you later. Maybe we can even go horseback riding next weekend."

"Maybe, but we might be heading to the mountains to ski again." Marin and her family started skiing. They didn't ask me, just like they never asked me if I ever wanted to go boating. That's OK. I've never skied before and I wouldn't want to embarrass myself.

"OK, just let me know," I said, walking her out to her bike.

"Bye, Marin," Mama yelled from the kitchen. "We'll be seeing you!"

"Bye, M," she said. Her hug was quicker than usual and when she rode off, she didn't look back. It didn't feel the same. I felt like I wouldn't see her again.

January 14, 1988

Things have been super weird with Marin since going back to school second semester. Don't know why.

Hoping to talk it out, I gave her a call. "Hello?"

"Um, hi, Mrs. Breiner, this is Maren. Is Marin available?" I asked, with a lump in my throat.

"No, Marin is not available. She'll talk to you later."

Click.

"Thanks," I said to the dial tone.

Later that night, Lacey had been on the phone with her friend Jamie for a while. When the phone rang, I thought Jamie was calling Lacey back. But when I heard the ceiling thumping, I knew it was for me.

"Hi, M!" I said, picking up the phone.

"Hey."

"Everything OK?" I asked.

"Yeah, why?"

"Well, you didn't wait for me at lunch today."

Silence.

"And, you ate with Duffy Palmer and everyone."

"Well, Mrs. Peters kept us after third period. So, we just went to the cafeteria and ate together."

"Just seems like you've been ignoring me," I said.

"Well, it seems like you've been ignoring *me*."

"Me? I've been calling and your mama always says you're not available. Just seems so weird because you've always been able to talk before. And, when I try to talk to you at school, you're always, like, trying to get away or something."

"I gotta get going."

Click.

She definitely takes after her mother.

"I hate this!" I yelled.

Fumbling through the menagerie of cassette tapes to play the perfect song for this awful moment, a knock on my door snapped me out of my muttering swear words. Stomping to the door, I yelled, "What?"

It was CJ.

"Um, Sister?"

"Aw, CJ," I said, crouching down next to my little brother.

"Can you pway with me?" he asked, showing me his baseball glove.

"Right now?"

"Uh, huh," he nodded, leaning into me, almost falling over onto my knee.

I exhaled. "Guess I can. C'mon."

A huge smile emerged as he made a bee-line for the backyard.

"Wait, gotta get my glove, too." On my way to the garage, I peeked into the living room. Lacey was upstairs, Mama was resting her eyes from a crazy day at work, and Clint was reading the newspaper.

CJ and I slipped out into the backyard where we threw the ball back and forth. But, only after CJ's insistence of singing the "Star-Spangled Banner" before we started. Mama said there was one time when he wanted to play and no one else was around, so he knocked on the neighbor's door and asked her to sing "The Star-Spangled Banner" with him. Fortunately, she had a good sense of humor and obliged since he said he couldn't play without it being sung first.

Scrawnier than his kindergarten classmates, CJ was quite athletic. I never liked balls, especially when they were flying at me, with good reason. But most of his throws had great aim despite having the attention span of a gnat. When he decided we were done, he ran up to me, since he hardly walks anywhere. "Sister, you are the best sister in the whole wide world."

"You really think I'm the best sister in the whole world?"

"The whole *wide* world," he corrected.

I knelt down next to him and threw open my arms, hoping he didn't feel my sweaty shirt. He ran into them, wrapping his little arms around my neck. "Thanks, I really needed to hear that today. You're the best brother in the whole wide world, too."

Couldn't have asked for a better ending to an awful day.

February 1, 1988

I just don't get it. Now Marin won't even call me back and totally ignores me at school. We don't even sit together at lunch anymore. She's always with Duffy Palmer and the other cheerleaders. I hate lunch now. I hate it so much, I wanted to talk to Mrs. Gardner more, but I don't know what to do.

My standard breakfast consisted of a handful of chips and a swig of Pepsi. Even though I was starving by lunchtime, I would have given anything to be anywhere else on Earth than the school cafeteria. It was hard watching Marin with all the other cheerleaders.

When the final bell rang after English class, I gathered my books slower than usual. The other students' mindless chit-chat on their way out the door and ricocheted off the hallway walls.

"Have a great night, Maren," said Mrs. Gardner, my English teacher. I never forgot how nice she had been the previous April when she walked me to the principal's office after I got hit in the head with the bat. I wasn't even her student, yet her kindness was reflected in her warm smile. Although clothes weren't ever my forte, I always loved to see what she wore. Her long-brown hair seemed to always be perfect and she didn't wear too much makeup. Couldn't say that for every teacher I had. "Great job on your test, too."

"Thanks, I studied. Well, maybe not as much as I should have. But things have been crazy."

She smiled. "You know how important it is to study for every test, but sometimes things come up. "Yeah."

They do. Just not always the things you want.

February 16, 1988

There's a new girl at lunch! And, we FINALLY got a new VCR! Things are getting better!

Lunchtime became a balance between creating an illusion that I was busy working on my faux homework, all while eating, and avoiding eye contact with others. However, on that day, I saw a girl I had never seen before sitting at the end of my new lunch table spot. She had just taken a bite of her sandwich when she looked up at me.

"Hi!" I said.

"Hi," she muttered.

"I'm Maren."

"I'm Jocelyn." Her tight, curly brown hair matched her glasses. "Are you new?"

"Yeah, just moved here from South Carolina."

"Well, welcome to Garner Junior High."

"Thanks," she said, eyeing my armful of books and notebooks.

"I usually do some of my homework here," I said.

She looked down.

"But I don't have to," I said, sitting down across from her. "Are you liking it here?"

"Yeah, so far. We moved here because of my daddy's job."

"That happens a lot."

We talked about moving, classes, and teachers. She was so easy to talk to. My heart sang when the next day she was sitting in the same spot again for lunch. And then the next day. And the next day. It was a relief to not have to pretend to work on my homework anymore. Lunch just got a little better.

A few weeks later, I went to the cafeteria but didn't see her. I was hoping she was OK. But, the next day, the same thing: no Jocelyn in the cafeteria. My eyes glanced over at some students a few tables away.

My heart fell.

Jocelyn was sitting at a full lunch table, talking to someone next to her. She didn't even see me or look over at me.

Since I had gotten into the habit of not bringing books or notebooks with me, I plopped down, staring down at my food, trying to block out all the kids talking simultaneously. Seemed so loud and inane. Who cares about who our baseball team is playing next or when the next pep rally will be?

Lunch had gone back to sucking. From then on, I would always be prepared, bringing my books and notebooks every day for lunch.

March 7, 1988

Dear Kiddo,

I'm so sorry to hear that the new girl at lunch. I'm especially sorry to hear about everything with your friend, Marin. You're right, it is hard, especially since you two were so close. And you both loved horses so much. I don't agree when you say that you'll never go horseback riding again, but maybe you'll find someone else you can enjoy horses with. In the meantime. I happened upon this movie that you loved and wanted to give it to you. Since you love *The Black Stallion* so much, now you can watch him on your new VCR whenever you want. Call it an early Hallomas or birthday gift. No need to tell Lacey or your mama about it unless they ask.

Sending you lots of love from Up North. Soon, the horses will be returning to Mackinac Island. Try to keep your spirit up!

Love you to the moon and back,
Aunt Mimi

March 10, 1988

Aunt Mimi's letter and gift were awesome and she really helped me to move forward. Or, at least try.

Since lunch had gotten unbearable, I decided to be creative and try to find a friendly soul. Mrs. Gardner had always been so nice to me so I thought she could help.

"Mrs. Gardner, can I eat my lunch in here today?" I asked, looking around at the empty desks in her English classroom.

"So sorry, Maren. I have to run some errands," she said, throwing her coat on.

"Oh, OK."

"But I'll see you last period, OK?" Her eyes glanced at her watch. "Bye, Maren!"

Shuffling my feet on my way back to my locker, I opened it as slowly as I could. Stretching to reach the top, I grabbed my brown bag and math book.

On my way back to the cafeteria, I was on overdrive scanning through the windows to find a place to eat. Once inside, the length of the lunch tables seemed to grow in size, while the availability of open seats decreased. Finally finding one that was far enough away from Marin and the cheerleaders, Jocelyn, or anyone else I knew, I sat down, ensuring my back faced a majority of the cafeteria.

Gripping my bologna and cheese sandwich with one hand, I pretended to answer questions in the back of my math book with my other. We actually didn't have that as our homework, but it looked as though I was busy doing something. I think it appeared that way, at least.

I felt like I was sitting alone on top of the slide again. Only this time, I avoided eye contact with everyone.

*L*unch was horrible that day, but that evening's dinner was agonizing. Near the end of the meal, Lacey announced, "Don't forget, it's two weeks until the Regional cheerleading competition. So, I'll need the final payment for the hotel."

My eyes rolled. Mama always said I could never hide my true feelings. Playing poker was never going to be a forte of mine.

Lacey's eyes narrowed. "By the way, Marin will be there."

Stopping midchew, I glared at her. "Why did you just bring her up?"

"Just thought you might want to know," she said, taking a bite of her barbeque.

"OK, girls," Mama whispered.

"Why would I want to know?" I asked, increasing in volume. "I mean, I don't care. Like, I don't care if she wants to prance around in a small skirt so everyone can see her. 'Oooo…look at *me!*'" I mocked. "'I can clap my hands and say, 'Go, team go!' Look at me and see how awesome I am! Aren't I just so very special'?"

"At least I don't have animal posters all over my walls. What are you—like ten years old?" she quipped.

"No, but it's better than drinking and sleeping around."

Lacey shot me a look. "Well, um, not…everyone does that," she stuttered. "And by the way, why don't you try wearing a little makeup once in a while. And, while you're at it, try not to smell like horse crap!"

"Hey!" Clint intervened. "Stop it now. Both of you."

"She totally insulted me!" I said.

"Both of you, stop it now," he repeated.

"She started it," I said.

"Now we're going to finish it."

I stared at Mama for backup, but she kept eating.

"So, it's OK if she does that? Oh my god," I said, shoving myself from the table, rattling the glasses.

"Maren, you sit back down, right now," Clint said.

"This is unbelievable!" I yelled on my way to my room.

"Don't you slam that door, Missy!"

"Just cannot believe this family!" I yelled, slamming the door behind me.

The sound of a chair being pushed out from the table led to loud footsteps down the hall. There was a banging on the door and the doorknob twisted from side to side.

"You open this door right now, Missy!" Clint yelled.

I trembled as I slowly opened it.

"Don't you ever leave the supper table like that again!" With each point of his finger, his face grew even redder.

"But she started it!"

"And, you kept it going."

"But—"

"You always have to get the last word," he said.

"But—"

"Just stop. It's coming out of your allowance if you ever break one of *my* doors from slamming. You hear me?"

The neighbors heard you.

"Yes, sir."

"What's that?" he asked, cupping his ear.

"Yes. Sir."

"All right," he said, shutting my door, which sounded more like a slam to me.

My red-hot anger morphed into tears. Collapsing onto the bed, I buried my head into my pillow so no one would hear. Especially not Clint.

<u>March 15, 1988</u>

Another day, another dreaded lunch period.

Although we weren't supposed to leave the cafeteria during lunch, I noticed others standing outside the entrance. I figured if I walked toward my locker as discreetly as possible, I could hang out there, pretending to get something before my next class. With my locker in sight, my Grand Master Plan almost succeeded when I heard a stern voice behind me.

"Miss Maren Markey!"

Slightly throwing my head back, I turned around to see it was Mrs. Cox, the largest, loudest, most annoying hall monitor on God's green earth. Her rogue chin hairs flapped in the wind when she spoke and her boobs stuck way out. Big boobs on an old person usually makes them look younger. Not on her.

"Let me see your pass," she bellowed.

I took in a deep breath. "Sorry, ma'am. I don't have one."

"You know you're not supposed to be in the hallways during lunch," she said, resting her thick hand on her hefty hip.

"I know, but please, Mrs. Cox. Just for today, can I just stand by the windows?" I pleaded.

"Can't let you do that." "I promise I'll stay right here. I promise I won't leave."

"You know the policy clearly states that you are not allowed to leave the cafeteria without a pass," she said, shifting her enormous weight.

"I know, but please. I promise you won't even know I'm here," I said, voice cracking as tears began to form.

"I can't let you do that. You march right back into the cafeteria. Now," she gestured. "And, furthermore—"

"—Maren, is that you?" A sweet voice cut through the painful encounter.

Turning around, my heart felt lighter to see Mrs. Gardner.

"There you are! I've been looking for you," she said, approaching us.

Furrowing my brow, I swallowed the forming tears.

"Remember, you were...supposed to come by at lunch today?" She raised her eyebrows and drew out her words.

"Oh, yeah!" I finally got her drift and looked over at Mrs. Cox. "Yes, ma'am. Sorry. I won't forget next time." I reveled in our mutual understanding.

"Luckily we still have a good part of the lunch period left. So, shake the lead out and let's go. I'm so sorry, Mrs. Cox, for any trouble."

I'm pretty sure Mrs. Cox didn't buy any of that, but it sure felt good to be free.

Shifting my math and English books to my other arm, I whispered, "Thank you so much, Mrs. Gardner."

"You're welcome." Her smile seemed to make all my anxieties disappear.

Turning the corner into her classroom, the room appeared three times larger without any students.

"I've been wanting to ask though. Are things OK with you?" she asked, motioning me to sit down.

"Um, well...."

She lowered her head, cocking it slightly, without losing eye contact.

"Well, not really," I sputtered, fidgeting in the chair. "Well, just that...I don't know."

Glancing back up, I was amazed. She was actually still listening, and smiling, no less. By now, most people would have looked away or found something more interesting.

"It's just...that I have this friend...."

She nodded.

"And, well, she..." I shook my head. "This is boring kid-stuff."

"Have you talked to your parents?"

"Well, my Mama and my *step*daddy aren't really that interested. Both work a lot and stuff. Have you ever met my mama?" I asked, resting my elbow on the desk.

"I believe so, yes. She came to the last Open House with your brother in tow."

"Awww, yeah. CJ."

"You really love him. Your face just brightened up."

"He's really a sweetheart. Love him to death. He's the only one I like in our family. Poor thing is a little smaller than the other kids. I wouldn't know what that was like at all since I'm usually one of the, well, biggest people in the room. I know from our pictures. I'm definitely bigger than my *step*sister, Lacey."

"Is she a student here?" she asked.

"No, but she was last year. Her name is Lacey Fletcher. See, she has her Daddy's last name and I kept mine."

"That's right, because your Mama's last name is Fletcher, too." She shook her head. "Nope, I don't know Lacey."

"I thought everyone knew her. She's so popular," I said, rolling my eyes.

"Guess not with everyone."

We both laughed. Mine had a hint of vengeance.

Apríl 1, 1988

I love Mrs. Gardner so much. She's super funny and nice. She really listens and looks at me when I talk. Feels like she really sees me. And, her room is so inviting. It doesn't smell like my history teacher's classroom. It actually smells good.

When the final bell rang, I gathered my books and asked, "Mrs. Gardner, do you ever need any help doing anything?"

"What do you mean?"

"Like running off copies or Scantron or anything like that?"

"Hm...," she pondered, eyeballing the stacks of paper piled around the classroom. "I guess I could use a little help doing that. Maybe you could even be a teacher's aide. Sometimes students can do that and get credit for it."

"Wow, that would be even better!"

"Let me poke around and see what we can do."

"Thanks, Mrs. Gardner," I said, pulling my backpack strap over my shoulder.

"You're welcome. Oh, and, Maren, anytime you want to come in here to eat your lunch, you're welcome to do so. If I'm not here, and anyone gives you any grief, you tell them I gave you permission and that I'll be returning soon."

I'm not sure what came over me. I threw my arms around her, trying to keep the lump forming in my throat from forming tears on her shoulder.

April 22, 1988

Mama said I could go horseback riding by myself! It was so awesome with Spirit and Mr. Bucky! I'm learning so much!

Once we arrived at Fair Oaks, I jumped out without Mama even getting out of the car. Or, coming to a full stop, for that matter. Ms. Patsy waved to Mama as she turned around in the driveway, disappearing into a cloud of dust.

"Well, look who's here!"

"Hi, Ms. Patsy!" She always made me feel like I was coming home.

"Just you today?"

"Yeah, just me. Marin said she couldn't make it," I said, avoiding eye contact.

She nodded. "I have a sneakin' suspicion I know who you wanna ride."

"Yeah, my Spirit."

"Who else?" she laughed. "Well, the Old Man's in the back working with Deuce."

I wondered why Mr. Bucky was "working" his horse before we rode? Wasn't going out on the trail work enough? Standing in the middle of the paddock, he held onto a long whip-like contraption and Deuce was cantering in circles around him.

"What's he doing?"

"Groundwork," Ms. Patsy said. "Very important."

"Why, what is it?"

"It helps to connect to the horse. Really strengthens the bond you have with them. They just need to know who's in charge. Not in a bad way, though. Not hurting them or anything, but they need to know that you're safe and will look out for them. Makes 'em calmer and more confident," she said, slightly smiling.

"Why does he use a whip on them?"

"That's no whip!" she guffawed.

Looked like a whip to me.

"The end of that thing is basically yarn. The Old Man would never intentionally hurt a horse. Never. That's not how you develop trust and respect."

Cantering around Mr. Bucky, the beautiful bay circled back, then trotted in circles, stopping by Mr. Bucky's side. The two seemed to share a special bond and it was awe-inspiring to watch the two of them together.

"He grew up seeing the wrong way to treat horses," Ms. Patsy said, lowering her voice. "Just killed him as a little boy to see the way his Daddy treated them. He saw him whip the tar out of 'em, tie their legs together. Sometimes punch 'em. Just hateful, and downright cruel," she said, shaking her head and pushing back some strands of hair. "He vowed he would never do that. He's always had a special place in his heart for horses."

Mr. Bucky stopped, rubbed Deuce's neck in long strokes before motioning to us.

"Hello, Mr. Bucky. We were just watching you. That was really cool!" I wished I had said something more profound.

"Yep." He rubbed Deuce's forehead which hung low, with heavy eyelids. "You ridin'?"

"Um, yes sir," I said, crossing my legs. Sometimes I felt a little nervous around him.

"Who you ridin'?"

Ms. Patsy smiled and shook her head. Took me a second to get Mr. Bucky's sense of humor.

"Spirit, sir."

"Figured."

Mr. Bucky made his way to the gate with Deuce walking behind him, without a halter or lead rope. We followed, but not too close.

"You two have fun. I'm off to run errands. Everything's locked up!" Ms. Patsy said, jingling her keys.

Mr. Bucky turned to me. "Time to tack 'em up."

"Yep," I said, giving a quick nod.

"Go get 'em," Mr. Bucky motioned with his head.

"You mean—?"

"Saddle and bridle, yep. The second one down from the top, right above Jubi's."

"So, I'm gonna—?"

"Tack him up. What you learned at camp. Here," he said, tossing me a lead rope, turning toward the paddock. "Let's go."

"Um, OK," I said, fumbling with the long rope. I restrained my desire to run after him.

"See him out there," he said, nodding his head toward Spirit.

"Yeah," I said, sighing. Just the sight of Spirit calmed me. His magnificent black mane glistened against his golden body. He was resting his back leg with his butt facing Jubi's face. Ebony stood off to the side.

"He's purdy good about comin'. So, call him."

"Spirit."

"Like you mean it. Ain't gonna come to that," he said, sucking through his teeth.

"Spirit!"

The sleepy equine lifted his head, pricked his ears forward, then shook his head, as if to say, "Nope."

"Dagnabbit. Here, try one of these." He reached into his pocket and pulled out three plastic-wrapped red-and-white round peppermints.

"Really?"

"Yup, loves 'em. Call him again."

"Here, Spirit," I said, crinkling the wrapper.

Pricking his ears forward again, Spirit gave a quick glance back at Jubi, then slowly lumbered toward me.

"Here he comes. Slower than molasses, but he's a' comin'. Heh, 'course Jubes is comin' too. Those two. Cast from the same mold."

I wasn't sure what that meant since I thought mold was something I was allergic to. I let it slide because of how thrilling it was to have these two large animals walking straight at us.

"Now, when he gets here, 'member flatten your hand. Don't wanna lose a finger."

"Are you riding Deuce?"

"Nope, he's done enough work today. I'll ride Jubi. Let them boys be together. Ebony is fine by himself." Throwing the lead rope around Spirit's neck, Mr. Bucky led Spirit out with Jubi following behind.

"Do we need a halter on them?"

"Nah, they'll be all right just standing here," he said, heading over to the tack area. Mr. Bucky rarely told me where he was going. I just had to follow.

Standing in front of the saddles hanging off on pegs from the wall, he said, "Spirit's stuff is right there. Grab his bridle. Hook it over the horn. I'll grab Jubi's stuff."

"Like this?"

"Lift the saddle off. Make sure the cinch and stirrups ain't draggin'."

"Oh, man," I grunted.

"Got it?"

"Yep." It took all my energy not to emit any straining sound.

"Saddle pad under your arm, like this," he said, with his back to me.

Waddling behind, I stopped momentarily to readjust, grateful that Spirit and Jubi weren't very far away.

Mr. Bucky turned around. "Make sure them stirrups don't—Here, don't let them drag," he said, folding them over the horn. Standing next to Spirit, I desperately wanted to pet him, but my hands were full and my arms were tiring from the saddle's weight.

"Always set the saddle on the ground, horn down. Could flatten out if you don't." He tossed it down like it weighed two pounds. "Gonna get the brush buckets."

I took a quick moment to pet Spirit, stroking his long neck. Ms. Patsy taught me to gently breathe into his nostrils as a way of identifying myself. He blew out and his soft eyes and cocked back hoof told me he liked it. Mr. Bucky handed me a bucket with a curry comb, brush, hoof pick, and other items in it.

"Curry him down. Then brush him."

Moving the curry comb in circular motions like I learned from camp made Spirit's back twitch. His ears darted around as his calmness seemed to fade.

"He don't much like the curry," Mr. Bucky said, currying Jubi. "Gentle."

"Sorry, boy," I said, lightening my touch. "I'll do it softer, then I'll use the brush, OK?" I'm not sure if Spirit understood me, but I just pretended English was his first language.

"Gonna get Jubi set up, then I'll show you," Mr. Bucky said.

As I used the soft grooming brush, Spirit lowered his head. Watching his bottom lip quiver relaxed me. It was as though there was a forcefield around him that sucked me in. Every part of my spirit just wanted to be near his. Madonna's song, "Angel" came to mind.

"Lift up his feet and pick out the crud in there." Mr. Bucky's words startled me from my meditative state. "Careful of the frog." I couldn't believe how well Spirit lifted his legs.

"Now, the saddle pad. Put it here on the withers, slide it down a bit," he said adjusting it. "Before puttin' on the saddle, throw the stirrup up on the horn. Gently place down on his back. Walk around to the other side so the saddle lines up with the pad."

"Looks good over here," I said.

"Bring the cinch down, just let it dangle. Don't want right in his armpit. Roughly a hand behind so he don't get sores. Walk back around.

Making my way back around to the other side, I forgot one thing.

"Always keep your hand on his rump," Mr. Bucky reminded.

Yep, that was it. I knew it. Just got excited.

"Reach underneath, grab the cinch and pull it through the D ring. Pull the strap snug a few times, wrapping it around and keeping it flat."

"Is this right?"

"Yep," he grunted. "Last thing you do, slide your fingers between his barrel and the cinch. Should wiggle a little bit. Not too much. Tight, but not too tight," he said, demonstrating. "Always check it before you get on. Want to make sure he can breathe but not so loose you'll be looking at the underside of his barrel."

I giggled, which seemed to momentarily break Mr. Bucky's focused face.

"Like this?" I said, pulling the cinch snug.

"That'll do it."

That's about as good a compliment as I'd get from Mr. Bucky.

"With the bridle, put your right arm around his neck, hand on his poll." Stretching onto my tippy toes to reach between his ears, I remembered they showed us at camp, but I never really did it myself. Bridling a horse always made me a little nervous.

"Take your middle finger and thumb. Guide the bit into his mouth from behind his cheek."

Although I wasn't jumping up and down to do this, Spirit's tiny whiskers on his muzzle endeared me.

"He's purdy good at takin' it. There, gentle now. Don't wanna knock the teeth," he said, slipping his hand over mine. I almost had the correct motions.

"There, OK. Let's git goin'," he said, mounting Jubi.

Grabbing Spirit's reins, I placed my left foot into the stirrup, hopping on my right for momentum. Nestling down into the saddle, I was grateful the stirrups fit. I told myself that was because I was the only one who rides him.

*E*ven though there was less talking when riding with Mr. Bucky than with Ms. Patsy, I reveled in the fact that I had tacked Spirit myself. Well, almost. I was thrilled that we cantered a few times, and I stayed on. Guess I got the cinch tight enough after all. As usual, the music from the Black Stallion played in my head as the image of Ruffian running her races came to mind. Spirit's spirited gaits sometimes made it difficult because he moved faster than Jubi, particularly on the way back to the barn.

"Now, don't let him go too fast. Always walk 'em back," Mr. Bucky said. "Don't want 'em gettin' barn sour."

I understood that to mean they didn't want to leave the barn. Sometimes I'd rather just stay at home, too.

Ms. Patsy was back from her errands when we returned.

"How'd you do?" she asked, reaching out for Spirit's bridle.

"Done good," Mr. Bucky said. Again, high praise indeed.

"We had so much fun—cantered and everything!"

"Possible gallop from this one here," Mr. Bucky said, motioning to me before dismounting.

Ms. Patsy mirrored my sheepish grin.

"I tacked them by myself. I mean, Mr. Bucky helped me, but he walked me through it!"

"Now you're a pro," Ms. Patsy said, smiling as I dismounted.

"Yeah, Spirit is the best horse ever." I couldn't stop petting his beautiful, muscular neck.

"He's pretty great," she said, scratching his forehead. "Now, loosen his saddle, go water him, and take everything off."

"Yes, ma'am, Ms. Patsy!"

Spirit gulped a few times from the water trough, looked around, then dove his head down again. I enjoyed watching his ears wiggle as he slurped. After his drink break, I slid his saddle off, and the weight of the monstrosity came screaming back to me. As I waddled back to the tack room, Spirit shook his entire body in contentment. When I came back for a final pet, he tried to gum me on the cheek with his lips. Scrunching up my shoulder in a weak attempt to block him, I squealed. It was amazing what they could do with their lips, since they're the closest things to fingers that they have. Must be frustrating, though. I stood in front of him, petting a small swirly cowlick between his eyes.

"Remember, Spirit here can't see you too well when you're directly in front of him," Ms. Patsy said, shaking me out of the Spirit-induced relaxation. "Yep, eyes on either side of his face. Because horses are 'prey' animals."

"Pray?" I asked, bringing my hands together.

"No, prey. As in predator-prey. Humans are predators, so we have our eyes on the front of our heads. Prey animals have eyes on the sides, so they can see predators coming."

"Wow," I said, craning my neck to get a closer look at his eye. "Yeah, they did say that at camp."

"Like rabbits, horses will always scan their environment looking for threats."

I could relate. I feel as if I'm always looking around to see who is safe and nice and who isn't.

"And, horses have one even better. They have the largest eyes of any land mammals. That's why they spook. Tryin' to get away. Sometimes they'll fight, but their greater instinct is to run. As herd animals, there is strength in numbers. But even if they like to be by themselves, they want to at least keep an eye on a buddy to feel safe. One big eye, I might add!"

I sure knew what it meant to not have a buddy and its importance.

"One other thing," she continued. "Don't slap them on the side of their neck. It feels like they're being hit. Rub on 'em instead. That feels good. Or, even tiny scratching. Have you ever seen them when they're standing facing each other and look like they're biting each other's necks? That's mutual grooming. They're saying, 'You get my itch and I'll get yours.'"

Another sense of calm washed over me as I gazed into Spirit's big, brown eyes with curly long lashes. It's as though Ms. Patsy pulled back a veil, giving me even greater insights into Spirit's world. She was sharing things Spirit, and other horses, wished people would know. The strange thing was, in many ways, it wasn't that different from mine.

PART
Three

<u>June 8, 1988</u>

I'm sooo ready to be done with Garner Junior High. But am excited <u>and</u> scared to start High School. No more lunch and stupid kids! They should be more mature in high school. I'm so sad to leave Mrs. Gardner. She is the nicest and prettiest teacher I know. She gave me a horse calendar that covers 1988 and 1989. And she said that she would be at my graduation in three years! I will miss her so much. But bye, bye, junior high—won't miss you at all!

<u>June 15, 1988</u>

I was really excited about summer since it used to be my favorite season, but I really miss Marin. I'm not sure what to do. I'm too old to go to Echo Lake as a camper this summer but I'm too young for my driver's license. Too old for one thing, too young for another.

Sometimes at night, thoughts of Ruffian haunt me. I sit up in bed, trying to get the image of her breaking *down and in pain out of my mind. During the day, it's easier for me to think about her winning her races, leaving all the other fillies in the dust. But sometimes at night, her death haunts me. Also wish I wouldn't eat so much, especially since my jeans are a little tighter again. Luckily, it's shorts weather so I'll just wear my stretchy ones. Can't wait to get my Driver's Permit though. I went to the YMCA's pool with Mama and CJ for his swimming lesson. He's just so cute playing in the water.*

June 28, 1988

I know Mama is trying to help me, but I just don't know.

Celebrating the new technological addition to our living room, I sat in the Lazy Boy chair, with my legs dangling off the side. My feet moved in time with every crunch of the potato chips I plucked from the large bowl on my lap. After watching the taped "Grab That Dough" episode of *The Golden Girls* for the fifth time, I laughed in all the same places and learned some new things. I marveled at how beautiful their house was, especially since I didn't see many houses decorated in wicker in North Carolina. Every episode enthralled me, particularly seeing the ladies' beautiful clothes, pajamas, and robes. My pink horse pajama top with the tiny hole and small stains and pink jogging pants were no match for their wardrobe.

Dorothy used the word "svelte" in one episode so I looked it up in the dictionary. It means "slender" or "elegant." I longed to feel that way. But at that time, my main activity consisted of extreme TV and VCR watching, accompanied by excessive eating. Tearing through potato chips and chocolate chips straight from the bags certainly did not make me feel svelte. However, I eventually used some of my allowance to buy a long, pink nightgown at Kmart.

Slipping into the nightie did make me feel more beautiful. Svelte, I guess.

In addition to my *The Golden Girls* viewing marathons, *The Muppets Take Manhattan* movie took a close second. Watching Kermit, Fozzie and the rest of the gang's antics always relaxed me. I saved *The Black Stallion* movie Aunt Mimi got me for the rare occasion when everyone else was gone. I didn't want them to see me crying.

Rewinding *The Muppets Take Manhattan* to the beginning from my last viewing, I picked up my half-eaten potato chip bowl and sat sideways on the chair.

"How goes it?" Mama asked, joining me in the living room.

"OK," I mumbled.

"Listen, Baby. I wanted to talk to you," she said, coming into my view.

I wished she had waited until the movie was over, but I got up and stopped the VCR since the remote wasn't working. "What?" I asked, plopping back down.

"Have you thought about volunteering or getting a job somewhere?"

"No, not really," I said, crunching on the remaining chips.

"Because either of those might help you to…Well, they might help you."

She didn't want to mention Marin's name, but we both knew what she meant.

"I don't know. Like, where would I go? What would I do?"

"Well," she said, sitting down on the loveseat. "You could try an animal shelter. Or, what about the place you ride?"

"Fair Oaks."

"Yeah, what about there?"

"Well, what if my allergies come back—really bad?"

"They're getting better with the shots and medication, right?" she asked.

"I guess, but riding horses is a lot different than actually taking care of them," I said, playing with the sides of the bowl.

"That's true."

"I mean, what if, once school starts, they can't work around my schedule. Or, my choir concerts. And, how would I get there?"

"I could take you. Or, Daddy Clint could."

I guffawed. "You really think Clint...er, I mean, *Daddy* Clint would do that?"

"Sometimes, if he knew ahead of time. When you get your driver's license, you could borrow the car."

"I cannot wait until then. Not much longer," I said, swirling my finger around the bottom of an almost empty bowl. "But, what if, you know, she shows up there."

"Then she'll see how lucky you are to work there. Also, wasn't there a horse there that you really liked?"

My face softened. "Spirit. He's the best horse ever."

"You could see him more. I know that would make you happy."

"Yeah, definitely. But, what do I say? 'Hi, Mr. Bucky and Ms. Patsy. I want a job'?" I set the bowl on the coffee table.

She laughed.

"Mama—I'm serious. What would I say?"

"Say that you've been going there for a while, and that you'd like to work there. I'm sure they know you."

That's what I was afraid of. It's weird, but sometimes it's easier for me to talk to a stranger than someone I really know. If they said "No," I wouldn't want to go back. Then, I could never see Spirit again.

"I'll take you and you can ask. Try it for a little bit and see," she said, walking into the kitchen.

"We'll see." I got up and turned the movie back on to watch Kermit and his buddies' shenanigans again.

June 30, 1988

After thinking about it a lot, I'm actually going to ask Mr. Bucky and Ms. Patsy! I am sooooo nervous. Please let them say "Yes"! I could have the job of my dreams!

The crackling gravel under Mama's tires and the Fair Oaks sign created anxiety instead of the usual excitement.

"Good luck, Baby. I'll be here waiting," Mama said, as I hopped out of the car.

Surveying the property for some sign of human life, I met Dodger and Moose who greeted me with excited barks. Dodger sniffed me with his usual inquisitive nose, while Moose stayed a little more distant. "Hey guys, have you seen Ms. Patsy or Mr. Bucky?" My eyes landed on Spirit and Jubi in the paddock and I felt a wave of confidence. The horses reminded me of why I was there.

Seeing a moving silhouette in the barn, I took a deep breath and marched in with two dogs following right behind.

Mr. Bucky was cleaning out Jubi's stall. His low-lying cowboy hat almost completely covered his white hair and mustache.

"Miss," he said, tipping his hat up. "You ridin' today?" The two dogs decided we weren't that interesting and left.

"Good afternoon, Mr. Bucky," I said, clearing my throat. "Well, actually, no."

"Where's your little friend?" he asked, scooping up a pile.

"She's not coming." I didn't know what to do with my hands.

"Ah," he said, wiping his brow and adjusting his hat. "What can I do you for?"

"Well, I was hoping…"

He stopped scooping to look over at me, grimacing his face.

I cleared my throat again. "I was hoping…"

"Spit it out."

"I was looking for a job, and was wondering if you needed any help around here." My words seemed to hang thick in the air.

"Huh. I think that'd be all right," he said, straightening his back. "'Specially since Sherry moved away."

"Thank you!" I didn't think it would be that easy. And, I can't say I was sad to hear Sherry was gone.

"Pays $4.00 an hour. You'll do the chores. Keep track of your hours and lemme know when you're here. Think you're up for it?"

"Yes, sir!"

"Reckon you'll want to ride either Spirit or Jubi."

"Yes, please. That would be great!" I tried to hide my enthusiasm, failing as usual.

He smiled. "Ride them when you want. But, first, clean out the stalls. Shovel into the cart and dump it outside," he said, motioning to a wheelbarrow in the corner. "You can start now," he said, handing me the shovel. "Lemme know when you're done. I'll tell you what to do next," he said, walking away.

I looked around, taking in the excitement of my new job.

Ms. Patsy came into the barn with Moose at her side and peeked into my stall.

"What ya doing here, Sugar? The Old Man gotcha workin'?"

"Yeah, I'm working here now! But only if it's OK."

"Of course," she chuckled. "With his bad back and my sciatica, and Sherry in South Carolina for school, we could use an extra hand around here."

"Thanks, Ms. Patsy."

"I know that Spirit and Jubi will be happier than a tick on a fat dog with you here. I'm not talkin' about you," she said, petting Moose's head. "Where's your friend?"

"Um, well, she's not coming."

"Today?"

"Yeah, and maybe probably not ever. I dunno," I said, my voice trailing.

She cocked her head. "You two have a falling out?"

"Guess you can call it that. She just, well, stopped talking to me, so…"

"That can happen. That's why I sometimes prefer animals to people. Don't let her ruffle your feathers." She patted the side of the stall. "Now, then, carry on," she said, walking out of the barn, Moose lumbering behind. "Welcome aboard!"

"Thanks!" Looking down at the heaping piles, I smiled.

Ms. Patsy poked her head back in the barn. "Sugar, is that your mama out there in the car?"

"Oh, my gosh, I forgot to tell her!"

<u>July 1, 1988</u>

Today is my first FULL day of work! I'm can't believe I'm really going to be around horses and especially my Spirit! I miss Marin, but I now have my dream job. Just me and the horses, dogs, cats, goats, and chickens. Not too shabby! This summer is turning out so much better than I thought it would!

Driving up the winding gravel road, all the butterflies of excitement returned. This time I was going there as an employee. I wasn't only excited, but a little nervous so they were more like caterpillars.

"Baby, have fun—again!" Mama said, shifting the car into park. "Just call when you're done."

"I will!" Again, every fiber of my being wanted to sprint to Spirit.

The welcoming committee consisted of Mr. Bucky, Ms. Patsy, Moose, and Dodger.

"Hey there, Sugar," Ms. Patsy said. She signaled to Mama that all was well.

"Miss," Mr. Bucky tipped his hat.

"Ready for this?" she asked.

"Yes, sir and ma'am!"

"Now then," she said, clapping her hands together as we moved toward the trough. "We'll start with water first." Mr. Bucky took off in the other direction without a word, but that was to be expected. "You can leave the hose on while you do things. But and this is a *big* but, keep an eye on it and do *not* forget to shut it off once the trough is full. Learned that the hard way. I've never run so fast as when I forgot and came back to the water bubbling over the sides, forming lakes on the ground!"

I could just picture all the horses standing around, wondering what to do.

"First thing's first, always make sure they have round bales at all times," she said on the way to the barn's food area. "Jubi, Beau, Frosty, Shadow, Ebony, and Kiwi are all easy-keepers, which means they don't need a lot to eat. They get the hay, the salt block, and a little bit of grain. They shouldn't graze as much, either. Deuce and Lady Bird are fed first. This order is important. They also get soaked alfalfa cubes and some soaked beet pulp shreds. They're both right here," she said, slightly lifting the bags. "They need to be fed separately from the others, as well as away from each other. They're both hard keepers, which means sometimes it's harder to keep weight on them. They're hard keepers and hard-headed!"

"Spirit is a hard keeper, too, but not hard-headed. Make sure he gets soaked alfalfa cubes and beet pulp shreds. Then some magnesium supplements and flaxseed," she said, touching the tops of the canisters on the shelf.

"Little Bit will eat as much, or more, than she should. Gotta watch her. Make sure she doesn't get any grain. She's little, but mighty," Ms. Patsy said, giving me a wink.

"Now this is important. They always eat on the ground. Good for their digestion. Not good for them if they eat too high. And, here," she said, handing me a pitchfork. "You'll need to muck the stalls."

"Muck?"

"Yeah, what you did before. Get rid of the horse crap. Also, make sure to give Penguin and his friends some of the Meow Mix. It supplements the mice they catch. We feed the dogs inside, so they're good. Dodger, here, will act as if he hasn't eaten in days, but don't let him fool you."

He looked up at her with his big, innocent, brown eyes and tilted his head.

"The goats get their hay, as well as a cup of grain every day," she said, directing me to their bag of feed. "Make sure they don't get more. They, too, will act as if they haven't eaten in weeks. Chickens will get scraps from our food and some feed, but we'll usually take care of them. Like today, they've already been fed. You'll also need to turn everyone out and bring them in as needed." She paused. "Any questions?"

"No, ma'am."

"We'll be in the house if you need us. We'll be by in a little bit. C'mon Dodger and Moose!"

It all seemed so daunting. But when I realized Ms. Patsy, Mr. Bucky, the horses, and all the animals counted on me, ironically it put my mind at ease. The soft noises in the barn were soothing: the running fans, the random nickering from horses. Once I got into a rhythm, my mind wandered and relaxed. I snapped back into reality when I realized how much Spirit and the others horses poop. The occasional farting also made me laugh.

After I finished the chores, I set the pitchfork against the wall when Ms. Patsy and Mr. Bucky returned to the barn.

Standing at the entrance, Ms. Patsy said, "Everything looks really good."

"Yup, real good," Mr. Bucky repeated.

"Do you want to see?" I asked.

"Sure," she said. We walked down the middle of the barn, peeking into the stalls. "Everyone good and happy. Stalls look good."

"And, here's my big guy," I said, opening Spirit's stall door. I reached out to scratch his neck and particularly enjoyed watching him eat, especially with a sprig of hay poking out from his muzzle.

"Let's see what we got here," Ms. Patsy said, craning her neck into the stall. Mr. Bucky stood right behind her.

"You did a great job with—"

But before she could finish her sentence, Spirit's tail raised up. Three large poop balls shot out, splattering on the ground.

Both of them erupted into laughter.

"He approves!" she said.

My face fell. "Oh, man."

"Oh, Ms. Maren," Ms. Patsy said, clutching her chest. "Don't you worry now. Stalls simply don't stay clean. It's just their nature."

At least I got their approval before Spirit gave me his.

July 10, 1988

I'm so excited! For my 15th birthday, I finally got my Driver's Permit! I still have to get my driving hours in and drive with an adult, but I'm on my way to freedom! I wonder what they do in other places, like Australia and England and Ireland? Do they go through what we do and do they get just as excited? I like thinking about other countries.

I wonder what Daddy is up to. Hoping he and the kitties are doing OK. It's like want to know how he's doing without him knowing I know. Wonder what Marin is doing, too. It's crazy that the summer started out pretty hard, but ending up awesome!

August 15, 1988

I am so nervous to go to Garner High School. Can't believe I'll be in the 10th grade! I miss Mrs. Gardner so much. I wonder if I can stop by to see her? It will be weird going from being the oldest in the school to the youngest. In junior high, I hated that Marin and I didn't have classes together, but now I don't want to see her at all.

September 7, 1988

School is really cool! It's so much bigger than junior high. I'm super happy that I don't have lunch with Marin or any classes together. Hope that continues until we graduate. I did see her on the other side of the hallway, but pretended I didn't. I'm just glad that our paths are going in different directions.

Lacey and I are at the same school again, but our classes are definitely not the same. Good news, bad news. I'm closer to getting my license, but bad news, once I get it, I have to share the car with her. I usually take the bus back and forth to school, but if I want, I can ride to school with her and then take the bus home. Sometimes it's just worth it to take the bus there and back. It's not all bad. Lacey gets the car because she's older, has her license, and has a job that she gets school credit for. I can't wait until Lacey is gone.

My locker acts weird sometimes, but luckily everyone has their own. Choir is going to be so much fun! I love that I have it first period and I love our teacher, Mrs. Darbinyan. She had to help us pronounce her name, since there aren't many Darbinyans in Garner. She's from Armenia and I am even happier that it means blacksmith in Armenian. Even my choir teacher's name is associated with horses!

There is a guy named Dustin Roberts in choir who had us all laughing. He's got a great bass voice, is kinda cute, and is hilarious! He's a bigger guy, bigger than Jake Creech or Matty Williams. Not fat, just solid. I can relate. He played football in junior high and I think he also plays with his friends. I'm pretty sure Brandi Lee in choir likes him, though.

There's a really nice guy named Jordan in choir too. He's super funny and knows so much about theater, movies, and music. He also acts in the plays and musicals at school. I ate lunch with him and a few other girls from choir. New people aren't the same as old friends but they seem pretty cool. Sometimes I really miss Marin and then other times I am so glad she's not around. I'm still eating more than I should and I'm still having trouble sleeping. But I got new jeans when we went school shopping, so things at least look a little better.

That morning before the first bell rang, Dustin's natural charm drew a few people to him.

"Then, I lit all the sparklers at once and totally burned my hand!" he laughed, emitting a strange honking noise when he did.

All of our mouths opened in surprise.

"You did?" Brandi asked, shining a coy smile.

We weren't sure whether to laugh or ask if he was OK, but he nodded and honked again.

"You honk when you laugh!" I said.

"Do I really?" Dustin asked. "Do (honk) I (honk) really?" I could hardly catch my breath from laughing so hard. He wrapped his arm around me as I doubled over, which felt really nice. The first bell rang and we all found our seats.

"OK, then. Hope everyone's doing well. Let's start on C," Mrs. Darbinyan said, walking over to the piano. Although I wasn't a fashionista, her clothing was always super cool and classy. But, in a different way than Mrs. Gardner. She didn't look like any other older adult I had seen. Her big brown eyes and shiny brownish hair complimented her soothing speaking and singing voice.

Choir was going to be the next best thing to horses.

September 19, 1988

I just don't get this family I'm stuck with.

The plan was to meet at the car in the parking lot after school since Lacey didn't have to work that day. As I waited for her, I talked with Angela, a fellow classmate, about the horrors of chemistry. It was a class that was kicking both of our butts. When Lacey finally emerged from the school's exit doors, she was laughing with two other girls. I'm not sure who they were, except they wore cheerleading uniforms and they weren't Duffy Palmer or Rachel Mellin. They headed toward their respective cars and Lacey sauntered towards us.

"You know Lacey Fletcher?" Angela asked.

"Yeah, she's my *step*sister."

"Wow. Isn't she the captain of the cheerleading team?"

"Yeah, she doesn't let me forget it either," I said, giving Lacey a quick nod.

"Let's go," Lacey said, passing by me, barely giving me eye contact.

"Thanks, Angie. See you tomorrow," I said, getting into the car.

I worked hard to bite my tongue when Lacey drove. But when she turned on the ignition, the radio immediately kicked on, blasting a song. The decibel level involuntarily forced me to reach for the radio dial and yell, "Dang, turn that down!"

"Just leave it!" she said. "I want to get outta here. Jamie is waiting for me." She turned the radio dial down one level.

The song was still up so loud, I couldn't even identify it. Half expecting to see blood trickle out of my ears, I pressed my face against the window, replaying *The Black Stallion* music in my head.

Putting the car into reverse, Lacey pressed down on the gas pedal.

A loud thud jolted the car.

"What was that?" I asked, snapping my head around.

"Dammit!" she yelled, peeking into the rearview mirror. "Stupid car!"

I craned my neck out the back window. My stomach fell when I saw Angela standing next to her car with her hands over her mouth.

"Oh, my god, Angela!" I said, throwing open the car door and sprinting over to her. "So, so sorry!"

Lacey rolled down her window and yelled out, "What does it look like?"

Angela and I crouched over, running our fingers up and down the bumper. In a fortunate twist to an unfortunate event, Lacey hit Angela's car straight on resulting in a tiny, almost imperceptible scratch.

"Looks OK. Can't really tell anything happened," I said, shaking my head.

"Good. Sorry," Lacey said. She gave a slight wave to Angela then rolled her window back up.

"I am so sorry. She is such an idiot."

"It's fine," Angela said. "Don't worry about it. Can't see anything anyway."

Angela walked by Lacey's window, "No big deal. Bye Lacey! See you tomorrow, Maren."

"Bye, Angela," I groaned.

Lacey flashed a weak smile in response.

"Well, that sucked," I said, sliding back into the front seat, buckling my seatbelt.

"Calm down. It's not that bad."

"Just didn't feel like getting into a fender bender today."

"You think I did? God, it's not always about you," she said.

I snapped my head around. "What is *wrong* with you?"

"Not that it's any of your damn business, but Chad broke up with me today."

"Sorry," I murmured.

"Yeah. Let's get the hell out of here so I can get to Jamie's."

Never had I been happier to live only a few miles from school than after that tense and silent drive home. It didn't help that when we arrived, Clint and Mama were smiling and embracing in the kitchen. Fortunately, they didn't do it too much, but seeing two old people do that was more than I wanted to see. Especially those two.

"Hey y'all, how was your day?" Mama asked, as Clint patted her butt.

"Clint!" she squealed and smiled.

I rolled my eyes.

"Fine," Lacey said.

"Maren, did you get what you needed for your speech class?" Mama asked.

"Yeah, but I think I forgot to bring my math book home."

"Maren's always forgetting things," Lacey said.

I shot her a look. "Well, I was talking with Angela from Chemistry class and was so focused on that, I forgot to bring my math book home."

"Do you need it tonight?" Mama asked.

"Nah, can get it tomorrow," I said.

"How's the gas for the car?" Clint asked.

"Should be OK," Lacey said.

"Be sure to keep it at least half-way full," he said, for the millionth time.

"Maren said she would fill it up, but she didn't. So, I went ahead and did it."

Cocking my head at her audacity, I was speechless.

"Maren, you really are forgetful, aren't cha?" Clint asked.

His comment was the straw that broke the poor camel's back.

"Lacey was backing up and hit my friend Angela's car in the parking lot!" I blurted.

"Are you all right?" Clint asked. "How is the car?"

"Everything's fine, Daddy. The car has like, nothing on the bumper," Lacey said. "Thanks for being a tattletale," she hissed at me.

"I'm not. I'm just saying it was *really* embarrassing."

"Well, her car was in the way!"

"She was still in her parking spot!" I argued. "She didn't have to move—you were supposed to!"

"How was I supposed to know?"

"You take a minute to adjust your mirrors and look around! That was taught like the first day of driver's ed. Doy!" I said, pointing a finger to my head, making the appropriate noise.

"All right, Maren, we get the picture," Clint said. "Let's see."

Following Clint to the garage, he crouched over the bumper. Licking his thumb, he rubbed the tiny scratch.

"Yeah, that's nothing," he said, groaning when he straightened back up.

"Yeah, but…?" I asked.

"But, what?" Clint asked, as we all returned to the kitchen.

"I mean, doesn't she get anything for this?" I turned to Mama for support, who looked down, slowly shaking her head.

"There wasn't any damage. And, it won't happen again, right?" Clint asked.

"No, sir," Lacey said.

"Sir." She only said that when she's trying to act innocent.

"Oh, my god! I cannot believe this."

"It's partly your fault, you know," Clint said, pointing at me.

"How is it *my* fault?"

"Because you keep talking about it and bringing it up."

I looked at him in disbelief.

"Mama?"

"Baby…" Mama said, averting her eyes.

Well, that told me everything. Shaking my head, I stomped to my room, slamming the door behind me. I didn't care if Clint came and yelled at me. I just could not wait until that "B" graduated and went God-knows-where. I couldn't give a flying-flip where just as long as it was as far away from me as possible. She could take everyone with her, too. Except for CJ. I'd take him with me. And, sometimes Mama—but not now.

Reaching deep into my closet where my secret stash of Doritos resided, I crunched on a chip and rummaged through my cassette mix tapes. After finding the perfect one, I cranked up the volume on "My Prerogative" by Bobby Brown, knowing that Erasure's "Give A Little Respect" and Johnny Hates Jazz's "Shattered Dreams" were up next. If anyone came and told me to turn it down, I didn't hear them. Or pretended not to.

November 7, 1988

I've tried to forget what happened a few months ago. It's obvious to me where everyone stands in this family and they aren't going to change. I tried to focus on my breath, like Aunt Mimi taught me. I just love my aunt more and more. Hallomas was fun this year. I just wish she could stay for actual Halloween night.

I dressed up as a witch for trick-or-treating, which I think Lacey should have been. It would have been more accurate. My head and belly hurt from eating waaayyy too much of my candy way too quickly, but I may have a new little buddy!

Sitting in the Lazy Boy, watching another taped *The Golden Girls* episode, I patted my protruding belly just as CJ barged through the front door.

"Sister, we found this!"

"What is it?" I rushed from the chair to the foyer where he and one of the neighborhood kids were standing. Something furry was wiggling in his hands.

It was a tiny tabby kitten.

"Where did you find her? Or him?"

"We found him underneath a tree over there," CJ's accomplice said.

"Where?"

"By that one person's house in the woods," the boy continued.

"Oh my gosh, he's the cutest thing I've seen!" I said, turning the kitten over. "But I'm thinking it's a little girl. Because I'm not seeing any, well, ..." CJ's eyes were as big as saucers. "Let's just say I think it's a little girl. But, you know, we can't keep her. Mama and Clint would never go for it."

"Aww," CJ said, shoulders slumping.

"Can you keep her?" I asked his friend.

"No, we already have too many. No way my mama would let me. I have to get home. Bye, CJ!"

The kitten nestled into the crook in my neck, purring in time with the wheels turning in my mind. My belly and head suddenly felt a little better.

"Hmm … let me think about this," I said, holding the snuggling fur ball next to my neck. Examining the backyard through the living room window, I had an idea.

"C'mon." Holding the kitten to my neck with one hand and leading my brother with the other, we walked to the treehouse in the backyard Clint had built for CJ. Climbing up the ladder, we crawled inside and I placed the wiggly kitten in the middle.

"Now I need you to do something for me, CJ. Make sure she stays right here. Don't let her jump down. OK?"

CJ nodded.

"I'm going to run and get some food and water."

Sprinting from the backyard to the kitchen, I grabbed a bowl of water and opened a can of tuna. Mama's famous casserole would just need to include less tuna next time. Grabbing a tattered towel from the bottom of the linen closet, I returned to CJ and the kitten. He sat giggling with her tucked under his chin.

"Aww, she loves you, CJ. Here, let's give her something to eat and drink. I'm sure she's hungry."

The kitten initially protested after leaving the warmth of CJ's chin, but gobbled up the tuna presented in front of her. Her slurping sounds made my heart melt. She was so grateful for so little. I thought about Jelly Bean and Brownie, the kitties I had when I was around CJ's age.

"Mama and Clint—Daddy Clint—will be home soon," I said, looking at my watch. "So, you go back in the house. I'll be there in a minute."

He climbed down the ladder and ran in through the garage door.

Swirling the towel around on the ground, I placed the kitten in the middle. "Now you stay there, Little One." She lapped up the water and probably didn't appreciate my petting her while she did so. I picked up the towel and placed her as far away from the tree-house entrance as possible.

"Be good, Little One. I'll be back later."

Please stay up here and don't leave.

Mama was in the kitchen, bringing in paper bags of groceries when I arrived. CJ stood nearby.

"Maren Theresa Markey. And, how was *your* day?" she asked, with one hand on her hip.

Uh-oh. My full name. I guess five-year-olds aren't known for keeping quiet.

"Um…good?" I said, grimacing my face.

"You know Daddy Clint won't approve."

"I know. We know."

"Someone might be looking for her. She needs to go back to where you found her."

"But CJ and his friend found her in the woods."

"Yeah, Mama!" CJ said. "All by herself."

"So, put her back."

"But, she's not safe out there alone," I protested.

"Where is she now?"

"In back. In CJ's treehouse."

"Yeah, my tweehouse!"

"That's not good for her. Try and find another place as soon as you can. Ask around," she said, reaching into a grocery bag.

"OK, Mama. I will."

Except that I didn't.

Since I had saved some money from Aunt Mimi and my job at Fair Oaks, I rode my bike to the Piggly Wiggly to get Kitten Chow, a small litter box, and a bag of litter. My ride home was a balancing act with the bag handles looped over the handlebars. I kept the opened litter bag in the back of my closet. That served two purposes: not only did it hide the litter, but was a deterrent from eating the opened bag next to it.

The perfect time for visiting hours in the treehouse was when

Mama and Clint were at work. Neither of them ever went back there and it was hidden behind some large oak trees. Their schedule was home, work, errands, sleep, and then start all over the next day.

A few days later, Poison's "Every Rose Has Its Thorn" served as the background to my studies when Mama knocked on my bedroom door.

"Hey, Mama! How are you?" I chirped, turning down the music.

She had that look of disappointment I rarely saw but tried to avoid. "You know—we can't keep her."

My heart fell.

"Who?" I knew my feigned ignorance wouldn't work. "I know, but she's so cute and so sweet."

"I know," Mama sighed. She seemed particularly tired.

"And, she loves to play, especially with strings. She bats at them, like this," I said, pawing at the air.

Mama studied me for a moment. "Well, I guess you could talk with Daddy Clint and ask him."

"*I* have to ask him?"

"Yes, tell him all the reasons you want to keep her and that you'll take care of her."

"Why do I have to?"

"Because *you* want her. Sometimes, if you really want something in life, you have to ask."

I tightened my mouth.

"Tell him why it would be good for CJ. And, don't forget to be positive."

"Guess I could." I wondered why Mama couldn't talk to him for me.

Clint always seemed so distant, practically living on a different planet. The next day, after practicing my speech numerous times in the mirror, I mustered the courage to talk to him. Waiting for the right time when no one was around, I approached him in the living room while he read the newspaper.

"Hi, Daddy Clint," I said, as cheerfully as I could, calling him something I never did unless Mama was around.

"Hey," he said, turning the page without eye contact. "What do you need?"

"Well, I was wondering...I was wondering..." I took a deep breath. "You probably know about the kitten."

"Yep, sure do," he said, glancing at me over the top of the newspaper.

"Well, I was wondering if we could keep her."

He folded the newspaper in half and set it on the table. "Now why would we do that?"

"Because I could take care of her. I can get food and a litter box for her. I would take care of her. You know, getting food and litter for her."

I'm repeating myself. This wasn't how I practiced it.

"I thought CJ found her with one of his friends?"

"Well, they did. But I can still take care of her."

He stared at me. Feeling my face flush and sweat form on my forehead, it was like he could see right through me.

"And I can take her to the vet and stuff," I added, clearing my throat. I averted my gaze, but it seemed as if he never blinked.

"And it would be good for CJ," I added.

"Well, I guess then."

"Thank you, Daddy Clint!" I bent over and gave him an awkward hug.

"But it would be CJ's cat, not yours."

"Um, OK." The jubilation quickly fizzled.

"What are you going to call her?" he asked.

"I liked the name Raisin. Or, Cinnamon. But whatever everyone wants."

"I think CJ was calling her 'Katie.'"

"OK, 'Katie' works," I said, repeating that name silently and getting lost in my thoughts.

"Then, Katie it is," he said, snapping me out of it. Better get her out of his treehouse."

My heart was simultaneously excited and broken. Katie wasn't a horse, but at least we got a kitten. Clarification—CJ got a kitten.

It sure was a lot easier at Daddy's to get a new pet.

December 29, 1988

This Christmas was the best! Every time I sing "Jingle Bells," I love the line, "Making SPIRITS bright!" My Spirit has his own line in a song! And, it was entertaining to watch Katie Kitty climb our Christmas tree and play with the wrapping paper everywhere. She is so cute! I laughed the most because not everyone was laughing. Mama finally put the Christmas tree in CJ's old playpen she still had. I still think about Jelly Bean and Brownie and about Morris and Rosie at Daddy's. But I'm glad we stayed home for Christmas because Katie is so much fun.

January 2, 1989

Winters usually are hard, but it's so much better having Katie here. She snuggles on my lap when I sit in the living room and sometimes she even sleeps in my bed. She likes CJ, but she definitely favors me. Thank God for my allergy shots since they really have helped. So glad to have this little ball of fluff in our life, even if she's not technically mine.

March 26, 1989

It was fun to celebrate Easter this year in a different way, even if not everyone was in a good mood.

That Easter, Mama and Clint took us to the Easter Egg Hunt at Pullen Park in Raleigh. Mama said it was Clint's idea, since he apparently loved Easter egg hunts when he was little. It was hard to imagine him really enjoying anything. True to form, he was even cranky on this day, complaining about everyone not being ready to go, not enough parking, and things not being marked well enough. Lacey decided not to partake. Fine with me. One grump was enough.

We all dressed in our Easter best. Mama was so pretty in her light-blue flowery dress and I wore my short-sleeved, peachy dress with the drop-waist and my small white heels. I think Clint wore his tan suit. But the best dressed was CJ, not only from our family, but of all the children there. He wore his tiny light-blue blazer, matching shorts and bowtie and his socks almost reached his knees. I don't remember him ever looking more adorable than on that day.

Well-dressed parents and children buzzed around the Park in their Sunday best as a white Easter Bunny mascot made his rounds.

There were three different Easter egg hunts: one for toddlers, one for four to six-year-olds, and one for seven on up. The one for the toddlers essentially had the eggs out in plain view, with each group's hunts becoming more advanced.

After we received our empty baskets and found the area for his age group, we lined up next to the starting line.

"OK, CJ," I said, kneeling next to him. "When they give the signal, all you have to do is run and find the eggs. Whatever eggs you find, pick them up, and put them in this basket. Got it?"

"Got it!" he nodded, swinging the empty basket.

"OK, go to that tree first and then the one right next to it," I said, pointing over at two oak trees.

"Let him do it on his own," Clint said.

"I just wanted to give him some ideas. Sheesh."

Clint shot me a look.

"All right, Easter egg hunters!" the announcer said. "On the count of three. 1…2…3!"

"Go, CJ!" I said, touching his back. Hardly able to contain my excitement, I jumped up and down, clapping and cheering him on as he darted from one side of the park to the other. Mama kept a keen eye on her son, but she didn't often show excitement when Clint was around, even though she probably wanted to.

From afar, we saw CJ squat down to pick up one egg when another child came and swooped right in, taking the egg before CJ could pick it up.

"Did you just see that?" I said, turning to Mama. "That kid just took CJ's egg. He was just about to get it!"

"Yeah, he needs to be tougher," Clint said. "He's gonna get walked all over."

"It's just an Easter egg hunt," Mama said. "He's fine and moved on. See?"

CJ stopped for a moment to wave at us.

"Keep going!" we all said in unison, motioning with our hands.

"Man," Clint said, shaking his head.

At the end of the hunt, CJ sprinted back with his basket, nearly tripping as he crossed the finish line.

"Good job!" I said, kneeling down to greet him. "Whatcha find?"

"I got lots of eggs!" He counted as he removed each one individually, and placed it on the grass.

All four of them.

I looked up at Mama, trying to shield my disappointment from my baby brother.

"Great job, CJ!" she said, clearing her throat.

"Um, yeah!"

His smile nearly took up his whole face.

"That was fun! Can we do it again?" he asked, swinging his practically empty basket.

"No, CJ," Clint stated.

"Here, bud," Mama said. "Let's go get our picture taken with the Easter Bunny." Fortunately, over the years, CJ outgrew his anxiety for Santa Claus and other big furried mascots.

"Can you watch my eggs, Sister?"

"Sure, CJ. I'll take good care of them."

Watching the three of them walk down toward the Easter Bunny station, I gripped his wicker Easter basket, almost feeling bad for the four lonely eggs inside.

June 15, 1989

Today is one of the worst days of the year. Father's Day. Bleh. Most years I've been able to just pretend and act OK, but for some reason this year has been harder. Luckily, Clint likes Cheez-its and those Dum-Dum suckers, so he's OK just getting those. I always dread trying to find a Father's Day card. The cards that say: "I love you, Daddy!", "Thanks for always being there for me," or "You deserve so much for all you give," just don't work for me. That's not what I feel. The stores don't sell the card that has what I really want to say. So, I try to find a card that sticks to the simple, "Happy Father's Day" and has some generic boat or sports on the front.

Even though I think about Daddy a lot, I'm OK with not seeing him. I do wonder what he's doing and hoping he and all the animals are OK. He's just so confusing, though, since it seemed like he was never really there for me. His love seemed so inconsistent.

I guess I technically have two Daddies, but it really feels like I don't even have one. Can't wait until this day is over.

July 10, 1989

It's my sweet 16 and I finally got my driver's license! I'm free! Well, almost. Lacey's still here. It's been such a busy summer. Hardly had time to write. For my birthday, I just wanted to see Spirit and everyone at Fair Oaks.

Ms. Patsy and Mr. Bucky recently got Spirit a big blow up ball, which he loves. It's fun to see him play with it. He's like a yearling. So, even if I didn't get a really big birthday gift, being with Spirit and seeing him play with his new gift was good enough for me!

September 20, 1989

11th grade has been fine so far. Nothing really too good or too bad. Just OK. I'm just glad I don't have to see Marin. That's always the big thing I worry about every year, but luckily, we don't have any classes or lunch together. Choir is still great and I'm glad that the same people are in it. Love that it brings music and happiness to my life.

They say a big hurricane is coming. There aren't many people around here who haven't lived through one before. But they're saying this one will be really big. Mama is stocking up on things, so we'll be fine. Hoping Spirit and everyone will be fine, too. It's weird, but it's kind of exciting!

Mama used to say, "Waiting for a hurricane to arrive is like being stalked by a turtle." It's true, but she should have gone on to say, "Then come to find out it's actually a snapping turtle."

Nothing about that late September day made it extraordinary. The birds chirped against the sunny sky and the September sun still warmed the air. It was hard to fathom a destructive storm was on its way.

After I cleaned out Spirit's stall, Mr. Bucky entered the barn with Moose and Dodger at his heels.

"Hi, Mr. Bucky. Have you heard about Hurricane Hugo?" I asked, returning the pitchfork to the corner.

"Sure have."

"Hey, Moose and Dodger," I said, petting their soft heads. Their usual greeting-almost-warning barks from months before were now tail-wagging. "Well, if you need anything, I'm here to help." I heard Daddy's voice saying, "Mare, whenever you can help someone out, you should."

"Good. Here," Mr. Bucky said, spilling a handful of small, multi-colored items in my palm.

"What are these?" I said, cupping my other hand to prevent them from falling.

"Cow tags. Write our information on 'em, then put 'em on the horses."

"Where?"

"Their manes. They gotta have 'em on. Ain't gonna be able to take 'em with us."

"Where are you going?" I asked, following him out of the barn to the paddock. Spirit and Jubi were resting their eyes and back hooves, standing face to butt in the paddock. Ebony stood near them watching the world go by. Spirit's head perked up when he saw me.

"We're taking the dogs and goin' to the wife's sister's in Tennessee."

The fact they were leaving made me simultaneously sad and anxious.

"What about the cats?"

"Eh, they'll be fine."

I started worrying about *Pingüino* and the horses. "Is everyone staying in the barn?" How is this going to work?"

"Gonna let 'em go. That's what the cow tags is for."

"Just let them go? Isn't that...kinda, bad for them?"

"If you keep 'em in the barn, something could fall. Barn could collapse. They get scared. Break a leg tryin' to bust out."

"Remove all the halters, 'cept maybe Lady Bird's. Hers is a breakaway. Only got a few of them. These horses can be hell on wheels to catch. Makes it easier if the halters can stay on. If not, they'll breakaway and won't hurt 'em."

He reached into his back pocket and chucked a can of bright blue spray paint to me. "Here. Spray 'Horses Inside' and 'Horses in Pasture' in big letters on the side of the barn."

"Why 'Horses Inside'?"

"Who knows what's gonna happen," he said, squinting up at the sun. "They might return back to the barn. Might take off. Who knows what we'll get. Or, what they'll do."

My previous excitement for the hurricane quickly transitioned into a racing heart, accompanied by a deep pit in my stomach.

September 22, 1989, 10:00am

Hurricane Hugo struck in the middle of the night last night. The strong winds and loud rain pelted our house and we lost power for a few hours. When I stepped outside, I saw trees down in people's yards and branches blanketing the street and sidewalks. But not the kind of damage I'm seeing on TV. We were lucky. Some people had trees through their houses and on their cars. And some were still without power. My only issue is having to be around Lacey, so I'm just trying to stay in my room, bringing Katie Kitty in with me and listening to music. I've been listening to "Right Here Waiting," by Richard Marx and "Back to Life" by Soul II Soul.

I really wish I knew how Spirit and everyone was doing. Still waiting to hear from Ms. Patsy and Mr. Bucky because I heard that people have actually died. I just keep wondering, is everyone OK? Is Spirit OK? Jubi? Did Ms. Patsy and Mr. Bucky make it out OK? Everyone else? I wish they'd call me.

<u>September 22, 1989 11:00pm</u>

I'm trying to fall asleep and I can't. We watched footage of the destruction from Hurricane Hugo all day. I think it's heading north where Mr. Bucky and Ms. Patsy were going to stay. And, I'm worried about Spirit and everyone left behind. I hate waiting. Hate it.

<u>September 23, 2:00am</u>

I still can't sleep. What if Spirit is trapped and can't get out? What if the barn falls on him? What if he sees Jubi or another one of his friends get hurt? What If the other horses or goats get hurt? What if the cats can't swim? Really wish the morning would come.

<u>September 23, 4:00am</u>

Still tossing and turning. What if I drove over to the barn now to see if everyone was OK? I'd probably wake everyone up but what if I snuck out? Then again, what could I do? It's the middle of the night. Hurry up, morning!

<u>September 23, 1989, 9:00am</u>

FINALLY heard back! Ms. Patsy just called and said they just got back and all the horses were just hanging out on the hill behind the barn. But they're fine and everyone is fine. The goats found a safe spot and the chickens were fine in their coop. They were surrounded by a lot of water, but had room to move. Mr. Bucky said that many of the horses had a little rain rot, a bacterial *infection they can get on their skin. Luckily, it's not a huge deal to get rid of. Pingüino and the other kitties hid in the trees. Now they'll just clean up and try to get them down. I asked if they needed help, but they said there wasn't too much to do and that they would see me soon. Thank God.*

At first, the weather people thought Hurricane Hugo was heading to the Triangle area after slamming Puerto Rico and Charleston, South Carolina. Even though it curved back to the Raleigh area and tore down many large trees, everyone was stunned when it hit Charlotte square on. I felt so bad for everyone who left the Triangle area to go to Charlotte thinking they were going to be safe, since it was further away from the ocean. But it actually was worse in Charlotte with even more downed trees and crushed houses. Hurricane Hugo ended up killing 86 people total, seven in North Carolina. The strange thing was, although Charlotte was devastated, no one died. By the time Hugo struck Charlotte, it dropped from a Category 5 to a Category 1. They said it might be days, even weeks to fully repair the storm damage. I would die if I had to be around Lacey and Clint that long. Thankfully, I didn't need to.

The day after Ms. Patsy called, I returned to Fair Oaks, wanting desperately to defy safety by running up to Spirit. Although the flood waters had receded by then, my boots sloshed in thick mud with every step. Some small trees had fallen on the barn and the side of the barn that still read "Horses Inside" needed some dented wooden panels replaced. Their property was littered with small branches and fallen leaves, but everyone was safe. After seeing Spirit and wrapping my arms around his neck, I was finally able to fully breathe again.

September 25, 1989

Choir was awesome today! I got to meet someone from Australia! I would love to visit. Wow, could I really go to another country?

After our short Hurricane Hugo break, returning to choir felt like I was home again. Before the school bell rang, everyone swapped hurricane stories, especially Dustin who, as usual, was able to make us laugh, even talking about a scary time. Hearing the others' stories really made me feel fortunate.

Among the buzz of the story-swaps, I saw a new girl talking with other choir members. My ears perked up when I heard her speak in an accent. Actually, she didn't sound like she was from the United States at all.

The bell rang and we all found our seats.

"All right," Mrs. Darbinyan said. "It's been quite an exciting few days! Glad to see everyone is back safe and sound. But, before we warm up today, we have a visitor with us. Valerie, do you want to introduce her?"

"Yeah, this is Victoria Turner. She's from Australia and she's been staying with us for the week."

"Hello, everyone." Her accent made her blue eyes and long, dirty-blonde hair even cooler.

"Welcome to America, Victoria!" Dustin yelled from the back.

"Thank you."

"You sure picked a good week to visit!" he added.

"Yeah," she blushed. "We get hurricanes in Australia too, but not usually like this."

"Well, welcome again," Mrs. Darbinyan said. "All right, let's warm up, starting on C."

I could hardly contain my distracting thoughts. All I wanted to do was talk to Victoria. Pick her brain. Hear about how she did things in Australia. Did she go to school as long? Did they get their driver's license at the same age? Why do they spell it "colour" and "realise"? My overflowing questions made it almost impossible to focus and sing, even the songs I knew like the back of my hand.

As everyone gathered their books before the release bell rang, I chucked my books into my backpack, practically running up to her.

"Hi, I'm Maren."

"Hey, Maren." Even hearing her say my name in her Australian accent made me smile.

"How do you like it here so far?"

"The States are heaps of fun. I'm keen on traveling. And this is my first time here, but it won't be my last!"

"I want to visit Australia so bad," I said, adjusting my backpack. "Where in Australia are you from?"

"New South Wales. I'm a Sydneysider."

"How long are you here?"

"I'm here today and then on my way back home."

"I have so many questions. Do you mind?" The buzz of the other students seemed to get louder.

"No worries," she said, sitting down.

"I know y'all use different words for things," I said, pulling up a chair next to her. "Like, I heard that 'bonnet' means the hood of a car."

"Yeah. And, 'lollies' are sweets and the 'loo' is the bathroom." I giggled again.

"And, we just cut the end of the word off and add a 'y.' Like, 'brekky' is breakfast and 'Chrissy' is Christmas. Oh! And here's a naughtier one. 'Fanny' means the front of a girl, not the back," she said, motioning to her lady bits.

"So, when someone is talking about a 'fanny pack'..." I said.

We both laughed. It fascinated me that, despite the fact we both spoke English, it seemed like two entirely different languages.

"Any words that are different for animals?" I asked.

"You like animals?"

Does a bear...? Thanks again, Aunt Mimi.

"Yeah, all of them, but mostly horses. Do you ride?"

"Sometimes. We usually ride English or the Australian Saddle."

"I've ridden English a few times, but mostly ride Western," I said, thinking about Spirit.

"What you might call mustangs, we call brumbies."

The sound of the word tickled me.

"And, we call cats who are mixed-breed, 'moggies.' And a 'bitzer' would be a mixed-breed dog."

Aww...Pingüino and his buddies are 'moggies,' and Dodger is a 'bitzer.' Moose wouldn't be called that because he's a purebred Great Pyrenees.

"I'm planning on majoring in animal science, or maybe even becoming a vet," I said.

"I think at university there are programs where you can study in Australia or maybe even in the UK and get credit for them."

"Really?"

"One of my mates is doing that and she says that there will be Americans in her class. Some of the programs are semester-long and others are shorter."

Traveling, school, AND horses? Where do I sign up?

"That would be Heaven. Have you ever been to the UK?"

"Yeah, been there a few times. We had a ripper of a time. Ireland, too," she said.

"You've been to Ireland? I can't believe you've been to places I want to go to so bad."

I thought my head was going to explode.

"Yeah, you should look into it," she said, standing up.

I glanced up at the clock. I had exactly one and a half minutes to get to my next class.

"Thank you again so much, Victoria. Safe travels back home!" I said, shaking her hand and heading out the door.

"Not at all. Cheers!"

*A*s I cleaned out Spirit's stall later that day, thoughts of actually going overseas swirled around in my head.

"How goes it, Sugar?"

"Hey, Ms. Patsy. Really good! In choir today, there was a girl from Australia. She taught me all these Australian terms for things, which was so fun. And, she said she mostly rides English."

"Other countries do that, too," Ms. Patsy said. "Ireland, England, and the like."

"Yes, that's what she said! All the places she's been that I would love to visit. She even said that you can actually take classes over there and get credit for it!" I said, setting the pitchfork back in the corner.

"Well, looky there! Sugar's going overseas, are ya?"

I shrugged. "We'll see. But it sure sounds fun. Traveling and horses would be a dream come true."

"I'm sure of that. We've done all the traveling we want to do, the Old Man and I. But I know you would love it," she said, winking at me.

"Have you ever ridden English?"

"Actually, yes. Quite a lot," she said.

"Really?"

"Yeah. In fact, I used to participate in dressage, but then I got an all-purpose English saddle."

I furrowed my brow.

"Those are different types of English saddles," she clarified. "Still got the all-purpose one and everything. Might have a foot of dust on it, but we still got it!"

"Why do you only ride Western here?"

"Well," she sighed, "When you marry a real cowboy through and through, that's what you get. Had to adjust to different things, but it's worth it."

"Do you ever miss it? Riding English, I mean?"

She sighed. "Sometimes, but I could always go back to it. It's like riding a bike. A half-ton one!" She laughed. "Have you ever ridden English before?"

"When I was in elementary school, I took a few lessons one summer," I said, thinking of Friday, wondering how she was doing.

"What did you think?"

"It's different, but I like it. I actually like them both, for different reasons."

She nodded.

"Um, Ms. Patsy…"

"Yeeesssss," she smirked.

"Um, do you think you might be able to teach me English?" I asked, biting my lip.

"Huh. Have to see about that," she said, adjusting her hat. "I've ridden Lady Bird before on it and Jubi, too. They both took to it. We could try it with you on Jubi but not Lady Bird. I want you to remain in one piece!"

"Yeah, I could ride Jubi. But what about Spirit?" I asked, crinkling my face, wondering if I had pushed too hard. "But, if you think he couldn't do it, then…."

"Some horses take to it, while others, after many attempts, just never do," she said, looking at Spirit in the paddock. "Not sure if he could do it. But I suppose we could try sometime."

"Thanks, I would love that!"

"Not promising anything. We'll put you on Jubi first and see how it goes first."

October 8, 1989

Today I get to learn English. Again!

Ms. Patsy greeted me with her two usual canine partners-in-crime.

"Hey, Sugar. Found our English saddle and bridle and shined them up real bright."

"Did you want to ride, too?" I asked.

"Might later. I do have to say, getting the things ready, I miss it more than I thought. But for now, let's get you going. Fetch Jubi and we'll get started."

Going to the paddock, it felt strange getting Jubi since it seemed like Spirit was being excluded. However, the peppermint I gave him seemed to ease some of my guilt and some of his sadness.

Walking Jubi up to the mounting area after a quick brush, Ms. Patsy said, "Go fetch the saddle. It'll be on the peg next to Lady Bird's bridle and saddle."

Some parts about riding English were tucked away in the dark recesses of my mind. Besides the obvious saddle differences, I had forgotten that the English bridle has a nose band, whereas most of the Western bridles don't. At least, Fair Oaks' bridles didn't have them. Even the saddle pads are different.

Bracing myself in anticipation of lifting a much heavier saddle, my balance was thrown off. Even with the saddle in my arms, saddle pad under my arm, and bridle over my shoulder, I didn't strain to carry them.

"Here," she said. "Let me take the saddle pad first. It goes on the middle of the horse's back, starting at the withers. Now, gently place the saddle down, as you know. Even though it's smaller than the Western, you still don't want to throw it down on Jubi's back.

Make sure it's level. Wiggle it, just a little bit. Some use a half pad and some have breast plates. We don't have either. Now we're going to attach the girth because most times people remove it from the saddle, unlike the Western saddle where it always stays on."

"Girth?"

"'Member it's called the 'girth' on an English saddle, not a 'cinch.'"

"That's right. I thought there were more differences than just the horn and nose band."

"Yeah, so attach the elastic side on the left side of the saddle and the leather side on the right side. Most people do the leather side first, but it's up to you. I leave it a little loose at first, but just make sure before you get on him, that leather side is tight. Put your fingers under the girth along his belly here and make sure once you tighten it, your fingers come barely off his body."

Pingüino decided to join us for this lesson. It was fun to have some of the other Fair Oaks' residents interested in learning from Ms. Patsy.

"Now, the saddle fits slightly on the shoulder blade. Some horses have really high withers, but Jubi's aren't too bad. Just make sure you can see daylight through the gullet or channel." She closed one eye, leaning over to look between the saddle and his withers. "Should be able to fit three or four fingers underneath the arch in front. The girth should always be right behind the horse's front legs. The saddle should always be in skin contact on the horse's back. And, voila! How do you feel there, Jubes?" she asked him, tilting her head.

I stood back to take a good look at him. His dark coloring was especially stunning in the English garb. It's not like he suddenly changed colors, but it was like the darker English saddle made his already dark bay coat appear like a glistening black. It's amazing how a different saddle and bridle could make such a difference. It's like how dressing up in a new dress, makeup, and shoes can make someone look different.

"Now bring him around here. Let's get you up." Moose and

Dodger seemed intrigued, watching me on a new horse with a new saddle.

I swung my leg over Jubi and squealed, "Wow, I forgot how close you feel to them. The Western saddle feels like a Lazy Boy compared to this!"

"Yessum!" Ms. Patsy said, holding onto Jubi's head. Being on a different horse felt odd. I tried not to look at Spirit, who stood at the paddock gate, ears pricked forward. Jubi shook his head and seemed more alert than usual, but he handled all these new contraptions well.

"Now, as you recall, you're not neck reining him anymore, you're direct reining him. That means you're going to pull the rein toward your belly in the direction you want to go. If you want to go to the left, you pull the left rein toward your belly. If you want to go to the right, you pull the right rein toward your belly. You see?"

I nodded. Couldn't help thinking about my first English lesson. Was Friday still alive? I had "moved up" in my skill level and confidence. I also moved up literally, because Jubi was taller than Friday.

"Make sure the rein comes between your pinky and ring finger and comes up out the top, between your pointer finger and thumb. Like so," she said, sliding the reins between her fingers. "Imagine there is a straight line from your elbow to the horse's mouth. Make sure your thumb is resting gently on the rein. Don't hold them like a gripped fist. Pretend you're holding two ice-cream cones."

I understand that.

Ms. Patsy got in closer. "Jubi here should be good to go. I just rode him in this saddle a few days ago. The Old Man doesn't quite like riding English as much, so I got in a little riding time on my own."

I took in a deep breath.

"Now, squeeze your legs and make him walk." My usual kissing noise usually moves Spirit, but Jubi required a few leg squeezes to move.

"How does that feel?" Ms. Patsy asked.

"Good, but weird!"

"Yeah, but you'll get it," she winked. Moose decided this wasn't worth his time and headed back to the house. Dodger stayed and *Pingüino* joined Ms. Patsy in the middle of the arena.

I could really feel each of Jubi's steps and his muscle movements under me. I also felt as though I were really exposed.

"That's good," Ms. Patsy said. "All right, now ask him to turn to the right."

I pulled the right rein toward my belly and he veered to the right.

"Now, the left."

I pulled the left rein and he turned to the left.

"Don't slouch. Sit up in the saddle."

After a few circles in the arena, Ms. Patsy asked, "Do you remember how to post?"

"Yeah, I lift my butt up at a certain point. Just don't remember when!"

She laughed. "When his outside, or right, front leg goes out, you go up! Got it?"

"Yeah!"

"OK, push your hips forward a little and ask him to trot."

Again, after relying on leg squeezes more than just kissing noises, we were trotting. However, it wasn't very smooth on my end, literally, my hind end.

"Now, bring him back to a walk." I praised Jubi by rubbing his neck and we slowed.

"We're going to try that trot again, and you're going to find his rhythm. It's a 1-2, 1-2 beat," she said. "I know you like music. And like music, there is a rhythm. So, find his!"

I squeezed with a little less intensity since I think he was waking up.

"Keep him going…. That's right. Very good…and up…and up…and up. Watch his front leg. Keep your legs still. There, you got it!"

This was such a joy.

"Make sure you're moving with him. Stay with his motion. If you tense up, it'll make you bouncy. Go with the movement. Like Goldilocks. Not too much, not too little."

We continued trotting in several circles and figure eights. "Let's bring him back to a walk."

I pulled back on the reins and we slowed. "Good job, Jubi. You're a really good boy," I said, stroking his dark neck. He blew out, shaking his head. It might have seemed like he was disagreeing with me, but I knew he wasn't.

"Can we canter?"

"You really feel ready?" Ms. Patsy asked, wiping her brow.

"Sure!"

"Then, bring him in here," she said, motioning me to the middle. "Let me show you something."

"Once you get to cantering, relax your hip joint," she said, poking my side.

I thought only old people thought about their hips.

"Just keep them loose. Keep them moving. And, don't push him forward with your shoulders or pump with your body. Just relax your shoulders. Keep them as still as possible. You see?"

"Yeah."

"Don't tighten your legs. Just go with his movement. Again, find his rhythm. You'll move around a little bit in the saddle."

"Yeah, but there's not much room to move in here."

"Right. Just keep your hips relaxed. If you tighten up your hips, you'll bounce and it will feel like a bouncy trot." She paused. "I'm throwing a lot at ya. You sure you getting this?"

"Yep," I said, hoping that once we started, it would make better sense.

"OK," she said, petting Jubi's neck. "Let's move him into a trot, then canter."

With just the tiniest of squeezes, we were in a trot.

"Squeeze again, and ask him to canter!"

Again, with a very small squeeze, we were cantering. The thrill factor jumped up a few notches to think about cantering in such a small saddle. I felt guilty it wasn't Spirit, but Jubi was a great mount.

"Keep your hips relaxed. Relax your shoulders," she reminded. "That's it—good! Keep your hands down."

Finding my position and balance: it's really what Life was all about.

"Yeah, that's it. See the difference? See how he's settled into the canter?"

"Yeah, I feel it!"

"He does, too!" she said. "Hands like a lady. Shoulders like a queen. Hips like a whore."

"What?" I asked, breathless from my concentration.

"Never you mind," she laughed.

I thought I heard her correctly. Based on her response, I think I did.

A half hour later, full of circles, lead changes, leg cues, and more games, the fun had to end.

"All right, that'll be it for today," she said, motioning me to the middle. "You think you got the hang of it? You think you'll be comfortable riding across the countryside in Australia? You sure got it in ya."

I tried not to smile too big, bringing Jubi to a stop in front of her and *Pingüino*. "Can we do this again?"

"Sure."

"When?"

She chuckled. "Soon. Just remember, shoulders relaxed, hips loose, and don't slouch. And, you're direct reining instead of neck reining. You're still communicating with him. Just a different way, is all."

Ms. Patsy's way of teaching was such a good fit for me. She expected you to do it, but she wasn't condescending if you didn't.

"OK, Jubes. Good job today," she said, stroking his neck. "You too, Sugar," she said, patting my leg.

"Thanks."

"He can go back with Spirit. Just give him some water and brush him down again."

I led Jubi back to the paddock where he smelled his friend, then stepped to the side and rolled around in the dirt. Spirit, who usually stands still when I entered, actually walked off.

"Come on, big guy," I said, following behind him. "You're not being replaced. I promise."

Spirit eventually stopped, allowing me to pet his neck and kiss his soft muzzle. His annoyance seemed to wane. I'm not sure if he was upset because he wanted to be part of the fun, missed his friend Jubi, or if he wished I were riding him.

I'm choosing to think it's the latter.

October 10, 1989

I just love riding Spirit English style!

Two days later, after finishing my chores, I went out to the paddock and greeted Jubi with a neck rub. Once Spirit walked over to me, letting go of some of disapproval from a few days prior, we started our new thing. I scratched his back and he extended his long neck, flipping his top lip up, nodding his head in agreement. After I laughed, I'd wait for him to crane his neck around, touching his muzzle to my shoulder as if to say, "Don't stop!" This went on for several minutes before Ms. Patsy showed up, escorted by Dodger.

"How ya doing, Sugar?"

"Great, thanks, Ms. Patsy."

"Sure, we're gonna head in. Thanks again and we'll be seeing ya soon. C'mon, Dodger." He jumped in the air, excited for any movement.

"Um, Ms. Patsy!" I said, trying to catch her.

"Yes," she said, turning around.

"I was wondering if we could…Um, if I could ride English on Spirit today."

"You really want to try it on Spirit?" she said, resting her hand on her hip.

"Yes, ma'am."

She laughed. "I thought you'd never ask!"

"Oh, man!"

"Bring him up around here, and let's see how he does."

Leading Spirit to the mounting area, I tied him to the post.

"Do you remember everything you need?" she asked.

"Yes," I said, trying to remember on the way to the tack area. Once I got there, all the correct answers flooded back.

Armed with the English saddle, pad, and bridle, I returned to Ms. Patsy who was rubbing down Spirit's legs. If I had gotten a dollar for every time I said, "Oh, yeah! I remember," I would be a very rich person.

Taking a step back and looking at Spirit in the English tack, I almost didn't recognize him. He played with the bit and shook his head a few times from the new nose band. His back seemed to quiver in opposition to the new saddle. But he was striking in his new garb and it really showed off his golden body and black mane and tail. Of course, I always thought he looked gallant.

"Great job, Sugar," Ms. Patsy said, smiling.

"Thanks."

"One very important thing, though, I need to point out," she said, stepping towards me.

I cocked my head to examine the saddle, pad, and bridle, trying to figure out what I had done wrong.

"Sugar, you need to take a moment and think about this real hard."

I couldn't imagine what she meant.

"I need you to take a good hard look at him. This is the first time Spirit's been in full English tack before. *Ever.* The fact that he stood so well for you when you put this foreign stuff on him means that he really trusts you."

I gazed into his soft eyes, keeping the lump in my throat from growing any bigger.

"Horses don't do that very often. And they certainly don't do that for just anyone. Really think about this moment and take this in."

I thought back to the Kentucky Horse Park when I realized how indebted we are to the horse, for so many reasons. Seeing Spirit standing there with a slightly raised head made me think about the tremendous responsibility I had to take care of Spirit's heart, like he had done with mine.

"Let's get you up," she said, patting my back.

Although it was different being on Spirit in an English saddle, it felt comfortable once I situated my legs and hands.

"Remember, direct rein. He'll probably take to it pretty easy. Most horses do OK, if they trust you. And he does."

With a slight squeeze of my legs and kiss in the air, Spirit raised his head and we were walking. His ears darted around, trying to make sense of the new apparatus. Yet, despite the new tack, he stayed steady and cool.

"Now, it's a big responsibility since he trusts you. He's looking to you for direction. Remember what you did with Jubi," she said, from the middle of the arena. "You're holding an ice cream cone in each hand, heels down, relax the hip. Just walk him around the arena a few times and work on direct reining."

I pulled on the left rein to go left. At first, he stopped, so I air-kissed again and he walked. Giving a gentle pull on the left rein while air-kissing, he turned to the left.

"Good job! You were nice and clear that time. Do it again."

Pulling on the right, he turned to the right, and after a few more times, we were making figure 8s. After walking in a few circles, we were trotting.

"Time to post. And, up…and…up…and…good! Find his rhythm."

I'm not sure if it's because I had trotted on Jubi before, or because we were in sync, but it was really easy to find Spirit's rhythm.

"You want to canter?"

"Yes, please!" I said, in between posts.

"OK, ask him to canter."

With another air-kiss, his ears darted around and we were cantering.

I was happier than a kitten chasing a leaky cow, as Ms. Patsy would say.

"Keep him there. It's too easy to let him go faster. We need to work on control now."

Even though I was disappointed we couldn't go faster, I knew she was right. There were some bumpy times, since I didn't always align my hand and leg commands to what he needed. But he was eager to please, and cantering on Spirit, in any saddle, was always the highlight of my life.

After another half-hour of trotting in circles, figure eights, and cantering, Ms. Patsy said, "All right, bring him to the middle. I think you've both done really well today. Don't want to work him too hard. It can be exhausting to a horse. Considering it's his first time, he did really well. Plus, he might have not liked seeing you riding Jubi. They can get attached to people, too! He really must love you," she said, scratching his neck.

"I really love him. He's simply the best. Ever!" I said, throwing my arms around his neck. I didn't realize how tired I was until we stopped.

"If we were going to do more advanced training or if you wanted to compete, we'd have his head positioned a little differently and work on his carriage and your form more. But, since you just want to learn on a trusted friend, this will do just fine."

That worked for me. I had no desire to compete.

Despite some of my mixed cues and leg commands, Spirit was so patient and eager to learn. It's amazing how much closer I felt to him and how much I appreciated his gentle nature even more. There is so much to learn from horses and I felt like I was just beginning.

January 8, 1990

I know it's been a super long time since I've written, but it was a great fall. Lacey was gone a lot at her friend, Jamie's, which was great because that meant she wasn't here. CJ is getting older and can do more now. He's now six years old and in the first grade. Halloween was a lot of fun and seeing Aunt Mimi at Hallomas is always a highlight for me. Thanksgiving and Christmas were especially awesome! Mama made all her famous food. I ate way too much, but the holidays only come once a year.

Still wonder how Daddy and all the animals are doing. But not enough to write. I did pick up the phone one or two times to call, but hung up. I think deep down, I really don't want to see him. Same for Marin. I miss her, but then I'm kinda happy she's not in my life anymore.

The most hilarious thing is that Lacey got a computer for Christmas! We already have one in the living room, and now she has one of her own. It was so obvious she totally didn't want it. She wanted more clothes. Ha! Plus, it took Clint and Mama forever to figure it out, with the TV screen, printer, and all the crazy cords! And, you have to make sure you line up the holes on the printer paper in the dot matrix printer. It just gave me a headache watching them. I don't even know what a dot matrix is. I swear, those computer people just make up words. Flipping through the TV channels today, I came across a show that talked about Australia. It said the seasons are switched and it's actually summer there now. I wonder how Victoria, the Australian girl, is doing? I really wish I was there now in the warmth.

February 22, 1990

I can't believe it. But, then again, I can.

Studying for my American Lit class on my bed cross-legged, Katie Kitty was curled up on my lap. The cassette tape played "Another Day in Paradise" by Phil Collins, "This One's For the Children" by New Kids on the Block and "I've Been Thinking About You" by Londonbeat. Mama knocked on my door. "Baby, can I talk to you for a minute?"

"What's wrong?" I asked, turning down Londonbeat's singing. Katie flew off the bed and sat in the middle of the room.

"Well, I have some news," she said, easing down on the bed.

"Oh, no. Is it CJ?"

"No."

"Is it Lacey or Clint? I mean, Daddy Clint?"

"Um...no," she said, rubbing her face.

"Then, what is it?" *Spit it out!*

"It's your Daddy Garrett."

I couldn't believe it. How long had it been since I heard from him? "What about Daddy? I mean, Daddy Garrett?"

"Well, Baby. He's gone."

"What do you mean 'gone'?" I asked, standing up.

"Apparently he moved out west."

"Oh! I thought you meant he, well...you know."

"Not that I know of anyway."

"How do you know he's gone?" I asked.

"It had been so long since you'd heard from him that I tried calling his number. But it was disconnected. Years ago, he and his band used to play at The Boulevard. So, I decided to stop by after work last week and asked if they had seen him or his band. Last they heard, they were moving out west."

"Like, where?" I asked, furrowing my brow.

"They weren't sure. He didn't leave an address or phone number."

I sat on the bed, shaking my head. "So, he just took off then?"

"Guess so. Sorry, Baby."

I think I hoped my head shaking would lead to understanding. "Whatever," I sneered.

"I was trying to find a good time to tell you. But, thought you'd want to know as soon as I found out."

I could feel my anxiety tighten my chest. "So, he just takes off. Just like that?"

"I know. I really do."

"That's so typical of him," My jaw began to tighten. "Is *she* here?" We both knew who I meant.

"No, Jamie came and picked her up."

"Is the car here?" I asked, on my way to the kitchen.

"I think so." Mama lifted her arms, presumably to hug me, but I just couldn't.

"I gotta get outta here," I said, dashing to door.

"Where are you off to?"

"Where do you think?" I said, slamming the door behind me.

I got into the silver 1983 Mazda GLC I shared with Lacey. From the driver's seat, I stared out the windshield at the lawn mower and push broom at the back of the garage, searching for an anchor to bring me back from what I just heard. Knowing I was supposed to have an adult in the car while I earn my driving hours, I turned the ignition before Mama forbade me from going.

Driving to the barn, I talked aloud, as if Daddy were sitting in the passenger seat. "You just take off?" I yelled. "When *you* were the one who was afraid I was going to leave *you*? You were gone *way* before! You were gone to me once you stopped visiting. And, 'forgot,' or 'let time slip away.' That's bull, and you know it!" I repeated, punching at the radio stations trying to find a good song. "Hope you're happy now out west. Wherever the hell you are! Thanks for leaving your information for me. Thanks for nothing!"

The vivid memories of his visits flooded my mind. All the horseback riding. Wildfire. Snickers. All the animals. The poor animals. Who's taking care of them now? I hoped they were OK. I remember playing air drums. The Christmases. Horseback riding on the Outer Banks and on Snickers and Wildfire. My stuffed animal Wildfire. Kentucky Horse Park. *The Black Stallion*. Talking about horses. Talking about music and singing with him.

Holding back my tears and trying to prevent the heaviness in my chest from growing, I saw Mr. Bucky coming and going from the barn, dispersing the evening hay and feed.

Flashing a quick, manufactured smile, I quickened my pace to Spirit's stall. The munching and pulling at the hay from their hay nets soothed me. Spirit turned his head toward me as he ate. A few pieces of hay protruded from his muzzle.

"Hey, big guy. How are ya?" I asked, with my voice cracking.

Mustering what little energy I had left, I opened his stall door and stood next to him. Slowly petting his neck, the calming sound of his munching was a stark contrast to the pain I felt. He was so innocent of everything happening in Life outside his world. I threw my face into the side of his neck, then slowly collapsed to the ground. Hay squished under me as I fell to my knees. Spirit swung his large head toward me, snorting and nuzzling me. His curiosity and interest prompted me to cry harder. I stroked his neck, muttering to myself. The sounds of my sniffs echoed through the barn.

"Miss? Ya in here?" Mr. Bucky asked. He folded his arms over the stall door, startling me.

"Oh, hi, Mr. Bucky," I said, snapping my head up and wiping my cheeks.

"Workin' today?"

"No, but I will tomorrow." I pushed up on the ground to stand up as quickly as I could, despite the fact that my legs felt like wet noodles.

"Y'all right?"

"Yeah," I sniffed. "Just a really bad day."

He grunted. "Got a good friend there," he said, nodding to Spirit.

"He's the best," I said, stroking Spirit's soft muzzle. "He's literally the best friend I've ever had."

Mr. Bucky nodded. "Holler if you need anythin'."

"Will do. Thanks, Mr. Bucky." I mustered all the energy I could to prevent more tears from rolling down my cheeks.

He smiled, tipping his hat.

Turning toward Spirit, I lost myself in his big, brown eyes and long eyelashes. "You really are my best friend," I said, in a hushed tone. He snorted in agreement.

March 10, 1990

It's been so hard to sleep since Daddy disappeared without saying goodbye. I wonder where he is. Sometimes I couldn't care less and then sometimes I would give anything to hear his voice again.

I still don't like being the last one asleep or the only one who's not asleep. It's like everyone else has gone away and they didn't take me with them. Like I'm left behind. One time, Ms. Patsy said that animals live in the "feeling world." I can relate. Sometimes that's how I feel I am—like one big nerve walking around that everybody steps on. The slightest wind that touches it hurts. I've been listening to "Oh, Father," by Madonna and "Hold On" by Wilson Phillips.

I'm happy Spring will be here soon and things will be better. Even if it's only the weather that's improved.

April 22, 1990

I really did it—Spirit and I did it together!

After Mama dropped me off at Fair Oaks, *Pingüino* was my greeter this time in front of the office. He rubbed his tail against my leg, then plopped over on his back for a rub.

"Hey, there," I said, crouching down to pet his exposed belly. "How's it going in kitty-land?"

Ms. Patsy came out from the office. "Hey, Sugar," she said, wiping her brow. "Ridin' today?"

For some reason, it hadn't really occurred to me. On that day, I just wanted to be there, away from everyone else.

"Sure, that would be fun."

She nodded.

"Are you going out with me, or will Mr. Bucky?" I asked, heading toward the tack room.

"C'mere for a second." Placing her hands on my shoulders, she said, "You are ready to do the trails on your own."

"Like, when?"

She looked at her watch. "How about right now?"

"Yes, please!"

"You and Spirit, I'm figuring," she said, smiling.

Does a bear...

"Now, I'm assuming you'll be riding Western, since you're both more comfortable in that. As you know walk when you take him out, maybe trot. But, when you get to the cleared area, on the other side of that big tree line—you know where I'm talking about?"

"Yeah, by that big oak tree?"

"That's the one. Really open him up there. Just go to town! I have a good feeling you'll be pleased with what you find," she said, giving me her traditional wink.

My smile was so big, I'm sure every last one of my teeth showed.

"But not on the way back," she cautioned. "Be sure to walk him then. Don't want him to get to be a really bad homebody or get—"

"—Barn sour. Yes, ma'am," I interrupted, hardly able to contain my excitement.

"You have fun out there. I know you will," she said, winking again.

"Thank you, Ms. Patsy."

"You're welcome, Sugar. Now, go get him!"

Retrieving and tacking Spirit up in record time, we made our way through the woods leading to the big oak tree. Once we entered the clearing, I kissed the air. Spirit threw up his head, trotted four strides, and broke into a canter. Collecting some of his dark mane, I sat deeper in my seat. With each air-kiss I made, his golden legs reached for the earth faster and faster until the strength and power of his strides moved us at a speed I'd only seen in movies. No other horse ever touched his speed and strength. Not Snickers, River, or even Wispy. Images of the Black Stallion on the island and Ruffian flying across the finish line flooded my brain and brought tears to my eyes. The moments when all four of Spirit's feet were off the ground suspended in mid-air truly felt like we were flying. I never felt more alive and joyful. Spirit and I were one, connected in a way that only a horse and horse person could understand. All the pain and hurt of Daddy leaving, Marin's rejection, and everything else evaporated. I was transported to a world of bliss that I never wanted to leave.

Although Spirit had physically done the galloping, I was out of breath. Those who think that horseback riding is simply about the rider hanging on are sadly mistaken.

On the way back to the barn, I repeatedly rubbed Spirit's sweaty neck and told him what a good boy he was. His ears turned slightly back toward me, letting me know he was listening.

Returning to the barn in a fast walk, Ms. Patsy stood in the middle of the mounting area. Her big smile mirrored mine.

"So, how'd ja do out there?" she said, reaching for Spirit's bridle.

All I could do was smile, shake my head, and allow the tears to flow.

"Aw, Sugar," she said, tilting her head to the side. "Glad it did you good."

It did more than "do me good."

It was like I found something that had been missing.

My Spirit.

June 15, 1990

Ever since my exhilarating ride with Spirit, I've been sleeping much better. And last night I slept the best because tonight is Lacey's graduation! She's leaving tomorrow to start a new job doing something. I have no idea what or where, but I don't care. All I know is she will be gone. I just cannot wait!

It felt like a lifetime in that hot, tightly packed gymnasium. Never-ending speeches. A million names announced from the podium. Clapping and whistling from adoring parents and family members as their beloved graduates walked across the stage. In reality, it was only an hour. Reminded me of being a bored spectator at Clint and Mama's wedding, only with more whooping and hollering. CJ got to stay with his friends because Mama said he would have been bored out of his mind. Lucky duck.

After the ceremony, everyone poured into the hallways, filling them with green-gowned students and gushing parents and families. The decibel level was even higher than during class changes. Lacey and I were in the middle of posing for an obligatory picture of the two of us when Jamie and a group of four or five girls came up, wrapping their arms behind Lacey.

The screeching girls lined up on either side of Lacey, pushing me down to the end. I stood next to the last girl as Lacey craned her neck from the middle of the group.

"Maren—move!" she barked.

I slid out of the shot and looked over at Mama. She mouthed the words, "I love you," but my embarrassment still hung thick. The other nameless girls tittered in nervousness at Lacey's insensitive comment.

After numerous hugs and well-meaning wishes of "I'll miss you! I love you! Keep in touch!", the herd of girls vanished into the sea of people.

"OK, *now* let's get that picture of the two of you," Mama said. She motioned to both of us to stand next to each other.

Lacey and I exchanged glances. "Nah, that's OK," we said in unison.

The first thing we ever really agreed upon.

Lacey, catching sight of another friend in the ocean of green, zig-zagged her way over to her. Three complicated people in my life were gone, Lacey, Marin, and Daddy. Lacey is the only one I was completely happy about.

July 10, 1990

I did it—on my own! What a perfect 17ᵗʰ birthday present!

Walking Spirit on a lead rope around the property next to Ms. Patsy leading Jubi next to me was like walking the biggest dogs you'd ever seen. The real dogs, Moose and Dodger, walked in front of us.

"This is a great way to spend time with horses," she said.

"Just walking around like this?"

"Sure. You don't always have to be riding them," she said. "Anything you can do to build trust and confidence with a horse is a good thing. Makes it a much better experience when you ride. Do you see how loose your rope is? That's a very good thing. The fact that Spirit moves and stops when you do shows that he's in tune with you."

Once again, Ms. Patsy shared information that Spirit and Jubi, or any horse, really wants humans to know. It was like she was a conduit from their hearts to ours. Stroking Spirit's neck, he quivered his bottom lip, indicating he liked what I was doing.

"Let's keep them walking," she said, giving a slight tug on Jubi's rope. I only had to take a few steps and Spirit followed me. "Oh, and happy birthday."

"Thanks, Ms. Patsy. There's no other place I'd rather be."

She smiled. "Sugar, it's time for you to be leading trail rides."

I stopped and Spirit did, too. "Like by myself?"

"That's what I mean. You've been on enough rides with the Old Man and me. You've even been out on your own. You know them backward and forward."

"But what if something happens when I'm out there?" I asked, clutching the rope.

"You'll know what to do," she said, stopping. "You can mount Spirit from the ground if need be, right?"

"Well, yeah."

"And, you know not to let the horses eat, right?"

"Yeah," I said, fiddling with Spirit's forelock.

"You wouldn't be going out on Lady Bird or Deuce. It would just be walking," she consoled. "Spirit, Jubi, and Ebony will be completely fine. They're not likely to spook and they also know the trails backward and forward. They'll always bring you back home if you forget!"

"Oh, I wouldn't forget!"

"I figured. That's why you're gonna do this. Now, the one thing you need to watch with Spirit is—"

"—Don't let him walk too fast," I interrupted.

"Right. You'll need to keep an eye on people behind you. Otherwise, you'll need to ride Jubi or another horse."

I was combing Spirit's black mane with my fingers along his neck when he shook his head. I agreed with him. As much as I loved Jubi, I always wanted to be on Spirit whenever possible.

"So, when would I do it?"

Ms. Patsy looked down at her watch. "As luck would have it, there is a woman and her daughter coming in about fifteen minutes."

"Fifteen minutes?"

"Yep, no need to look like you've seen a ghost. You'll do just fine. We've just warmed up Spirit and Jubi, let's bring Ebony around. He's good with these two."

After watching Ms. Patsy on the trails, my plan was to copy what she did. She always asked the guests where they were from, how long they lived in the area, and how much they had ridden. All questions to make people feel at ease, but not so many that it interfered with the ride and scenery. Ms. Patsy always had that quality about her. She always seemed so comfortable in her skin.

When the little girl arrived, her excitement was palpable from her nonstop chatter. It was difficult not to see myself at her age—being so excited anytime a horse was near, much less on one. Still feel the same way now. I asked a few questions, and found out it was the little girl, Miss Dory's, birthday, too, and her first time riding. Her mom, Ms. Diane, went horseback riding on her first date with her husband. They're from North Raleigh and lived there their entire lives. Ms. Diane spent a little time in Michigan and knew about Mackinac Island, so we had even more things to talk about.

Although we walked the entire time, being the leader was exciting, yet scary. Turning around to see Jubi and Ebony felt surreal, but I trusted them to take care of Ms. Diane and Miss Dory. I just needed to trust myself in the same way.

Ms. Patsy was waiting for us when we returned and helped Miss Dory, who continued her narration of any thought that crossed her mind. I dismounted from Spirit and helped Ms. Diane. As they gave their thanks and said their goodbyes, Ms. Patsy turned to me. "Well, whatcha think?"

"That was awesome! They were so great. It was Miss Dory's first time on a horse and Ms. Diane's husband is overseas in the military now. So, she wanted to celebrate their little girl's birthday the way Miss Dory wanted. She was so excited to be on a horse and loved everything about them."

"You both have the same birthday." She smiled. "Like looking in the mirror."

Couldn't have said it better myself.

*A*fter we removed the tack and returned the horses to the paddock, I stood next to Spirit, scratching his neck.

"Sugar, you'd be good with horses who help other people, too," Ms. Patsy said.

"What do you mean?"

"One of my friends runs a facility called Horse and Buddy that matches horses with people who have special needs, like Cerebral Palsy or Down's Syndrome. Horseback riding helps with their balance, coordination, and confidence. Makes them feel better, too. You know how much being around horses can make you happier than clams at high tide. I think you'd be really good at helping them over there."

"It sounds like a really great program. But, I'm really better with horses than with people."

She smiled at me. "You're better with people than you think. Plus, you could always be the person who gets the horses tacked up and leads them rather than the person who walks next to them."

I looked at Spirit, thinking about others who love horses as much as I do. The love is deep and pure, regardless of physical or emotional differences.

"The program is mainly run by volunteers. I'm going to give

you the name of my friend and her phone number. She's expecting your call."

Apparently, it was a done deal.

"Remember, Sugar, nothing is better than helping others." I heard Daddy's voice in that sentence.

They're both right.

August 5, 1990

Ms. Patsy was right! Yesterday, I went to Horse and Buddy, the therapeutic riding center and met Ms. Sally, Ms. Patsy's friend. She was awesome and it's an incredible place! They have seven horses, and two ponies for the shorter students, which I can understand. Usually people have to attend a volunteer training to help out, but since Ms. Sally knew my background, she just gave me a tour of their beautiful facilities before we started. She explained that every student has a volunteer who leads the horse and then someone who walks alongside.

After showing me the large covered outdoor arena where the lessons were held, they gave me a gorgeous horse named Dice to tack up. His coloring is what they call a Buckskin Tobiano Paint. I had to ask since I had no idea. He has Spirit's build, but his coloring is stunning! The white, black, and chestnut colorings of both his mane and body reminded me of a caramel and fudge sundae swirl! Of course, Spirit is still the most beautiful horse in the world, but Dice sure comes close. I talked to a mom before her daughter's lesson and she said that her daughter looks forward to coming here more than anything else—even Christmas!

Then, I was introduced to Gavin, the student I would be leading around, and his parents. Gavin's mother told me so many good things that Horse and

Buddy had done for her son, including giving him more strength and self-confidence. It really touched me that she said the first time she saw Gavin smile was on the back of a horse. I certainly understand that.

Tacking up the horses is much different than what I'm used to. At Horse and Buddy, many horses are led around with a lead rope attached to a halter, not a bridle, since some of the students don't take the reins. And, whereas some students ride in a full Western saddle, others ride in basically a thick saddle pad, which is what Gavin needed.

As I led Gavin and Dice around, I don't really remember too much of what the side-walker, Judy, said to him and vice versa. I could just feel her warmth and that she loved what she was doing. Just couldn't get over what a special place this was. The staff and volunteers are loving and generous and have the biggest hearts. The students are committed and determined despite their challenges. They're working on their coordination and balance, among other things I take for granted, yet their hearts are so open. I need to remind myself to think about them when things suck, even if it's hard to do.

Most of all, I got teary-eyed thinking about how much these horses give of themselves. They don't understand why they continually walk in circles inside an arena while one person leads them, another sits on their backs, and another walks by their sides. Horses do it because they are amazing beings. If they trust what is happening, they will give it their all. I can also understand that. Sometimes, I think that we don't deserve horses. As I realized at the Kentucky Horse Park, nothing we do can ever repay them. We are forever indebted.

<u>August 13, 1990</u>

I simply cannot believe I'm going to be a senior! My last year at Garner High School. I'm somewhat sad to leave, but also ready to move on. Maybe even to another country!

And, my Senior pictures are coming up! Lacey's pictures were so good because she had the best clothes. And, it does help when you're a size 4 rather than an 8. OK, 10. But, my hair has gotten really long, which is fun. I'm somewhat excited, but it's a lot of pressure to get everything right.

Katie Kitty helped me rummage through my closet for potential outfits when Mama tapped on my unlatched door.

"Baby, I heard you mumbling and wondered if you needed any help." She glanced over at my bed, scattered with most of my closet's contents.

"I just don't know what to wear, Mama," I said, holding a different shirt in each hand. "Lacey had such great clothes. I wouldn't even know where to start."

"You've got them, too. How about this one? You always look great in this one," she said, holding a purple top under my chin. "You wore that for the Honor Awards night. I know Mrs. Brooks complimented you on how nice you looked."

"Yeah, I guess," I said, examining myself in the mirror on the back of the door.

"Now, this would look really good on you." She picked up a striped sweater with black pants. "And, if you wear these sandals or pumps with it. Yeah, this is what you should wear."

"I can actually have two or three outfits."

"OK, let's see here." She slid the remaining hangers in the closet over the pole. Apparently, nothing on the bed interested her. "Where is that one you wore for...here it is!"

She pulled out a deep blue shirt with a nice pair of jeans.

"Oh, yeah," I said, reaching up and touching the sleeves. "I remember this. You got me this shirt for my thirteenth birthday."

"It was way in the back. Try it on. See if they both fit."

I instantly felt a connection to all the girls who held their breath anytime they tried on clothing that hadn't seen the light of day for a while. "See, they look great on you!"

"Thanks, Mama." I was pleased I only had to suck in my gut a little.

"And what about asking the stables if you could have your pictures taken there? You know, with the horse you like."

"With Spirit? That would be unbelievable! Do you think they'd let me?"

"Only one way to find out," she said, hanging some of the clothes back into the closet. "Give them a call and see if that could be arranged."

I couldn't get to the phone fast enough. What made it better is I didn't have to fight Lacey for it.

October 1, 1990

They said "Yes!" I am so grateful that Mr. Bucky and Ms. Patsy said I could have my pictures taken with Spirit. Today is the big day! And Mama said the extra fee for the photographer to go out there wouldn't be a problem! I was exactly where I wanted to be: at Fair Oaks with my Spirit.

Ms. Patsy must have been a photographer in her former life. Her numerous suggestions included "Y'all come over here," "How about this pose?", and "Let's try it where her arm is around Spirit's neck?" She definitely gave feedback, solicited or not.

I was appreciative of her ideas, since a variety of pictures were taken. One was me on Spirit's back, both of us looking off into the distance. Another one had us touching forehead to forehead. In that one, his eye was so soft and his head was relaxed and lowered. Another picture I liked was me sitting on the ground with Spirit standing over me, smelling my hair. Ms. Patsy loved the one of me kissing his soft muzzle. Right after that particular picture was taken, Spirit's top lip moved around in a circular motion, as if trying to grasp something.

My favorite picture wasn't posed at all. The photographer took a candid shot at sunset. Both of us were silhouettes, and I smiled as I scratched Spirit's chin with his ears pricked forward. We were in the process of posing for another picture, but I just loved how natural this was. I couldn't stop smiling. Seeing Spirit always did that for me.

After an agonizing ten-day wait, the senior picture proofs were finally ready. I drove Mama to the photographer's shop, driving at a speed that wasn't completely legal.

We both sat down at a black-felted table top, and the photographer laid out all the pictures for us to choose. I literally gasped. Mama was right: my deep blue top against Spirit's golden color was striking.

"Wow," we both said in unison.

"Yeah, they really turned out well," the photographer said.

I had to agree, even if he was complimenting himself.

These pictures only confirmed what I always knew: Spirit was the most beautiful horse I'd ever seen.

January 26, 1991

A new year! I know I haven't written in a while but Hallomas with Aunt Mimi was so much fun. The Trifecta of Holidays were great, too. The fruit sale was an awesome great way to start the new semester!

Every year in choir, there was an orange and grapefruit sale to raise money for our robes or anything else we needed. When cars drove up to the school on that brisk Saturday morning, we took their ticket and loaded the car with their purchases. Selling things, especially fruit, was not my favorite pastime, but I actually didn't do too badly. Mama was very generous in buying boxes and sharing with teachers at her school.

Since there was a lot of down time between customers, several of us stood around, laughing and talking in the choir room. I stood next to Jordan, Brandi, and Dustin. In his usual leadership role, Dustin led a discussion about *Les Miserables* since we were singing one of its songs, "I Dreamed A Dream." Out of the blue, he bent down and picked up Brandi. Her petite figure made it easy for him. However, it was awkward watching him twirl her around as she wrapped her arms around his neck, pulling herself closer.

"Weeeeeeeeeeeeeee," I said.

What else were we supposed to say?

Dustin set her down and she touched her head, pretending to be dizzy.

"We need some help out here!" Mrs. Darbinyan said, motioning to the cars lined up. Dustin darted out the door.

"I think he likes you," I said to Brandi.

"Nah, he's not my type."

"Really?" I asked, legitimately surprised.

"I mean, he's nice and all. And, sorta cute."

"And, funny."

"Oh, yeah, he really makes me laugh."

"He makes all of us laugh. Especially when he honks when he laughs."

"Yeah, but I'm just not looking for anyone right now," she said, crinkling her nose.

You could do a lot worse.

I actually liked Brandi. She was very sweet, almost mousy. She covered her mouth when she laughed, hardly making a peep. It seemed to me like she was playing coy, but I guess some guys like that. Sometimes it annoyed me.

Dustin dashed back inside, smelling of citrus and flexing his muscles. "I am He-Man!" We laughed, which was the usual response to Dustin.

Jordan whispered to me, "You know what the song 'In the Mood' is about, don't you?"

"To dance?" I asked.

"Um, yeah. If you want to call it that."

"Jordan, you have such a dirty mind!" I said, elbowing him.

"You never know what the composer meant. He's dead!"

Jordan's witty comments always made me smile. We sat next to each other since I was an alto and he was a tenor. He taught me about theater and what was happening in Hollywood. We'd often chat in class, not always staying on topic about what Mrs. Darbinyan was teaching.

I was still laughing from Jordan's remarks when Dustin jumped right in front of me, threw me over his shoulder and spun me around. I couldn't catch my breath for two reasons—dizziness kicked in and I couldn't believe it was happening. No one could *ever* pick me up, but he did it without any grunts or groans, which amazed me.

"Dustin, put me down!" I faux-protested, gently slapping his back for emphasis.

When he set me down, I didn't have to pretend to be dizzy. Memories of the Dizzy Stick back at Echo Lake Camp returned. Fortunately, this time I hadn't just eaten Mexican food.

"Let me know if you want me to do that again!"

"Yeah, sure," I said, smiling and wobbling around. I rested against the wall as Dustin sprinted out the exit, presumably to help more potential customers. He had more energy than anyone I ever knew.

"You OK?" Jordan asked, touching my back.

"Yeah, I only see one of you now," I joked. "Dustin is so funny. And, kinda cute."

"Yeah," Jordan sighed.

I looked over at him.

"I mean, I can see why girls would think that," he said, clearing his throat.

The rest of the day consisted of laughing, singing, and more standing around. I was grateful to have found choir and a group of people where I fit in. It was my own safe herd.

February 6, 1991

Winter is usually hard, but I don't seem to be inhaling chips like I normally do this time of year. I'm still eating more than I'd like and I have days where I'm just not as motivated. Then I think about Gavin and everyone from Horse and Buddy and try to remind myself that if he can push through things, so can I. Plus, this winter isn't as hard as past years. Part of it is I got accepted to NC State and will be going there in the fall! And, I got my roommate's information and will be writing to her soon. I'm so excited! I wonder if I really could go overseas to study for a while. Wouldn't that be awesome?

March 1, 1991

Hey Kiddo,

Congrats on getting into State! Do you know what you want to study?
I'm just kidding. I don't need to ask! Something to do with animals.
Yes, it will be hard to be away from CJ and Katie Kitty, but it will be
such fun! And, you'll learn so much.

 As you well know, Mackinac Island's most treasured residents
will soon be returning. And, again, that means spring is coming. Your
spirit is up now, I'm sure!

 Hope springs eternal and so does Spring itself!

Love you to the moon and back,
Aunt Mimi

April 10, 1991

Mr. Bucky and Mrs. Patsy are some of the most big-hearted people I know. So grateful to be working there.

Ms. Patsy once said, "Mucking out stalls is 10% cleaning, 10% talking to your horse and 80% making life decisions." I found that mostly true, but I would subtract 10% from the making life decisions part to either humming, singing and/or talking to myself. Spirit's lowered head, half-closed eyes, and loose bottom lip signaled he enjoyed my humming while I scooped out the pile he had made.

Thoughts of going overseas still dominated my mind. I'd love to do it as soon as possible, preferably my freshman year, if Mama said it was OK. It wouldn't be more than a semester. The thought of traveling out of North Carolina, as well as the US, would be the ultimate freedom. The details and possibilities swirled around in my head as a voice snapped me out of my thoughts.

"Hey, Sugar. Looking good in there."

"Thanks, Ms. Patsy," I said, petting Spirit's neck. "He's really good about pooping. Picks one spot—and that's *the* spot!"

"Yeah, he's one of the neatest horses we've had. Not many of those around!"

Almost on cue, Spirit raised his tail, letting out a long fart. I still think farting is one of the funniest things in the world. But I held back my laugh in front of Ms. Patsy so I wouldn't appear juvenile.

"That's his way of thanking you!" she exclaimed.

Once she said that, I doubled over in laughter. "Then they thank me a lot!"

"Endless gratitude from these guys!" she said.

Spirit turned his head toward me and I almost couldn't catch my breath from laughing. That moment reminded me of the fun times with Marin. Although I missed her, I'm glad this time was with Ms. Patsy.

"Sugar, can I get you a Pepsi?" she asked, with a few residual chuckles.

"No, thank you."

"Just holler if you change your—"

Interrupted by a vehicle's back-up beeper, we both turned toward the barn's opening. Mr. Bucky was backing up his black Ford F-150 pickup truck with an attached horse trailer. "Wow, where did Mr. Bucky go?"

She sighed. "The Old Man decided to rescue another horse. Like we don't have enough around here! I'll tell you what, and he probably wouldn't want anyone to know this," she said, leaning closer to me. "That man's heart is bigger than his bank account and hat—combined. Yes, sirree." Nodding emphatically, she looked out at the truck and trailer, then wistfully smiled, "But that's why I love the old goat."

She tapped the side of the barn. "Let's go see what we got here."

"Hey!" Ms. Patsy yelled, walking up to the driver's side before Mr. Bucky put the truck in park. "Who ya got in there?"

"What?"

"Roll down your window! Who'd ya got in there?" she asked, when he parked the truck.

While the two of them decided if they were ever going to answer one another, my focus shifted to inside the trailer. Taking a large step onto its tire cover, I peeked inside. The sun hit my eyes creating shadows and darkness, making it harder to focus. Stretching up on my tippy toes, I was able to discern the outline of a dark-colored horse. Its head hung low and its raspy breathing accentuated its extremely high withers and visible ribs.

"It's OK, big guy. It's OK," I said, whispering into the trailer. The poor thing seemed so scared, but just too exhausted to respond. "Mr. Bucky and Ms. Patsy are going to take good care of you. It'll be OK now."

I'm not sure if my words or soothing tone helped or not. They didn't seem to hurt.

"All right," Mr. Bucky said, opening the trailer's back door, causing the horse to slightly startle. "She loaded right up," he said. "Got halter on her. No problem."

"Oh, it's a 'her,'" I said, jumping down from the trailer tire.

"Yep, callin' her Lily," he said, climbing in and untying her. "Easy, girl."

Despite Mr. Bucky's gentle, calm voice, Lily's ears darted around. The poor thing looked as if she was using every ounce of energy to understand what she was supposed to do. She struggled to place her back legs behind her, as if she had never walked backward before.

"Easy, girl. Eeeezzzzeeee," he reassured again.

Once she unloaded, I gasped. Her bay body was a living, breathing dichotomy. Although her ribs and spine were protruding and her neck lacked muscle tone, she had a huge belly.

"Oh, man," Ms. Patsy said, wiping her forehead. "Whatcha doing bringin' home a soon-to-be mama?"

I thought the bloating was from worms. Guess not.

"They found her tied to a tree in a field," Mr. Bucky said. "Not leavin' her there."

Ms. Patsy scanned under the mare's barrel and her teats. "You *do* realize, it could be any day now."

"Probably so," he said, turning the bay mare around. "Let's get you to your own place."

Ms. Patsy shook her head and smiled.

Mr. Bucky looked back to watch each hesitant step Lily took, creating a stiff and stilted manner to her gait. A persistent cough seemed to plague her, too.

"Bless her heart," Ms. Patsy said. "She's trying so hard. People gave up on her, but he won't. The Old Man will be good with her. And, to her."

"What happens now?" I asked, following them to the barn.

"We'll have Dr. Wheeler come out. She definitely needs a deworming to see what parasites she's got."

Guess I was partly right, after all.

"And, we'll need to draw a coggins on her. Probably has it, but need to have proof."

"What's 'coggins'?"

"It's a blood test to make sure they don't have some diseases. Very common procedure." Ms. Patsy quickened her pace. "She'll probably need antibiotics for her cough. Also, her body score is super low. We measure that on a scale from one to nine with nine being obese and one being skin and bones."

"So, she'd be a one or two?"

"I reckon so. She is really emaciated and will need buckets of love. But, there's a trick to that. Can't just throw tons of food at 'em. They could get colic. Or, worse, die."

"Oh, no!"

We caught up to Lily in her new stall as Mr. Bucky signaled he would be right back.

"And, with her young 'un on the way, that would be devastating. For everyone. So, nasal and IV fluids will most likely be in order. I'm sure Dr. Wheeler will recommend other things. Who knows what else she'll need?"

I watched Lily standing eerily still in her stall, with a wary and wrinkled eye, and darting ears.

"Will she be OK, Ms. Patsy?"

"You mean besides the fact she's no bigger than an ant and weighs about the same? She'll be OK. Just a lot of commotion for her. She has to learn to trust us. Being young and in the family way is even more stressful."

I couldn't help but stare at this creature who simultaneously exuded desperation and gratitude. "How old do you think she is?"

"You can't know for sure unless you look at their teeth. I'm spit-balling it here, but maybe two or three. No more than four."

"That's so young! Spirit is ten and he's still considered young."

"That's exactly right. A baby having a baby. My guess is it wasn't planned either. Maybe that's why she was abandoned. Who knows? But, she's here now, and at least has a chance."

"How do you know so much about all this?"

Ms. Patsy winked at me. "This ain't my first rodeo."

<u>April 26, 1991</u>

Prom is coming up! I want to ask Dustin Roberts because we just have so much fun talking and laughing. He even sent me a valentine rose for our school fundraiser. It was a white one, which is for friendship, but at least he sent one to me. He is a friend, but I admit it, I do have a crush on him. But I think everyone likes him. I better ask him quick.

The sounds of chatter filled the choir room before the starting bell.

"Hey, Maren," Dustin said.

"Hey, everything OK?"

"Yeah, wanna ask you something." He smiled, motioning for me to follow him.

This is it! I can't believe it. I was working up how and when to ask him, but he's making this so much easier!

We walked to the back of the choir room, past the empty orchestra teacher's office, slipping into the end of the hall. Reaching into his pocket, he pulled out a small box, creaking it open to a beautiful, sparkly necklace.

"Oh, my gosh, Dustin. This is gorgeous!" I quickly covered my mouth after my voice echoed down the empty hallway.

"So glad you like it."

"Yeah," I said, biting my bottom lip. "I do. I really do." I shook my head, realizing I had repeated myself.

"Awesome! 'Cuz I'm gonna give it to Brandi when I ask her to Prom."

My hand reflexively recoiled from the opened box.

"I wanted to know what you thought before I gave it to her. Man, can't believe I'm so nervous," he said, rolling his head from side to side. "Do you think she'll like it?"

I opened my mouth to answer.

"You don't need to answer that again." He closed the box and placed it in his pocket. "Thanks so much." He hugged me with a faint smell of Eternity for Men on his shirt.

When the starting bell rang, he sprinted back to the choir room ahead of me. "You're the best!"

Stunned, I ambled down the hall, trying to gather my thoughts. Feeling like Eponine from *Les Miserables*, I returned to my seat in the choir room, fighting back the growing tears.

"You OK, Maren?" Jordan asked.

I looked over at Dustin. "Yeah, just bad allergies." I even faked a sneeze for added flare. I didn't want to go to Prom after that. So, I didn't.

*T*he school day dragged on forever. Every hour of class felt like a year. The only male I wanted to see was a gelding named Spirit. When the final bell rang, I headed straight for my best friend. It didn't help that, on the way to the barn, the radio played "You're in Love" by Wilson Phillips. The lyrics couldn't have been more appropriate.

Giving a quick wave to Ms. Patsy on the phone in the office, I grabbed the soft brush from the tack area, and unlatched Spirit's stall door.

"Hey, big guy." He raised his head and turned it back, blowing out. "You up for a little brushin' now?"

Even though I knew he wasn't a huge fan, he tolerated it for me. The trick was not to brush too hard. I understood what it was like to have thin skin.

"Guys are just so aggravating." As I gently brushed his neck, he lowered his head again, and rested his back hoof. "They only like the really cute petite girls. Or, the ones with really big boobs. Or, ones that laugh at their stupid jokes, batting their eyes at them. Or, are super perfect Christians. Or, ones who love to have sex a lot."

Spirit blew out, making me chuckle.

"You're so lucky. You don't need to worry about guys—or, girls. Or, whatever you used to like before you were gelded. Doesn't matter to me." Spirit shook his head, stretching down to rub his front hoof.

I sighed, dropping the brush and scratching down his neck. "I'm none of those. Guess that's why I'm not with anyone."

Spirit stomped.

"That's what I think, too."

Wrapping my arm around his neck, I gently brought his large head to mine. "Being with you is better than any stupid guy, anyway. Just want to stay here forever." I stood at his side for a while, even doing our thing when I scratched him and he extended his neck, flipping up his top lip. "Guess I better go see what Mr. Bucky and Ms. Patsy are up to." Kissing his soft muzzle, I giggled when his whiskers tickled me.

I joined Ms. Patsy who was watching Mr. Bucky inside of Lily's stall.

"How is she doing?" I asked, studying Mr. Bucky's concentrated face.

"We were just about to call you over. Baby's coming real soon," Ms. Patsy said. "You OK to stay later tonight?"

"Yeah."

"Good," Mr. Bucky said. "Spread hay all over the bottom of her stall. This is happening soon."

"Oh, I don't think I can be a part of the birth though." My eyes darted around, trying to find a way out of this.

"Ain't got no choice now," Mr. Bucky said.

I bit my lip and took in a deep breath.

"Ever seen a baby being born, Sugar?" Ms. Patsy asked, nodding toward Lily.

"Yeah, when I was little. But it got weird at the end."

"Best thing to do is stay real quiet," Mr. Bucky said. "Too many folks is right up in there, tryin' to help. If Lily ain't a good mama, then we go in. Otherwise, let her be. Nature knows best."

"But we have Dr. Wheeler's number on speed dial just in case," Ms. Patsy added.

Lily spun in tight circles, then fell to her knees. Rolling around on the hay, she stood back up, shook herself off, and paced around the perimeter of the stall. The sound of the hay under her hooves was soothing. I kept thinking about Gypsy and the foal, wondering what really happened. I think Gypsy probably died and Daddy didn't want me to know. Who knows what happened to her foal, Spirit.

"Make sure no one gits in there. Moose. Dodger. Goats. Cats. She needs to be alone," Mr. Bucky said.

"Dogs are inside. Goats in their barn," Ms. Patsy said. "I know they hate to be away, but it's for the best. Cats will have to shoo," she said, nudging *Pingüino* away. "That curiosity thing can lead to using up all their nine lives in one night!"

For several hours we stood watching Lily in labor. Propping myself against the stall door, I fought the sleep that wanted to take over. It had been a long day. As with Gypsy, it was hard to see Lily in pain, but knowing there would be a cute little addition made it all worthwhile.

Mr. Bucky and Ms. Patsy kept their focus on her the whole time. The heaviness pushing against my eyelids almost completely shut them when Mr. Bucky said, "Here it comes."

Sure enough, there were the beginnings of a foal. Almost half of it was out already and its head protruded from the amniotic sac, back legs still inside. A few more pushes and the foal whooshed out, along with a great deal of fluid.

"It's a little girl." It amazed me that Mr. Bucky could tell so quickly.

"Great! We sure as heck didn't need another stallion around here," Ms. Patsy said, winking again.

I stood in awe at the beauty of this little being. She lay for a few minutes before she tried to stand up, as if trying to get footing on ice while the rest of us were firmly planted on solid ground. Her tiny ears pointed east and west as she struggled to stand but the amniotic sac was still attached, seeming to weigh her down. Lily occasionally licked the nearly black foal as she walked in circles around her baby, protecting her from an invisible foe. The foal lunged forward, finally disconnecting the sac from her mama. She looked like a drunk bunny.

"Placenta will come out in 'bout an hour or so. Let her do that on her own," Mr. Bucky said.

"Aw, cute little beauty. Doin' just fine," Ms. Patsy said. "And Lily is such a good mama, aren'tcha girl? Sugar, what do you think we should name her?"

"Oh, I don't know," I whispered, trying to catch my breath from how amazing it was to be a witness to this experience again. I know Lily did all the hard work, but watching her and simply staying out of her way was harder than it seemed.

"Maren's Spirit," Mr. Bucky said.

"Really?" I looked up at him, then at Ms. Patsy, whose warm face made me tear up. I tried to hide my quivering lips.

"You heard the Old Man."

"Yep, Maren's Spirit," he repeated.

"What a tremendous honor," I said, reaching up and hugging Ms. Patsy. I wasn't sure if Mr. Bucky wanted a hug, so I clasped my hands and said, "Thank you so much."

He nodded.

Watching this tiny foal struggling to stand, the name just seemed to fit.

May 11, 1991

Watching tiny Maren's Spirit with her mama, Lily, is the cutest thing I've ever seen. I'm just amazed at how coordinated she is on her spindly legs. It's incredible to watch her progress from a tiny, wobbly foal to one who's constantly running like someone is chasing her. All the while keeping her mama, Lily, in her sight. I'm just so honored she has my name.

It was an extraordinary experience to sit and observe Maren's Spirit who was basically a gangly, fuzzy dog. Moose and Dodger weren't as sure about her, but they accepted her as part of their new pack. Due to his overwhelming curiosity, *Pingüino* was driven to smell Maren's Spirit as she slept with Lily watching over her. Proceeding slowly on his belly, the cat approached the foal, smelling her crossed, spindly legs. Lily is an intuitive mother and is thriving from Mr. Bucky and Ms. Patsy's care. She kept her eye on the feline as *Pingüino* stared at the foal for any possible movement. Maren's Spirit raised her head, and slowly blinked at the cat.

In the wild, the baby needs to stay with its mama for survival, so the communication between the two is immediate and clear. Anytime Lily moved, Maren's Spirit was practically glued to her side. Whenever Lily trotted, Maren's Spirit cantered right alongside her. Whenever Lily stopped, her foal stopped with her. One time Maren's Spirit decided to leave her mama's side, she broke into a full gallop trying to see what she could do with "those things that kept her up." However, the law of inertia took over and she wasn't able to stop in time. Boom—right into Lily's butt. Down she went, back legs splayed out. I struggled to restrain my laugh as her innocence and exuberance pulled at my heartstrings.

Mr. Bucky really worked with Lily, who was the most mild-mannered horse I'd ever met. As he says, "There ain't no way a half-ton animal can be told to do anything. We have to be respectful. All the respect you give, gets returned in spades." Considering the unknown, black hole that was Lily's past, she was incredibly loving and accepting. I thought Spirit was docile, but Lily had him beat.

June 9, 1991

Graduation day is finally here! I can't believe it. Hard to believe I'll soon be leaving Garner High School and becoming a proud member of the NC State Wolfpack. Good thing I like wolves and the color red.

The graduation ceremony didn't seem nearly as long as Lacey's, but it still dragged. Seeing CJ in his little brown suit and bowtie was one of the highlights. It seemed as though Mama never stopped smiling, even when her eyes were wet from tears. It was obvious Clint wasn't thrilled to be there, but he was polite when I introduced him to people.

After the ceremony, all of us wearing green gowns with gold trim filled the hallways. Once again, the decibel level skyrocketed when our friends and family joined us. It was like any other day between classes, except there were more tears, hugs, presents, and balloons.

Getting a familiar whiff of Eternity for Men, I turned around to see Dustin heading toward me with arms extended. Wrapping his arms around me, he picked me up, gown and all. Brandi was by his side.

"Congratulations!" I said, catching my breath in his tight grip.

"You, too. We're off to East Carolina!" Dustin said.

"Yep, ECU Pirates—arg!" I said, twisting my face.

"Gonna miss your sense of humor," Dustin said, giving Brandi a quick kiss. "Stay in touch, Maren. Good luck at State!"

"Bye, Maren," Brandi said. Dustin grabbed her hand, leading her through the sea of people.

"Maren!" I heard behind me.

Turning around, I saw Jordan maneuvering his way over to me.

"Jordan, so glad you're here!"

"Of course. Wouldn't miss it. I'm going to miss you, though. Choir won't be the same."

"I'll miss you, too. But next year, you'll get to rule the school and choir will be your kingdom!"

"Sure," he laughed.

"Listen, Jordan," I said, taking his hands. "I really hope you find what you're looking for. You deserve to be happy and like whoever you want. Even if others don't completely understand. You deserve it."

"Love you, Maren." He hugged me tighter than he ever had before. "You keep in touch. I better go."

"If you ever want to get together this summer, just give me a call."

He nodded as he disappeared into the wall-to-wall people. Feeling a gentle tug on my arm, I turned around and my heart leapt.

"Ms. Gardner, you came!"

"Of course! I wanted to wish a very special student all the best." She handed me a horse-themed gift bag. "Here is a little something for you."

I reached inside, removed the multi-colored tissue paper, and pulled out a horse-themed diary. "I knew how much you adored horses and keeping a diary."

"I love it. Thank you so much!" Hugging her, I slightly crinkled the bag and hoped the forming tears wouldn't land on her shoulder. "Thank you again for being there for me."

"You are so welcome, Maren. You were such a big help to me, too."

We smiled at each other. There was so much I wanted to say, but the words just weren't coming.

"Well, listen, you have a wonderful time at State and stop by whenever you're back in town," she said.

"Thank you again, Ms. Gardner!"

She waved and also disappeared into the sea of green.

Looking around for Mama, Clint, and CJ was like trying to find a needle in a haystack. I finally spotted Mama near the lockers, calming my nerves.

"Mama, over here!"

She zig-zagged towards me through the crowd, practically running. Mama rarely ran. "Baby, we're just so proud of you."

"Thanks, Mama," I said, hugging her. "Look what Mrs. Gardner gave me! Can you hang onto it?"

"Sure," she said. "What a great gift."

"Good job, Maren. Congratulations," Clint said. Fortunately, the obligatory hug to Clint was over quickly, allowing me to immediately turn to CJ.

"Hey there, what do you think of your sister now?"

CJ wrapped his arms around me and I swooped him up, kissing him on the forehead.

"That sure was long. It was like 100 years!" he said.

"Yep, sure was. But now I've graduated!"

When I set CJ down, my eyes saw Marin and her family standing not too far away. She was laughing with Duffy Palmer and a few others. I gave a quick smile and wave which she returned. Our first communication in a few years. It felt odd during the ceremony when I heard her name called and glanced up at the bleachers to see her family cheering and clapping. A large part of me wanted to ask where she was going and what she was doing after graduation. A bigger part was OK with not knowing and just wishing her well.

Turning back toward my family, I choked back the tears when I saw two very familiar faces.

"Hey there, Sugar."

"Miss," Mr. Bucky said, tipping his hat.

"Mr. Bucky and Ms. Patsy, I can't believe you came! Thank you so much."

"No need to thank us. Your mama called us up and invited us. Wild horses couldn't keep us away!"

"Mama, you remember Ms. Patsy and Mr. Bucky."

"Sure, I'm so happy you could make it."

"And, this is...Daddy Clint," I said, mumbling the "Daddy" part.

"Pleasure," he said, holding out his hand.

"You remember my favorite little guy, CJ," I said, hugging him, rocking him back and forth.

"Of course! We remember you rode Little Bit at Miss Maren's birthday party a while back," Ms. Patsy said. "How ya been there, Cowboy?"

"Good," CJ said. His eyes looked up at me for a clue on how to respond.

"Here," Mr. Bucky said, handing me a package. "This here's from us."

"Thank you! Do you want me to open it now?"

"Sure!" Ms. Patsy said. Mr. Bucky gave a quick nod under his cowboy hat.

Ripping open the green graduation wrapping paper with gold trim, I gasped.

In my hands was an 11x14 professionally framed picture of the silhouette of Spirit and me from my senior pictures. His ears were pricked forward as I'm scratching under his chin.

Touching my fingers to my mouth, I tried to keep the welling tears from dripping on this tremendous gift.

"Thank you so much. I absolutely love it." I handed it over to Mama so I could hug this special couple.

"We asked your mama when she called what picture she thought you might like," Ms. Patsy said. "She said this was your favorite. We think it's the best. Something to remember us by."

Although I had a smaller proof at home, this framed version helped to honor the photograph in the way it deserved.

"We know you'll be off at college, but be sure to come by when you can," Ms. Patsy said.

"Of course I will. I wouldn't just leave you!"

Ms. Patsy and Mama exchanged smiles.

"I'll be busy, but never too busy for y'all and Spirit and Little Spirit and everyone."

"Just come by when you can," Ms. Patsy said, giving me a quick hug.

Words could not convey the depths of my gratitude. I just hope they knew that.

July 5, 1991

I am soooo excited! For the first time ever, I get to visit Aunt Mimi in Michigan! Just the two of us. It's her birthday and graduation present to me. Can't wait! Guess where we're going? Mackinac Island! It's pronounced Mackinaw Island, but spelled with a "C". I went when I was really young, but don't remember anything except the pictures Mama took. When Aunt Mimi is here for Hallomas, she has shown me some pictures of the Island, since she doesn't live too far away. She's so lucky. Just the two of us, with water AND horses? Life doesn't get any better. Again, there are no cars allowed on the Island, so everyone has to get around either by bike or horse. If I had to choose one, which one would I choose? Let me think! I just love traveling. There is so much to see in this world. One last hurrah before I become a freshman again.

Driving across the Mackinac Bridge, known locally as "The Mighty Mac," we arrived at the ferry stop. Boarding the ferry for the half-hour ride to the Island made me even more excited. I love it when the engines revved up as we rode underneath that magnificent bridge. Waves slapped against the boat's sides, almost beckoning us to the Island. It felt as though we were going back in time. When we disembarked, the downtown included rows of shops and restaurants, but in my excitement, I didn't even know where to focus. Here a horse, there a horse, everywhere a horse, horse. Entranced by it all, Aunt Mimi had to occasionally tug on my arm to move me along. The aroma of lilacs filled the horse-drawn carriaged streets, creating a fragrant bubble around us. The scent was heavenly, which was appropriate since I felt like I was in Heaven.

The most incredible building on the Island is the Grand Hotel. The magnificent white pillars stand upon the 660-foot-long porch, making it the "World's Largest Front Porch." It sits high on a hill creating spectacular views, especially those of the Mighty Mac. I'll bet it was even more beautiful at night. The steep hill in front of the Grand Hotel bustled with horse-drawn carriages, bikers, and other horseback riders. Despite everyone walking on the sidewalks, the horse is king on the Island, always having the right of way. Plenty of "road apples" dotted the street, but the employees were fast to clean up the piles. Although I've never seen it, the movie, *Somewhere in Time*, was filmed there. A small plaque commemorates where they filmed one of the scenes, and the Island has an annual weekend celebrating the movie.

Mama has a photo from when we visited when I was little. In the picture, a woman is riding her horse alongside our Percheron-pulled carriage. I would have given anything to be that woman. Years later when Mama gave me the picture, I cut the girl out. Just wanted the horse anyway. When Aunt Mimi and I started our carriage tour, I imagined myself as a little baby sitting on Mama's lap so many years ago. I smiled when a woman passed us riding on a horse. Although the photographed woman's image was removed by scissors years ago, I liked that the moment was recreated.

Lost in my thoughts, I almost missed some of the interesting history the guide shared. Mackinac Island was the second national park, after Yellowstone. Then, about twenty years later, it was decommissioned and became Michigan's first state park. Our first stop was at Arch Rock, an amazing site overlooking Lake Huron. Then onto the historic Fort Mackinac, where cannons were fired almost every hour. It was my least favorite part of the Island and I was glad we were never close to the Fort when they went off. I've never liked gun shots, really loud fireworks, or anything that startles me. I'm like horses in that way.

Numerous Victorian houses along the shoreline stand guard on the Straits of Mackinac. Lake Huron also adds to the beauty of the Island. As thrilling as it would be to live there, I reminded myself that most of the horses leave for the winter. And, the snow fall is so high, the whole Island can get close to shutting down. Considering the fact that winter already depresses me, living there probably wouldn't be good for me.

The highlight of an already incredible day was when we went horseback riding. Even though it was just walking, the hills and picturesque views were enough to keep my attention. I was grateful it was just a guide with Aunt Mimi and me. I rode in front on a dark bay named Rio and Aunt Mimi rode behind with a standard bay named Slim, who was definitely the follower, reminding me of Jubi. Rio was a full hand taller than Spirit and his ears remained pricked forward the entire ride. It was as though he was seeing the Island for the first time. He only startled once when we walked by the residential area where carpenters were working on a roof. Although he was fun to ride, it made me miss my Spirit. Slim moseyed behind, but was a good fit for Aunt Mimi, because it was obvious she was just riding for me.

Since it was a "No Adults Day," according to Aunt Mimi, we ended our day by feasting on homemade Mackinac Island fudge until our bellies practically burst.

Holding our middles and waddling back onto the ferry, we found our seats. The ride back to the mainland was much bumpier than the one on the way to the Island earlier that day. Fortunately, some of the fudge had digested on the drive back to Aunt Mimi's house. By then, it had gotten a little easier to hoist ourselves out of the car.

Her beautiful home had a guest room that featured a "Beach, please" pillow on the bed and a "See you at the beach" picture on the wall. The aroma of the room was fresh and uplifting, just as I pictured the color of light turquoise would smell.

After my nightly shower in the attached bathroom, I had just slipped into bed when she knocked on the door.

"How ya doing in here?"

"Good. Thanks, Aunt Mimi." I smiled and snuggled down into the fresh, teal sheets.

"Let me know if you need anything, all right?" she said, holding onto the doorknob.

"I will. Thanks again for *everything!* You are the best. I love you."

"I love you, too, Kiddo. I never asked you, though, how are you doing?"

"Um, good. You just asked me that."

She chuckled. "I meant, how are things going?"

"Today was the *best* day. Ever. But I really don't want to go back home. And, I'm still more anxious than I wish I were."

"I wondered," she said, easing down onto the side of the bed. "Remember what I taught you. Take a deep breath. Inhale for four, hold for four, and exhale on eight."

Sometimes some of her things seemed so "woo-woo," but I really felt better when I did what she suggested. Just need to remind myself to do it.

"Thanks. And, I'm still a little upset at Daddy at taking off and stuff."

She rolled her eyes and snorted.

"And, I'm nervous about going to school. I still miss Marin."

"Your friend?"

"Yeah. And, I'll miss CJ, too," I said, leaning my back against the headboard. "I hope Katie Kitty is being taken care of. Clint…meh. But it seems like Mama is so excited for me to go to college. She said she's going to miss me, but I'm not so sure. Probably wanting it to just be the three of them. Ever since they got together, it's been like that."

"Caroline had her hands full when they first got married. New husband. New kids. Then, baby CJ came along. You got lost in the shuffle." She paused. "It doesn't mean she doesn't love you."

I twisted my face to keep the growing tears from falling.

"She loves you very, very much. She's been pulled in many different directions and you were always such an easy kid. So mature. You always did the right thing. Plus, you were so independent."

I played with the sheets with my thumb and forefinger.

"Sometimes a person's focus and energy go where problems lie, and skips over the good stuff. I know it is hard for you, because you remember the time when it was just the two of you together."

"Yeah, I call them the 'Golden Years.'"

She laughed. "Maybe for you, but not for her. She really worked extra hard to make sure you were taken care of, especially after the divorce."

"What do you mean?"

"She had to get a place to live, transportation, and try to re-build her life," she said, counting on her fingers. "And, Garrett still showed up, whenever he felt like it, upsetting what she had tried to do."

I had never really thought about Mama's experience through all this.

"And, she didn't really have anyone to help her because we lived so far from North Carolina. She went the extra mile. Even getting a cat. What was her name again? Candy Corn? Gummy Bear?"

"First there was Brownie, and then Jelly Bean."

"Yeah, Jelly Bean. She sure had a lot of kittens," she guffawed.

"Well, that could have been avoided. She should have been fixed."

"Well, it was a different time," she said, picking at her sleeve. "Just remember that your mama loves you, and will *always* love you. Sometimes the ones we love the most don't always show us love the way we want. Or, need."

"I guess."

"The love is always there. She would have moved mountains for you."

"Then why didn't she? I mean, why didn't she act like it?" I asked, sitting up.

"Maybe she didn't want you to see how hard she was working at it. Or, maybe she did, and you never saw it. You'll get a better idea when you have kids."

"I'm not so sure I'm going to have kids."

"We'll see."

"*You* don't have any!" I snapped.

"Right," she said, pointing at me. "But your path might be different. At any rate, just think about CJ. Think about how much you love him."

I smiled. "My baby brother. He's just the sweetest little guy."

"Hold that in your heart," she said, touching her chest. "Now, your mama's love is even greater than that. Can you imagine?"

"I guess. But sometimes CJ can get on my nerves."

She laughed. "Of course! Just because we love someone doesn't mean they don't ever annoy us. Sometimes they're the biggest offenders!"

"Arg! It's still so hard, though," I said, plopping back down.

"Don't I know it."

"Sometimes I want to spend time with Mama, and then other times I just want her to get the hell away from me!" I paused. "Whoops, sorry. I mean 'the heck' away from me."

"You're also in the time of your life where this is normal."

"Does it get any easier? I mean, sometimes I think, like, why the hell do I do that? Whoops, sorry again."

"Eh, don't worry about it," she said, waving it off. "Might not be OK around others, but it's sure as hell OK with me."

"But, does it ever get easier?"

"'Does it ever get easier?' she repeated, touching her chin. "Well, no."

"Awesome."

"But, then again, sometimes it does," she said.

"So, which is it?"

"Both."

I exhaled loudly and threw up my arms. "This is exactly what I mean."

"You just develop better ways to cope, is all. Of course, there's the deep breathing. That's one. Exercising is another. Getting good sleep is another. One of the most important things is to try to see things from the other person's perspective."

"That's hard, especially when you don't feel like they're trying to see yours."

"Yep," she sighed. "We want so desperately for others to see it through our eyes we forget that they might have an entirely different vantage point."

"It can be so hard."

"I know, Kiddo. I know. This is Life," she said, stretching up. "We had a really full day today."

"Yeah, I know. Horses, history, and water—the best! Oh, Aunt Mimi, which would you rather—"

"—Uh, Kiddo," she smiled. "It's time to go to sleep. You have an early flight tomorrow."

My shoulders slumped. "I know. I don't want to go back."

"Well, you can be thankful that you were able to come."

"I guess. Would you ever move to North Carolina?" I asked.

"Nah, my life is here. I love living in Traverse City and going to Florida in the winter. Plus, the summers in North Carolina are way too hot and humid."

"They're not too hot," I protested. "Plus, we don't get the snow that y'all get up here."

"I love the snow and skiing, and—"

"—North Carolina has skiing!"

She sighed and smiled. "Come here." She wrapped her arms around me and the faint lilac smell on her shirt soothed me. "Love you, Kiddo."

"Love you too, Aunt Mimi."

"G'night." She switched off the lamp with the seashells in the base, and closed the door behind her.

"G'night." I pulled the turquoise, shell-laden quilt over me, snuggling further down into the bed. The day's activities, horses, great conversation, and good food led me to quickly find Dreamland.

*C*losing my diary, I pressed my hand against the cover and placed it on the nightstand. I glanced at the clock.

3:20am.

Staying up almost all night reading and reminiscing cut my packing time short. But I didn't regret one minute. It reminded me how important it is to write about what's going on. It's so easy to forget the details of Life.

The diary from Ms. Gardner is around here somewhere. Even though my last entry in this diary was from July, I plan on using the one she gave me in college.

As I had done at Aunt Mimi's house, I climbed into bed, pulled my old familiar horse-themed comforter over me and fell asleep. Tomorrow I start a whole new chapter.

PART
Four

August 19, 1991

First day on NC State campus. Here we go! That's all I
have time to write about today!

*A*fter the short night and four hours sleep, Mama's knock
on my door jarred me awake.

"Baby, you up?" Mama asked through the closed
door.

"Yeah, Mama," I said, yawning.

"Do I want to come in there?"

"Um...well, I'll be ready by the time we go," I said.

"We have about an hour."

Rushing, I poured the final remnants of my room into the remaining empty boxes. I smiled at the framed picture of Spirit and
me, as well as Wildfire, Billy Bob's Texas Turd Bird, and my Breyer
horses still comfy in my room. It's better for all of them to stay here
and not get tainted by college.

*A*fter saying goodbye to my room, Mama, CJ, and I followed Clint's packed truck to North Carolina State University's campus in the car Lacey and I had shared. I was grateful to be able to keep the car on campus. We found an area to park and began unloading.

"Got it?" I asked CJ.

"Yep!" he chirped.

In his attempt to help, my little brother reached into the packed truck, pulling out my pink table lamp.

"Just be careful, because I need that when I study." I wrapped the dangling cord around its base.

He set it down on the sidewalk next to Sullivan Residence Hall, a twelve-story brick dorm.

I exhaled, looking up at my new home. "Here we go."

Mama accidentally bumped my shoulder and adjusted the bin of clothes she was carrying. My new college-sized refrigerator filled Clint's arms while I carried two boxes of cassette tapes. CJ picked the lamp back up from the sidewalk and the four of us created our small parade into the dorm.

"I'm in room 116," I said, reading the numbers on the doors. "108, 110, 112, 114… this is it."

Inside the room, a girl was arranging her items on the shared dresser.

"Hi, are you Shannon?"

"Hi, Maren!" she said, hugging me as though we were long-lost friends.

"After all the letters, it's so good to actually meet you!" I said.

"I know!" Shannon could have gone to Old Dominion University in Norfolk, Virginia. But her dad went to North Carolina State and now she will be part of the Wolfpack, too.

"Is your mama here?" I asked.

"No, I totally forgot my boombox, so she went to the store to get me another one. She shouldn't be long."

"Shannon, this is my mama. And little brother, CJ. And, Daddy Clint." She smiled, nodding to everyone.

"Nice to meet you, Shannon," Mama said, setting the bin of clothes down. "CJ, just set the lamp down here."

"Sister, you're really going to college!" CJ exclaimed. Everyone laughed and appreciated his announcement.

"I think the refrigerator would be good here," Clint said, setting it down in a little corner nook.

The unpacking commenced as the boxes and clothes piled up on the bed, in the corner, and on the desk area. Although I missed my room with the old-fashioned desk, it was fun creating a new space with Shannon.

After several trips to the car and CJ's "help" in his own way, the room looked as though a tornado ravaged through it.

"It's kinda coming together. Kinda," I said. "You ready to do this?"

"Yeah, but it's hard to be so far away from home," Shannon said. "I miss my boyfriend, Randy, already."

"Your 'HTH'. Hometown Honey!" I joked.

"I really miss him."

"I'm sure."

I'd miss my boyfriend too, but it's hard to miss someone who is nonexistent.

"I wanted to tell you I'm going to be in Australia for a little while next semester."

"You really got it, then? You had mentioned in your letters that you hoped you'd be able to go."

"Thanks, I'm really excited about it."

"Glad you get to go. I can't imagine leaving North Carolina. I really don't even want to," she said, looking out our window.

"Well, Packapalooza is coming up. I hear the bands are awesome and so is the food."

"Not sure I'm going to go. I might even be going back home this weekend."

But we just got here.

"Baby, I think we're going to get going," Mama said.

Again, we just got here!

"You're leaving now? You're not even going to stay for lunch?" I asked.

"Unfortunately, I have a workshop this afternoon and Clint has to get to his game."

My face fell. Mama's arms engulfed me, making her departure even more painful.

"CJ, say 'Goodbye' to Sister," she said, her voice slightly cracking.

I crouched down to CJ and he wrapped his arms around me.

"Bye, Sister! Are you coming home?"

"Yeah, of course," I said, choking back some tears. "I'll be home before you know it."

"Have a good semester," Clint said. "Be careful with the car. Remember, it's on loan." I gave him the usual quick, obligatory, side hug.

"She will," Mama said. "Shannon, it was so nice to meet you. Hopefully we can meet your mama sometime."

"Nice to meet you, too, Mr. and Mrs. Fletcher."

"Bye, Baby," Mama said, turning to me with wet eyes.

"Bye, Mama." I looked around at our disheveled room. Shannon and I both wondered how we would ever get this mess to feel like home.

<u>August 23, 1991</u>

Packapalooza was so much fun! The bands and food really WERE great! I wish Shannon had gone too, but I have no problem going places by myself. She is so homesick and calls Randy every night. Sometimes she calls him during the day and again at night. Then, she's on the phone with her mama. I mean, do they have to talk every day, too? We have a phone in our room, but sometimes she gets calls on the hall phone, too.

Wonder how Daddy and his band are liking being out West and if he misses me. Wonder about Marin, too. It's funny that I don't get as sad thinking about her. I'm really hoping if she did go to college that she's doing well.

As I arrived at the lecture hall for my first class, the buzz of chattering people echoed down the hallway. I could hardly believe I was there. Picking an empty seat near the back, I sat down, fiddling with my psychology book and notebook.

"Hey."

Looking up, I saw a cute guy with dark hair and blue eyes. He sat down in a seat to my right.

"Hey." I smiled, slightly biting on my lower lip.

"I'm Brody."

"I'm Maren."

"Maren," he repeated. "That's a great name."

"Thanks."

"So, um…this class should be pretty cool. I hear the professor should be all right, too."

"Yeah, I liked my psychology class in high school."

"Why are you taking it again?"

"It didn't transfer."

"That sucks," he said.

"But I probably would have taken it again anyway. I just love psychology." I figured it was OK to be a little nerdy. We were there to learn, after all. "What's your major?"

"Business, with a focus on marketing," he said.

"Wow, I don't know much about business."

"There's so much out there now. I just want to help companies get their names out and develop relationships. What's your major?"

"Animal Science. I want to be a veterinarian and next semester I'm going to study in Australia for a little bit," I said.

"Look at you, Miss World Traveler."

I laughed and bit my lower lip again. "Yeah, well, I love to travel. So, when the opportunity to go overseas came up—"

"—You took it."

"Yeah. Do you like to travel?" I asked.

"Nah. There's way too much in North Carolina to do. We got the ocean *and* the mountains."

"There is a lot to do here, but I figure since I'm young, now is the time to travel. And I get credit for it," I said, gaining some confidence from who-knows-where. "So, are you living on campus?"

"Yeah, we're in Bragaw. You?"

"I'm in Sullivan."

"Roommate, or not?" he asked.

"Yeah, Shannon. She's really nice and is majoring in elementary education."

"Yeah, my roomie seems cool. Charles, I think. Or, Chad, maybe," he said.

"You don't know his name?"

"Guess not! I do know he is probably pre-vet. Not sure, though. He should be because he really likes animals. Especially horses."

"Really?" I perked up.

"Not me. Way too big."

I chuckled, picturing him bouncing on a horse with his reins all over the place. Poor horse.

"I'm stickin' to baseball. I played shortstop, even played Varsity."

"Cool." He might as well have spoken Greek because what he said made no sense to me.

"Anyway, we're having a party on Friday. We're in room 307. Y'all should come by." He paused. "Your boyfriend, too."

"Actually, I don't have a boyfriend," I said, basking in this moment when he thought I had one.

"You should," he smiled. "So, Friday, come on by!"

"Sure, I'll try to stop by," I said, biting my now sore lip, trying to keep my cool.

*T*he smell of beer permeated Bragaw's hallway and the thumping bass resonated in my chest. "You ready?" I asked Shannon as I reached for the doorknob. She smoothed out her skirt and gave a quick nod.

The darkened room was almost wall-to-wall bodies on that humid, summer night. It was just like the hallways in Garner High after graduation, only with kegs strategically placed in each corner.

"Hey, Maren!" Brody jumped from the side, landing right in front of us. "You came!" His potent beer breath overwhelmed my senses, and I could practically taste what he had in his Solo cup. He waved over a few other people.

"Maren, meet April. This here's Colton, and Nolan and his girl-friend, Tina," he said, yelling over the Nirvana song. "Nolan and Colton live down the hall. And the girls live in Lee Hall."

"Hey, y'all," I said.

Another guy standing there drew me in with his inviting smile. "This here's my roomie. His name is Chase. I remembered!" Brody exclaimed. "Aren't you proud of me? Chase, this is Maren."

I studied Chase's face, struggling to focus in the room's dim light.

"Hey, Maren." He furrowed his brow and looked as though he was studying me too. "Don't I know you from somewhere?"

"No, don't think so," I said.

"Ah, man. Get a different line!" Brody exclaimed, slapping Chase on the back.

"Lame, dude!" Colton said.

I narrowed my eyes. The blondish hair, deep brown eyes, inviting smile. But it couldn't be. That was Matty, not Chase.

"Did you ever go to Echo Lake Camp?" he asked.

My heart nearly stopped. "Yeah—Oh, my god."

Now I know what those romance novels are talking about.

"Y'all know each other?" Brody asked.

"Yeah, from camp," he said. "Wow, how have you been?"

At that moment, every word I had ever learned in my life exited my brain. Every. Last. One. It was like seeing a ghost, which was also probably the color of my face. I wondered if my zipper was down, or if I had lipstick on my teeth.

Answer his question, Maren!

Summoning up the courage and wherewithal, my brain finally kicked into gear. "Good. I've been good. How have you been?"

Dang it, that's already been asked.

"Good, good," he said, smiling, bobbing his head.

As he took a step closer to me, all the feelings from years ago flooded back. It was as if the boy I knew had grown up to be a man with darker hair, more muscles, squared jaw, and an even more inviting smile.

Brody said something behind me, but I didn't see him, nor did I really care at that point.

"This is crazy," Chase said, shaking his head.

"Yeah, it is. So, you're 'Chase' now?"

"Yeah. Matty was from my middle name, 'Matthew.' I took my first name, which is the same as my father's."

"Oh, OK." I felt relieved that I hadn't forgotten his name. Lord knows I had not forgotten him. Or, that night.

"This is so amazing, seeing you again," he said. "You look great. I wondered what happened to you."

Every fiber of my being wanted to skip around campus, scream-ing that very thing.

"Thank you, but I always thought you liked that Shae girl. From camp."

"Who's Shae?"

"She had blonde hair and big—"

"—Oh, that girl? Not a chance."

"That's weird because she bragged about how you liked her and kept watching her, every time she'd walk by. And, other stuff."

"Well, she was hard to miss. But way too high-maintenance for me."

I smiled.

"Besides, I'm not even sure she liked horses," he said. "Why are you at a camp with so much horseback riding if you didn't like horses?"

My sentiments exactly.

"Lucky for me, my girlfriend Brittany likes horses, too."

Damn.

"Yeah, she's at UNC-Greensboro so we both come home to Raleigh as many weekends as we can."

Brain locked again. Come on words!

"That's good."

At least, I think that's what I said. What else was I supposed to say? His words became distorted as if I were under water anyway.

"This is just crazy, though," he said.

"Definitely. Well, good to see you. I think I'm going to head out."

"Oh, OK. Good seeing you again, Maren," he said.

I averted my body to avoid his hug and my eyes landed on my roommate, standing alone in the corner.

"Shannon—I'm so sorry. Are you ready?"

She nodded with slightly pouty lips.

"Let's go." I never really said goodbye to Chase, or anyone, but I wasn't going back.

"What did you do, Chase? You scared off the chicks!" I heard Brody say as we closed the door behind us.

Once outside into the hallway, I asked, "You doing OK, Shannon?"

"I really miss Randy," she said, almost jogging to the dorm exit. "He's the best boyfriend."

Must be nice.

<u>September 3, 1991</u>

I just can't believe I saw Matty, I mean, Chase again! It's like he came back from the dead. All that time I spent thinking about him and here he is! Maybe he didn't kiss Shae from camp, but who knows. Anyway, it's just so great to see him again and I feel like I have someone here from "home." Of course, he has to have a girlfriend. Bleh.

I met with my advisor today to discuss possibilities for the Study Abroad program. Even though they have semester-long programs, I can't do that as a freshman and get credit for it. So, we discussed the details of going for the first part of the semester, then finish the semester out at NC State. There are so many places to go, but I already know I want to go to Australia! They have an awesome program at University of Adelaide, which is northwest of Melbourne. They don't usually allow many students to go second semester. However, because of my high school grades and GPA, Mr. Bucky and Ms. Patsy's recommendations, and Mama's permission, I'm allowed in the program. Even though it's not until next semester, I'm getting excited! Shannon isn't around too much since she's been commuting from her grandparents' house in Wake Forest. It's becoming more real—I'm really going to a different country!

September 4, 1991

Dear Kiddo,

I'm so sorry I won't be able to make it to North Carolina this year for Hallomas. I'm really disappointed, but I have to take care of some things in the condo in Florida as soon as I can. To make it up to you, when you get to Australia, I want you to have an experience on me! Go on a tour, go visit a historical site, go horseback riding on the beach—your choice! Whatever you want. Just make sure you have fun!

  Keep your spirit up!

Love you to the moon and back,
Aunt Mimi

September 4, 1991

I'm bummed that Aunt Mimi won't be here for Hallomas, but I'm not even sure I'll get home this semester anyway. I'm loving college! Matty, I mean, Chase is so much fun. It's just so hard to call him that.

"Hey, World Traveler!"

Leaving Talley Student Union after grabbing a quick bite, I turned around to see Brody running toward me. April, Brody's new girlfriend, and Chase were walking behind.

"We're heading over to Zaxby's to catch a bite," Brody said, out of breath.

"Now?" I asked, pulling at my backpack strap.

"Yeah, you should come. C'mon, let's go!"

"Oh, man. I just ate." I glanced over at Chase and April who had caught up to us.

"Oh, too bad," Brody said.

"Join us anyway," Chase said, smiling.

"OK," I said.

"Last one there is a loser!" Brody yelled, running away with April hot on his tail.

My heart rate shot up walking next to Chase and I bit my bottom lip to try to contain my anxiety.

"You took off the other night. That wasn't cool," he said.

What do you care? You already have a girlfriend.

"Sorry about that. It was just getting stuffy in that room," I said, pulling again at my backpack strap.

"Uh, huh. So, did you ever go back to Echo Lake?"

"Yeah, I went back another year. Anything to be around horses!" I immediately regretted how dorky that sounded.

"It was a fun place."

"Wasn't the same without you," I said, regretting my honesty. Again.

Without looking over at me, he smiled.

As everyone feasted on their Big Zax Snak meals, I was glad I had already eaten. There was no way I would have eaten in front of Chase. I'm not a big fan of eating in front of other people anyway, much less him. Even April got in on the fried meal. The competition between her, and her new boyfriend, Brody, seemed to have no bounds, including how much they could eat.

"Hey, let's head over to Lake Wheeler!" Brody suggested.

"Yeah!" April said.

"Sure. Maren, you in?" Chase asked.

"Yeah." Although I was exhausted from the day and lack of sleep with an English paper still waiting for me to write, there weren't many other places I'd rather be.

"We'll need to take your car," Brody said, smacking Chase in the stomach.

Even though I was grateful Mama and Clint gave me the 1984 Mazda that Lacey and I had shared, I was equally grateful Brody didn't suggest using my car. The stray remnants of hay, horse clothes, books, and other things spread around would have made it difficult for another human being to sit anywhere.

In the parking lot, we stopped in front of a practically new Honda Accord.

"This is your car?" Brody asked.

"Yeah," Chase said, almost embarrassed.

"What year is she?" he asked, running his fingers against the dark blue finish.

"1992."

"Next year's model. How'd you pull that off?"

"Got it for graduation," Chase said.

"Sweet!" Brody exclaimed, climbing into the backseat next to April. "Where are you from again, man?"

"North Raleigh."

It amazed me how little Brody knew, or cared to know, about his roommate. Of course, I wanted to know anything and everything about Chase, so I was on the complete opposite side of that coin.

Sitting next to Chase in the passenger seat in a brand-new car made me feel as though my cool factor jumped about 1000 notches.

*E*ven before Chase put the car in park at Lake Wheeler, Brody jumped out, sprinting toward the water with April doing her darndest to keep up. Another competition between them. The Big Zax Snak Meal tends to slow most people down, but Brody seemed to get even more energized. That's how he stayed so thin and lanky. Chase and I followed the two, who were now clear on the other side of the lake.

"Are you still riding that horse you really loved? What was his name?" Chase asked.

"Spirit, yeah. I'm impressed you remembered!"

Chase smiled.

"Spirit is the absolute best. Easy keeper, practically bomb proof, goes wherever you point his nose. And, he's forward."

"I like that," he said, clearing his throat. "Ray is like that—my Quarter Horse and Morgan cross. Olive, my Thoroughbred, not at all. You would think she would be. She's pretty fiery, but most mares are."

"That's not true!"

"I've been around horses my whole life, so, yeah, it is," he said, trying to hide a smile.

Brody and April zipped back over to us, breathless. She bent over and rested her hands on her knees while Brody contorted his mouth in an attempt to get more oxygen. *I guess even he has his limits.*

"So, you think you know so much about horses?" I asked.

"Um, yeah. I do," he said, with a glint in his eye.

"Ooooo..." Brody scoffed, momentarily shifting his focus away from trying to catch his breath.

"OK, Mr. Big Shot. Here's a question for ya," I asked, with my hands on my hips. "When did Secretariat win the Triple Crown?"

Chase looked up at the sky, pulling on his chin. "1974."

"Wrong Bucko! It was 1973," I said, poking his chest.

"Nope, 1974."

"I know for a *fact* it was 1973," I said.

"I'll bet you that I'm right. And, if I win, you're going into the water."

"And, if I win?" I asked, puffing out my chest with a grin to match. "Which I will."

"If you win....well...you *still* go in!" He swooped me up, carrying me several feet. After I kicked and flailed my arms, he plopped me down in the water. I splashed up some water, trying to soak his face. When that didn't work, I grabbed his waist, knocking him off balance, and dragged him into the water with me.

Brody and April, observing the whole interaction, doubled over again, this time in laughter.

Once Chase and I emerged, I yelled, "You know I'm right!" Little droplets flew from my mouth for emphasis.

"If you say so," he grinned and winked. When he ran his fingers through his wet hair, less-than-Christian thoughts flooded my mind. *It was time to get out.*

"You OK?" Chase asked, reaching out his hand to help me.

"Yeah, I'm fine," I smiled.

"Get a room, you two!" Brody yelled.

Although shame filled my head, it didn't fill my heart.

September 17, 1991

College is a blast so far! It's so much fun hanging out with everyone, especially Chase. It definitely helps that I've always been pretty independent, like Aunt Mimi said. Shannon, however, is having a harder time. She's still on the phone a lot with Randy and says how much she misses home. I miss home too, but I don't have the yearning that she has. I have that feeling more with Fair Oaks.

   I was just happy to get back to the barn today. I can't believe it's been almost a month since I was there. I've really missed seeing everyone, especially Spirit, of course. It made my heart sing that he came to me in the paddock, sans a peppermint! Initially, he shook his head, but eventually came on his own. Since it had been so long, I gently blew into his quivering nostrils, like Ms. Patsy had said. He blew back out, so I felt we were good. Admiring his long black eyelashes and golden color, I wrapped my arms around him, smooshing my nose into his neck. The horsy-smell is hard to describe, but it's one of my favorite and most relaxing smells. I'm also grateful for my allergy shots since they helped to make my time around horses less sneezy and even more enjoyable.

   Little Maren has really grown. She's getting steadier on her feet which seems to be the same for me, too. I'm still trying to get my feet under me from being at college. Ms. Patsy was on to something when she told me not to forget them at graduation. Guess she knew. I'm just grateful that they still let me work there, even if I can't get there as often as I did in high school.

<u>October 1, 1991</u>

Well, it happened. Shannon finally left. It was just too hard for her to be away from her boyfriend and family. She was a nice girl and I wish her well! It'll be strange not having Hallomas this year, but I love that I have my own room now!

I was able to get to the barn again. Mr. Bucky and Ms. Patsy are working to wean Maren's Spirit from Lily. They've started separating them for longer periods of time. They're getting Maren's Spirit used to touch by petting her all over and touching her legs and hooves. They let me do it, too. I love when the foal leans into me, even though they say not to let her get away with too much. Sometimes I'll sit on the ground and Maren's Spirit, or Little Spirit, as I call her, will come and join me. Nothing like a few hundred pounds plopping on you! She is so fuzzy, loving, and playful. How can I say no to that?

<u>October 15, 1991</u>

What a day! I got to the barn AND talked to Chase— like REALLY got to talk to him!

Later that evening, I yawned as I pushed through the double-doors of the campus library onto dimly lit sidewalks. Studying for Calculus was kicking my behind. I was determined to not let it get the most of me and studied until the library closed. A slight crispness to the night air almost made me forget the previous week's warmth. Wrapping my arms around myself to stay warm, I noticed a familiar silhouette approaching from the parking lot.

It was Chase.

"Hey, what are you doing out so late? Isn't it past your bedtime?" I asked.

He smiled, throwing his head back. "Hey! I'm just getting back from celebrating my sister Amy's birthday."

"Happy Birthday, Amy! How old is she?"

"Sixteen. We all ate at Angus Barn and then sang to her. It was fun. She seemed to enjoy it, too."

Since Angus Barn is one of the most expensive restaurants in the Raleigh area, I could only imagine what it was like. It took every ounce of energy not to ask if Brittany was there for the party. I assumed she was, so I didn't ask.

"Do you have any other brothers or sisters?" he asked.

"Nope, just me and Amy. You?"

"I have a stepsister, but we're not close. We don't even have the same last name. Everyone has 'Fletcher' except for me. I kept my Daddy's last name."

He nodded.

"I do have a brother, well, technically a half-brother, CJ. He's the cutest thing. Just love him to pieces."

"That's really cool." He took a small step closer to me. "What about you? It's past your bedtime, too."

"I'm just coming back from the library prepping for my Calc exam tomorrow," I said, clearing my throat.

"Mine is later this week."

"I was at the barn late, so it pushed my study time back. A different barn than where you were. It was an actual barn!"

"That's great. I know you haven't been able to get there as much as you'd like," he said.

"Yeah, it's crazy how busy college is. But I really miss everyone there, especially Spirit." I squeezed my crossed arms tighter.

"I miss riding my two monsters, too."

"So, you really know," I said, locking my eyes on him longer than I should. "Plus, there's a new foal there that they named after me."

"Wow, how much did you pay them?" he said, elbowing me.

"They did it on their own!" I pretended to protest.

"Sure."

"Believe what you want," I said, giving him a wink, thinking of Ms. Patsy. "Plus, I've been working on learning to ride English. It's different, but I like it."

"I never learned English. Western was enough. My Pops taught me how to rope to increase my strength. And, baling the hay and chores at the barn. Then playing tennis and baseball helped, too." His voice fell. "I was kind of a scrawny kid."

"I've never been scrawny in my life," I joked.

"Well, for a guy, it's not a good thing. So, my Pops suggested I try different things. It really helped."

"Good."

My response resembled nothing like what I really wanted to say. Why does my brain freeze up around him? What I really wanted to say is how I never thought he was scrawny, despite what Marin repeatedly said about him. And, now he's filled out even more—nicely, I might add. But none of that seemed relevant to the conversation we were having—only the one in my head.

I shuddered.

"You OK? Here, have a seat." He unzipped his jacket and placed it over me. The faint smell of Drakkar Noir on it gave me comfort.

"Thanks. It's gotten chilly—fast!" I said, sitting on the curb.

"Why are you learning to ride English?" he asked, sitting next to me. "Just because?"

"Well, that too, but since I'm going to a country where they don't ride Western too often, I thought I'd learn what they do."

"That's right. When are you leaving again?"

"A few days after Christmas. December 27."

"Oh," he said, chucking a small pebble to the side.

"I'll have the weekend to get settled in, then I'll celebrate New Year's Eve down there," I said. "Since Australia is in the Southern Hemisphere, it will be summer. It'll be weird that it's warm in

January, but fun, too! I love it when it's chilly for Christmas, but once Christmas is over, I like it warm again. I don't do as well when it's cold and dark."

Why did I go on and on? He doesn't need to know all that.

"That's really cool."

"Just don't miss me too much!" I said, giving a slight nudge with my elbow.

"OK," he said, smiling and holding his glance longer than usual.

I cleared my throat. Again.

"I was just thinking about that time at camp when the 7Up overflowed in your cup," he said.

"Oh, my gosh! So embarrassing. And you handed me the napkins. That was so sweet."

"And, you really rode that horse in that race, too."

"You mean against Shae?" I asked.

"Yeah, her."

"Wispy was such a good boy," I said. "That was really fun, for many reasons. Don't forget, I won at the tag on horses, too!"

"Gotta tell ya—I let you win."

"You did not," I laughed. "I won fair and square!'

We smiled at each other and he nudged my knee. Looking at his watch, he said, "Well, it's about 1:00am. Guess I should head out."

Is it that late already?

We covered many topics—family, growing up, and school. The conversation flowed so well, I guess it made sense that two hours had passed.

"Good luck on your exam tomorrow. I know you'll do great." He stood, and reached out to help me up. Feeling his strong hand in mine, I wanted to wrap my other hand around his.

"Thanks," I said, returning his jacket back to him. "Good luck with whatever you're doing!"

He snorted. "Thanks. G'night, Maren."

"G'night, Chase."

I don't think my feet touched the ground all the way back to my room. I ended up doing OK on my exam, but it wasn't because I slept well. It's obvious that didn't happen.

<u>Friday! October, 18, 1991</u>

I'm so happy that Chase is staying on campus this weekend! I think I'll go over to his room after my Bio lab today. I've been on Cloud 9 since Tuesday. Brody and April are interesting, but it was awesome talking to Chase alone. I just love being with him. It's been a busy week. You would think there would be a slight slowdown after midterms. Nope! It should be fun because Halloween is coming but it's sure been a strange Fall. No Hallomas, haven't been home, and new college life. I'm happy that I've been able to see Spirit and little Maren's Spirit but it still hasn't been as much as I would have liked. Of course, if I'm not at the barn a few hours every day, it probably isn't as much as I want!

<u>Sunday, October 20, 1991</u>

Well, it wasn't as good a weekend as I thought it would be. It kinda sucked. Wish I hadn't gone over there. Just made it all too real.

Going over to the guys' room filled me with excitement, partly because I always looked forward to what Brody and April would do or say next. But even though he was technically off-limits, seeing Chase was definitely the highlight. By the time I arrived, it was still early in the evening, so their hallway didn't wreak of sweaty bodies and beer. Not yet, anyway. The familiar smells of Drakkar Noir, Eternity for Men, and Obsession for Men hung thick in the air, making me wonder if every guy shopped at the same place for their cologne.

From their open door, I heard an unfamiliar voice coming from the room. It was female and she was laughing.

I peeked around the corner. Brody and April were snuggled together on their bean bag chair and Chase had his arm around a blue-eyed girl with short blond hair. She had more makeup caked on than I'd seen in a long time.

"Hey, Maren's here!" Brody yelled, startling me. "Meet Brittany, Chase's Hometown Honey!"

"Hey," she said.

"Hey, Brittany." I gulped to swallow my deflated excitement and went in.

"She's here until tomorrow!" Brody yelled. He rarely speaks at a normal decibel level.

Trying to keep myself from bursting into tears, I asked, "Where do you go to school?"

I knew full well it was UNC-Greensboro because Chase already told me, but I needed to ask something.

"Great, what's your major?" I asked, using every ounce of energy to make my smile seem genuine.

"Communication Studies."

"Oh…great."

Brody, yell something out again. Chase, April—somebody say something!

"Yeah, I'm planning on going into television. Maybe interning at WFMY in Greensboro or better yet, ABC11 or WRAL here in the Triangle," she said, as Chase embraced her tighter.

"Very cool."

Just trying to keep my vomit down.

"Let's head over to Zaxby's," Brody said, hoisting himself out of the bean bag chair. "So these two can make it to their movie," he said, gesturing to Chase and Brittany.

"What are you seeing?"

"*Don't Tell Mom the Babysitter's Dead*," Brittany said.

"Oh, wow," I said, trying to suppress a laugh.

"Yeah, this one here wanted to see *City Slickers*," she said, nudging Chase.

"I would love to do a cattle drive like that!"

"Yeah," Chase said.

Brittany raised her eyebrows. "Really? Not me."

"All right—off to the Chase-mobile!" Brody said, offering his hand to April.

"Well, actually," I said, clearing my throat. "I just stopped by to say 'Hey.'"

"You're not bailing, are you?" Chase asked.

"Well, I have, like, tons of work to do this weekend," I stammered. "So, yeah. Sorry."

"Oh, man." Chase unwrapped his arm from Brittany.

"Y'all have a great time at the movie. And, uh, nice meeting you, Brittany."

"You, too," she said, giving a small smile.

"Bye, y'all!"

On the way back to my dorm room, my last ounce of energy was used to keep my welled-up tears from falling. I guess he really does like prissy girly-girls. That's definitely not me. He said he didn't like or kiss Shae from camp, but maybe he really did. Guess he really is that shallow.

October 24, 1991

I needed to get to Fair Oaks to try to forget what happened with Chase and Brittany. Maren's Spirit is getting bigger and cuter every time. No one tops Spirit, of course, but Maren's Spirit is definitely more darling. I've been able to take my books there and work on my homework while Spirit lies down next to me. Jubi stays nearby, watching over us and Ebony is more in the distance. I liked talking with Mama and CJ today. I do miss them, but I guess not enough to go over and visit. If I have any extra time, I want to be at the barn!

"Hi, Mama," I said, calling from my dorm phone.

"Baby, how've you been? Let me put you on speakerphone!"

"Sister!" I heard CJ yell in the background.

"When are you coming home?"

"Well, Halloween is coming. And, I'll be home for Christmas before I leave," I said, twirling the phone cord around my finger.

"You're leaving?" CJ asked.

"Yeah, to Australia, remember?"

"Can I go, too?" he asked.

"Not this time. But we'll have fun dressing up for Halloween and trick-or-treating. Can you take me off speakerphone?"

"Sure," she said, with more clarity despite the sound of CJ playing with cars in the background.

"The last payment for Australia and this semester's tuition is coming up," I said.

"Sure, I can get that to you."

"Thanks so much, Mama. How are things with you?" I asked.

"Well, Lacey just called from Florida."

So that's where she ended up.

"She said she wouldn't be home for Christmas this year."

"Thank God," I said. "This really *will* be a great Christmas!"

"Now, now," Mama laughed. "How's the semester going?"

"Busy, but I'm loving it," I said. "Hope that my roommate is doing OK at home, but it's been nice having the place to myself."

"Glad to hear. You always enjoyed your own room."

"Yeah. Whoops, sorry, Mama. Just saw the time. Gotta get to class. But I'll see you soon."

"OK, Baby. See you then."

<u>Over Thanksgiving break 1991</u>

Even though we didn't celebrate Hallomas this year and I missed Aunt Mimi, Halloween was a lot of fun. Mama and CJ always make it so. It's strange, but I've been thinking about random things. I think college makes you do that. Like, what motivates adults to do things, like go to church? We never really went, but I think it's like an insurance policy. And, why do people eat after a funeral? The grandma of one of the girls in my Biology class died. She told me about all the food afterward. Why is that? Why do people have to eat every time they're together, especially after a funeral. It's like we have to stuff our feelings right away. Those are just some of the things that I've been thinking about.

It's been unseasonably warm this Thanksgiving break. My visits to Fair Oaks are still the highlight of my life. There is so much to be grateful for.

Joining Spirit, Jubi, and Ebony in the paddock, I found the spot on Spirit's neck where he loved to be scratched. It's like finding that special area on a dog's butt where they delight in pressing their backside into your hand. We did our thing again, where Spirit extended his long golden neck, flipping up his top lip. If I stopped, he would touch his lips to my shoulder so I would start again. Jubi was at his usual position of watching over us, and Ebony observed from afar.

Once he had enough, he pawed at the dirt and his knees folded under him. Emitting a long and slow groan, he eased down onto the ground. I grinned, just happy to be standing next to him and not sitting on his back this time. With soft eyes, he stretched out his neck, smelling the dirt.

This huge animal who normally towers over me now was lying down like a lamb with his legs tucked under him. Easing down next to Spirit, I placed my head on his shoulder. He stretched his neck around to smell me, touching his muzzle to my cheek. His warm breath emerged through his tiny whiskers and flaring nostrils. I gently kissed his muzzle and his lips quivered. Since horses evaluate a situation through their sense of smell, Spirit must have felt fine because he laid his head back on the ground, releasing a huge sigh.

Pingüino trotted out to us, joining the lazy horse and human on the ground. After touching his vertical feline tail against my cheek, he tucked his tail under him, curling against Spirit's chest.

I sat up, looking down at Spirit's large, magnificent head resting on the ground with his feline companion nestled next to us. Rubbing Spirit's long neck, it surprised me how much different he looked and even felt from when he's standing. I pushed parts of his mane to stand up making it appear as though his mane were flowing. The beauty of the moment overtook me. As strange as it was, giggles were the only way I could express my gratitude and full heart. A tinge of guilt washed over me because I didn't want it to seem I was laughing at him. Every move I made, I checked in with Spirit to make sure he was OK.

Giving his neck a final rub, I nestled my head into his shoulder. Gazing upward provided me with a completely different point of view. My mind wandered, finally landing on horses' contributions to history; how much they've done for us and given to us. The passing clouds in the endless sky seemed to symbolize each passing moment and I felt both simultaneously enormous and minuscule.

It was Heaven there with my Spirit.

<u>December 4, 1991</u>

I can't. I just can't.

Spirit normally stands quietly in his stall, facing the back corner. However, this time he was shifting his weight and kicking at his stomach.

"Hey, big guy. How are you doing?"

I thought there was a fly on his stomach, so I crouched down and ran my fingers over his sweaty belly. Didn't see anything. He turned his head around, touching his muzzle to my hand. I scratched his forehead and lifted up his forelock. I even found his special spot and scratched but he still shifted around. Plus, I didn't see any pile. I never thought I'd miss them that much.

"Here's your food."

His neck was soaked with sweat and he pawed at the ground, repeatedly turned his head to his stomach. Again, I examined his belly, but nothing felt or looked different. Something was definitely wrong.

I ran to find Mr. Bucky inside the house paying bills since I knew that Ms. Patsy took the dogs and was visiting friends on the Outer Banks. Even though I defied one of the Golden Rules, it seemed the best thing to do at that moment.

"Mr. Bucky," I said, breathless. "Something's wrong with Spirit."

He looked up from his desk. "How figure?"

"When I got there, he didn't greet me. He keeps pawing at the ground and looking at his belly. And, he's super sweaty and not interested at all in his food."

Mr. Bucky rose up from his desk so fast a few of his papers flew off. I had to run to keep up.

He unlatched Spirit's stall door and stroked Spirit's belly. Taking a step back, he took a second to watch the unsettled horse. "Don't look good," he grunted.

Mr. Bucky rarely showed emotion, so hearing those words flooded me with overwhelming fear.

"Be right back. Gonna call Doc. Take his food and water away. Put the halter on him and walk him around. Do not stop and do not let him lie down. *Do Not,*" he emphasized, pointing his finger at me. "Ya understand?"

"Yes, sir," I said, nodding through wet eyes.

I wanted to ask him what was wrong, but I didn't even see him leave.

My shaking hands reached for the hanging halter. I had done this tons of times before, but it felt like it was the first time. I fumbled around, occasionally using my shoulder to wipe my tears.

After finally getting the halter on, I unlatched his stall door. Usually, he'd walk right behind me, but it was a struggle to get him to follow me.

"C'mon, big guy," I said, jerking on the lead. Eventually, he moved, but at such a slow pace, we might as well have been stopped. I craned my neck looking for any sign of Mr. Bucky's return.

I decided to talk sweetly to Spirit like I had done so many times before. This time I narrated what I was doing and seeing.

"Here we go," I said, finally pulling him out of the stall. "Just going to close the door behind you." I caught a glimpse of his full food bucket in the stall.

"We're just going to walk through the barn now," I said, listening to the munching of happy horses. As we passed by Jubi's stall, he stopped eating and poked his head out. "Hey, Jubi, how are you doing?" I tried to keep my voice from cracking. "There's your buddy, Spirit. See him? There's Jubi-man." Jubi extended his neck and smelled Spirit, who hardly raised his head. Jubi blew out and neighed, startling me as it reverberated inside the barn.

"You're right, Jubi. Spirit *is* a good boy." I tugged on the lead again. Still moving at a snail's pace, I continued my narration. "And, over there is where we keep the brushes. You don't like the brushes, do you? No, you don't."

I was so relieved when Mr. Bucky returned. "Yeah, keep him walking."

"I forgot to get his food and water."

"I seen that. I'll get it. Keep him walking," he said.

A truck with a horse trailer rattling behind raced up the crackly gravel drive. Dr. Wheeler emerged, a slender, gray haired man with a deeper voice than Mr. Bucky.

"Doc," Mr. Bucky said, shaking his hand.

"Bucky. Let's see what's going on."

Dr. Wheeler lifted Spirit's lips. There was no expression on his face or words uttered as he pulled out his stethoscope to listen to Spirit's heart.

"Racing," Dr. Wheeler said. "Load him—Now."

"Where are we going?"

Wish I hadn't blurted that out.

"To the hospital. He needs to have an ultrasound. Could be colic. Or, worse."

Spirit's front knees began to shake.

"Hold on there," Doc said, jumping over to Spirit. "Pull him up and keep him moving. Go directly to the trailer. We don't have much time."

Spirit was usually an easy loader. This time, however, it took several attempts to get him in. I could almost hear the clock ticking.

"Can I stay in back with him?" I asked, shutting the trailer door.

"No, come up with me," Mr. Bucky said.

We drove to North Carolina State Veterinary Hospital where they were waiting for us. It was all a blur, but I remember the friendly staff worked quickly to unload him.

They escorted us to a waiting room. It should be called the "Eternity Room," because that's what it felt like. A nurse emerged, motioning for Mr. Bucky and I to go back to meet the vet.

"I'm Dr. Malek," a thin, dark-haired man said, extending his hand. I wasn't sure where Dr. Wheeler went.

"Doc," Mr. Bucky nodded.

"We did an ultrasound and X-Rays. Unfortunately, it's colic," Dr. Malek said.

Mr. Bucky sighed and shook his head.

"His intestines have strangulated. He's already lost six feet of intestine."

"But he seemed completely fine. How can this happen?" I asked.

"Sometimes colic can be a small blockage and other times it can be like what Spirit has. Many cases are idiopathic, or of unknown origin. We simply just don't know. Horses can be fine one day, and not the next. Seems to come out of the blue."

"Will he be OK?" I asked.

"Unfortunately, it's the leading medical cause of death in horses."

I gasped.

"I usually recommend surgery. However, Spirit's strangulation has progressed so quickly and severely, his chances are almost nil."

He paused.

"I don't recommend it. He's suffering too much."

Even though I understood the words the doctor was using, I looked to Mr. Bucky to help me interpret.

"I'm so sorry," Dr. Malek said.

Mr. Bucky tipped his hat and cleared his throat. "Gotta do right by him."

The doctor gave a quick nod as he took down the ultrasound and X-ray results.

"Can we see him?" I asked, clearing my throat.

"Sure. He's been given a small sedative to make him more comfortable, but you can see him."

It took everything I had not to ask a gazillion more questions. Mr. Bucky is such a quiet man and seemed to prefer it that way. But I had to say good-bye to my best friend. Shallow breathing came from the stall where this beautiful buckskin lay.

I knelt down next to him, gently lifting his large golden head into my lap. "Spirit, my big, wonderful guy. My Spirit. I love you." I gently blew into his nose and pet his soft muzzle.

Mr. Bucky crouched beside me, rubbing Spirit's neck. "Really good horse," he said, through a tight jaw. "Damn good horse."

I couldn't tell you what happened next or what was even said. All I could see in my mind's eye was the beautiful face of this majestic horse. His distant eyes still held a glimmer of life. Memories of riding, sharing my school days with him, galloping alone with him, and resting in the paddock inundated my mind. Although there were many horses before him: Trixie, Snickers, Friday, River, Dolly, and Wispy, Spirit was my best friend and my heart's horse. He always will be buried deep in my heart.

I nuzzled my face into his neck, muffling my tears. "You're such a good boy, Spirit. You are my best friend. I love you so much."

"Miss."

I flinched, feeling a hand on my shoulder. Time moved simultaneously too slow and too fast since it was now dark outside.

"It's time," Mr. Bucky said.

It will never be time. There will never be enough time.

With Spirit's head in my lap, I pleaded, "Just one more minute? Please, Mr. Bucky?"

"Time to go."

I sniffed, giving this tremendous horse one more kiss on his soft, velvety muzzle where his tiny whiskers tickled my face. One last time.

Mr. Bucky helped me up since I was shaky rising to my feet.

"OK?"

I nodded.

"Don't look back."

I knew he was right, but that was the only place in the world I wanted to be. All I wanted to do was stay with my Spirit. My heart felt like it was broken wide open and I was bleeding out.

I just couldn't believe it.

My Spirit died today.

*L*ost in a crippling haze on the sidewalks of campus, my heart led the way to Chase's room, since my head was nowhere to be found.

"What's up? Haven't seen you in like, forever," Chase said. "Right Here, Right Now" by Jesus Jones played in the background of his dorm room. I think he saw my blank stare and asked if I was OK.

"Um, not really," I said, shifting my weight back and forth. "I'm not really sure why I'm here."

"Wanna come in? Brody's out." He stepped aside to let me in, closing the door and turning down the radio. "What's going on?"

"It's been the most terrible day. Spirit died last night."

"Oh, man. How did—?"

"He colicked. We took him to the Vet School right away. Wish it was one of those times where they can be saved, but not with him. It was too late."

"Oh, man, Maren. So sorry," he said, moving toward me. "I know you loved that horse."

"Yeah," I said, choking back tears. "He was *literally* the best horse. Ever." I looked out his window. "Always there for me."

"Yeah, I get that. I lost my favorite horse, Dakota, to colic, too.

Seemed like one minute he was OK, and the next, we had to put him down."

"So, you know."

"Yeah. People who don't have horses don't understand. Just really sucks."

"It really does," I said, my voice cracking. "I'm sorry."

"Don't be. Come here." I collapsed into his open arms. My heart ached for Spirit, but being there with Chase felt so safe.

My arms were still wrapped around his waist as his hands began running up and down my back. Staring up into his warm, brown eyes released something in me. He glanced down at my lips and his head moved in closer. The levee that held all the memories from camp and suppressed my feelings for him all semester finally collapsed.

His kiss felt familiar yet gentle and tender. I was grateful that both of my first real kisses were from him. The momentary bliss was fleeting as the guilt began to build thinking of Brittany.

I pulled away, touching my lips. "Sorry, just can't do this. You have a girlfriend."

"Ugh," he said, plopping down on the bed.

"I'm sorry. Shouldn't have come over here," I said, running to his door.

"No wait! Please don't go," he said, standing up.

Closing the door behind me and sprinting back to my dorm room, I repeated in a choked whisper, "I'm just so sorry."

December 1991

I'm not even sure how many days it's been. Part of me feels as if it didn't really happen and that Spirit is still here. I really don't want to go back to the barn, but I know I need to go. I need to touch his bridle and see his empty stall to make sure it actually happened. But the other part of me wants to run far from Fair Oaks, never looking back. I feel bad that I haven't checked in on Ms. Patsy and Mr. Bucky. I'm sure they're hurting, too.

I feel numb, like I'm in a cloud. It's hard being at school. Everyone else is living their lives and I'm stuck living in slow motion. It's hard to breathe and my nightmares are invading my waking hours. It's like I'm in a deep hole that I keep trying to dig out of, but each time I try to pull myself up, the dirt around me collapses, driving me deeper down. Even finding songs I like is hard.

And, now I've screwed things up with Chase, the only person I can even talk with about horses now that Daddy and Marin are who-knows-where.

December 11, 1991

I think it's been a few days since I last wrote. I still can't seem to find my footing and I still feel so lost. Feels like I could cry until I literally run out of tears. Can't sleep. I can't seem to get moving. I'm so scared that I might be going crazy. I hope to God I'm not going crazy. Am eating way too much and my classes seem pointless. Kinda how I felt when I first learned about Ruffian and after learning that Swale died, only much bigger. I've tried so hard not to think about Ruffian and her death now, but it's really hard. They had to make a decision to put her down, too. It's excruciating, even if it's the best thing for the horse. I'm not sure I really want to be a vet now.

Feel so guilty about the fact that Chase and I kissed. I'm not telling anyone about that. Just don't know what to do. I'm going back to Fair Oaks to pay my respects, but it will be so hard.

The gravel under the tires that once filled my heart with excitement now filled me with dread. An unusual hush fell over the usually busy farm as I scanned the property. The sound of my steps toward the barn resonated against the trees.

Peeking into Spirit's empty stall, I clutched the stall door as the reality of Spirit's death made my legs buckle.

"Miss."

The deep voice startled me.

"Mr. Bucky," I said, straightening myself.

"You loved that ole' buckskin."

I think I said "I really did." My voice cracked so much I'm not sure he heard me.

"He was special. Really was your horse."

Mr. Bucky's words touched my heart and my legs buckled again. "Oh, my god, Mr. Bucky," I wheezed.

"You'll be OK," he said, linking his arm underneath mine as the world began to spin.

I placed my hand over my mouth and silently screamed into it.

"Hey, now. Settle. It'll be OK."

"No, it won't!" I snapped, surprised by my own reaction. Attempting to take in a deep breath, I whispered, "Spirit is gone. I just can't believe it. He's really gone."

Repeating those words felt like a knife sinking deeper into my chest. "I hate everything about this. I hate that he's gone. I hate that I couldn't be there for him the whole time. I hate every damn part of this!"

Mr. Bucky put his arm around me, pulling me into a hug, letting me sob in his arms.

"Take it easy. Wasn't nothin' anybody coulda done." He pat my back in an attempt to calm me.

Despite my dry mouth and tear-soaked cheeks, I was able to squeak out some coherent sentiments. "Spirit was my best friend. He was here for me when my Daddy and Marin left. He was my heart."

"Yup. His heart was just too big to be here for long."

"It really was." I stood back and blew my nose.

"Hardest thing any horseman got to realize is their horse don't live forever."

No truer words have been spoken.

"We all got horses that get us here," he said, pointing to his chest. "Gotta move on. Always another one that needs us. Come to find out you need 'em more than they need you."

I wiped my cheeks with my sleeve.

"S'pose you don't feel much like workin'."

"Not sure," I said, sniffing and staring out the barn door. My eyes landed on Jubi, Ebony, and Little Bit in the paddock and felt a little better. "I guess I can do it. I probably need to do it."

He gave a quick nod and left.

"Thought I heard a familiar voice. How are you, Sugar?" Ms. Patsy asked, with Dodger at her side.

I shrugged, twisting my face.

"Yeah, I know," she said, looking off into the distance. "He was a great horse. But little Maren's Spirit is doing well and advancing the way she should."

I didn't give a damn about her at first. Then I felt guilty for not caring about my namesake. She really was so sweet and innocent. "That's great, how's Jubi doing?"

"He's had his ups and downs, but he'll be OK."

"Is he still in the paddock?" I then realized that I passed him on the way to the barn, but my grief blurred my memory.

"Yeah, he's got Ebony and Little Bit in there to get 'em by. But I know he would be happy to see you," she said, handing me a peppermint.

"Thanks, Ms. Patsy." She nodded, turned, and headed back toward the house with Dodger following.

My eyes struggled to find the dark bay horse in the pasture again. Each step I took seemed to require more energy. Unlocking the gate, I reached inside my pocket and pulled out the peppermint. "C'mere, Jubi."

The dark bay snorted as he plodded toward me with his head hanging lower than usual.

"So sorry about your buddy, Jubi. He was a special guy," I said, tearing up again. "I know you love and miss him, too." As I stroked his long neck, his eyes appeared to soften. I think we both were crying.

December 9, 1991

Dear Kiddo,

I am so, so sorry to hear about Spirit. I know you loved him dearly
and he loved you, too. You were both good for each other. He's still
with you in your heart. Your Spirit will never leave your spirit. I
wanted to get this letter mailed to you sooner, but since Thanksgiving
was so late this year, all the Christmas festivities started immediately.
It's OK to cry and it's OK to feel unsettled. Your heart is so big and I
hope it's healed a little bit, even though the pain will stay with you for
a while. Your spirit might not be up for a while, but that's OK. Don't
forget to take deep breaths.

Love you to the moon and back,
Aunt Mimi

December 14, 1991

It helped to go back to Fair Oaks, even though it was one of the most painful things I've ever had to do. Seeing Jubi, Maren's Spirit, and everyone as well as talking with Ms. Patsy and Mr. Bucky took some of the fog away. I was able to sleep a little better, leave some remaining Doritos in the opened bag, and get through the night without sitting up in bed. But my heart is still broken and sometimes I still feel as though I will never stop crying.

My life will never be the same without this amazing horse, who I feel was mine. I'm so grateful for all horses do for us, even if it means they take a piece of our hearts.

Something inside me just drove me back to see Mama and CJ.

"Hi, Baby, what a surprise! Aren't there a few more days left in your semester?" Mama asked, greeting me at the front door. It was a Saturday morning, so I knew Clint would be at his touch football game.

"Yeah, just a few more days and we're done." I bent down and picked up fuzzy Katie Kitty.

"Sister!" CJ said, running up to me.

"Hey," I said, grunting when he ran into my stomach. "Missed you so much." I couldn't believe how big he had gotten. It was like he was a real person now. "It's just been a while since I've been home," I said, cradling Katie, enjoying her soothing purr.

"Uh, huh," Mama said, with a half-smile and furrowed brow. "We've been busy around here."

I gently laid Katie Kitty down. Mama said a few more things, but it all sounded like she was underwater.

"Oh, Mama," I said, as my bag slid down my arm. "Spirit died."

"Baby, I'm so sorry." She opened her arms for an inviting hug.

Cozying into Mama's arms felt like a warm blanket making me feel like I was a kid again.

"Who's 'Spirit'?" CJ asked.

"My favorite horse."

"CJ, bud, why don't you go outside and find your baseball and mitts," Mama said. "We'll be right out to play with you."

"OK," he said, skipping to the door leading out to the garage.

Mama motioned to the couch. "You OK?"

"Not really. Just don't feel like doing anything. I'm doing OK in my classes. And my last finals will be fine, but it's been so hard to concentrate."

"This *has* been really hard for you."

"Yeah," I said, looking right through her.

"Do you want to come home the last few days of the semester?"

"Nah. I mean, no offense."

"None taken," she said.

"I just…I don't know. Just so hard sometimes," I said, fiddling with the couch cushion.

"Do they have people on campus you can talk to?"

"They do," I said, taking in a big breath and forcefully exhaling. "It's just…I don't want to be like 'him.'"

We both knew who I meant.

"Baby, you're not like him."

"How do you know? What if I'm crazy, too?"

"You're not crazy," she repeated.

"I mean, isn't that genetic? Like, if your parents have it, then you can get it sort of thing?"

"Who knows? All I know is that you *are not* him," Mama said. "You're brighter, smarter, more focused, and dedicated. And, most importantly, more loving to those who love you."

"I don't know." I shook my head, pulling out a slightly used Kleenex from my pocket.

"Oh, I do. I know what I'm saying is true. I'm just really sorry that we never really explained it to you. We really didn't understand manic-depression ourselves, but that's no excuse. So sorry."

I shrugged. "We did learn about it in my Psychology class."

"But as far as your sadness, I do know what you're feeling. In my freshman year of college, one of my friends died in a car wreck. Everyone was back home: Nanny, Bumpa, Aunt Mimi, and my friends. I was so lonely at school. It seemed like there wasn't anyone I could connect to. To make it worse, a month later Nanny died." She cleared her throat. "Broke me wide open. It was soon after that I met your Daddy Garrett. His charm, sense of humor, zest for life and devilish good looks took away a lot of my pain. At first, anyway. He was going to a nearby school at the time. We started dating and the rest is history, as they say."

Thinking about Mama as a girl my own age was strange, but made me feel even closer to her. Less lonely and anxious, too.

"Y'all coming?" CJ asked, charging back into the living room.

"Oh, sorry, bud! Sister and I got to talking in here," Mama said.

"Here," he said, tossing me the baseball. "This will make you feel better."

As I gave him a big hug, it was so hard to believe my tiny brother was now in second grade. He had the biggest heart of any little guy I knew. Or, any guy, really.

December 17, 1991

This time, when I got to the barn, I was immediately drawn to Maren's Spirit. Although she's growing quickly, she's still young and has a lot to learn. I can relate. Plus, she's still so adorable. Talking to Ms. Patsy always helps, too.

"Hey, Sugar," Ms. Patsy said, peeking her head into the paddock. "How goes it?"

"Hey, Ms. Patsy. It's still hard," I said, petting Maren's Spirit's soft, dark neck.

"I reckon you'd say that. These things take time."

"Jubi is still having a hard time, too," I said.

"He still misses his buddy but he's been hangin' more with Ebony and Little Bit. If things don't get better for him, we might get him a donkey. Lord knows all we need around here is another ass!"

I smiled, still stroking Maren's Spirit's fuzzy neck.

"I know you'll be goin' overseas soon. When is that again?"

I sighed. "Don't know if I'm going."

"Not goin'?" she said, putting her hand on her hip.

"I just don't know how I can leave everyone. And, I don't know how I can be a vet if I can't even handle this."

"We all break down when we lose our horses. Even Dr. Wheeler, so that's nothing to lose sleep over."

Too late.

"I can always go overseas another semester," I said. "They already have all my paperwork and stuff," I said.

"It'll be a cold day in hell before that happens."

"What?" I said, snapping my head to look at Ms. Patsy.

"Remember the time when you were knee-high to a grasshopper and that horse at camp jumped and you went flying? And that time when that horse lay down with you still on him?"

"Yeah."

"Well, this is like that. You've fallen off. You lost your seat and mount and now you're clutching the ground like your life depended on it. But a horsewoman won't be happy just staying on the ground, watching other people ride. What you really need to do is—"

"—Get back up," I finished, with a slight eye roll.

"Right," she said, pointing at me.

"But things are so crazy right now. Plus, it's going to be so hard to leave y'all. And, Little Spirit here."

"Yeah, you won't recognize her when you get back!" Ms. Patsy said, giving the foal a small rub. "She might even be a different color."

"Exactly. And, what about Jubi and—"

"—You're not going be gone forever! C'mere, let me show you something."

My curiosity was piqued as we headed up the slight hill behind the paddock, an area I rarely went.

"Look around—the barn, stable, horses? All of that is everything I ever truly wanted. My life with the Old Man. This is it," she said, spreading out her arms.

Seeing everything from that vantage point offered a different perspective. Dodger trotted up to us while Moose stood off to the side, observing us.

"Yes, even you, Dodger," she said, giving him a quick pet. "When I left home after the Old Man and I got married, I never thought I could do it. Being so far away from Mama and Daddy and Meemaw and Poppy was hard. But I slowly got to where I couldn't *not* be away. It was my path. Going to Australia is yours." She wiped her brow.

"Horses have always been in your blood. They are an important part of you. I knew that the very first time you rode here years ago. Traveling is also in your blood." She paused. "I seem to remember a girl who once said, 'It's a dream come true to go over seas.'" Sometimes you need to fly the coop. When you come back, you'll be all the better for it. You have to go. You *need* to go. Not going would get in the way of what you really want—to be a wonderful vet."

Tears welled in my eyes.

"You OK?"

Words failed me as I fell into her arms.

"Oh, Sugar, you've done dealt with so much. You lost your best riding pal. You lost your Daddy. You lost the possibility of getting your own horse. Now you've lost your best friend, Spirit. It's OK to break down. Lord knows we've all done it before."

I knew she was right and I was tired of fighting everything: the pain of losing Spirit, the need to go to Australia, the guilt I felt about kissing Chase, Marin doing her own thing, and Daddy leaving.

We stood in silence, except for my muffled sobs. "It's OK,

Sugar," she repeated, rubbing my back. As the tears poured out, I finally felt a release of my overwhelming grief; like a pipe had burst. These tears felt unlike all the tears I had cried before.

They felt healing.

She gave me a quick tight embrace. "Feeling a little better now?"

All I could do was nod.

"You're doing just fine," she said, wiping away the tears on my cheeks. "Just remember, you've lost your seat. All you need to do is get back up. You've done it before and you can do it again."

"Thank you, Ms. Patsy." They were the only the words I could muster through my wet cheeks and swollen eyes.

"You go over there and have yourself a ball, Sugar," she said. "We'll be here waiting for you, with bells on."

December 19, 1991

That day with Ms. Patsy is one of the most important of my life. It was two days ago but I'm still exhausted from it. It's like I had all this stuff I just needed to let out. Things aren't perfect, but I do feel better about being a vet. Guess I really could be a good one. And, I'm not worrying as much about being crazy anymore, even if I still feel that way from time to time.

I'm totally ready to get back home for Christmas and leave this horrible semester behind. I turned in my final English paper and the final paperwork for Australia today. I got 2 Bs in my classes that should have been As, but it's enough for the GPA I need to go to Australia. Still feel guilty about what happened with Chase. These past couple of weeks have sucked but soon I'll be out of North Carolina and in a whole new country. I didn't think I'd say this before, but now I'm really getting excited!

Ravaged with guilt over what I had done, for the last two weeks of the semester, I had strategically and successfully avoided Chase. It helped that I spent a lot of time holing myself up in the library in preparation for finals. Knowing I'd soon be home with Mama, CJ, and Katie Kitty for Christmas vacation was also a relief. I was packing up a few last items in my dorm room, when there was a knock on the door.

I opened the door to see the only person I had evaded, yet truly wanted to see more than any other.

Chase.

"Hey," he said, with his hands in his pockets.

"Hey," I said, trying to keep my nervousness from being too obvious.

"Can I come in?"

"Uh, yeah."

"Thanks," he said, looking at the empty desks and room full of packed suitcases. "Looks like you're ready to go,"

"Yeah."

"Well," he said, turning to me. "I just didn't want the semester to end without saying 'Goodbye.'"

"Thanks," I said, biting my lower lip. "I'm just so sorry about… Well, you know."

"You really don't have to be sorry."

"Yeah, I do. I don't want to be *that* girl. It's just not me and just not cool. I never want to hurt anyone."

"You didn't. I've wanted to tell you that we broke up."

"You did? When?" I asked, my eyes widening.

"The weekend we got back after Thanksgiving."

"So, you just weren't going to tell me?" I asked, with a small sense of frustration.

"Well, with finals and everything, I've hardly seen anyone. Plus, it seemed like you were avoiding me anyway."

I sighed. "Honestly, just thinking about you two dating, and then seeing you two together…it just got too hard."

He plopped down on Shannon's bare mattress. "I get that.

Brittany lived down the street from me growing up. Our parents went to the same church and our mothers were in the same women's prayer group together. They fixed us up, and we started spending more time together. Before you knew it, we were going out." He paused. "She's a great person."

"Yeah, I know," I mumbled.

"But she's not that great. I could never talk about horses and other things with her like I could with you. And have fun, too. Like, when I threw you into Lake Wheeler and talking to you that one night after my sister's birthday." He stood up.

I vividly remember. Happy to know you do, too.

"After you left that night, I thought about everything. Everything that happened this semester. Who I was when I was with Brittany. Who I was when I'm with you and how much I, you know, really like you." He scratched his nose nervously. "I wasn't sure if I should come over. But it was either tonight or never. Wanted you to know before you left."

Smiling, he took a step closer, forcing me to look up into his big, brown eyes. "Man, when I saw you that first weekend of the semester, all those camp memories came flooding back."

"You have no idea," I said, shaking my head, touching his chest. "I've liked you since camp and thought about you so much."

"You did?"

"Yeah! You were my first kiss," I said.

"Mine, too."

The tingly feelings, though quite buried, quickly returned.

"I have to say, though, um…well, I kinda need to take it a little slow," I said.

"That's fine," he chuckled.

"Really?"

"I mean, don't get me wrong!" he said. "But we can take time to get to know each other a little better."

"Maybe we *are* actually looking for the same thing."

"Sounds like it." He leaned down, gently wrapping his arms around my waist, and gave me another one of his kisses. Out of the three kisses, this was definitely the best. Maybe because a camp counselor or girlfriend weren't weighing heavily on my mind.

"And now you're leaving," he said, his hands still around my waist.

"Yeah, but I'll be back before Spring Break. And I'll write."

"You better," he smiled, hugging me closer.

"Or, you'll what?"

"Or, you might have another incident in Lake Wheeler when you get back!" he said.

"Hey, it wasn't just me that got wet that night! Remember?"

"Oh, yeah. I definitely remember," he said, nodding his head. "You can hold your own. That's what I love...like about you."

"That's what I love...like about you, too," I said, smiling.

December 25, 1991

It was a different Christmas. Even though my heart still felt so tender from my Spirit being gone, talking to Chase on my own phone line every day was surreal. Being at home with Mama, CJ, and cuddling Katie Kitty, sans Lacey was awesome. Even Client tried to be nice, in his own "Clint-like" way. My big Christmas gift this year was money for my trip, which is perfect— unless it was another stuffed animal, which I'll never have enough of.

December 26, 1991

My last time at Fair Oaks for a while. I'm really going to miss everyone.

Peeking into the barn, Mr. Bucky and Ms. Patsy were talking to each other with Moose and Dodger by their sides. *Pingüino* seemed to teleport from the tack room to greet me.

"Hey," I said, crouching over to rub the kitty's belly.

"Hey Sugar—Merry belated Christmas! Aren't you supposed to be on a plane?"

"Tomorrow," I laughed. "I just wanted to say good-bye before I left."

"You'll be back before you know it," she said.

"C'mere," Mr. Bucky said, motioning to me. "Wanna give you this."

Squinting, I adjusted my eyes to focus on a black-haired braided bracelet with a gold clasp and heart charm that said, "Spirit."

"Oh, my, g—" I said, reaching for it.

"I done heard that they can use horse hair and make it into a bracelet. Thought you might want one to remember him by."

I garnered enough energy to flash him a quick smile. A few trailing tears landed on the memento honoring my best friend.

"Thank you so much, Mr. Bucky. This is incredible. It's just…. incredible." I couldn't think of what to say. No words seemed to fit.

I gave him another quick hug and he patted my back with a force that was stronger than most. Mr. Bucky had his own ways of doing things. He blew his nose as he walked toward the house.

Ms. Patsy smiled. "You know, Spirit really was your horse. I'm just sorry we couldn't have made him officially yours. As you know, he technically belonged to Sherry, his daughter. But the Old Man really wanted to give the bracelet to you. It was all his idea. I think he felt guilty," she said, rubbing her forehead. "Especially when you didn't get your horse from your Daddy."

I was overwhelmed with gratitude, biting my lip to prevent more tears from falling. I'm not sure why, but I momentarily placed the bracelet next to my cheek. I could almost feel Spirit's spirit.

"Ms. Patsy, could you help me put it on?"

"Sure," she said, unfastening the clasp.

I straightened out my arm to see it on my wrist. Wrapping my fingers around the beautiful bracelet, I kissed it.

"Just remember, anytime you lose your seat, you get back up. Horses have always been in your blood and an important part of you. Now Spirit will always be a part of you." She paused. "And, little Maren's Spirit is looking for someone to be her special person, too. Someone who will love her, train her, become someone's horse. Someone, maybe, who might have the same name as her."

I snapped my head up to meet Ms. Patsy's smiling eyes.

"We'll talk when you get back," she said.

I almost knocked Ms. Patsy over to hug her. The soothing smell of hay on her clothes was almost another hug in itself.

I had cried so much my eyes burned and my tear ducts practically dried up. Clearing my throat, I asked, "So, are you going to get more help around here?"

"Nah, me and the Old Man are slowing down a bit," she said, rubbing her forehead.

"Everything OK?"

"Oh, yeah, nothing to worry about. We're just not doing as much as we used to. A trail ride here and there. If we don't feel like getting the horses all tacked up for others, then we don't. If we feel like a trail ride just for us, then we go. We're just enjoying our horses and farm now. It's a hoot watching Maren's Spirit grow up. She brings a lotta joy."

We both watched Lily graze in the paddock and Maren's Spirit darting around in her own paddock.

"If you want, you can come with us tomorrow to the airport," I said.

She shook her head. "Think we'll just say 'See ya real soon' now, Sugar. We'll be waiting for all your stories when you get back. Tell us how they do it Down Under."

"Oh, OK," I said, fighting the lump forming in my throat. Observing the playful foal for a minute, I asked, "Can I still work for y'all when I get back?"

"Of course! We're not going anywhere," she said, placing her arm around me. "You came along at the perfect time."

I was thinking the exact thing about them.

December 26, 1991

Dear Kiddo,

(Do you mind if I still call you that?)
Merry Christmas! Hope Santa was good to you this year. You'll be leaving for Australia soon! Can you believe it? I know you're nervous, but you will do well and they're lucky to have you. Keep reminding yourself that you're in Australia and treasure every moment. Remember: take deep breaths. Inhale for four, hold for four, exhale on eight.

You really know horses and they will appreciate your kind and loving way. They know a good person when they see one. I'm so proud of you and the woman you've become. You're sharing your gifts with others as well as learning more about the animals you love more than anything in the world. Maybe they'll even let you ride a horse like The Black Stallion on a beach! Australia is full of them.

We will miss you back home, but are looking forward to hearing all about it when you get back! Don't ever hide who you are. Let your beautiful light and spirit shine for others.

Love you to the moon and back,
Aunt Mimi

<u>December 27, 1991</u>

Well, this is it. My last journal entry in the United States for a while. I'll miss everyone here, but having Chase, Mama, and CJ to see me off at the airport means the world. I wish Ms. Patsy and Mr. Bucky could have been there, too, but I'm glad Clint will be working. Been listening to the song, "All Together Now" by The Farm. I think it fits.

Gathering my suitcases at the front door, Mama said, "Before Chase gets here, I want to give you something."

She pulled out a slightly bent and tattered envelope. It read "Mama" on the outside, surrounded by drawn hearts, Christmas trees, and stars.

"Can I open it now?" I asked.

"Of course!"

Peeling back the warped envelope, I found a $5 bill.

"Remember that Christmas, way back when you gave this to me?"

"Oh, my gosh, Mama. I completely forgot about this."

"I said I'd hold onto it until you needed it. This is as good a time as any," she said, smiling to hold back her tears.

I hugged her then slipped the envelope into my backpack. We both jumped a bit when we heard a car door shut. "Sounds like he's here," she said. Gathering Katie Kitty in my arms, I was able to give the kitty a goodbye hug.

"Good morning, Chase," Mama said, greeting him at the door.

"Hello, Mrs. Fletcher."

My heart usually skipped every time I saw him, but this time heart skipped and hopped from the mixture of excitement and anxiety.

"Hey," I said, cradling Katie Kitty in my arms.

"Hey you," he said.

"Hi!" CJ said.

"Chase, this is Katie Kitty and my brother, CJ."

"Hey there, little man," Chase said, bending down and shaking his hand.

"Sister is going to Austwalia! That's a different country!" CJ shouted.

"Yes, she is," Chase said, looking up at me.

"When are you comin' back?" CJ asked.

"I'll see you when the daffodils bloom."

CJ furrowed his brow.

"I'll be back in a few months and then we can throw the ball around," I said, setting Katie Kitty down. "I know you'll be the best pitcher this side of the Mississippi River!"

His brow relaxed into a smile.

"Here," Chase said. "I wanted to give you this as a belated Christmas gift. Just a little something." He handed me a little box decorated with horses and holly wrapping paper. "My sister helped me pick it out and also wrapped it for me." He slightly laughed and put his hands in his pockets.

"Sorry I didn't give you anything!" I said.

"That's OK."

"No, it's not. I'll bring something back from Australia then."

"Sounds good," he smiled. "Do you want to open it?"

Does a bear…?

Unwrapping the present, I found a smaller box inside. Unlike the one Dustin showed me in high school, this gift was for me—I was sure of it. Inside the creaky box was a galloping horse pendant on a silver chain.

"It's beautiful!" I said.

"Let me see!" CJ said. Mama peeked over his head.

"That *is* beautiful. Just what you love, Baby. And that's a good chain that will hold up."

"Can you help me put it on?" I asked Mama.

"Sure," she said, unfastening the clasp. "There. Perfect," she said, taking a step back.

"Thank you, Chase," I said, giving him a quick peck.

Seeing her son wince at our public display of affection, Mama said, "CJ, we need to pack up. Can you show Mr. Chase the car and maybe grab a small bag?"

"Here, let me get those," Chase said, picking up both of my big suitcases.

"Thank you so much. That's so kind of you," Mama said.

"You're welcome, ma'am."

"Mr. Chase, follow me to the car," CJ said.

"What a special young man," Mama muttered, shutting the door behind the two guys. I'm not sure if she knew I heard her.

"Got your tickets?" Mama asked.

"Yep," I said, patting my backpack.

"Now don't lose them. You have what you need for your layovers. First to Los Angeles, then to Sydney, then to Adelaide. Keep them in the little envelope here."

"I will," I said, delighting in Mama's motherly attempts.

"You ready?"

I took a deep breath. "Yep, I think so."

"Sure gonna be quiet around here without you."

"I was away this whole semester!" I said.

"I know, but you were at least still in the same state and country. I'm so proud of you, Baby. You should be proud of everything you've accomplished."

On the approach to the airport, the roar of the jet engines and driving under the belly of the descending airplanes thrilled me. The hustle and bustle of parking, as well as finding the right gate reminded me of trying to find my dorm room on moving-in day.

"Here we are," Mama said.

"Flight 451 to Los Angeles is now boarding. Please have your ticket ready," the announcer said.

"That's me," I said, turning to Chase, hugging him tight.

"Go get 'em," he said. "You'll be awesome."

"Thank you," I said, locking lips just long enough for CJ to notice.

"Ewwwww, kisses—Yuck!"

"Now it's your turn!" I joked, reaching down to him.

"No!" he protested.

"OK, no kiss. But, how about a big hug?" He wrapped his little arms around my neck, squeezing tight.

"Bye, Sister."

"Love you, CJ. You be good," I said, sneaking in a quick kiss on his arm.

I stood up. "Love you, Mama."

She hugged me with a strength I'd never felt before. When I went to pull away, she pulled me in even closer.

"Goodbye, Baby Girl," she said, kissing the top of my head. "So proud of you."

After showing my ticket to the lady behind the counter, I turned around and waved to three of the most important people in my life. Chase flashed his warm smile, while Mama placed her fingers to her mouth, in a failed attempt to hide her trembling lips. CJ enthusiastically waved goodbye.

As hard as it was to leave, my spirit rose thinking about fulfilling one of my Life's dreams. Swallowing hard, I ran my fingers over Spirit's bracelet around my wrist, feeling his gentle, loving presence, anchoring me as I took my next step. My Spirit was guiding my spirit and the next chapter brimmed with promise.

Turning back around, I walked down the ramp toward the plane, drawing in a deep breath on four, holding for four, and exhaling on eight.

Did you like FINDING HER SPIRIT?
Please tell your friends and family, and leave a review on
Amazon and Goodreads.
It doesn't have to be long—just enough to share your thoughts.
Many thanks for supporting an Indie author!
Paperback and Kindle available on Amazon.
Please check out my other novel,
BURIED DEEP IN OUR HEARTS

www.TracieBartonBarrett.com
TBartonBarrett@gmail.com
www.facebook.com/TBartonBarrett

Reflective Discussion Questions

(These questions contain spoilers)

1. Talk about the different meanings of the title, *Finding Her Spirit*.

2. When Mama asked Maren, "What is it about girls and horses?", Maren didn't have a definitive answer. How would you describe this connection? Do you agree with Mama when she said, "You never forget your first love"?

3. The book is set in the 1980s and early 1990s. How do you think things might be different if it were set nowadays? In what ways is it the same?

4. How might the book read differently if you're a parent versus a teenager?

5. If you come from, or are living in, a blended family, what are your relationships like with your stepparents and/or stepsibling(s)? Are they similar to how Maren feels about Clint and Lacey, respectively? If you're a stepparent, did you ever have a stepchild like Maren?

6. At first, Maren is disappointed that she got a new baby brother instead of a sister. In the end, however, she becomes close and develops a deep bond with CJ. Has this happened to you?

7. How would you describe Maren's relationship with Daddy and his love for her? Can you love a parent even if it's complicated?

8. What hints were provided that Daddy most likely suffered with Bipolar Disorder, or Manic-Depressive Disorder, as it was more widely known then?

9. The book, *Ruffian: Queen of the Fillies,* and the movie, *The Black Stallion,* both had a profound impact on Maren. What book(s) and/or movie(s), horse-related or not, have you kept close to your heart?

10. Maren's relationship with Spirit helped her become more confident and less anxious. Have you ever had a horse in your life that mirrored the special relationship between Maren and Spirit? Was it a horse you had or, in Maren's case, one that belonged to someone else?

11. How many of the horse scenes happened to you? (i.e. Horse rolling over while you're still on; horse jumps suddenly and you fell off; lying down next to a horse in the paddock)

12. The people with whom Maren could share her love of horses ended up leaving, which is a strong theme in the book. For example, Daddy begs Maren not to leave, when he, in fact, leaves; not getting a horse from Daddy; Marin ends up leaving, and ultimately, Spirit leaves. What other examples of leaving and/or loss are shown? A different meaning of "leaving" is when Maren left for Australia.

13. Aunt Mimi is a supportive and loving confidant and advocate for Maren, as is Ms. Gardner, her teacher. Have you ever had a family member, or teacher, who was that for you?

14. Was there anything in the book (an event, such as the 1984 Kentucky Derby; a specific horse, such as Ruffian; or a place, such as Mackinac Island) that you Googled to learn more about? If so, what was it?

15. Chase (Matty) was special to Maren for a few reasons, including her first kiss. This was especially meaningful because she sometimes felt guys just looked at her as a friend. Has this ever happened to you?

16. Did you ever have a close friend growing up, but one of you drifted away like with Maren and Marin? How did you deal with it? Some people say "breaking up" with a friend can be harder than breaking up with a girlfriend or boyfriend. Do you agree?

17. How would you describe the marriage between Ms. Patsy and Mr. Bucky compared to the marriage between Mama and Clint?

18. Although horses were the primary love of Maren's life, cats also played a role. This was evident in her first experiences with Brownie and Jelly Bean, *Pingüino* at Fair Oaks, and then Katie Kitty. What other thing(s) in your life do you love as much as horses?

19. Maren had difficulties in the winter, suggesting Seasonal Affective Disorder (SAD), as well as anxiety and issues falling asleep. Have you, or anyone you know, ever experienced either of these?

20. At the end, Maren is concerned that she might be "like him," her Daddy. Have you ever worried that you might be like one of your parents?

21. After Spirit's death, Mr. Bucky said, "Hardest thing any horseman got to realize is their horse don't live forever." How have you dealt with losing a beloved horse?

22. Ms. Patsy says to Maren that she's "lost her seat and just needs to get back on." When have you experienced this, literally and figuratively?

23. Music was something that connected Maren and Daddy. It was also an ongoing part of Maren's life when she listened to it in her room, in the car, and in choir. What music do you enjoy and do you feel like it connects you to others?

24. If you primarily ride English or Western, have you ever tried learning the other discipline? Why or why not?

25. Maren is interested in traveling to other places and learning other languages. Is this something you enjoy, or are you more like Ms. Patsy when she said, "(This is) all I ever truly wanted. My life with the Old Man. This is it…It was my path. And, goin' (to Australia) is yours."?